To P... ...
Best
[signature]

Read Em and Weep
book one

SERIAL KILLER

PAT MILLS · KEVIN O'NEILL

MILLSVERSE
BOOKS

Read Em and Weep
book one

Serial Killer
Pat Mills
Kevin O'Neill

This first edition published in 2017

Copyright © 2017 Pat Mills and Kevin O'Neill
All rights reserved.
ISBN 978-0-9956612-0-2

Published by Millsverse Books 2017
Published in the United Kingdom

Cover design by inspiredcoverdesigns.com
Interior formatting by Author E.M.S.
Edited by Lisa Mills

First Printing, 2017

The authors greatly appreciate you taking the time to read our work. Please consider telling your friends or blog readers about this work to help us spread the word. Thank you for supporting our work!

Millsverse Books
Apartado 2009
C/ Montemayor 34
29688 Cancelada
Malaga
Spain

www.millsverse.com

To Lisa

For making it happen – Pat

PART ONE:

OCTOBER 1975

'Who's that Bumpy Man, sir?'

CHAPTER ONE

Stoke Basing Star August 16th 2016.

BODY IN BASEMENT IDENTIFIED

Two weeks ago, homeowner and builder John Trigger was horrified to discover a dead body while he was renovating his house. As the *Star* reported last week, Trigger, 54, knocked down a basement wall revealing a small secret room behind it. Under its York stone floor were the remains of a woman who, police have confirmed, was strangled with a fur boa found lying beside her.

It's thought to be Mrs Jean Maudling, 32, who lived in Stoke Basing and was reported missing in 1957. Police have appealed to her daughter, Annie, 71, and son, David, 67, to get in touch with them.

The location and identity of the previous owner of Trigger's property has not yet been disclosed as police enquiries are still continuing.

There was one further discovery for Trigger. Stuffed in the wall he demolished, along with old newspapers, he found a 1957 British comic *The Fourpenny One* which he described as 'very rare, in mint condition'.

'My eyes lit up when I saw it,' Trigger, told the *Star*. 'I just know it has to be worth a great deal of money, but I have no idea just how much. After all, you hear about old copies of *Superman* and *Spiderman* selling for thousands and thousands of pounds, so I really believe I've found treasure hidden in the wall.

'I've put it up on eBay. Bit of a slow start so far, but now the word's out there, I'm just waiting for those serious bids from collectors to come rolling in. I'm sure there'll be an improvement on 10p.'

CHAPTER TWO

It was 1957 and eight-year old Dave Maudling was hoping for the best, even though he feared the worst. When he looked back on those formative Saturdays of his childhood, he didn't recall them through a warm, nostalgic haze of sepia-coloured photography with a reassuring brass band playing. Neither did he remember them with endless rain spattering down on humble, gloomy, endless terraced streets as violins bitterly lamented life in the 1950s.

No, all he could ever remember was a white void, empty of meaning and of sound, with the newsagent's shop floating menacingly in the centre of it.

Enticing him to enter. Demanding he entered.

Its window was crowded with magazines, jars and boxes of sweets, made-in-Hong Kong toys and home-made slogans all competing to catch his eye: "Authorised agent for biro pens and refills ... Take home a family brick – delicious Neapolitan ice cream ... Stop here for men's magazines, biggest selection in East London. On sale to adults only." He lingered for a moment, taking them all in, delaying the evil moment of entering the shop, but knowing he must; knowing, deep down, it really was best to get it over with.

Then he took a deep breath and went inside.

The doorbell jingled, betraying the boy's presence, as he descended one step down into Hell.

Hell took the form of a dingy, cramped, damp-smelling, dimly lit room; actually a living room converted into a shop.

He looked up in wonder at all the adult magazines attached to bulldog clips, suspended by strings from the ceiling, away from children's eyes: *Two-Pennorth, Thruppeny Bits, Wink!, Members Only, Birthday Suit* and *Casino for the Man About Town.* Then, on the shelves below: *Stately Piles, Kith and Kin, Forces Sweetheart, Slippers and Shawl, Pram and Oven, Sabrina, Tranny,* and *Twinset.* All of the magazines had their own distinctive smells which combined with the confectionery and the damp to give the shop its unique, fusty, and not entirely unpleasant signature aroma.

He scanned the lowest comic shelf, looking past the bright, enticing logos of *Basher, Scarper, Blimey!, Bazooka, Pinafore, Radio-Active, Goggle Box, Spunky* and *Homework,* for the comic he was really after. The *only* comic that would do. The comic his playground peers insisted he must have if he wanted to be part of their in-crowd. Not to possess it would mean being cast out from the inner circle of five-stone players, flick-carders and marble shooters.

And then he saw it. Or rather he didn't. There was a *blank space* where his beloved comic should be.

His face dropped.

The silence in the shop was suddenly broken by a harsh voice that Dave recognised all too well. The voice of Mr Cooper the newsagent. 'You stupid cow!'

A female voice cried out in pain.

The newsagent continued, 'I've got a customer. I'll deal with you later. I'll come back and black the other one. You see if I don't.'

There was a rustling sound from a beaded curtain that hid the back room from the shop and a man wearing a short brown jacket stepped through it.

He looked sourly down over the counter towards the boy with his severe short back and sides and lop-sided fringe, his face and feet barely projecting out of the raincoat he was still growing into, his woollen gloves dangling down from the cuffs by pieces of elastic.

Dave stared back up at him with Bambi-like eyes and a gap-toothed, nervous smile, silently appealing for mercy, not realising that this only whetted Mr Cooper's appetite.

'Ah, young Dave. What can I interest you in, young man?'

Dave couldn't find the words to reply. He was paralysed with fear. To deaden his fear, he read the words on a box of *Sherlock's Liquorice Pipes*. Silently repeating them over and over to himself. 'He chews *Sherlock's*. We choose *Sherlock's*. Everyone chooses *Sherlock's* pipes. They're elementary. He chews *Sherlock's*. We choose *Sherlock's* ...'

'Caps for your cap gun? New spud gun? Ten Park Drive for your mum? Twenty Kensitas for your dad? Copy of *Slapper* for your sister?' interrupted the newsagent, nodding in the direction of the magazines.

Slapper was Mr Cooper's nickname for the glossy *Sabrina* magazine, aimed at girls who dreamt of becoming movie stars, and was a typical example of his rapier wit. He liked to comment on the publications his regulars purchased, and particularly enjoyed humiliating those brave enough to buy *Birthday Suit*, "The magazine for serious naturists", and the only available photographic source of full-frontal, female nudity. He liked to warn purchasers of *Birthday Suit* they'd go blind or grow hair on the palms of their hands. He loved seeing them cringe with embarrassment.

But, out of all his customers, the one he enjoyed humiliating the most was young Dave.

Dave stopped his liquorice mantra and looked desperately again along the line of comics. Hoping against hope.

'It's not there.' Mr Cooper produced a copy of *The Fourpenny One* from under the counter and held it between his heavily nicotine-stained fingers.

Dave felt a pang at the sight of his special comic with its bold red and yellow logo and that familiar huge fist smashing out through the '*O*' in the '*One*'. It was all-action, it was fun, it mocked teachers, parents, park-keepers and other figures of authority, it was full of catch-phrases to be endlessly repeated in the playground.

'I've kept it back for you special, see?'

Dave's eyes lit up. He had no choice. He was under his comic's spell. Summoning all his courage, he approached the counter, quietly repeating to himself, 'He chews *Sherlock's*. We choose *Sherlock's* …'

'It's a free gift issue. You know what the free gift is?' The newsagent enquired, looking knowingly at Dave who nodded apprehensively as he leaned forward to take his comic.

His tormentor slyly moved it just out of reach.

'You know the routine,' he smirked. He slid a ring off his finger in readiness and prepared his fist, clenching it in anticipation. Then, as Dave still said nothing, punched it impatiently into the palm of his other hand.

'I'm waiting.'

For a moment, Dave was distracted by the lurid covers of the sweat mags for men on a spinner rack with endless battles between man and beast and titles like *Man's Man*, *Hard Man* and *Man Size*. It was an image on the cover of *Man Size* that had caught his eye. A sadistic Nazi smiled as a crocodile was about to bite a tied-up, scantily-clad glamour girl, while a heroic American soldier fought his way to her rescue.

'Step away from the spinner. I've told you before.'

Dave obeyed. But it had given him new courage. He knew what he had to do now. Like that square-jawed G.I. on the cover, like all the other Real Men snarling out at him from the spinner, facing overwhelming odds, facing certain death, showing him how to behave: he, too, must be a Hard Man, a Man's Man.

'Now come along, Davey. What is it you want?'

The boy's resolve faltered again. He tried to say the words, but they just wouldn't come.

'A … F … F … F … F…'

'What's that …? "Fur … Fur …?" We don't sell fur-furs here.'

Then, finally, he had the courage to say it.

'Please, sir, I'd like a *Fourpenny One*.'

With a sadistic leer, the newsagent slammed his fist into Dave's face.

CHAPTER THREE

'Aaagh!'

It was 1975 and Dave was sitting at his desk, struggling to eat a gobstopper.

He gingerly felt his face. 'This is breaking my jaw. If it wasn't free, I wouldn't bother.'

Greg, his assistant editor, looked up from proof-reading some artwork pages and sneered.

Dave removed the gobstopper and returned the sneer. 'I see you disapprove of my breakfast. But I haven't had to pay for my breakfasts since 1973. The cost to my health has been heavy; but it's a price I'm prepared to pay: nothing.'

He reached into a large box of assorted free sweets given away with comics since the 1950s.

'So let's see what else there is in the bilious buffet.'

He extracted a packet of sweet cigarettes with an illustration of a cruel-looking teacher in mortar board and gown on the front. A medal hung from his mortar board and a cigarette from his mouth as he wielded his cane.

Dave read the brand-name. '*Caning Commando* Sweet Cigarettes.'

There was a further caption on the side. 'For Tomorrow's Smokers'.

'Did you know these are worse for you than the real thing, Greg?'

Greg didn't bother to reply. 'I approve of that,' Dave added.

He rummaged further. 'Black jacks … Flying saucers … Aniseed balls. Once you've sucked off the outer layer, they make lethal mothballs … *Yo Ho Ho* liquorice chewing tobacco … *Kojak* lolly. "Who hates you, readers?" I do. And I always will … Edible false teeth …'

Greg lit a Black Russian Sobranie cigarette and shook his head disdainfully, continuing to ignore Dave. The cigarette completed his Man in Black image, with his black hair, black polo neck, black cords and blue and black, patent leather platform shoes. Dave disapproved, but at least it was preferable to Greg's other look: Billy Liar, complete with flying jacket and boots.

'Bit queer,' Dave commented on the Black Russian cigarette.

'No.' replied Greg. 'I smoke them to annoy you.'

'You succeeded. Now. Whatever you do, Greg, don't lose this box,' Dave continued. 'You wouldn't like to see me when I'm not on my fizzy pop.' He found a blue paper cylinder with a liquorice straw. 'Ah! The choky sherbet given away with *Gulp!* It lasted just three months. Let's drown our sorrows in sherbet.' He sucked up the sherbet enthusiastically through the liquorice straw. 'Mmm … the sweet nectar of failure.'

As promised on the label, he started choking, scattering sherbet down his Marks and Spencer white safari suit. As he dusted himself down, Greg finally smiled. 'It's those bloody things you're smoking,' scowled Dave and opened the window wide, letting the chilly Autumn air fill the office.

It was the suit Greg had recommended after Dave realised he needed to improve his image if he was to find himself a girlfriend, which he reluctantly thought he should. After all, he had been single for a long time. Forever. And he was an editor, even if it was only editor of *The Spanker* comic.

Greg had told him he'd look like Roger Moore's James Bond in a safari suit.

'You'll look so cool. You'll be the Editor With The Golden Pun,' he assured Dave.

'You really think so?'

'Definitely. Especially with your Hai Karate aftershave.'

'There's an instruction booklet of karate self-defence moves with it, to help me fend off lustful women driven crazy by the scent. I haven't been attacked so far.'

'You will be in a safari suit. Trust me.'

And Dave had fallen for it. It was necessary to be slim and trim to wear a safari suit; Dave was neither, and Greg knew that, which is why he suggested it. The suit looked terrible on Dave, just as Greg hoped it would. Dave's old fashioned, old man's haircut didn't help.

This gave Greg enormous pleasure and made the experience of being his assistant tolerable.

Dave was unaware of just how unflattering it was. Cost was his first priority. The safari suit wasn't expensive and that's what mattered. Not least because he was saving up for something far more important.

It is said that we fight our inner demons or surrender to them. Dave had hung out a white flag to his a long time ago. After his traumatic childhood, he liked to boast that he was possessed by more demons than the Gadarene swine.

These traumas were no minor 'character-building' misfortunes. There was his mother's mysterious disappearance, Mr Cooper's 'games' every Saturday morning, his father's break-downs, and more.

It was his demons who had built his character so that he had *become* the newsagent.

Or as near as possible, as the editor of *The Spanker.*

The Spanker had absorbed *The Fourpenny One,* the comic of Dave's dreams and nightmares, some years before. Its name was still visible on the comic's masthead in small type: *THE SPANKER* and *The Fourpenny One.*

There were other similarities between Dave and Mr Cooper. Both were involved in publishing: one at the beginning, the other at the end of the process. Cooper's hatred of his customers mirrored Dave's hatred of his readers. Cooper's sarcasm inspired Dave's sarcasm. Dave played secret games on his readers that surpassed even Cooper's games. History was repeating itself. All that was missing was the newsagent's brown jacket and the nicotine-stained fingers. Dave preferred a liquorice pipe.

Fortified by the knowledge that he was the embodiment of Mr Cooper, the purveyor to kids of all things cheap and usually rather nasty, Dave turned to Greg. 'Today's literary challenge. Did you come up with a new name for our great free gift?'

Dave held up a piece of red plastic that crudely resembled a delta-winged aircraft. 'This example of finest Hong Kong plastic.'

Greg consulted his notes as Dave prepared to fly the plane with an elastic band.

'Super Stuka?'

Dave scowled. 'Loada crapper,' he responded. It was typical of Greg, he thought, to suggest a Nazi plane. Greg was obsessed with all things German.

'Bionic Bomber?'

By way of response, Dave fired the plane directly at Greg. It flew across the large, high-ceilinged Edwardian room, Greg ducked and it crashed into the frosted-glass partition wall that separated them from the Spanker art department. 'Watch it! You could take someone's eye out with that thing,' Greg protested.

'Good,' said Dave. He smiled evilly as he picked up the futuristic aircraft. 'We'll call it The Super Nuker: The Red Terror from the skies.'

Greg looked appalled. 'What? You'll be giving kids nightmares about nuclear annihilation.'

'I live in hope. Although I personally look forward to nuclear annihilation. No, really. I do. Sadly, *The Spanker* would survive it. I'm sorry to say it will survive a nuclear winter.' Dave considered his comic's future. 'Although we might have to chisel it out on a rock. There'll be two-headed readers queuing up for it. We'll be able to sell the little bastards two copies at once.'

Greg sighed, 'Why can't we have decent free gifts like Angus, Angus and Angus's comics? The Whirly Bee. Or The Thunder Cracker. I loved those as a kid. They were great.'

'You didn't rate our last free gift? A conker with detailed instructions and free string?'

Dave fired the Super Nuker at Greg again. It flew past him, through the open window, and landed on the flat roof extension outside.

Dave scowled and continued. 'Our readers don't deserve a free gift that actually gives them pleasure. It has to be shite. I did suggest they give away real shite. I would have been happy to have made a donation.'

He went to the window and climbed out.

'There must be something more interesting we can give them?' pondered Greg.

Dave looked back at him. 'There is. Something they'll find useful all their lives. A free P45. I'd like to sack the lot. They'll get no reference from me.'

Dave made his way out along the roof.

Fleetpit Publications, who published *The Spanker*, were housed in an imposing six-storey former Edwardian hotel on Farringdon Street just off Fleet Street. Many of Britain's popular culture magazines were produced here. Women's magazines like *Darling, Twinset, Mumsy for Today's Young Mums* and *Heroine Chic*. Teenage girls magazines. Comics. Specialist magazines from *Stately Piles* to *Advanced Caravanning*. Sexy magazines like *Casino for the Man about Town*. Household names. The publications that had once filled Mr Cooper's shop.

The wind blew the Super Nuker further along the roof and Dave followed it. *The Spanker* office was located on the third floor at the back of Fleetpit House, looking down on an inner courtyard. Across the void, he could see the offices of the teenage magazines: *My Gang* with tartan scarves and feather boas hanging up in the window; *Hot Pants* with a poster of Farrah Fawcett and Lee Majors; *Get It On!* with a dreamy image of Gilbert O'Sullivan.

He glanced up to the sixth floor attic rooms. They were used mainly for storage and were unoccupied, except for Dave, who had been furtively living there for some months in the turreted tower at the very top of the building. He was content to see there was no sign of activity, so his secret was still safe.

He continued his rooftop stroll. He felt no sense of

embarrassment at being out there, staring into everyone's offices. Nothing ever fazed him, he was used to spying on people and to getting away with eccentric behaviour.

Nothing except …

From an office on the second floor below, he heard a long, whinnying, bleating laugh, instantly depressing, like the whine of a soul in eternal torment, and he trembled.

There it was again. It was hideous. Like the endless, monotonous drone of a buzz saw. It made him felt sick to the pit of his stomach and he had to steady himself against the wall and take deep breaths.

The hellish sound came from the editor of *Laarf!*, the most unfunny comic ever created. It filled Dave with dread, because, whenever he screwed up on the *The Spanker*, which was often, he was threatened with a six-month sentence on *Laarf!*

Sweating and shuddering at the thought, he carried on. He headed past *Pinafore*, edited by the tweedy, forty-something Bridget Paris. It was a rather dated, 'nice' comic, the kind parents and teachers approved of. A cigarette dangling from her mouth, she seemed utterly bored by the comic proofs she was checking and was oblivious to him passing by her window and leering in at her. He always felt there was something familiar about Bridget. He was sure he had seen somewhere before, but just couldn't work out where.

Beyond *Pinafore* was the top-selling, not-so-nice *Shandy*, edited by Glaswegian Joy Glass. The Super Nuker had now completed its bombing run and landed outside her window. Picking it up, he casually glanced into her office.

Joy was in her underwear, trying on clothes. Her light-fingered friend Sofia, who worked at the legendary Biba's, had 'liberated' some stock in August, just before Dorothy Perkins pulled the plug on the ailing store. Joy had bought three outfits from her at bargain prices: A gingham shirt and matching waistcoat and skirt. A pink, satin-weave, cotton trouser-suit. Cotton dungarees with a yellow and black Art Deco pattern, reminiscent of the Biba logo.

Unaware she was being watched, the striking twenty-four-year old tried on the pink trouser-suit. It fitted her perfectly. She imagined herself in a *Nova* fashion spread – the famous women's magazine that had more male than female readers. That would show Daddy. She knew her Australian father wrote for *Nova* sometimes – alongside Graham Greene, Lynda Lee-Potter and Christopher Booker – giving readers his legendary, eye-witness accounts of wars in far-flung corners of the globe. She imagined the awed expression on his handsome, tanned, chiselled face as he saw his daughter staring out from its pages as he sipped his Pimms in the Long Bar in Raffles Hotel, Singapore. She had made it on her own.

Then she recalled *Nova* had just folded. Like Biba.

And all the time she dressed and undressed, Dave watched through the window, open-mouthed, slack-jawed, unable to avert his eyes from the object of his desire. His loins were stirred as never before. Joy was so intent on trying on her bargain-price purchases, she was unaware that she was giving Dave a long and intimate private floorshow. She pouted and posed in a mirror, imagining the effect on Greg, her current boyfriend, who seemed to have lost interest in her recently.

'This should light your fire,' she teased her lover in the mirror, her man in black, who was actually better looking than the *Cadbury's Milk Tray* man in black. Greg could swing across the rooftops for her, anytime. She imagined him landing cat-like on the roof, deftly opening the window and entering her bedroom, and ... Lost in her fantasy, she stepped out of her dungarees and turned seductively towards the window, running her fingers through his luxuriant, stylish black mane, murmuring, 'Take me now.'

And there, indeed, on the other side of the glass, was a man staring in at her. Dave.

Her expression quickly changed to shock and fury and it was no-good Dave lamely pointing to his Super Nuker to explain why he was spying on her. His glazed expression and open, drooling mouth told her otherwise. In vain he covered his eyes, pretending he couldn't see her in her underwear.

Then he shook his head, miming the words 'No. No. You've

got it wrong. It's not you I'm interested in! No! Not you!' and desperately pointed to *something else* in her office. The real focus of his lust. But she shook her fist, angrily pulled down the blind, and in a moment it was lost from view.

His fantasy was hanging from a coat hook within. Sexy, slinky, grey and white, with a generous, warm, soft, inviting collar. It was everything he had always wanted. Everything he had ever desired.

Joy's vintage Arctic fox fur.

CHAPTER FOUR

Knowing Joy, she would shortly be coming round to *The Spanker* office to give him a seeing-to, but not in a good way, rather, in a Glaswegian way. Unless, of course, she was wearing her fox fur at the time. Then it might be a good way, but he couldn't take that risk. He rapidly made his way back across the roof, climbed through his office window, deposited the Super Nuker, told Greg he wasn't feeling well and he was going home early, and was out of there. He'd be feeling extremely unwell if he met up with Joy.

He decided to hang out at The Hoop and Grapes over the road, then, once all the Fleetpit staff had gone home, climb the fire escape to the top floor, let himself into the building with the duplicate keys he had cut, and go up to his turret in the roof.

Over a pint, Dave wondered about telling Joy of his strange preference for fur. How much could he get across, and how much would she believe before she delivered her first punch or headbutt?

He had recently confided his story to Greg. Dave had been editing *The Spanker Wild West Annual* at the time, and had held onto the Davy Crockett hat used for a photo feature. He stroked it fondly. 'A coonskin cap as worn in *Davy Crockett, King of the Wild Frontier*.'

'And John Wayne in *The Alamo*,' reminded Greg.

'Yes,' said Dave dreamily, looking far away. 'It reminds me of my first love ...'

'A girl you went to see *The Alamo* with?'

'No, I went on my own.'

'Your first love wasn't John Wayne …?' Greg asked suspiciously.

'No, I leave the bum-boy stuff to you. When I got home, I went up into the loft for the hat.' Dave's eyes gleamed as he remembered. 'It was up there with my Davy Crockett moccasins, lunch-box and cap gun…'

'I had a hat, too,' recalled Greg.

'But yours came from Woolworths, right?' said Dave.

'Everyone's did.'

'Oh, no. My mother made mine *specially*,' said Dave triumphantly. 'She loved anything to do with fur.'

'It meant a lot to you?'

'Oh, yes. I actually lost my cherry to my Davy Crockett hat.'

'To a hat …?' Greg was gobsmacked, this was weird, even for Dave.

'It was the best night I've ever had. It wasn't exactly the opposite sex – it was the opposite species.'

'That is … unusual,' Greg said diplomatically.

'Yes,' Dave reminisced, continuing to stroke the coonskin. 'I also dated my mum's fur coat for a while.'

'What did your mother say about that?'

'It happened after she disappeared.'

'I remember you saying. One Saturday she just …vanished?' Greg asked curiously. 'So is she actually dead then …?'

'No one knows,' said Dave lost in thought. 'Her body was never found.' He sighed and shrugged his shoulders. He had told the story so often, it was no longer painful to him. Or, rather, he told himself it was no longer painful.

'It sounds like she could be dead?' said Greg gently.

'We never heard from her again, so I suppose she must be.' Dave grimaced, despite himself.

'That's really tragic,' said Greg, feeling some rare sympathy for Dave.

'So …I was looked after by my big sister and my dad.'

'You seem okay about it?'

'You've got to be, Greg. And it was a long time ago. Nearly twenty years ago now. You can't go on grieving forever. I don't like grief, you see?' Dave struggled to explain feelings he resented. 'It makes me feel ... sad.' He was starting to look very sad.

'Well, yes, it would do.' Greg tried to distract him. 'So what did they think of your interest in fur?'

'My sister first noticed when the nap of the fur went a bit flat ...' Dave said meaningfully. 'We never discussed it, but she left the key to mum's wardrobe out ...'

'That was thoughtful of her.'

'Then my dad saw what I'd been doing with it and he went mad: "You never even took it off the hangar!" He said there'd never been anything like that in his family.'

'What did they do about it?' Greg was curious.

'They talked about sending me for treatment. But the doctor had never heard of it.'

'I suppose it's not really bestiality,' said Greg, reassuringly, 'because it's not alive.' Then added, as an afterthought: 'It's having sex with a *dead* animal.'

'The doctor preferred not to talk about it,' recalled Dave. 'There was no pamphlet for what I had. And he didn't want to write one either. I was very disappointed when I grew up to discover that women weren't all furry like a grizzly bear. I would long for a woman with a back like a Turkish deck-hand. I wasn't sure I was alone with these feelings, but apparently I am.'

'So what happened to the fur coat?'

'It packed me in,' Dave frowned. 'It was pretty terrible. The wardrobe dumped me.'

'Dumped you?' Greg's eyes widened.

'Oh, yes.'

'How?'

Dave shrugged. 'She just said I don't want to see you anymore.'

Greg's interest was definitely piqued. This could be useful for future 'Dave stories' down the pub. His odd ways were already the subject of considerable gossip. 'Wait a minute. Let me see if

I've got this right. Your mother's fur coat actually *spoke* to you …?

Dave nodded, as if it was the most normal thing in the world.

'What did it say?'

'It told me it was over.'

'You actually hear voices …?'

'Oh, yes,' said Dave without a trace of embarrassment. 'All the time.'

'You've never thought of seeking professional help?'

Dave shook his head. He'd seen what the psychiatrists had done to his dad. 'I also have fond memories of her crocodile-skin handbag. From Nigeria.'

'Her handbag?' Not just mammals then, but *reptiles,* Greg thought. This was getting better and better. This was more than office gossip, it was valuable ammunition. If Dave kept this up, he might be able to get him sectioned and take over his job as editor.

'And we won't talk about her ferret stole,' continued Dave, lost in his memories. 'I couldn't bear those dead, accusing eyes looking at me on the pillow. It didn't have the glint I was looking for. But at least it was something. I gave it a French kiss and nearly choked on the mothball.'

Greg nodded understandingly.

Dave looked bitter. 'My sister stopped me taking it to the pictures once.'

Greg nodded again, successfully hiding a smirk behind his hand.

This was brilliant, he thought. If his secret plan to produce a new comic didn't work out, getting Dave certified would be an excellent alternative.

* * *

Later, sitting in his rooms at the top of Fleetpit House, Dave was still in a melancholic mood. He looked out the window towards St Paul's to cheer himself, but there were two 1960s brutal, shimmering glass office blocks in the way.

He had one of those annoying chains of thoughts he could have done without. Joy's Arctic fox fur reminded him of his mum's furs and how much he missed her.

Then he thought of how his father, Peter, had lavished those furs on his wife, and this set him thinking how much he missed his dad, too.

To make it worse, the past had been carefully censored by his sister Annie, his aunt and his dad; they would never discuss it, so he only had a vague idea of his family history.

He leafed through a photo album Annie had passed onto him, trying to make sense of it.

He knew his mother Jean had met Peter during the war in a Soho club, where she'd been working as a singer and there was a photo of them together. It was fairly obvious she was a hostess, although the family always said she was a singer. It was his David Niven looks and manners that first attracted Jean, according to the agreed history and he was very handsome in the photo, before he started drinking heavily.

There were more photos of their wartime marriage before they went out to the colonies. Peter was a scientific adviser to the Department of Agriculture, and there was a nice shot of Annie just after she was born in Nigeria in 1945. But then a quarter of the photos in the six pages of their time in Africa had been carefully removed for no apparent reason. The remaining images were just typical, colonial sight-seeing images of Africa and told him nothing.

Two years later, they were sent home and Peter was dismissed for reasons that no-one would ever explain properly to Dave. All they had to show for their stay were a few carved African statues and the crocodile-skin handbag.

Jean never talked about Nigeria, but when Dave had been naughty she would sometimes say, 'Go to your hut, boy' instead of 'Go to your room.'

Peter got a new job as a chemist in a laboratory at a grain merchant's, M&R Pell. There were rows with Jean, but there were happy memories too, and Dave needed to hold onto them. There was a photo of Dave excitedly unwrapping his first chemistry set one Christmas – The Radioactive Laboratory – bestowing him with a love of science that would prove useful in later years. He treasured it alongside his Electrodes Set ('Fun with Electricity') and Glass Blowing Set, which involved softening glass to 1,000 degrees Fahrenheit (blow torch supplied). The Radioactive Laboratory really did live up to its name. It contained isotopes of polonium, ruthenium, uranium ore, a Geiger counter, and a cloud chamber to check radiation levels.

There was a photo of Peter patiently showing seven year old Dave how to avoid a nuclear meltdown.

Then Jean vanished, and everyone said she'd gone off to start a new life with one of her mysterious lovers. Peter fell apart and got heavily into debt. He spent periods in hospital where they fried his brains. In between hospital stays, he would make home-brew beer with a high alcohol content. M&R Pell unwittingly supplied the cereals, hops, yeast and laboratory equipment.

He took over a derelict, bombed-out house just down the street from their home for his illicit factory. An out of focus photo, doubtless taken by a drunken customer, showed him proudly brewing a *Bockbier* there with secret malt combinations and an impressive 18% alcohol content. He jacked it up to 30% through fractional freezing using the 'mad-scientist-ice-in-the-bath' method. The result was popular amongst friends, neighbours and pubs. A pint of the local strong stuff was easily eclipsed by Peter's 'blackout'. It was the crystal meth of its day.

The trouble was, he was drinking 'blackout' faster than he could make it. Under the influence of still-fermenting beer, in September 1968, Peter finally exploded. He and Dave were watching Bernard Shaw's *St. Joan* on the BBC. The effect on Peter was electric. He staggered drunkenly to his feet, lurched forward to the television screen, shook his fist at the Inquisitor who had sentenced Joan to death and hissed, 'You bastards. You *evil* bastards.' Dave was mystified, even though it *was* a brilliant performance by Sir John Gielgud as the Inquisitor. With angry tears streaming down his face, Peter started to punch and kick the set. When that proved ineffective, he went and found Dave's old cricket bat and smashed the screen.

This time, they really fried Peter's brains. He was gone for two months. Dave had some idea what he went through – he had once tried out the electrodes from his electricity set on himself.

Two years later Peter blacked-out forever in the derelict house, surrounded by sacks of wheat and barley, after sampling his revolutionary new *40%* brew. Some local Germans had come up with a rival toxic *Doppelbock*: 'Von Ryan's Express' and Peter had been determined to top them. His answer to his home-brew rivals was 'From Here to Eternity'. It carried out its promise. It was a cereal killer.

CHAPTER FIVE

The next morning, in The Spanker office, Dave was in better spirits. He had made his peace with Joy, thanks to a craven apology he delivered over the phone to her. She was amazed that he was more interested in the fur than her, but finally, grudgingly, accepted his unlikely explanation. So he no longer needed to keep his office door locked.

He just wanted to forget his awful past. It was why he enjoyed working on *The Spanker*. He could be a Peter Pan his entire life and never have to grow up.

Unfortunately, Greg didn't feel the same way. He looked up from reading the pages of *The Caning Commando, The Spanker's* number one story.

'Dave, what are we doing …? Two grown men editing *The Caning Commando*. It's embarrassing.'

'*What's* embarrassing?'

'A teacher with a cane who single-handedly defeats the Germans?'

'You forget we won the war. So we have a right to cane them.'

'There must be *something* we can do to improve it.'

Dave shook his head.

'Changing the Major's story requires effort, which I'm not prepared to make and our readers are not prepared to read. We could shuffle the pages in any order and they wouldn't notice, as long as there's caning and there's Germans.'

Greg steeled himself to look at the story again, shuddered, and shook his head sorrowfully. 'I'm just praying I can find a publisher for my novel.'

'Greg, you've only got one unpublished novel. I've lined my loft with mine. I'm sorry to say you look like a lifer to me. You have a comic pallor. You're here for the long stretch. Come to terms with your sentence. It's always best.'

'But we're writers,' Greg insisted. 'We've got to keep trying.'

Dave sucked on a liquorice pipe, trying to extract imaginary smoke from the pink 'embers' in the bowl. 'But what is a writer, Greg ...?' He nodded at their Imperial typewriters. 'It's a typist without prospects. Face it, we're failures. In fact, we are over-qualified as failures.'

'Don't you ever have dreams, Dave?'

'Wet dreams, once. But not anymore. I'm getting old.' Dave smiled. 'From now on, Greg, it's a nice long slide towards the grave.' He reflected on this for a moment and then added: 'Actually, I'll get to the cemetery twenty years ahead of our readers. They'll have to endure two more decades of this shite.'

'I know what you mean ...' agreed Greg. 'I never tell anyone I work in comics. I always say I'm in publishing.'

'I share your sense of shame. A chimpanzee would be ashamed of this job. At least they can organise a tea party. Our readers drink out of the tea pot.'

In fact, Greg, had been secretly planning his exit from *The Spanker* for some months. The Fleetpit board had asked him to prepare a new, realistic war comic, but he had been ordered to keep it hidden from Ron Punch, their managing editor. Ron, a D-Day veteran, would never approve of shootings, bayonetings, and men being blown apart. Especially the real war comic Greg had prepared.

However, now all the work was done, he felt he could risk showing it to Dave. He knew Dave was sly, but he also knew there was no way he could sabotage his project now.

Greg proudly took a dummy comic out of his briefcase to show him. 'Look. *This* is what we should be doing.'

Entitled *Blitzkrieg!*, the cover showed a German stormtrooper firing towards the reader.

Dave repeated the top line, 'Achtung! Achtung! The Great New War Comic for Boys!'

There was a tin-foil free Iron Cross attached.

He leafed through *Blitzkrieg!* and the pipe dropped from his mouth. '*German* heroes!"

'Why not …?' grinned Greg triumphantly at the young fogey in the safari suit sitting opposite him. 'It is the seventies, for God's sake.'

'Greg, you do know you live in Britain …? In El Alamein Close, Colchester? Or is it Montgomery Drive? Or Normandy Avenue?

'Churchill Way, actually.'

'Not Stalingrad Crescent? Von Rundstedt Lane? Or Erwin Rommel Road?'

'I'd be honoured to live in a road named after Rommel. He was a great general,' said Greg, deliberately provocative.

'Ron hates Germans. He fought them for two years.'

'Well it's time he got over it.' Greg said irritably. 'The board said I don't need his approval.'

'But Ron was a *D-Day* veteran. He was younger than us when he stormed up the beaches and *killed* Germans.'

'I don't give a shit. He's held up progress long enough. It's time he was put out to grass.'

'You haven't got some secret Nazi temple at home …?' asked Dave suspiciously.

'Don't be stupid. There were good Germans, too, you know,' said Greg.

'Not according to Ron,' replied Dave. He handed *Blitzkrieg!* back. 'He never talks about it, but I'm told he had a bad war. If I were you, I'd keep that well out of sight. You don't want to bring out his thousand-yard stare.'

Greg took Dave's advice and carefully slipped *Blitzkrieg!* back into his briefcase.

But he felt he had to explain his great vision further. He talked like an advertising man, because that was his previous job, in Fleetpit's competitions department. 'For the first time a British comic will have *authentic* war stories. It's going to be groundbreaking.'

He leaned forward and looked meaningfully at Dave. 'It's time for a new broom, Dave. Time to get rid of the detritus.'

Dave didn't like the sound of that. It reminded him of new broom Mrs Thatcher who had been elected Tory leader earlier in the year, defeating Ted Heath. Mrs Thatcher had actually waved a giant blue feather duster at the party conference, ready to sweep away the cobwebs of the past. He knew he was a cobweb, he knew he was detritus.

As Greg showed off about his creation, Dave gave no hint he was impressed.

Looking at the dramatic layouts and hard-hitting stories of *Blitzkrieg!*, he feared it had the makings of a hit. There were German heroes fighting on the Russian and African Fronts and one token British hero, *Longest Day Logan*, fighting his way out from the Normandy beaches. Compared to *The Caning Commando*, it had the realism young readers were desperate for; answering that question they were always asking: 'What was it *really* like in the war?'

Blitzkrieg! might sell a million copies a week, compared with *The Spanker's* worrying 120,000 copies a week and sinking. In fact, it was sinking so fast, it was quite likely the board would change their mind about a free gift Super Nuker issue to boost sales and the comic would be axed.

If *Blitzkrieg!* did top the comic charts, Greg's rise from the ranks would be meteoric. He was disgustingly ambitious, a young man on his way to the top. That's why he was still living at home with his parents. So he could spend all his spare time working on his novel.

Dave had no illusions what would happen if Greg became his boss. He'd already seen just how ruthless he could be: he was only dating Joy because he thought her famous journalist father could be useful to him. Dave had to find a way to sabotage the new comic,but he'd bide his time, until the right opportunity came along.

'*Blitzkrieg!* is the Future!' concluded Greg, imagining he was sitting down to thunderous applause like Mrs Thatcher, at the Tory conference.

Dave picked up the pages of Caning Commando artwork and shrugged nonchalantly, hiding his true feelings far better than Ted Heath. 'Let's just stay in the past for now, shall we?' He settled back comfortably in his chair to read another cosy episode of *The Caning Commando*.

The picture strip story was told at frenetic speed, and began with an introductory caption:

'Because of his legendary caning skills, the War Office recruited
schoolmaster Victor Grabham to be –
THE CANING COMMANDO.'

The more ludicrous the story was, the more Dave was going to enjoy it.

CHAPTER SIX

An army despatch rider rode his motorbike through the rural leafy lanes of wartime England, past the village of Lower Belting Bottom, and down the long drive that led to The Golden Hind Academy for Boys.

As he parked his machine outside the stately Victorian building, he could hear the swish of a cane from within, and the resulting cries of pain.

In the housemaster's study, a schoolboy was being caned by a teacher: Victor Grabham, a menacing figure in mortarboard and gown, tall and gaunt, yet with the strength of ten gym masters. He had a hawk-like nose, a cruel mouth and the cold, dark eyes of a Satanic exam inspector. A military medal instead of the customary tassel hung down from his mortarboard.

The schoolboy, Alfred 'Half' Mast, a gormless-looking scamp with 'begging bowl' eyes, had a somewhat ape-like physique, and was talking as he was being caned.

'*Oww!* I likes being caned, Sir. It gives me a touch of class. *Yaaah!* Six of the best makes me feel like a toff, Sir. *Aaah!* Remind me again, Sir, what I did wrong.'

'Just keeping my caning arm in, Alf Mast. So you're contributing to the war effort.'

'Thank you, Sir. *Ooh!* I'm a bit slow today, Sir. Why don't we just shoot the Jerries instead?'

'We don't waste precious British bullets on the Hun. We send them back to Berlin with a red rear.'

The despatch rider, still wearing his goggles and gauntlets, entered with a telegram. 'Caning Commando? Secret message from the War Department. Eyes only.'

Victor Grabham read the message impressively fast. 'Bad news, Alf. Your nan's street was bombed last night. She's homeless. They're sending us into occupied France to give the sausage-noshers a taste of their own medicine.'

He flexed his cane menacingly. 'This calls for rearguard action.'

That night, the Caning Commando and Alf Mast were dropped behind enemy lines. Hiding in bushes, they observed a nearby French chateau with a swastika draped over it. It was the German H.Q.!

Grabham was now wearing an officer's army uniform with his mortarboard and gown over the top of it. He turned to give an order to his assistant, Alf Mast, now dressed in a corporal's uniform. Over his shoulder, Alf was carrying a golf bag containing a selection of canes.

'Ready to lay down your valueless life for King and Country, Corporal?'

'Yes, please, sir.'

'Then hand me the *number three* cane.'

'*Number three*, Sir? Are you sure, Sir? Isn't that a bit strong, Sir?'

He passed across a cane that came in three separate sections. The teacher connected them together so it was like a chimney sweep's extended brush. 'Just think of your poor old nan, lad. Did the Boche show her any mercy?' He flexed the super-cane. 'When I've finished with them, their arses will be so red-raw, they'll be able to guide our bombers in.'

Suddenly, they were surrounded by German soldiers. 'Drop your cane, Englander schwein! The war is over for the Caning Commando and Corporal Punishment!'

Soon after, the plucky pair found themselves in a damp, dripping prison cell in the basement of the chateau.

'What'll they do to us, Sir?' asked Alf. 'Will they thrash us in a Hunnish way, Sir? I can take it, Sir.'

'Don't worry, lad. If they make the caning unbearable for you, I'll throw myself in front of the seat of your pants and take the striping for you.'

'Will you, Sir? You'd do that for me? You're a hero, Sir. A real toff.'

'It will require split second timing. We'd better practise now. Bend over.' Alf duly bent over a chair. The Caning Commando bent over Alf.

Suddenly, a section of the stone wall slid open, revealing a secret corridor beyond.

'A secret corridor!' exclaimed Alf Mast.

Yvette, a beautiful French Resistance fighter in a tight-fitting sweater, appeared. 'I am Yvette of the French Resistance.' She took in the sight of the two of them bent over. 'You British have different ways. But moving on, you must come quickly. You are to be caned at dawn. There's a caning squad waiting and I am sorry to say it's a dishonourable caning. How you say? "Strides down".'

'The swine!' muttered the Caning Commando.

Alf could not keep his eyes off Yvette. 'Who's that Bumpy Man, Sir? Why is he speaking funny, Sir? The Bumpy Man, Sir. He's giving me a tingle, Sir. Is that right, Sir? Is it, Sir?'

'You young scamp,' scowled Grabham. 'If I had my cane with me, I'd make you tingle.'

They headed down the secret corridor.

Alf was still looking open-mouthed at Yvette. 'I can't help it, Sir. I'm getting that tingling feeling below decks again, Sir.'

'That's it. You're in credit for a thrashing.' growled the Caning Commando.

'Perhaps Mr Yvette could thrash me, Sir? I think I could take a thrashing from Mr Yvette, Sir.'

'You'll get no thrashing from Mr Yvette. That would not be contributing to the war effort.'

By now they had exited the corridor and entered the grounds of the German H.Q. Yvette retrieved the Caning Commando's bag of canes from behind a bush. 'We managed to get your canes back. There is a light plane waiting to fly you across the channel. Now please – we must hurry.'

The teacher took out a cane. 'Our business here is not done, Yvette. We have to avenge Alf's dear old nan. She was bombed out last night.'

Yvette looked concerned at Corporal Punishment. 'Oh, you poor boy. You have lost your home?'

'No, I stay with Sir at the school, Mr Yvette. I've got me comfy hammock in the boiler room. 'Cos I'm too common to sleep in the dorm with the other boys.'

Suddenly, German soldiers ran towards them. 'Achtung! Achtung! Englanders escaping!'

Grabham turned to Yvette. 'Stand aside. There's caning to be done. Come dawn, their arses will be redder than your lipstick.'

Then the Caning Commando charged into the German ranks. Before they could take aim, he struck them a series of devastating blows with his cane, and their guns went flying.

As the Germans fled in terror, the Caning Commando pursued them, endlessly thrashing them with his cane. 'Howzat for a Bouncing Bum raid?' he snarled.

'Nein! Nein!' they pleaded over the sound of birch on buttocks.

'Yes. Nine of the best for you, Fritz! Yvette! Turn away! Put the tea on! It's time to Carpet Bum the Hun!'

The Germans were hurled through the air by the sheer ferocity of his attack as he roared: 'I'm going to boot you up the Brandenburg Gate, you shifty-eyed schnapps drinkers! I'll give you "strides down", you Munich mutton munchers! You'll get it up the Unter Den Linden, you panzer pansies!'

'Aaaghtung!' they screamed.

Alf had joined in, hurling blackboard dusters and booting fleeing Germans. 'Take that in the South End for the East End!'

'Nicely put, young Alf!' smiled Grabham, then turned to Yvette. 'How's that tea coming?'

Later that night, their plane landed them safely back at the Golden Hind Academy. It was a good night's work well done. In the housemaster's study they listened to the proud and stirring words of Winston Churchill on the radio:

We shall defend our honour whatever the cost. We shall cane them on the breeches. We shall cane them on their heiling hands. We shall cane them over chairs, over knees and over desks. We shall never surrender.

A little misty-eyed at hearing the great man's stirring words, Grabham began marking exercise books while Alf Mast started his day's chores to pay for his keep. 'Whitewash the latrines, lad. Make them fit enough to eat your dinner from. As usual.'

'Thank you, Sir. It'll be my pleasure, Sir.'

Their adventure concluded with a final caption:

'Fall in for more caning capers with The Caning Commando in next week's *Spanker*, chums.'

CHAPTER SEVEN

The Caning Commando was the brainchild of the Major. He had a *Carry On* film sense of humour, which Dave and the readers shared. 'It's time to Carpet Bum the Hun!' was the most popular catchphrase in school playgrounds, alongside smirking references to female teachers as 'Bumpy Men', which sometimes led to real-life thrashings.

From its first appearance in the number one issue of *The Spanker* in 1960, the series was hugely popular, which owed much to the artwork by Roger Baker, a disabled ex-serviceman, originally discovered by the publisher when he was producing impressive chalk pavement art and begging for change in Farringdon Road market. Roger brought 'something of the night' to the Commando, a vampiric darkness and mystery that made him a scary bogie-man for many boys, so they were relieved he was 'on our side' and caning for Britain.

The Major had been a prisoner of war of the Japanese, that much was certain, but the rest was in some doubt. His rank and scholastic qualifications, for instance, which enabled him to obtain the post of housemaster in a public school, and inspired the character of Victor Grabham. Dave suspected he'd never risen above corporal.

He wore a threadbare camel hair coat with a velvet collar, but was always immaculately turned out, sporting a magnificent handlebar moustache. He lived life 'on the hoof', on the run from wives, debt collectors, bookies and 'the rozzers'. He carried a portable typewriter around with him and could write a story, have a conversation and make a bet all at the same time. Dave remembered their first meeting. The Major had looked up from completing a script and introduced himself: 'My name's the Major and I earn more money than the prime minister.'

Then he checked his watch:

'Fifteen minutes. Two minutes off my existing record.' He handed the manuscript across to Dave who was pleased that it was not typed on the back of a court summons like the last one. Although the summons was not in the Major's name. Dave wondered how many names the Major had. He was impressed by his speed. He hoped that one day he would be able to write complete crap that fast.

'Thanks, Major,' he said. 'Another literary masterpiece.'

''Cos I used to teach boys, you see? And thrash 'em. Before taking up writing.'

'After you had that problem with the school fees?'

'Not so good with the old arithmetic. Easier to subtract than add.'

'And the lead on the school chapel roof that got blown away in a storm.'

'Nothing the Beak could make stand. Rather like the roof, eh?'

He was always paid in cash, so he headed on to Ron's office, announcing in his booming voice, 'I've come for my readies.'

He eyed up Sharon, Ron's secretary and, in the worst tradition of the seventies, commented within her earshot, 'Look at the form on that. I could get my oats there. Ride her to the finishing post. Have you rogered her yet, Ron?'

Sharon scowled. Ron said nothing.

Then, adding insult to injury, the Major removed the detachable collar from his shirt. 'Got some lipstick on it last night.'

Ron turned to his secretary. 'Sharon, could you do the Major's collar?'

A glowering but acquiescent Sharon had no choice but to take the offending item away to clean it.

Ron then handed the Major a thick wad of pound notes for the scripts he'd written, complimenting him: 'You're still number one, chum.' The Major looked at the money but never counted it. He could tell from the feel it was all there. He'd nod and put it away. 'Come in handy. You've got to feed and water them to get them to drop their drawers.'

Then the two of them went off for a liquid lunch at The Hoop and Grapes, onto the Cheddar Cheese, followed by Ye Olde Cock Tavern opposite the High Courts in the Strand. Finally, the two cocks would end up in The Eight Veils in Soho.

As a result, the Major was often more unwell than the legendary drinker Jeffrey Bernard and this was to Dave's advantage. The Major kept no carbon copies of his manuscripts, never read them back or looked at the finished version in the comic, and often had no idea what day of the week it was, let alone what he had written about. He was the perfect patsy for Dave. Because, for some time, whenever a suitable opportunity presented itself, Dave had been secretly altering the Major's stories, writing in evil ideas for his own pleasure that he hoped the readers would try at home with lethal results.

He was aware just how influenced they were by comics. There had been complaints from parents about other stories giving kids dangerous ideas: the firework-fuelled, kid brother-piloted, dustbin spaceship. Playing submarines in an old abandoned fridge, and using mum's tablecloth as a parachute while jumping off a council flat roof. No brains required.

He'd started by adding a scene where the Caning Commando and Corporal Punishment go swimming at night in the old quarry near their school when they see German paratroopers land.

Then the plucky pair visit the War Office in London and Alf Mast was taken ill after eating his beloved fish and chips. Dave added him drinking Thames water 'for medicinal purposes'.

As there were no complaints, he'd upped the ante by having the Caning Commando make gas bombs from household cleaning products. If there was any comeback he could always say, 'I didn't know kids could make mustard gas. At least not in dad's shed.'

It was funny. Just like getting a punch in the face every Saturday was funny. He knew Mr Cooper would think it was hilarious. When Dave talked about hating the readers, everyone thought he was joking and couldn't possibly be serious. They assumed it was just part of a grouchy act, like W.C. Fields, who was believed to hate children. But it was no act. He was hiding in plain sight.

His dream was to edit his readers, a hundred here, a hundred there. It was true he would never see the results of his work, but neither does a bomber pilot when he drops his payload.

Dave's need for revenge for his childhood humiliations had to be satisfied. His readers were going to pay with their lives and the Caning Commando was the perfect murder weapon.

If there was an investigation, he'd blame it on the Major. No one would believe his denials. It wouldn't be Sharon feeling the Major's collar, it would be the rozzers.

Greg looked over expectantly for Dave's reaction to the latest episode of the Commando. 'Okay, Danno, what have we got …?'

Dave scowled at Greg's quote from *Hawaii Five-O*. 'Do you think you could possibly not talk in TV clichés today, please?'

'The story about the number three cane and Mr Yvette. It's crap, isn't it?'

'Ah, Greg … Greg … complete crap is our goal,' Dave smiled. 'If I can ever achieve a completely crap issue, I'm a happy man. I wouldn't wipe my arse with *The Spanker*. That would be disrespectful to my arse.'

'The Caning Commando is unfunny and pathetic,' said Greg venomously.

'It's what our readers deserve, Greg. They're not carbon-based sentient life forms.'

'They're still our readers. They're paying your wages, Dave.'

'I'd rather they paid my redundancy. And I think we should stop referring to them as "readers". We are catering for the hard-of-looking, you know.'

He grinned gleefully as he continued. 'I should remind you

the Caning Commando comes from a long tradition of stories catering for the British working class's unhealthy obsession with caning and public schools, which goes all the way back to the classic *Fags Army* published in 1914.'

'*Fags Army*!'

'Four Fags, the servants of the senior boys, decide to join up under age and fight for King and Country.'

'Sounds awful,' said Greg.

'You liked *If.* That was about public schools and caning.'

'I preferred *Privilege*,' Greg replied, suddenly brightening up. 'Did I ever tell you about that movie?'

'Let me think ...' pondered Dave. 'Yes ...yes, I believe you might have done,' said Dave, his sarcasm lost on his assistant.

'It's about a rock star, played by Paul Jones, who becomes a messiah for the masses.'

Dave pretended to look interested. 'And, er, wasn't that the film you saw with your best friend, Bernie?'

'Yes. The night before he was sent to a detention centre for stealing cars.' Greg looked sad. 'How did you know?'

'Oh, you may have mentioned it,' said Dave breezily. 'Once or twice.'

'I haven't been going on about him again, have I?' asked Greg, looking guilty.

'No, not at all,' reassured Dave.

'Bernie was much better looking than Paul Jones, you know?'

'I believe you said.'

'He was so handsome,' recalled Greg, thinking back to happier days.

'Yes. I remember from all those photos you showed me,' said Dave kindly.

'Would you like to see them again?' asked Greg, reaching into his case. 'I've actually got them right here with me.'

'No,' said Dave hastily. 'Maybe we could look at them later?'

'They didn't really do him justice, you know?' said Greg enthusiastically.

'No ...?'

'Yes. He could have easily been a movie star.'

'Well, he certainly ended up like one,' said Dave. 'James Dean. That car crash.'

'Yes …' said Greg sighing. 'He was addicted to cars. Stole an E-type Jag and lost control.'

Dave could see Greg's eyes filling with tears, as they often did, when he talked about his friend's death. Dave wondered if he was secretly gay. He suspected he was; he never seemed to be that into Joy or other women. If so, he might be able to use it against him in the future.

Dave liked to have secret files on people, and regularly went through Greg's waste-paper bin, looking for evidence of hidden sides to his character that he didn't want his colleagues to know about.

'It was so tragic what happened to Bernie,' said Dave gently. 'Any time you want to talk about him, mate, I'm here for you.'

* * *

Ron Punch entered, irritated and harassed by an interruption to his usual sedentary life. But he still walked with a proud military bearing: shoulders back, chin forward, sporting a blazer with his veteran's badge. 'Just had publicity come to see me. A German kid nearly killed his British pen friend and they're blaming it on *The Caning Commando*.'

'No? Really?' said Dave, hiding his delight.

'Seems the British kid played the Commando and the German played his arch enemy …'

'The Oberspankerfuhrer?' interjected Dave. 'Leader of the feared Wackem SS, he drives around in his Underpanzer.'

Greg raised one eyebrow and continued in an arch, German accent. 'His much feared canes ver attached to ze periscope of a U-Boat for six months, so zey're hardened in brine.'

'Also known,' Dave concluded, 'as ze Blue Man becos his arse vas frozen solid on ze Russian Front.'

'Pack it in, you two,' snapped Ron. He shook his head, baffled. 'I don't know what the Major was playing at, but he had a scene where the Oberspankerfuhrer interrogates the Commando by shoving him underwater in a bath.'

'What's wrong with that?' asked Dave.

'Nothing. But the Commando survives by pulling the plug out, and breathing air through the plughole.'

'Ah, yes ... I remember,' said Dave.

He remembered very well. It was one of numerous scenes *he* had added to the Major's stories.

'Well, the kid only had to go and imitate the Commando, didn't he?' said Ron.

Brilliant, thought Dave, just as he had hoped. But he looked up, sober-faced, at his managing editor. 'So what happened?'

'What do you think?' said Ron.

'I have no idea,' said Dave innocently.

'Suction pulled his face against the plughole, smashed his teeth in.'

'Oh, my God,' said Dave, hiding a smirk with his hand.

'Which he swallowed,' continued Ron.

'That's ... terrible!' gasped Greg, trying to hold back a guffaw.

'Yes, it is,' said Dave, hoping his own smirk had gone. 'I feel ... really bad. Still, at least he'll get a lot of money off the tooth fairy.'

'Although ...' queried Greg, 'if he swallowed his teeth, that's not much fun for the tooth fairy.'

You're right,' agreed Dave, 'After the kid recovered them, he wouldn't want to put them under his pillow, would he?'

Ron scowled at their levity.

Dave tried to look serious. 'I should have taken that scene out, Ron. It was stupid of me.'

'Not half as stupid as the kid,' reassured Ron. 'And the Major. He should have taken more care.'

'Even so,' said Dave, 'is the boy all right now ...?' The expression on his face was serious and concerned, even as the demons inside him were laughing their heads off and singing, 'All I want for Christmas are my two front brain cells.'

'Apparently. Although I'd like to know what was he was

doing with a *German* pen friend in the first place?'

'Good point,' said Dave, glancing meaningfully at Greg. 'Fraternising with the enemy.'

'Anyway, James Barber wants to do a fucking interview.'

' "The Demon Barber of Fleet Street? He always goes for the jugular"?'

'That's him,' agreed Ron. 'Sounds like he's going to make a big song and dance about the Commando caning Germans.'

'It's pathetic,' said Greg indifferently. 'Who cares?'

'Some people have no sense of humour, Ron,' commented Dave, looking in Greg's direction. 'German arses were funny. Are funny. And always will be funny.'

'Well, you're going to have to do it, Dave.'

'Me?'

'I can't. If he starts saying we shouldn't be making fun of Germans, I'll just get mad.' Ron looked far away. 'I lost all me chums on Sword Beach. A one-man reunion is no fun, Dave.'

Dave nodded sympathetically. Then added as an afterthought, 'But it's a cheap round.'

Ron pursed his lips, and continued. 'We had this sort of trouble back in the days of the *Fourpenny One*. Kids complaining about getting black eyes and punches in the gob 'cos of the title. Moaning nancy boys. Part of growing up. Punch up the throttle was character building. From your old man, it was a sign of affection.'

'Yes,' said Dave, remembering. 'A punch in the face was great.'

'So he's going to interview you.'

That was all right, thought Dave. He would express regret, but blame everything on his writer. Barber might want to talk to the Major, but he led too dubious a life to ever talk to the press. So Dave could say anything he liked. And a lot of people would find the kid trying to suck air out of the plughole as hilarious as he did. It was just a pity he couldn't claim credit for his ingenious idea.

'Then he wants to look through all the Major's recent scripts to see exactly what he wrote.'

'What? Why?' Dave was taken aback.

'Well, to make sure there's nothing else kids could imitate and hurt themselves with.'

'Why would there be?' asked Dave defensively.

'I know. I know. But we're living in changing times, Dave. The world's gone fucking mad. There's all these stupid Health and Safety rules coming in. Kids have to be protected now. For fuck's sake. They keep this up, kids won't be allowed to play in the street or climb trees anymore. It's all bollocks.'

'Yes. Yes. It's all bollocks,' agreed Dave.

Dave was thinking desperately. Maybe he could lose all the scripts? Burn the evidence? Yes. That's what he would do. So there would be nothing to incriminate him. The missing Major scripts would be like the missing Nixon Watergate tapes. There'd be no smoking gun here.

'I'll get all the scripts out now, ready for him,' said Greg helpfully.

'No, no, now wait …' said Dave hurriedly, but Greg had already gone to a filing cabinet.

'Here we are,' smiled Greg, producing a fat wad of Caning Commando stories.

'Good lad,' said Ron.

Dave watched horrified as Greg put the files on the desk. This was not going according to plan.

But all was not lost. He decided he could come down to the office in the middle of the night and bin the files. Blame it on the cleaner. No problem.

'Here. D'you want to take them away now?' said Greg, offering the files to Ron.

Dave looked aghast and gasped, 'Wait …' but too late.

'Thanks, Greg.' Ron picked them up, then turned to Dave. 'Oh, yes. And he definitely wants to interview the Major, too.'

'Ha,' said Dave smugly. 'Good luck with that one.'

Dave just knew that was *never* going to happen.

'Barber insisted. So I said I'd arrange it and make sure the Major was stone-cold sober to answer questions.'

'The Major …? Sober …?'

'It has been known. And, when he is sober, he can be surprisingly coherent and he actually has excellent memory. Are you all right, Dave? Your face has gone white. That's not a problem, is it?'

'No, no.'

'You're not all right? Or it's not a problem?'

'It's not a problem.'

Ron patted the files under his arm as he departed. 'Just the Oberspankerfuhrer driving round in his underpanzer. Nothing to worry about, eh, son?'

* * *

Dave hadn't thought it through. He had never figured on a Fleet Street investigation by someone as relentless as Barber. The ace reporter would see all the places he'd changed the Major's story and written in endless ways the readers could harm themselves. Not just breathe air through the bath plughole, but drink the Thames for its health-giving properties, have a relaxing swim at night in the old quarry, make Molotov cocktails, chlorine gas, potassium nitrate rocket missiles, calcium chloride guns, mustard gas bombs and ... he was screwed. He couldn't even say they must have got the formulas from his source; The Radioactive Laboratory. Following complaints from parents, it had been withdrawn from sale in the late 1950s, possibly because it was in breach of the Geneva Convention prohibiting chemical weapons.

There was no way out. No escape.

CHAPTER EIGHT

Dave nuzzled his face deep into the folds of Joy's fox fur and whimpered to himself. He had waited until Joy went out for lunch then slipped inside her office. A liquorice pipe was not enough. He needed real comfort as he faced the prospect of his guilty secrets being revealed. And her fur felt so good, so warm, so loving, and he prayed it was going to make everything all right. It was a classic, and he was something of an expert on the subject.

In his belfry, he'd spent many happy nights watching films and furs from the lost age of elegance. *Baby Face:* Barbara Stanwyck. Fur cape and muff combo. *Lady Be Good:* Ann Southern and Eleanor Powell. White fox fur coats plus a *bonus* silver fox wrap! *Party Girl:* Cyd Charisse, sublime in a silver fox trimmed mink. He knew them all. Intimately. There was nothing to beat the glamour, the romance, the *relief* of fur.

On the subject of relief, he had thought about it, but one of Joy's mannequins, wearing a black and white sixties dress from *The Knack,* was sitting in the chair opposite him and her wide-eye stare was putting him off.

Nearby, there was also Mothra, Gorgo, Godzilla, Lady Penelope and Parker in her six-wheeled pink Rolls Royce FAB 1, looking down accusingly from Joy's bookshelves.

Joy was a geek in an age before the word became widely used. Before geeks there were anoraks, but Joy was too stylish to be an anorak, so her obsession had no name. It began when she started collecting memorabilia from film sets while she waited around for her actress mother who starred in British films in the fifties and early sixties. She now had enough nostalgia and toys to open her own shop which she was, in fact, considering.

In the end, Dave decided to ignore the mannequin's accusing eyes. The fur coat's slight fusty smell took him back to gentle, far off, happy times, even as it mingled with the faint perfume of the current owner and ... It was good ... *Soooo* good ...

The perfume was stronger now as his hand unzipped his trousers ...

'You are fuckin' disgusting, Dave.'

Shit! He turned, panting heavily, to see Joy standing, glaring, in the doorway, a shopping bag in hand. 'I'm scunnered wi' ye!'

'Hi, Joy,' he said. Limply.

'If you've got jizz on my coat, you're paying for the dry cleaning.'

'No chance of that. Now. Now you're here.' Joy had had an instant deflationary effect on him. Her looks and perfume may have been seductive (Charlie, she'd been given free samples by My Gang), but her Glasgow accent and menacing manner had the opposite effect.

'Good,' she glared at him as she crossed the floor and dropped the shopping bag behind her desk.

Dave breathed a sigh of relief. It didn't look like she was going to deck him. Although he was actually one of those people who enjoyed being caught *in flagrante.* Or, in his case, *in furgrante.*

'So you weren't kidding about lusting after my coat?'

'It is a beautiful fur,' he said, giving it a final wistful stroke.

'Aye. It was mum's,' she said sadly. 'Present from dad.'

'That's nice,' said Dave.

'She didn't want it anymore after he left her for that fuckin' bitch.'

'Right,' said Dave, relieved that Joy's anger was directed towards someone else. He zipped up his trousers. *'Morning Glory,'* he explained.

Joy looked down at him and sneered. 'Dinna flatter yourself. I dinna see much glory there.'

'No, no. Not *me*,' he corrected her. 'The film. Starring Katherine Hepburn. Your jacket. It reminds me of the fur she wore. From the lost age of Hollywood glamour.'

'Ah. Thanks. Hollywood glamour, eh?' Joy smiled. 'I must admit, it does go well with my tennis shoes.'

She sat down at her desk and looked curiously at him. 'So what is it with you and fur, Dave?'

'You don't want to know, Joy. But I could tell you anyway ...?'

Joy considered his offer for a moment and then made a decision. 'No. I'd rather you didn't. You need help, Dave. Have you thought about talking to Cross Line?'

Dave was nonplussed. 'Why would I talk to Cross Line?'

'Because they say "Whatever your cross, we'll help you carry it." And it's *free*.' Joy looked excited at the prospect of a bargain. 'Think of the money you'd save on therapy.'

'But in my case it's a very big cross, Joy. I could be on the phone to them all night.'

'Doesn't matter.' She quoted Cross Line. ' "When you're hanging from your cross, we'll never hang up on you." '

'I know,' agreed Dave. 'And "When you're on the road to Calvary, we're the cavalry." ' He looked at her with a classic Dave hang-dog expression. 'But I'm afraid my past is just too awful, too painful, Joy. It's my cross to bear alone.'

'In that case, fuck off, Dave.'

He was about to exit, but then he remembered, in his earlier excitement, he had dropped a pen on the ground and he now went to retrieve it from in front of her desk.

She leaned over to watch him scrabbling around on all fours on the severe, polyester-carpeted floor. 'You do know I've had a modesty panel fitted ...?' she warned him.

It sounded like a strange and discreet Victorian gynaecological device that might appear in the small ads in the back of an old magazine. The reality was stranger. The browncoats, the feared maintenance staff, fitted modesty panels to the front of all the desks of female staff following the dawn of the miniskirt. After numerous complaints from women, they were designed to disappoint hordes of male pen-droppers.

He looked up at her over the desk. 'No, no. I really did drop my pen, Joy. When I – you know …'

'Aye. A likely story.' Despite the modesty panel blocking Dave's floor-level view of her thighs, she still checked and pulled down her skirt.

He collected his pen and stood up, straightening his safari jacket.

She scowled at the sight of it. Joy could forgive Dave being a Peeping Tom and his strange preference for fur, but what she could never forgive him for was that safari suit.

She had such fond childhood memories of her father, 'Lawrence of Fitzrovia', the height of sartorial elegance, dashing and debonair in his hand-tailored safari suits. And now those precious memories had been replaced. By Dave. There was a photo of her father on her desk, wearing such a suit, reporting from Vietnam. She would never look at it in quite the same way again.

'Actually, Joy, now I'm here, there was something I wanted to talk to you about.'

'Oh?' she said without enthusiasm.

Dave looked around for somewhere to sit, but the only chair was occupied by the mannequin.

'I need to get some standing legs for Stella Jeanne,' Joy explained.

'Shall I move her?'

'I'd rather you didn't.'

'You'd rather I stood?'

'Yes,' said Joy, lost in thought as she looked at the shop dummy. 'It's a worry, you know?'

'What?'

'Her hands are cracking and she was so perfect in spite of her years.'

'Poor Stella Jeanne,' said Dave coldly.

'Yes. She's drying out and her skin is crazing. I think close

45

proximity to central heating is bad for her. She'd be better off at home.'

Dave was surprised. 'You don't have heating at home?'

'Oh, no. My girls don't like it.'

'I didn't know you had children, Joy?' Dave was surprised.

'Oh, yes,' said Joy proudly. 'Stella Jeanne and Stella Louise.'

'Ah.'

He looked nervously around him. 'What happened to that wheelchair from *Whatever Happened to Baby Jane?*'

'No one felt safe in it, so I took it home again.'

'Maybe I could get a chair from from *Pinafore?*'

'You want to live dangerously? If the browncoats found out you'd moved furniture, they'd call a strike. What do you want, Dave?'

'I just wanted to know what you thought of my latest submission.'

Dave had had been saving up for a fur from Sacks and Brendlor, but now he needed the money to hire a hot-shot lawyer. After the Demon Barber's investigation, when the full enormity of his crimes became known, he would need someone first-rate to defend him. And the only way he could earn extra money was to write freelance stories for *Shandy.*

Joy didn't reply. She was too excited by her recent purchase. She took several pairs of thick-seamed stockings out of her bag and admired them. '1950s stockings. Still in their original packets. Aren't they brilliant?' She tucked them away in a drawer.

'Yes ... brilliant,' Dave said uncertainly. He wasn't sure whether she'd bought them to save money or because they were retro. He knew she had an eye for a bargain. When she visited her mum in Scotland, she would bring bundles of firewood back on the plane because they were cheaper in Glasgow.

Standing awkwardly in front of her desk, he reminded her. 'My latest story, Joy. What did you think?'

'I had a problem with credibility,' she responded.

'Why? You run serials with blind tap dancers, blind horse riders and blind swimmers.'

'I think a blind javelin thrower is stretching credibility too far, Dave. *Una Never Saw the Umpire* didn't really work for me.'

'I see.'

She took a hairbrush out of her bag and went over to Stella Jeanne. 'Anyhoo … it was an improvement on your previous proposal: *My Dead Little Pony*. A lassie meets a gypsy who persuades her to swap her record player for a dead pony that appears to her as a ghost.' She looked up from brushing Stella's hair. 'That's too weird.'

'I don't agree. I myself have regular conversations with the dead.'

Joy looked quizzically at him. 'Yes. With your mum or something?'

'How did you know?'

'Greg told me.'

Dave grimaced as she took a joint out of a tobacco tin.

Dave felt he needed to explain further. 'Yes. I often hear her voice inside my head.'

'What do you talk about?'

'Usual mother son things. She's always giving me good advice.'

'And do you take it?'

'Of course not. She's my mum.'

Joy opened the window and sat on the ledge smoking, lost in her own private thoughts. Dave's eccentricities were really not that interesting to her. She offered him the joint. 'Want some?'

'No thanks. I'm a pipe man.'

She took a long draw on it. 'I need realistic stories, Dave, relevant to girls' lives in the 1970s. Hard-hitting. Social realism, showing the kind of Britain we're living in today.'

'Less Ken Barlow, more Ken Loach?'

'Yes. If you like.'

'Then I think I've got just the story for you, Joy. How does this sound? *Tower Block Tessa*. She's homeless and sleeps in the lift. Her mother's a bag lady and her father lives in a burnt-out car. She wants to be an Olympic swimmer. So she's training in the water tank on the 30th floor. Maybe she has a disability, too, and is using her crutch to sweep aside the dead pigeons. She could find her alcoholic mother in the tank as well.'

Dave saw Joy's wide-eyed face. 'I'm not reaching you. Too over the top? Not enough? Give me some guidance here.'

But Joy was speechless.

Greg swaggered in and Joy lit up. 'Ah. Maybe Greg can help.'

She indicated a multi-coloured story popularity graph that contrasted with the drab vanilla office walls. 'Greg's *Feral Meryl* has been number one for six weeks running.'

Dave scowled at his assistant's success. His graph line easily overtaking the others and shooting to the top of the chart.

Greg sat on the corner of Joy's desk and opened his hands in a gesture to receive Dave's applause, but none was forthcoming.

'Tell Dave where you get your ideas from,' suggested Joy. She passed him the spliff.

Greg took a drag and explained. 'Meryl's a wolf girl. So obviously I drew on Kipling's *The Jungle Book*. But James Joyce has always been a big influence, of course.'

'Of course,' said Dave.

'And Thomas Hardy.'

'I'm more Laurel and Hardy myself,' said Dave.

Joy looked amorously at Greg, 'He writes about such strong women. Powerful women. Real women.'

She indicated the original art pages of the latest *Feral Meryl* episode. 'Have a read of them and you'll see what I mean.'

'I probably should be going,' said Dave, starting to slope off. 'Another time, eh?'

'Read them,' said Joy menacingly.

'Okay,' said Dave reluctantly picking them up. 'Let's just review this literary masterpiece.'

The opening caption read: '**Feral Meryl was a wild girl, brought up by wolves in the wilds of Berkshire. She was rescued by her friend Mandy who was trying to stop her being sent to a Special School.**'

The art depicted two realistically drawn girls in school uniform chatting in a bedroom. Or rather Mandy was chatting: Meryl was growling.

CHAPTER NINE

Mandy was a typical, wide-eyed heroine but Meryl was a female Mowgli. She looked normal, apart from dishevelled hair and sharp canine teeth. She was on all fours and Mandy was brushing the tangles out of her hair. 'Soon be done. Just a little more.'

Mandy saw some chewed up possessions. 'Oh, Meryl. Not my Marc Bolan records. And my best sling-backs.'

Meryl made a throaty, doggy sound.

'I know. It's not your fault. You don't know any better.'

Meryl balanced back on her hind legs and Mandy was pleased. 'It's those wolves that made you do it. Now keep balancing on your hind legs, because today is your first day at school and no one must know your secret.' She threw a biscuit in the air. 'Here.'

Meryl jumped up and caught the biscuit in her mouth. 'That's a good girl.'

Mandy turned and looked appealingly towards the readers. 'I was so lonely before I met Meryl. I needed a friend and Meryl is so kind and wants so little in return: just two tins of dog food a day. I hate telling lies, but I can't tell Mum and Dad the truth about Meryl or she'll be sent to a Special School and I'll lose her forever.'

Meryl was still standing on two legs, although a little unsteady. Mandy checked her over, adjusting her uniform. 'You ready, Meryl? Now, when we get to class, remember you mustn't mark your territory and no more drinking out of the lavatory bowl.'

Meryl made a doggy sound by way of response.

Mandy observed some strands of wool on her uniform. 'Meryl … what's that wool doing there? Oh, you didn't? Please say you didn't?'

Meryl's tongue hung out. She panted and leered at Mandy, exposing her wolfish teeth. 'Oh, Meryl. This is very bad, Meryl. And in the lambing season, too.'

The front doorbell rang. Meryl suddenly became alert, growling, sensing an enemy.

'Ssssh!' Mandy went close to the door to overhear who it was.

Down below she could hear a man's harsh voice. 'Mrs Jones? I'm from Cider-Acre Farm just down the road. We've got a problem with wolves.' Meryl growled. 'I traced the spoor to here.'

Mandy heard her mother reply, 'I'm sure you're mistaken. There's only my daughter and her friend upstairs.'

Meryl started scratching at the door and growling loudly.

'Meryl! No!' implored Mandy.

Now the farmer was shouting below, 'Stand back, Mrs Jones! I've got strict orders – it's got to be shot. It could have rabies.'

Mandy heard his heavy footsteps thundering up the stairs.

She looked fearfully at a snarling Meryl. 'Oh, no! How … how am I going to save Meryl? She's done a bad thing and deserves to be punished. But there's lots of lambs and only one Meryl. My special friend.'

She stared towards the window. 'One chance! The window!' She swiftly locked her bedroom door, then turned to her friend, 'Come on!'

They opened the window and climbed out onto the shed roof, just as they heard the farmer hurling his weight against the bedroom door.

Moments later, Mandy and Meryl fled from their house and ran down the street.

Mandy had put a home-made muzzle on Meryl and a dog's choke chain and lead. 'I'll have to take you back to your wolf parents, Meryl. They understand you and you were happy there. It was wrong of me to take you away from them.'

Meryl growled and lunged at passers-by who backed away in alarm. Mandy pulled her away from them. 'I hated putting that muzzle, made of satchel straps, on you, Meryl, but I had no choice. Please don't make me use the choke chain on you.'

The Farmer appeared at Mandy's open bedroom window. He was clutching a shotgun. Mandy's terrified mother was beside him.

'Mandy Jones, step aside! The Wolf Girl must be destroyed!'

He fired.

Mandy's mother screamed.

Meryl was wounded in the shoulder.

She fell to the ground.

Mandy knelt beside her friend who was moaning in pain.

She removed her muzzle and tried to comfort her. 'Oh, no. Don't die, Meryl. Please don't die. You're my best friend. I ... I couldn't bear to lose you.'

She held a whimpering Meryl close. Unfortunately, too close because it was hurting Meryl's wounded arm so she whimpered even louder.

She looked down at her friend. 'We'll never get away to the wilds of Berkshire now. How can I stop that farmer? And if I do save you, will they send you to a Special School? And ...where will it all end?'

The story concluded, 'What does Fate hold for Feral Meryl? Don't miss next week's *Shandy.*'

* * *

Greg's success made Dave feel bitter, competitive and angry. And he hated the story, too, not understanding why it was a success. So it was several moments before he had calmed down enough to respond to it. Finally, he asked, 'As a matter of interest, did you research this story, Greg? Are there, in fact, any wolves in Berkshire?'

'It's dramatic license,' said Joy, coming to his defence.

'Originally it was a herd of lions,' said Greg. 'But Joy thought wolves were more appealing to girls.'

'And "Berkshire"?'

'In-joke,' winked Greg.

'It doesn't affect the *social realism*?'

'Not at all,' said Joy. 'Readers don't care. Anyway, they probably pronounce it 'Burkshire'.

'So what did you think?' Greg smiled at Dave.

'Well, talking of burks ...'

'Doesn't really matter what he thinks,' Joy interrupted Dave. She pointed again to the popularity chart. 'Girls love wolves. Greg understands that.' She looked pointedly at Greg. 'He just knows what women need.'

Greg winked at Dave again. He kissed Joy. 'See you tonight.'

Then turned and grinned at Dave. 'Oh, yes. You've got your interview with the Demon Barber. In The Cock Tavern? We'll be there.' He leered. 'Wouldn't miss it for the world.'

'I'll be wearing one of my Biba outfits,' Joy promised him.

'Can't wait,' said Greg. He smiled insincerely at Dave. 'Good luck, mate.'

'Anyhoo ...' said Joy turning her attention to Dave. 'You know what I'm looking for now.'

Dave looked for a way to shoot Greg's story down without making his jealousy too obvious.

'I still have a problem with Greg's realism,' he said critically. 'Meryl didn't look very hirsute to me.'

'She's brought up by wolves, she's not half-human, half-wolf. Pay attention.'

'Sorry. I was so riveted by the sheer power of his writing, I didn't realise.'

He looked at Joy's bare arms. It was the first time he'd noticed them. 'You're quite downy yourself, aren't you? I hope you're not a slave to the razor?'

'I'll give you razor. You want to be chibbed?'

That was Dave's cue to depart and, losing interest in him, she started to water one of her plants. He idly wondered if it was a Triffid. If it was, it had better behave itself.

As he looked back, he was surprised by a sudden stirring in his loins at the sight of Joy's lithe, svelte body. Her dark, lustrous eyes, heart-shaped face and beautiful, if rare, smile. She was so like her film star mother who had seduced cinema audiences with her beguiling beauty as she courageously faced alien monsters, the undead and Vincent Price.

The only difference between the two women was that Joy was the scary one.

Yet, despite her scariness, he realised he fancied her, which was a first. It had never truly happened to him before. He was lusting after a woman. Not a fur coat. Rather than pretending to lust, to keep up appearances, like when he was a teenager, so other teenagers didn't discover how strange he really was. Until he reached his twenties and then he didn't care anymore. Even though he knew it was an impossible lust: Joy was in the first division and he wasn't even on the league table. The Subbuteo table, maybe.

But lust was lust and he could dream of what might be. The two of them, locked in each other's arms, caressing and …

Although, ideally, she'd need to be wearing her fur coat, of course.

CHAPTER TEN

After work, Dave left the imposing, Edwardian building that was Fleetpit House, with its splendid Neo-Baroque ornamentation, two magnificent Dutch gables and an accompanying tower, and went over the road to The Hoop and Grapes to gain some Dutch courage before facing the Demon Barber.

On the wall next door, someone had daubed 'George Davis is Innocent'. To Dave, it seemed to read, 'Dave Maudling is Guilty.'

Inside the pub, standing at the bar with his pint, he just wanted to fret. His arrested development was about to lead to his arrest. He thought about all those parents who had written to *The Spanker* to complain about what had happened to their Little Johnny after he imitated the Caning Commando. The pain, the tears, the visits to A&E. He'd laughed about them at the time, then thrown their letters in the bin. But once they'd read Barber's exposé, they'd make the connection and contact the police. What if it had gone further? What if ... a kid had already died? He'd wanted that, hadn't he? He hated the readers. He felt lightheaded, and wiped his sweating brow, trying to marshal his thoughts. Yes, of course he'd wanted it, he hated them. But the parents would now realise the Caning Commando was responsible. He was responsible. Maybe there were several deaths. Maybe ... He clutched at the bar, holding onto it, breathing deeply.

But then the reassuring words of Stevie Wonder's "Don't You Worry 'Bout A Thing" cut into his thoughts. Fat chance. He knew his mother was the DJ because she often communicated with him through songs.

She was trying to help, but it wasn't helping. The reassuring lyrics did not reassure him. He *didn't* know how to handle it. He *was* reaching out in vain. He *wanted* to feel bad.

But she paid no attention and kept playing the track over and over, insisting he stop worrying. She didn't understand: he *needed* to worry.

So he tried to silence her by thinking more lustful thoughts about Joy. How cute and sexy she was. Yes, the editor of *Shandy* had definitely turned him on. She'd finally thrown that rusting 'on' switch in his brain. Although, he then thought despondently, what chance would he possibly have when she was into Greg? No chance.

He was doomed to imagine jealously them doing all sorts of things from the confines of his dank cell in Wormwood Scrubs, where he'd be serving life and trying to keep out of the way of sexually frustrated axe-murderers.

He shuddered, enjoying the familiar feeling of failure. Yes, that was better. 'Hello, darkness, my old friend.'

'You're wrong,' said his mother. 'Their relationship is not going to last much longer.'

'How can you know that, mum?'

'A mother knows these things. Trust me.'

'That is ridiculous. Look at me. Okay? Then look at Greg. All right? What do you see? He looks like Terence Stamp and she's a gorgeous Chelsea girl.'

'Marble Arch girl, actually, dear. You're getting confused with the magazine.'

'What difference does it make? I still haven't got a hope in Hell.'

'Like I've told you so many times, all you have to do is get rid of that terrible safari suit. Greg set you up. He wanted you to look like a dog's dinner. I did warn you about him, didn't I? I never really liked that young man. And then you just need to lose some weight, and the right opportunity *will* come along.'

'It's never going to happen. Get real, mum.'

'Well, you keep telling me I'm *not* real.'

People in the pub were starting to stare, noticing him talking to himself, so he drank up and left.

He had enough weird fantasies of his own without paying attention to his mum's fantasies that he would somehow one day – against impossible odds – score with Joy. This was why he didn't like spending too much time on his own with his mother. They'd always end up getting into these arguments.

'Why don't you pick a more appropriate song?' he muttered under his breath as he walked down Farringdon Street. 'How about "Slippin' into Darkness?"' '

That seemed to silence her and he was pleased to be left alone in his slough of despond as he turned right into Fleet Street.

It was a surprisingly warm October evening, and he found himself sweating in his safari suit. He pushed his way through the dark evening throng of hard-drinking, drug-taking, scoop-hungry hacks spilling out of newspaper offices and heading for their locals.

He was briefly comforted by the ad on the back of a red Number 6 bus: "Swears and Wells. The world's largest furriers." He had spent many a happy hour browsing in their Oxford Street store.

He passed the Punch Tavern over on the other side of the street; its colourful and welcoming tiled exterior also cheered him up. It reminded him of fairgrounds, trips to the seaside, and the happier days of his childhood.

And then he saw the massive, gleaming, black and green, Art Deco 'Black Lubyanka', the *Daily Express* and *Sunday Express* building, and his heart sank once again. It was the H.Q. of the newspapers the Demon Barber worked for.

He wondered what sort of prison he would be sent to. It wouldn't be as bad as the Soviet Lubyanka, of course, but it would still be bad, especially when the other cons found out what he had done. He'd have to spend his sentence in solitary.

Soon after, he approached the equally forbidding, red brick London offices of Angus, Angus and Angus of Aberdeen, the great publishing rivals to Fleetpit, and his previous employer. Inscribed on the side of the building in appropriately fading letters were the words *Kith and Kin*, the name of the austere magazine for the elderly he was seconded to when he worked for the company in Scotland.

It was while he was a sub-editor on *Kith and Kin* that Dave had discovered he was a narcoleptic, prone to fall asleep at any time of the day. Reading a *Kith and Kin* romance would do it. It hadn't kept him on the edge of his seat, rather he had fallen off it. That was before that unfortunate business with Mrs Angus's fur coat. It was so cold up in Aberdeen, and Mrs Angus had loaned him one of her old fur coats to put on his bed and, well, he couldn't help himself. The minx. So to speak. That incident had brought his employment with the Scottish publishers to an abrupt end.

He didn't really want to walk past the building: there were too many uncomfortable memories. He was depressed enough already. So he crossed the road, stopping at a traffic island in the middle. There was a dank gents public lavatory in its depths and wafts of stale urine billowed up from below. Avoiding an *Evening Standard* red and white zebra-striped van, a competing *Evening News* truck in bright yellow livery, and a bolshie Robin Reliant, he crossed to the far side.

Finally, he reached the narrow-fronted Ye Olde Cock Tavern opposite the Royal Courts of Justice.

He glanced across at the vast, forbidding Gothic pile with its statues of Jesus, Solomon, and Alfred the Great, staring disapprovingly down at him, and shuddered. It seemed more like Dracula's castle than the Law Courts. All that was missing was a flash of lightning and a roll of thunder. Its pollution-blackened façade looked particularly uninviting and sinister in the dark, even though acid rain had washed the rows of its arches white. Like it was baring its fangs in anticipation of his fate.

Then he took a deep breath and plunged into the dark,

smoky, cavernous interior of the tavern. For hundreds of years, famous writers had used it as their watering hole: Samuel Pepys, Doctor Johnson, Lord Tennyson, Charles Dickens – and now the soon-to-be-infamous Dave Maudling.

He squeezed his way past gowned barristers and portly judges to join Greg, Joy and Ron, who were already on their second round.

'He'll call you when he's ready,' said Ron, nodding to the snug that served as the Demon Barber's office.

Ron was wearing his demob mac, unfashionably belted high around his waist, contrasting with Greg's grey Aquascutum leather trench coat, and Joy's fur coat. She was now in her pink satin trouser suit and talking vehemently to Ron's mini-skirted secretary Sharon.

'Ron's warned me not to wear this tomorrow. Can you believe it? It's the seventies and trouser suits are *forbidden*. Coming to work in hot pants is fine, but wear long pants, and you're sent home. What next? No pants?'

Ron, Greg and Dave noted her vehemence. 'Look at her filling Sharon's head with rubbish about trousers,' said Ron. 'My dog doesn't wear trousers, so why should they? Makes as much sense. Pint of falling down water, Dave?'

'I think I need a pint of blackout, Ron.'

'Blackout?'

'Sorry, I was miles away. The usual's fine.'

Dave found himself drooling over Joy. She looked almost as gorgeous as the fur coat she was wearing.

Greg went over and interrupted her in mid-rant. 'Is your dad back in the country?'

'No. I think he's in Cambodia.'

'Did you send him my last manuscript?'

Joy looked puzzled. 'Why would I?'

'Because a nod from him could really open doors for me.'

Joy smiled lovingly at him. 'You've got talent, Greg. You don't need my dad. And neither do I. We can make it without him.'

'Are you sure about that?' asked Greg uncertainly.

'Yes,' reassured Joy. 'It's 1975. There's no glass ceiling anymore. Everything is possible today.'

For a moment, a trace of anger crossed Greg's face, then was quickly erased. 'Cool.' He reached down into the briefcase at his feet, pulled out a notebook, and scribbled something in it.

'What are you doing?' asked Joy curiously.

'Jotting down ideas for my next novel.'

'Excellent,' she said.

Actually, he was writing angry words about Joy. Angry, four-letter words.

This was why he always kept his notebook close by. He couldn't risk tearing out the pages once he'd released his feelings about what a stupid, unhelpful, rich, arrogant, privileged cow she was who always believed she was in the right. He suspected Dave went through the wastepaper bins after he had gone home.

What he didn't realise was that Dave already knew about the notebook, had taken photocopies, and was biding his time for the right opportunity to use it against him.

'Yes. Just you and me, darling,' smiled Joy. 'That's all that matters.'

'You're absolutely right, darling,' agreed Greg, returning her smile. 'Do you have your dad's address in the jungle?'

The Demon Barber looked out from his 'office' in the snug. 'Maudling ...?'

Dave nodded.

'Five minutes.'

Five minutes to his doom. Another wave of paranoia passed over Dave. He stepped away from his cheerful companions, needing some time to compose himself.

He became aware that a drunk, red-faced judge was staring in his direction. Try as he might, Dave couldn't seem to avoid the judge's accusing, all-knowing eyes.

In his guilty mind he could hear the judge saying, 'David Maudling, the jury has found you guilty of murder. You have claimed your inner demons ordered you to kill, however the Police and Crown Prosecution Service do not accept this, and have rightly rejected your plea of manslaughter on the grounds of diminished responsibility. You have also claimed that the real culprit is a certain 'evil newsagent', who every Saturday, when you were a little boy, would punch you in the face as a joke. Whilst I do not condone such behaviour, unfortunate events happen when we are young and we learn to put them behind us. They do not give you the right to inflict your bitterness on a new generation of innocent children. You are a cold, calculating serial killer. You will go to prison for life and, in your case, Maudling, life will mean life. Take him down.'

Dave backed fearfully away from him. The judge must have recognised the expression on Dave's face from his long years on the bench because he suddenly pointed a perfectly manicured, but claw-like finger in his direction. 'Yes. You are guilty, sir. You *are* guilty.'

'M-me? I'm sorry. I don't understand,' burbled Dave, looking guiltier than ever.

The judge smiled knowingly. 'Oh, I think you do, sir. I think you do. I have been quietly observing you and I know that look so well. I don't know what you've done, sir, but you've done something.' He pursed his thick, ruddy lips. 'Something … *very* bad.' Dave's horrified face confirmed it. 'Oh, yes. I've seen that look so many times on the faces of defendants in the dock.'

His red, malevolent face was now very close to Dave's. 'Just before I sentenced them to ten years' imprisonment.'

'Fuck,' thought Dave. 'It must be written all over my face.' Normally, he prided himself on never giving anything away.

'I-I have no idea what you're talking about,' he said lamely.

The judge stabbed his finger three times into Dave's chest. 'Guilty. Guilty. Guilty.'

A female barrister intervened. 'I must apologise,' she said to Dave. 'He's intoxicated.' She took the judge by the arm. 'Now come along, Cecil. Let's get you a taxi.'

'I'm not drunk, Joan. I'm fortified with brandy,' protested the judge as she led him away.

It was not a good omen.

James Barber emerged from the snug again. He was a huge

man wearing a flamboyant pinstripe suit that George Melly would have admired, with a napkin around his neck.

Joy rolled her eyes and whispered to Sharon. 'The Demon Barber. He's a monster. They say Tolkien based Sauron on him.'

'I'm ready for you now, Maudling. Step into my office,' he boomed.

Dave obediently entered the snug.

His life was ruined. He'd have to bring forward his plans to end it all. Go to Helsinki, the suicide capital of the world, and come back in a pine overcoat.

CHAPTER ELEVEN

Inside the snug, there was no room to move and Barber and Dave – hunter and prey – were uncomfortably close. Barber swivelled a shielded green wall light round into Dave's face to begin the interrogation. 'I'll make this short, but not painless.'

He continued eating his pub meal as he spoke. 'I hope you don't mind? I can eat and eviscerate at the same time.'

He didn't wait for Dave's approval. 'So ... you're Dave Maudling, editor of ... *The Spanker*?' He lingered on the name, enunciating with relish.

Dave nodded penitently.

'You know my reputation?'

'You're the most feared man in Fleet Street.'

'I broke the Profumo scandal. Christine. Mandy. Stephen. I knew them all.' He raised a bushy eyebrow meaningfully. 'Intimately. I made my excuses and stayed.' He smiled arrogantly, enjoying his little joke.

Dave tried some light-hearted banter, hoping to keep things jokey and get on Barber's good side. 'Perhaps if we spanked Christine Keeler, I'd be in even more trouble?'

Barber ignored it. 'Tell me about your comic for Borstal bum boys, Maudling. This Caning Commando individual who says, "I see Germany as one big arse that needs a colossal thrashing." '

'Well, it's a fictional character. And a fictional arse.'

'Do you now plan to stop peddling this filth to our nation's children?'

'That's not up to me. I'm only obeying orders.'

Dave quickly realised how unfortunate that sounded. 'I mean –'

Barber recited his copy to himself; he never wrote anything down. 'A spokesman for *The Spanker* said "We intend to carry on peddling this filth." All in bold.'

'I didn't say that,' protested Dave.

'So now an innocent young boy has been cruelly injured, are you satisfied?'

'Of course not.'

' "We aren't satisfied with just one child being injured," the spokesman added. Exclamation mark.' Barber smiled to himself. 'This is good.'

'I didn't say … I never … It's meant to be a funny war story, not *The Diary of Anne Frank*,' protested Dave.

' "At least our comic is funnier than *The Diary of Anne Frank*" added the heartless editor. Full stop.'

'Could that be "*Handsome,* heartless Editor"?' suggested Dave, trying to make the best of his impending destruction.

'With the headline: "Playground turned into Killing Fields by comic-crazed thugs." '

'Actually, make that "*Single, available,* handsome, heartless editor," ' said Dave, looking across at Joy, Sharon, Ron and Greg watching him from the bar.

Maybe Joy would come and visit him in prison? He'd heard that seeing men helpless and in trouble sometimes turned women on. His sister Annie once told him she had lustful thoughts about a handsome, half-naked, helpless Jesus nailed to the cross, and at her mercy.

Maybe *that* was the way to nail Joy?

Once again he heard that Stevie Wonder song "Don't You Worry 'Bout A Thing".

Then a great idea came to him in a flash: how to turn the tables, how to win out against all the odds, how to finally stand up and be counted. How to be an *alpha* male. Even if it was his mum's idea.

'Any final words from the condemned man?' asked the Demon Barber.

'Oh, yes,' said Dave with newly discovered confidence. 'Wouldn't you prefer a *front* page story?'

The reporter's eyes lit up. 'Always.'

Dave stalked across and grabbed Greg's briefcase before his assistant could stop him. 'If you think *The Spanker* is bad ...' Barber emerged from the snug as Dave took out the dummy copy of *Blitzkrieg!* and passed it to the journalist. 'See what my colleague, Greg here, is planning.'

Barber read the cover. 'Achtung! Achtung! The Great New War Comic for Boys. *Blitzkrieg!*' He leafed through six, powerful, exciting, illustrated war serials: *'Panzerfaust. Angerman of the Afrika Korps. Stormtrooper. Legion of Verdammt. Graf Fear. Prussian Blue.'*

His eyes narrowed. *German* heroes!'

A worried Greg joined them. 'There is *Longest Day Logan* as well,' he pointed out lamely. 'At the end.'

'Perhaps he should be called *Lonely Day Logan*, because he's outnumbered by his Wehrmacht chums,' suggested Dave unhelpfully.

He pinned the tin foil medal to Greg's black polo neck and quoted. 'Free Iron Cross with Issue One.'

'Yes,' agreed Barber. 'This is much better.' He considered possible headlines. 'Puss in Boots to Jack Boots Horror! ... Nazi comic shocker! From Ha Ha to Haw Haw!'

He looked Greg up and down in his black outfit and leather trenchcoat. 'Blackshirt editor invades Britain.'

Ron had joined them. 'What's going on, chum?'

'Obergruppenfuhrer Greg has been secretly planning a new comic, Ron,' said Dave.

Ron flicked through the dummy, then handed it back to Barber without a word, pursing his lips as he stared grimly at Greg.

'It could be worse, Ron,' said Dave helpfully. 'He was going to call it *Stormtrooper*.' Then, just to really rub it in: 'I guess we didn't win the war, eh?'

A guilty and embarrassed Greg turned nervously to Ron. 'Ron ...I can explain ...Let me buy you a drink.'

Ron just looked contemptuously through him and walked silently away with a proud, stiff military bearing, like a veteran on Remembrance Day.

* * *

So Dave was off the hook. It would be back to business as usual on *The Spanker* now, he told himself, as a little later, he strolled triumphantly back through Fleet Street toward Fleetpit House. The spotlight would be on *Blitzkrieg!* instead. Nationwide negative publicity from the Demon Barber would trigger uproar from parents, Mary Whitehouse and the British Legion, and the board would definitely kill the war comic. It was history.

Greg's dream of becoming his comic overlord were over.

It had all turned out rather well, he thought. Although he would need to work on his guilty face, which had nearly let him down. That guilty expression was not because he felt bad or ashamed of what he had done. It was because he thought he was going to be caught.

'Play up being a buffoon,' he told himself. 'It's the perfect mask that no one can see through. So they have no idea who I really am. Everyone thinks I'm a harmless asshole, whereas, in fact, I am an extremely dangerous asshole.'

He smiled evilly. 'Oh, yes. It's not a good idea to make an enemy of Dave Maudling. Not with my inner demons. The Gadarene swine are on my side and they are Legion.'

Dave could hear Lou Reed's "Perfect Day" playing inside his head as he walked back. A good choice by his mum, for once, he thought. She had taken it from his memories and probably didn't know about the drugs connection, it would have been after her time.

He didn't pay any attention to those softly spoken words at the end of the song, 'You're going to reap just what you sow.'

CHAPTER TWELVE

That night, he relaxed in an armchair in his comfortable quarters in the attics of Fleetpit House. Why pay rent when he could live in a hotel in central London for free? He had to keep the lights low and the blinds drawn in case the police thought there was a break-in, but otherwise it was perfect. Better than Greg, who had to commute back to Colchester every night, except when he was staying at Joy's in Marble Arch.

A fur boa, symbolising his mother, was draped over the armchair opposite. It was a bit moth-eaten; he'd bought it from a thrift shop, but it was all he could afford at the time. The glass eyes would stare beadily back at him from the darkness as he told her about his work, his adventures and now how he was falling for Joy, as well as her fur coat. The kind of thing that any boy might talk to his mother about.

And they weren't always one-sided conversations; she would respond and, all too often, disagree with his opinions. Like her insistence that, one day soon, he was going to make it with Joy.

The boa triggered one of his last memories of Jean Maudling. As he chewed on his liquorice pipe, he could almost smell her Sirocco perfume, her face powder, her bright red smile, her long blonde hair cascading in waves onto her shoulders. They had been going to see *Blue Murder at Saint Trinian's*. The flicks was the only time he ever got to spend any real time with her. She checked herself in the dressing table mirror and asked him if she looked okay and he replied, tugging at her coat, 'Yeah, yeah. Come on. Or we'll miss the start, mum.'

'Doesn't matter,' she smiled. 'We can always sit through and watch it again.' They often did this. The year before, they'd sat and watched *Reach For the Sky* three times from the afternoon right through to the evening performance that ended with the cinema-goers' stampede for the exit before the national anthem.

Ronald Searle's creations were already creating blue murder as they followed the usherette's torch down to the front stalls and were shone to their seats. For a moment, his young mother's beauty was inadvertently caught in the spotlight of the torch: her movie-star looks, fur jacket, high heels and platinum blonde hair. There was a sharp and collective intake of breath from the male members of the audience, momentarily distracted from the deranged schoolgirls on the screen by this apparition of loveliness in her early thirties. His mother always knew how to make an entrance.

A man who hadn't mastered the useful art of looking at other women out of the corner of his eye without moving his head, was elbowed in the ribs by his wife. 'Stop staring, you. She's all fur coat and no knickers, that one.'

And now, for the first time, it seemed to Dave she was actually sitting opposite him in the darkness of his room. The beady-eyed, moth-eaten boa was now new and lustrous and draped around the bare shoulders of her tight-fitting black dress. He'd always seen her in his imagination, but this was different. Her figure was more sharply defined, her scent richer, her looks more lustrous.

'Mum!' he gasped.

She was real.

Even though she was dead.

He knew she must be dead. It was one thing for her to go off with a lover and not be in touch. She had disappeared before, usually for a few days. Then that terrible day when she disappeared forever. At the time, he believed his father when he told his anxious young son she must have found someone else.

67

But it was quite another thing for her not to have been in touch with her family for nearly twenty years. Something awful had to have happened to her. It was a question he had asked her, of course, when he heard her voice in his head, but she had never given him an answer.

Alive or dead, she always knew how to make an entrance. Not a day older than the day she vanished, she smiled across at him. A *femme noir* in her tight-fitting black dress. A *femme fatale* who had surely met a terrible fate. He chewed hard on his noir pipe. There had to be a reason why she was appearing to him now.

'What's happened, mum? Why are you back? What is it you want?'

The smile left Jean Maudling's beautiful lips.

'I want you to find out who murdered me.'

PART TWO:

NOVEMBER 1975 TO JANUARY 1976

'No McGuffin, no nothin'.'

CHAPTER THIRTEEN

Stoke Basing Star August 23rd 2016.

COMIC MAY HOLD KEY TO MURDER MYSTERY

The police are examining the copy of *The Fourpenny One* that builder John Trigger, 48, found in the wall of the secret room where the body of Mrs Jean Maudling was discovered. It is now thought she purchased the comic for her eight-year-old son, David Maudling, around the time she disappeared.

Police believe *The Fourpenny One* was in her shopping bag, found buried next to her body, and the murderer had stuffed it in the wall he built, along with old newspapers, as insulation. The comic is dated Saturday 9th March 1957, three days before records show she was reported missing.

Mrs Maudling's daughter, pensioner Annie Ryan, 71, who came forward in response to a police appeal, said, 'I'm surprised the comic was in mum's bag. Dave usually got it himself from the local newsagent, but, for some reason, she must have bought it for him that Saturday.'

Police are examining the fur boa used to strangle Mrs Maudling, and her shopping bag, and completing DNA tests, which they believe could identify the murderer. They expect to make an announcement soon and disclose the location of the house where the body was found.

They would also like get in touch with the victim's son, David Maudling, 67, but his current whereabouts are unknown.

CHAPTER FOURTEEN

A week after his mother had first appeared to him, they were in Selfridges together and it was going badly. Very badly. Admittedly, it was early November and the Christmas shopping crowds were out, but shopping with his mother was a stressful experience, and Dave was concerned things were getting out of hand.

At first, he had been thrilled that his mother could physically manifest herself. It was so good to see her again after all these years. And if she was an illusion, it was a consistent illusion that made him feel better about himself and his life. He was no longer alone.

He was well aware she could be a figment of his imagination, an elaborate and unknown construction of his subconscious that psychiatrists knew nothing of, some benign cousin of insanity. He told himself that writers often have imaginary conversations with their characters. It was well known that they would talk back to the writer and 'take on a life of their own'.

But this was so much more. Once he started having hallucinations and talked about finding his mother's killer, in the words of Mandy from *Feral Meryl*, where would all it end?

Because of his father, he had read everything he could about madness: R.D. Laing, Janov's *The Primal Scream*, Thomaz Szasz's *The Myth of Mental Illness*, as well as books on conventional psychiatry, and finally reached the profound conclusion that, whilst they might earnestly claim otherwise, no-one really had a clue about the true nature of the human mind.

His guess was as good as R.D. Laing's, in fact, possibly better, as Laing used LSD as his 'spiritual laxative' whereas Dave used liquorice. And he wouldn't describe, as Laing might well have done, that his father had 'a shamanic journey' into enlightenment. Peter had been manic, rather than shamanic.

But he feared that if anyone discovered he was actually *seeing* his dead mother and claiming she was murdered, they'd section him, fry his brains, feed him drugs and make him really crazy, like his dad.

So he had not been comfortable with his mother following him around like the ghostly partner of the detective in the TV series *Randall and Hopkirk (Deceased)*. It was also a matter of privacy and giving him his own space. She was no longer a voice inside his head that wouldn't leave him alone. She was now an apparition who wouldn't leave him alone.

First up, she had told him the safari suit had to go; it was gone, and she was looking for its replacement. Replacements, plural. Jacket. Coat. Trousers. Shirts. Shoes. Everything.

'Try that raincoat on again, Dave.' He dutifully obeyed. She looked at him thoughtfully. 'Let me see. Turn around. Stand up straight.' She shook her head. 'No.'

'What's wrong with it?'

'Nothing, it looks excellent on you, sir,' said the assistant, unaware Dave was talking to his mother and not him.

'It makes you look like Columbo,' said his mother.

'I thought the idea *was* to make me look like a detective in preparation for my assignment.'

'I don't understand, sir,' said the assistant.

'You want to look cool as well,' said his mother.

'I don't know what all the fuss is about,' he sulked. 'I'd have been happy with a demob mac like Ron's.'

'I'm not sure I know Ron, sir. Is he a regular customer here?' asked the assistant brightly.

'Don't be silly, dear,' said his mother.

'Have you seen the prices here? They're very silly.'

She pointed to another rack. 'Now this one.'

He tried it on and the assistant hovered expectantly.

'Shoulders back. Don't slouch.' She smiled. 'Oh, yes. That's nice. Your dad used to wear one just like it when he'd come to The Eight Veils.'

'The Eight Veils? I didn't know you were at The Eight Veils?'

'I don't know the Eight Veils,' said the puzzled assistant.

'No. Not you. I'm talking to my mum,' explained Dave.

'Ah. I see,' said the assistant, looking a little worried.

'There's a lot about me you don't know,' Jean Maudling said. 'Yes. I think this is the one. Keep it on as well.'

Dave nodded to the assistant whose pleasure in making a sale over-rode any concerns about his customer's sanity.

They left Selfridges with Dave clutching an endless assortment of glossy yellow bags containing his old clothes and shoes.

He had complained bitterly to her about the cost of an entire new wardrobe, but she'd pointed out he had been saving up for an expensive fur coat and he was living rent free. But he would still have to write a lot of episodes of that new serial he was going to propose to Joy: *Paula Never Saw The Pool*, about a blind high diver.

He had to admit he looked and felt good in his Yves Saint Laurent trench coat. Her sartorial advice was certainly better than Greg's. Even so, it was the last time he went shopping with his mum.

She regarded him critically. 'Now we really should do something about your hair.'

'What's wrong with my hair?'

She looked across the road from Selfridges. 'There's a salon in Aldford Street. Maybe they could fit you in.'

'That's in Mayfair. I don't go to hair salons in Mayfair. I go to barbers,' he protested.

There was a cancellation and an hour and a half later he emerged with a George Carter *Sweeney* look. It went well with his brown corduroy jacket, cream polo neck and black and burgundy shoes.

But not so well with the liquorice pipe, even if it was a Sherlock Holmes briar. 'Stop chewing liquorice in the street,' she admonished.

'Why?'

'Because it's not nice, dear.'

Despite, or rather because of, his mother's positive influence on his appearance, Dave was scared. She was changing his life; his comfortable, cosy, boring, buffoonish, sedentary, rent-free, woman-free, challenge-free life. He liked having nothing to do, nothing to think about and the days and weeks and months all merging into one with nothing to remember them by. He certainly didn't want to think about tracking down murderers from twenty years ago. It could be dangerous.

He decided he was going to refuse the quest.

And he knew just how to make her go away.

So this was why, with his mother struggling to keep up with him in her high heels, he strode purposefully to the Catholic church in nearby George Street and entered its vast, echoing, dimly-lit Gothic interior.

Inside, Dave lit a candle for his mother and put a pound note in the box. He told her it was to honour her memory.

But it was actually to exorcise her.

So her soul, or whatever was responsible for her appearance after two decades, could be at peace. And, more importantly, he could be at peace.

He could see her waiting apprehensively in the darkness at the back of the church. For some reason she seemed uncomfortable being in a church. That was a good sign. It could mean she was scared of being exorcised. Maybe she really was an evil spirit? A witch who had to be invited over the threshold? Or was she simply a figment of his fevered imagination?

Whether he was mad or haunted, either way he had had enough. She had to go.

He looked up at the altar, 'If she's a demon, Lord, could you tell her to be gone please? I've put a quid in. Is that enough?

Then he added hastily, 'But not my regular inner demons.

Not the Gadarene swine. I'm used to them. I'd miss them. They can stay.'

She clacked down the aisle and sat next to him. They stared in silence at the flickering candles for several long moments while he waited expectantly for the exorcism to take effect and for his mother to fade away back into the ether.

Nothing happened. He wondered if it was because he hadn't said the words in Latin. Maybe it wasn't possible to conduct a DIY exorcism. Perhaps he had to consult a professional exorcist? Finally he was forced to admit:

'Damn. It's not working.'

'What's not working?'

'My exorcism. Your head isn't spinning round, you're not vomiting green bile and you're not going away.'

'And I don't intend to. I need you, son.'

'But I'm no detective, mum.'

'I know, dear, but you're all I've got.'

'But I don't want to do this. I'm refusing the quest.'

'Now there's several suspects you need to look at.'

'You're not listening to me. I don't want it.'

'I won't let that stop me.'

'If you're real, then you already know who killed you.'

'Of course I do, but I need you to know.'

'So why don't you just tell me?'

'Because it doesn't work that way. There's all the poison that needs to come out first.'

'How much poison?'

'More than in your old chemistry set.'

'That's a lot of poison.'

An elderly priest had crossed from the sacristy to the altar and looked curiously down at the big man in the front row muttering animatedly to himself. The cleric had unlocked the tabernacle and was about to transfer the reserved sacrament, the hosts and the wine, to a small container for taking communion to the sick.

He turned and put a finger to his lips and Dave nodded obediently in his direction. 'Sorry, father.'

'He's moving it to the pyx,' he whispered to his mum.

'How do you know it's a pyx?' she whispered back.

'I used it in Scrabble and got loads of points.'

'Dave,' said his mother looking uncomfortably around her, 'D'you think we could leave now? I'm really not comfortable in a church.'

'No. I need to have a word with the priest. I want to see if he will exorcise you for me. Send you back wherever you came from.'

A sinister look crossed Jean Maudling's face. 'That would be a mistake, David ...' He noticed her normally soft, feminine voice was suddenly harsh, almost masculine. It must be all that smoking. 'A big mistake ...'

'I'm sorry, mother, but you've got to be exorcised and there's no more to be said.'

She looked at him with a stern expression that he remembered from his childhood when he'd done wrong, but it wouldn't do her any good now. She was dead and he had the power.

'I'm not in a good place right now, mum. Greg and I are doing a stretch on *Laarf!* It's a living hell.'

'Because of what happened to *Blitzkrieg?*'

'Of course. The board blamed both of us for the bad publicity in the Demon Barber's article and the comic being cancelled. We were given a three month sentence on *Laarf!* I just can't handle you *and* working on the most unfunny comic in Britain.'

'You did the crime, you do the time,' she said unsympathetically.

'And *Laarf!* readers love it. Can you believe it? They have zero taste.' Dave leaned back in his pew and sighed. 'It's why I hate them. God, I hate them so much ...'

'Yes ...Yes ... Hate is good ...' agreed his mother, her voice still dark, rich and menacing.

'It's why they deserve to die,' continued Dave. 'No,' he corrected himself. 'No. That is unfair. It's just one of the *many* reasons they deserve to die.'

'To die …' repeated his mother huskily to herself, savouring the words, 'to die …' as Dave and his inner demons ranted on.

'Yes, I told Tom Morecambe the editor, "Tom, the right to humour lobby are pressing you hard to actually produce a funny strip. You surpassed yourself with that last issue. I put my head in the gas oven after reading it. If I'd paid the gas bill, it would have been fatal." And you know his response?'

'Tell me …' Jean smiled in anticipation.

'That hideous, whining, grizzling, mind-numbing laugh of his.'

'Do it, David,' she encouraged him. 'Do the laugh.'

Her eyes stared hypnotically as she leaned over him. 'For me, David …'

'I can't.' He looked rather embarrassed and backed off, sliding along the bench away from her. 'We're in a church, mum.'

'Doesn't matter.' She slid after him. 'Do it, son …' He slid to the far end of the pew. So did she. She smiled archly as she pressed up next to him. 'You do it so well …'

'All right.' There was nowhere left to slide.

Dave gave a scary imitation of Tom Morecambe' laugh. It was more like a long-drawn-out baby's lament than a laugh. The echoing acoustics in the church made it sound even more nightmarish, giving it an inhuman, demonic resonance.

The priest turned around and angrily *shushed* him.

His mother smiled appreciatively. 'Oh that's very good … Again.'

He hesitated, she insisted, so, once more he laughed Tom's painful, banshee, buzz-saw laugh that surely came straight from the bowels of Hell.

The priest turned again and now there was concern on his face now at such a hellish sound.

'On *Laarf!*' Dave continued, ignoring the priest, 'the rules are: No fireworks. No playing on bridges. No bare bums. No flatulence. No drawing pins up the arse. No disfigurements. No jokes about fat people. Thin people. *Any* people!' he shouted.

Grim-faced, the priest came down from the altar. He was

still holding onto the chalice. There was a white silk cloth and gold platter with the consecrated hosts on top.

Dave imitated Morecambe's hideous laugh again.

'What is wrong with you, young man?' the priest hissed, oblivious to the presence of Dave's mother. 'This is the House of God.'

A wave of fury came over Dave, a feeling of absolute shock and outrage that he had never experienced before, that stunned him with its sheer ferocity.

He was possessed.

His face was a greenish pallor in the dim light of the stained glass windows, as he grinned evilly at the old man. The priest realised that this was no ordinary intruder. 'What…what do you want?' he whispered fearfully.

Dave stood up so they were face to face with each other in the aisle.

'I want a drink.'

He snatched the chalice from the priest and quaffed every last drop, discovering that, surprisingly, it was not red wine at all.

'Mmm. South African sherry. Not worried about the boycott then?' said Dave.

The platter and the hosts had gone flying. The priest was dismayed.

'Five second rule,' a leering Dave reassured him. 'They're still holy.'

He bared his teeth, revealing his black lips and black tongue. It had been a tough morning. He'd done a lot of liquorice.

The priest took in the black-mouthed, demonic sight.

'Truly you are the Son of Satan!' He was equal to the occasion and roared in a voice Max Von Sydow in *The Exorcist* would have been proud of.

'By the authority of the Lord, begone, Demon! I cast you out!'

Dave smiled his black-lipped, black-toothed smile again. 'Try it, priest.'

Then his mother stood up and pointed an accusing finger at the old man. 'YOU!'

The cleric was unaware of her presence and her voice.

So she repeated herself, her face suffused with rage, once more stabbing a finger at him. 'YOU!'

Once again, the priest heard nothing and carried on with his exorcism. 'Most glorious Prince of the Heavenly Armies, Saint Michael the Archangel, defend us in our "battle against principalities and powers" ...'

Then she merged with Dave and he found himself pointing at the priest and repeating, 'YOU!'

The old man heard *that* all right, and recoiled in horror, snarling defiantly, ' ... against the rulers of this world of darkness, against the spirits of wickedness in the high places ...'

Dave knew what the accusations and the pointing fingers were all about. After his father had smashed the TV in with a cricket bat, his sister had foolishly called the local church for help, as well as their GP. As Canon Williams hurried up the street, a tall, elegant, and rather dashing figure with his red trimmed, expensively-tailored, high-waisted black cassock swirling impressively around him, Peter had stood at his front door and pointed down at him and roared, 'YOU!'

The Canon, an ex-military man, looked up, but was unafraid. He continued to advance, ready for trouble.

And he got it. Peter charged towards him, pointing and screaming, 'YOU! YOU! *YOU*!'

He was almost upon the priest. 'You're going to pay for what you did. She told me. I know. YOU!'

Then Dave brought his dad down with a splendid rugby tackle; his expensive, if short-lived college education paying off. The kind of tackle Dave imagined Carstairs, the Fag-Master, star of *Fags Army*, performed every day.

Dave held his father down until the men in white coats came to take him away. As his dad looked back from the steps of the ambulance, he once again yelled accusingly back at the Canon, 'YOU!'

The fear of ending up like his father brought Dave to his senses. His homicidal rage faded and, gathering his purchases, he pushed past the priest and stumbled out of the church.

Hurrying down the steps, he tried to make sense of the intense and unexpected anger that had flooded his mind. His mum's rage? His dad's rage? His own?

'Hi, Dave. What were you doing in a church?' It was Joy, looking gorgeous in her fur jacket, trouser suit and tennis shoes. Mainly in her fur jacket.

He looked at her, dazed. 'What are you doing here?'

'The trouser suit,' she grimaced. 'Ron sent me home to change.'

'Of course,' said Dave. 'You live round here, don't you?'

'Aye. Marble Arch. Fancy a drink?'

'Er … no thanks, Joy. I've already had one.'

'I'm really pleased you've been to church. So you're finally sorting yourself out.'

'Yes, I've just seen a priest, Joy.'

She looked towards the church. 'Is that him up there? He seems to be waving a cross at you.'

Dave looked back. The exorcist was framed in the church doorway and was, indeed, brandishing a cross at him.

'No, he's just waving goodbye.' Dave put down his shopping bags and waved back. 'Thank you, father. Same time next week …?'

Joy cast an appreciative eye over his new-look clothes. 'And Yves Saint Laurent. Get you!'

'How did you know?' asked a mystified Dave.

'I used to hang out in the wardrobe department on sets. I know my Burberry from my Aquascutum. I like it. And your hair. Your shoes.' She looked him up and down in disbelief. 'This is such an improvement, Dave. You must have a girlfriend?'

'No, Joy. There's still a vacancy.'

'But how could you possibly have chosen all those cool clothes on your own?'

'I have hidden depths, Joy.'

'So I see. I'm impressed! Anyhoo … I'd better get going. I'll see you later.'

She gave him a quick, appreciative smile and disappeared.

'You see?' said Dave's mum, emerging from a shop doorway. 'It was worth going shopping with me.'

CHAPTER FIFTEEN

On the Central Line, Dave leaned back and relaxed. His mother was sitting next to him, but as it was a busy compartment, and they were talking about murder, it made sense to converse by thought.

'You don't need a detective after all, mum,' Dave thought. 'Dad said it was the Canon. Case closed.'

'I'm afraid there's a little more to this case than your father's accusation,' thought his mother.

'Can't you just confirm he's right. It was the Canon. Right?'

'Dave,' she replied angrily. 'You're not only the world's laziest serial killer, getting kids to harm themselves without lifting a finger, you're also the world's laziest detective.'

'I think that's a little harsh, mum,' he responded. 'I do have other things on my mind right now. Apart from you.'

'I'm aware of that: Joy. And I'm pleased about that, at least. She's a big improvement on chasing after fur coats.'

'And I don't think you appreciate the whole raison d'être of my crimes is that I don't have to be physically present at the murder scenes.'

'Yes. You're not just a lazy serial killer, you're a cowardly serial killer.'

'And an undetectable one. The heat's off me on *The Caning Commando* now. All the attention is on *Blitzkrieg!* Banned before it was born.' Dave smirked. 'So I can slip easily under the radar.'

Jean Maudling looked at him with derision. 'And that's the height of your ambition, is it? To be an anonymous, invisible killer?'

'That's a little unfair. Think of God. He is everywhere and he is nowhere. Like myself.'

'Don't you have any real ambition, son? Don't you want to achieve something? To get on in life?'

Dave thought about the question between Oxford Circus and Tottenham Court Road. Finally, he gave his answer, 'No.'

His mother looked exasperated. 'But you're interested in Joy. So you've got to ask yourself: what do you have to offer an ambitious young woman?'

'A boil-in-the-bag lifestyle and all the laundry she can lift?'

'She's going to expect you to move up the career ladder.'

'Well,' pondered Dave, 'my ultimate ambition is the editorship of the *Mirror*.'

Jean looked excited. '*Daily Mirror?*'

'*Budgie Mirror.*'

She groaned and looked away.

'Look, mum,' he thought. 'I really would like to help you solve your murder.'

'You're my son. It's your duty,' she insisted.

'I'm sure that's true. But if I'm really honest …'

'Be honest.'

'I'm just too much of a shit.'

The compartment was filling up now, and, as if to emphasise his point, he remained seated while an elderly man and a pregnant woman with a toddler and lots of shopping were standing directly in front of him. His mother also gave up her seat and joined the strap hangers.

'Yes,' he thought comfortably. 'I'm afraid I have to refuse the quest.'

His mother glared down at him. 'You're not interested in who killed me? Or how?'

Dave shrugged. 'Not really.'

'You don't care whether I was shot? Poisoned? Strangled?'

'Dead is dead. I got over you, mum. I moved on.'

'Well, you *can't* refuse the quest.' She looked menacingly at him. 'You saw how I could control you in the church? I can do that any time I like.'

He scowled up at her. 'Oh, so it's like that, is it? Mind control. Like *The Manchurian Candidate*. Laurence Harvey's mum did the same thing to her son.'

'Sometimes that's what it takes, when boys don't do what their mothers want.'

'That's okay. Then I won't be responsible for my actions. I can plead diminished responsibility.' He smiled gleefully. 'I can say my mum turned me into a zombie.'

'Good luck with that one,' she smiled thinly. 'Now. I want you to think back to what you remember about the Canon. Remember the church procession ...?' The Virgin Soldiers ...? The Knights of Saint Pancras ...?

'Bloody hell, mum. Homework?'

* * *

The church procession at Dave's primary school. His mother was a Virgin Soldier, 'Soldiers for the Blessed Virgin', a women's organisation linked to the Knights of St Pancras. The Soldiers were dressed in blue and white robes and head-dresses, like nuns, so they looked like sexy nuns. To Dave, anyway, who spent a lot of time evaluating grown-ups for their looks and sexiness.

Two of them, at least: his mother and Mrs Czarnecki. Both were young mums, wore make-up with their outfits, and looked rather fetching. 'Mrs Czar' as everyone called her, was a Pell, a member of the grain merchant family, and had married a solicitor and coroner. The other two Virgin Soldiers, however, looked like Mother Theresa, although not as attractive.

The four Virgin Soldiers carried a statue of Our Lady on a bier, leaving St Mary's church, next to his primary school and the convent of the Sisters of Sorrow, and heading in the general direction of King Edward VIII dock, because Our Lady was also the Star of the Sea, and they were going to drop flower garlands in the water for her.

They were flanked by the Knights of St Pancras. Dave was very impressed by them, although they looked more like funeral directors than Knights. He thought they guarded the train station. They wore top hats, black suits and cloaks with splendid red, gold and blue linings, and carried silver top canes. Every one had a different coloured lining. Dave would have loved to have collected them as cigarette cards. When they weren't guarding the train station, Dave knew they worked with the Virgin Soldiers, helping the poor of the parish.

They included Mr Czar and Canon Williams, their chaplain. He was wearing a beretta and a most stylish, flared, long black cassock, which showed his tall figure off to great advantage. For this special occasion, he wore over his cassock a white, pleated, embroidered rochet tunic with lace inserts, which reached down to just below his knees. A gold cross added a finishing touch.

Dave was amongst the small boys and girls, marching in pairs, dressed all in white, with the girls looking like miniature 'Brides of Christ', escorted by the Sisters of Sorrow. Sorrow was the nuns' speciality, so Dave was on his best behaviour for once. It was claimed that rumours that the headmistress, the ancient Mother St Vincent, 'Vinegar Bottle', used a bicycle pump to punish bad children was just a silly story made up by her pupils, but Dave knew better.

Women of the parish wearing their Sunday best, dutifully proceeded after them. A long Brueghel-like procession of the sorriest and ugliest lost male souls in Christendom followed. Many of them were as afflicted as Brueghel's 16th century peasants. Dave thought of them as Opportunity Knocks for lepers. A young police constable was also on hand, to divert traffic.

The procession brought out the anti-clericalism in the crowd. They started jeering at the Canon: 'Look at that priest in his petticoats and his long black dress.' … 'Mystical mumbo jumbo! It's just an excuse to get out the dressing-up box' … 'Yeah. They're all nancy boys!'

Then a Wycliff preacher addressed the crowd. 'They keep

their nuns prisoners in their convents. And *him*,' pointing to the Canon, 'he has a harem of nuns.'

There was a shocked gasp from the onlookers. 'Yes,' the preacher continued, 'I've heard cries of newborn infants from that convent, but no babies have ever been seen.'

'How dare you?' retorted the Canon. 'Why, my own sister is a Sister of Sorrow.'

He appealed to the crowd. 'It's all lies. Look at Mother St Vincent here. Look how happy she is.'

The nun confirmed his words, giving the audience a vinegary glare, clutching her bicycle pump, hidden in the dark recesses of her robes, ready to deal with anyone who disagreed.

The preacher persisted with his accusations. 'They say the priest's body is sanctified, so it is not a sin for him to have carnal relations with a nun.'

This was too much for the outraged Canon. His father had been a Lieutenant Colonel in the Indian army and he himself had been a cavalryman before taking holy orders. 'Right! You've asked for this, Fletcher!' he snarled.

He laid into the preacher, delivering a hefty blow to his jaw. The preacher retaliated and knocked the Canon's beretta off, which caused Dave great amusement. The fracas was wildly entertaining for all the children in the procession. Dave couldn't stop laughing, despite his mother urging him to stop, and even the Brueghels seemed to be enjoying it in their own way. Dave was hoping Vinegar Bottle would get her bicycle pump out. Women in the procession fainted and were lifted away over the heads of the onlookers to safety. The Canon and the preacher continued to lay into each other until, eventually, the Knights pulled them apart.

The young policeman was completely out of his depth and unable to restore order, and a police inspector was called and there was a heated three-way conversation between the inspector, the Canon and the preacher.

Finally, the preacher was forced to acknowledge the truth. Some weeks before he had made similar accusations in his prayer meetings. In response, the Canon had invited him to visit the Convent of the Sisters of Sorrow. He had to admit he had found the nuns were happy there, being sorrowful, and there had been no impropriety. He had made it all up.

'You see why I was so angry with him, Inspector,' explained the Canon.

The preacher added lamely, 'But they're still ignorant of Christ's teaching to shut themselves away like that.'

It was a victory for the Canon and the Church. He strode on triumphantly, his LBC – Long Black Cassock – flapping in the wind, and the procession obediently followed in the direction of King Edward VIII dock, singing "Faith of our Fathers". The Knights, their canes at the ready, formed a protective cordon in case of further trouble.

Faith of our fathers, living still
In spite of dungeon, fire and sword.

At the dock, as seagulls wheeled and shrieked overhead, everyone posed for a photo for posterity. At the front there was the bier with the statue of Our Lady, and the children, the Sisters of Sorrow and the Virgin Soldiers positioned themselves behind it. The Canon stood behind the Virgin Soldiers with his back to the water. The Knights flanked them on both sides. The women of the parish and the Breughels were not considered important enough and milled around behind the photographer.

As a punishment for laughing, Dave was also left out of the photo. He wandered off sulkily, following the edge of the dock, balancing on the heavy chains, staring into the oily waters to see if there were any fish, and watching the swans cruising in the open water beyond the ships. Then he turned back to return to the group who were still being photographed.

Looking across the water at the backs of the posed company, he stiffened with outrage and clenched his fists at what he saw.

How ... how *dare* he?

The Canon was fondling and squeezing his mother's bottom.

CHAPTER SIXTEEN

As Dave left the Underground at St Paul's, he still recalled that sense of outrage. No one was allowed to touch his mum. He barely tolerated his dad touching his mum. Yes, it still looked like an open and shut case to the Liquorice Detective. Something had clearly been 'going on' between his mother and the Canon. And his father had pointed an accusing finger at the cleric. The Canon was definitely implicated in his mother's murder. He was still the prime suspect.

His mother had not elaborated further on the subject, but that was because Dave had blocked her from his mind.

Right now, he had more serious matters to attend to: working on *Laarf!*

Even though the comic proudly claimed it was 'Number One for Fun! A Mirthquake every week, Pals!' it was, sadly, anything but. He'd pleaded with his boss, Ron Punch for a suspended sentence. 'I can't face being demoted to *Laarf!* The next step down is *Sewer and Septic Tank Monthly:* I think I'd prefer that. Or *Incontinence Quarterly.*'

Ron was immune to his pain. 'That'll teach you, son. A few months on *Laarf!* will wipe that fucking smirk off your face.'

'Don't take that away from me, Ron. Humour is all I've got.'

'Well, you won't find any on *Laarf!* They take their comics seriously.'

'It's like a mortuary down there. I've seen more life in a funeral urn.'

But now, walking along Farringdon Street, the jaunty, triumphant theme tune of *The Great Escape* was endlessly being repeated in his head. He really didn't need that. It just made him feel worse. How inappropriate, he thought. There he and Greg were, doing a three-month stretch on 'Mirth Row', and his mother was playing *The Great Escape*!

He entered the dismal, silent *Laarf!* offices and his fellow prisoner looked up. Greg was taken aback by Dave's fashionable new image, but tried hard not to show it. Instead, he sneered, 'Dentist's appointment went well then?'

Dave didn't reply and sat down opposite. They had barely spoken since *Blitzkrieg!* Greg was still seething after his dreams were destroyed by Dave's treachery.

Dave took in his terrible new surroundings. There was a poster on the wall of a popular cartoon character, *Dirty Barry*, covered in sewage. Barry wore short trousers and a red and black striped jersey. Every week he started off clean and ended up dirty. The cartoon's catchphrase was inscribed on the poster, 'It's all right! It's only Dirty Barry!'

On the wall opposite there was Andy of *Andy's Anorak* fame – whom Dave especially despised – giving him a cheery thumbs up. His magical anorak could turn into whatever Andy wanted it to, such as a suit of armour, enabling him to beat up bullies.

There was a clock on the wall with the caption FUN TIME above it. It ticked slowly and ominously.

The low-wattage light bulbs seemed to give the smiling cartoon characters a grotesque and sinister quality.

There were two other empty desks. These were normally occupied by other old lags doing hard time for serious editorial errors of judgement.

Dave wanted to bury his head in his hands and sob. Instead, he made a neurotic bleating laugh, just like Tom Morecambe.

He was starting to crack already.

Greg and Dave worked on in sullen silence, reading page

after page of *Laarf!*, checking for lettering mistakes and occasionally looking up to scowl at each other.

They also had to open and read *Laarf!* readers' letters. They wrote in regularly and enthusiastically to say how much they enjoyed *Dirty Barry* and *Andy's Anorak* and couldn't stop laughing at them.

What was the matter with them, Dave wondered. Were they brain-dead? Was it something in the water, like fluoride, that dulled their senses so they actually enjoyed these crimes against comedy?

No, there could be no excuse and no mercy for the readers, Dave thought bitterly.

Greg held up an original cartoon page of *Dirty Barry* art and shook his head. 'I'm not passing this page.'

'Why not?'

Greg looked accusingly at Dave. 'Because I don't want to be accused of peddling filth. Again.'

'What's wrong with it?'

Greg handed the page over. 'It's obvious.'

Sighing heavily, Dave started to read *Dirty Barry*.

* * *

Looking smug, with a jaunty cartoon character walk, a clean Barry approached a building inscribed with the unlikely name: 'Common Cold Cure Research Lab'.

Then he saw a totally implausible elephant's trunk drooping down out of a window of the lab.

'Gosh!' said Barry. 'They must be testing their Cold Cure on that elephant!'

The elephant's trunk suddenly stiffened, inflated in size, rose up, and swivelled to point in the direction of Barry. Slime was dripping ominously from the end.

A 'reader's voice' from off picture warned: 'Jumbo's got the flu! Look out, Barry!'

Next moment, the elephant sneezed violently and Barry was knocked to the ground by a huge mass of quivering snot blasted out of its trunk. 'Ooer!' said Barry.

There was one further lethal squirt from the extended trunk before it deflated and drooped down again.

A worried man in a white coat ran out from the laboratory. He saw the figure lying on the ground, covered in slime. 'Oh, no!' he said.

Then he recognised Barry, just visible under the pile of snot, and he looked relieved.

'It's all right! It's only Dirty Barry!'

* * *

Dave recoiled from the vacuous nature of the strip. All the cartoons were just like this. Truly awful.

He started to bang his head on the desk.

Greg waited patiently until he had finished. 'You see?' he said. 'It could seem like the elephant has ejaculated all over Dirty Barry.'

'I suppose so,' said Dave despairingly, 'you'd better replace it with another strip.'

'Yes,' repeated Greg. 'It definitely looks like the elephant has ejaculated all over Dirty Barry.'

And he smiled knowingly at Dave.

Dave wondered what that smile meant. What was he getting at? It couldn't be that Joy had *told* Greg how she found him with her fur coat and –? Oh, no, she wouldn't have?

'Yes,' insisted Greg with a big grin. 'That looks like elephant cum to me. What do you think, Dave? Does that look like cum to you?'

Joy *had* told him.

Dave nodded, defeated. 'Yes. Yes. Yes.'

'But it's all right,' sneered Greg and leaned forward to sneer in Dave's face. 'It's only Dirty Dave.'

'Okay, okay, leave me alone,' said Dave, slumping forward across the desk.

Greg hadn't finished with him, though. 'There seems to be a lot of jizz about at the moment. Take *Andy's Anorak*.' He picked up an Andy page and gave his own freely-adapted version of the character.

'Don't you envy me, readers? When I'm wearing my anorak, there's no chance of my meeting girls. But when I pull my toggle, my anorak changes into whatever I want. I've been pulling my toggle for ages, readers. It's always worked in the past. Two tugs and I'm away.'

Greg paused to allow his sarcasm to sink in, then: 'What do you reckon, Dave ...? Two tugs on his toggle enough? I gather you're an expert in these matters.'

Dave said nothing, but Greg wasn't going to let it go.

'So how are the fur coats, Dave? Had any hot dates lately? A foxy fur? A *bear*-skin? A nice beaver?'

Dave suffered in silence, his misery complete.

He was used to furrist abuse. In fact, the underlying reason for Dave's hatred of *Laarf!* may have been that there were no furry characters in it. They were mainly bland 'reader identification' kids. Part of Tom's winning formula. So there were no talking bears, cats, dogs or rabbits. No one Dave could identify with.

It would be another decade before furry fandom was established, and the furries could start to come out of their hutches. Dave was ahead of his time. So he had to endure this kind of abuse about his preferences, like other persecuted minorities in the seventies.

But maybe, one day, things would change and it would no longer be possible to make furrist jokes about Billy Bobtail, because it was offensive to a man in a rabbit suit.

* * *

Fun Time passed endlessly slowly between 'Mirthquakes' on the Devil's Island of comics. Each key on their typewriters hit the page like a prisoner's pickaxe breaking rocks on Dartmoor. They dragged themselves into the *Laarf!* offices every morning, every day shuffling a little slower, a little more downcast, their mood made worse by their hostility to each other.

Dave was ordered to write a fill-in *Billy Blower* episode as the regular writer was off sick (he often seemed to be sick), and it was crucifying him. Billy was a boy with super blowing powers. He could, for example, inflate balloons in seconds that would lift a house off its foundations and this hugely amused the readers and made him one of *Laarf!*'s most popular characters.

So Dave wrote a story where, in the punchline picture, Billy Blower had blown vapour words up into the sky that read, 'Billy Blower blows your mind'.

Tom rejected it with the comment, 'Hippy angle not wanted.'

Dave's other suggestions for Billy Blower stories and his blowing powers were unrepeatable and even less appreciated by Tom.

Tom was an affable, likeable, suited and booted editor with a sober fashion sense that did not defer to the sixties or seventies, except for a discreet and very mild Beatles haircut. But his pleasant, easy-going manner hid a steely resolve to enforce his vision of Fleetpit fun factory humour comics.

Not everyone knew how to deal with Dave's aggressive jibes and cruel comments. They were designed to get under people's skins and provoke an angry reaction. But Tom was different. He had the perfect defence to Dave's verbal onslaughts. He just laughed them all off.

As the days painfully passed, Dave tried to explain to Tom what the problem with *Laarf!* was, and why the comics of Angus, Angus and Angus were infinitely superior.

To which, Tom simply laughed and laughed and laughed.

Dave could see he was getting nowhere, so he tried to find a weakness in Tom's armour.

'Humour has never knowingly touched you, has it, Tom?'

Tom once again laughed his strange bleating laugh in response, impervious to the insult.

Dave got ruder yet. 'Tell me – when exactly did you pass away, Tom? Perhaps I should be contacting you by ouija board?'

Once again, Tom leaned back in his chair, slapped his thighs and laughed. A distinctive, grating, bone-jarring whine, like an infant's long, drawn-out grizzle. It left Dave impotent with rage.

'Perhaps you'd like to write *William the Conkerer* instead …?' suggested Tom, a sinister gleam in his eye. 'That writer is also off sick.'

'Also known as William the Bastard?' said Dave. 'On account of how mind-numbing it is to think up stories about a boy who plays with his conkers all day? Nice try, Tom, but I think I'll stick with good old *Billy Blower*.'

Tom's buzz-saw laugh whirred once more into life.

Dave and Greg's minds were, indeed, being blown. Dave discovered that after just one week on *Laarf!*, he could no longer read *The Guardian, Private Eye* or *Punch*. It was just too hard making out the big words. Even *The Sun* newspaper was becoming a stretch. And BBC2, the up-market TV channel, was now way beyond him.

There was definitely brain damage.

Dave went in to see Ron to suggest that he got an early release from *Laarf!* leaving Greg to carry the can and serve out his sentence. Greg was, after all, the creator of *Blitzkrieg!*, the offending comic. But Greg had been in earlier to blame it all on Dave, so Ron was having none of it. They both had to serve out their sentences.

'But I can't face another *Billy Blower*,' Dave protested. 'How can you possibly be proud of a strip like that, Ron?'

'Course I'm fucking proud of it.' Ron stubbed a cigarette out, lit another, leaned forward and confided in Dave.

'It is a work of genius, Dave.'

'Genius!' Dave looked incredulous. 'You mean "genius" as in Shakespeare? You're putting *Billy Blower* in the same category as Shakespeare? Tolstoy? Goethe and Cervantes?'

'Well, you can't count foreigners, Dave,' scowled Ron.

'Cervantes wrote *Don Quixote*, Ron.'

'That's what I mean. He's a dago. So he's out for a start. And never mind Shakespeare neither. He's overwritten and not punchy enough.'

'This is a nightmare,' thought Dave. 'Maybe I'll wake up and it will all be different.'

'You see, Tom is the real genius,' continued Ron, 'because

he has the Formula. Reader identification, Dave. Every reader can identify with *Billy Blower*. Once you have the Formula, anyone can produce it. Even a fucking chimp.'

'Even me ...' echoed Dave, the full horror of Ron's words sinking in.

'Yeah, even you, Dave. You feed it in at one end and it comes out the other.'

'I ... I am lost for words, Ron.'

'Well that's good, Dave. Working on *Laarf!* is obviously doing you a power of good.' Ron smiled and prepared to return to his racing papers. 'Just remember all you have to do is repeat the Formula endlessly. Because that – *that* – Dave, is *true* genius.'

'Fair enough, Ron. Okay, I'd better rejoin the undead.'

'You do that. And, Dave. I've got my eye on you, son. Don't get any ideas.'

'I'm on *Laarf!*, that doesn't seem very likely.'

'Well, I'm warning you, son. Watch yourself.'

* * *

The days continued to drag by. The FUN TIME clock seemed different to and so much slower than a regular clock. It delayed to the very last possible moment recording every second, every minute, every hour of their sentence.

Joy came to visit them in their cell.

'How are you boys holding up?'

'Could be worse,' sighed Greg. 'We could be on the *Laarf! Crossword Specials.*'

'The Hole?' Joy shuddered. 'Aye, that would be hard time. I've smuggled you in an Angus, Angus and Angus comic. I thought you might appreciate some genuine humour?'

'Yes, indeed. You are talking to two desperate men starved of humour, Joy.' said Greg, 'What have you got for us? *The Corker? Bazooka? The Tosser?*'

He scowled at Dave with his head slumped forward over the desk. 'Dave ...? Dave ...? *The Tosser?* You might like that?'

Dave didn't bother to look up.

Greg stared malevolently down at him. 'Or ... *Spunky,* perhaps?'

Dave still showed no signs of life. He was a lost soul.

Joy looked furtively around her and then quickly pulled a comic out from under her top. Rival comics were frowned upon in the fun factory.

'It's ... *The Corker.'*

Dave suddenly came to life. '*The Corker?* Oh, that's brilliant! Thank you, Joy! Thank you! Thank you so much!

The desperate, humour-impoverished convicts excitedly went through the precious example of real comedy together.

'Yes. Yes. This is more like it: *Scratch and Sniff,*' said Greg. 'Love the way that cat and dog knock hell out of each other!'

'*Spat and Monocle,*' smiled Dave.

'*Knuckles Duster.* Look! Look at the size of his deer pie!'

'*Cap Puccino,* the crazy Italian.'

'*Wee Cheeky.'*

'This is so good,' said Greg, happily looking up, 'after the crap that's been sucking our souls dry.'

'But there's a problem,' responded Dave, '*The Corker* is *so* good, it's actually making me feel worse.'

'Worse ...?' asked Joy. 'I don't understand.'

'Yes. It's just rubbing it in. You may need to put me on suicide watch if I read anymore.

'He's already rung Cross Line six times,' explained Greg.

From the next office they could hear Tom's strange laugh.

'What ... What's that *neighing?* Is there a horse in there?' asked a bewildered Joy.

The sound continued, reaching a consistent tempo now. Joy listened carefully. 'Actually, you know, it's more like the whine of a buzz saw,' she decided.

'That is Tom Morecambe laughing,' explained Dave.

'It's ... horrible,' winced Joy. 'It's so ... depressing.'

'Yes. Now you know what we're going through, Joy,' agreed Dave, the pain written across his face.

'I should go,' said Joy. Just five minutes in the room, and she could already feel the corrosive atmosphere of the fun factory eating into her very being.

'No. Please stay,' begged Greg.

'Don't go,' implored Dave.

'Please don't leave us,' they appealed in unison.

Joy heard Tom Morecambe's buzz saw laugh again. 'I'm sorry. I … I have to go!' and bolted for the door.

Then she turned back and smiled at them, the relief obvious on her face that visiting time was over.

'Keep your heads down, boys, and don't drop the soap.'

* * *

Dave and Greg were in a bad way and then Tom came in and delivered the knock-out blow.

'Sad news. Kenneth Royce has just died.'

Dave and Greg looked shocked.

'At his drawing board,' Tom added.

Both of them were huge admirers of the artist's work. 'I loved that strip he did for *Angus, Angus and Angus* about a character who sinks ships every week,' sighed Greg.

'Yes. *Albert Ross – the Ancient Mariner*,' said Dave. ' "You wouldn't want him landing on your deck." '

'He was working on *Ebeneezer the Tight Geezer* when he died,' said Tom.

'He was the Rolls Royce of cartoonists,' remembered Greg. 'He did *Billy's Belly*, a kid who had workmen living in his stomach. They looked a bit like the Tetley Tea Folk. They were always on strike, so Billy was constantly constipated.'

'That's right,' agreed Dave. 'It was like a factory inside his belly. All these workmen sitting around reading newspapers and drinking tea.'

Greg and Dave were united in their grief, their differences for now, at least, behind them.

Dave nodded at Tom. 'He thought it was disgusting and axed it.'

'Lavatorial humour is *not* required,' said Tom primly.

'We should remember Ken in some way,' mused Dave. 'Maybe a special commemorative issue of his work? With a percentage of the profits going to his widow?'

Tom was taken aback. 'Are you on something, Dave? Apart from liquorice?'

'I just think it would be a nice gesture. For all the faithful years of service he put in.'

Tom looked blankly at his prisoners. 'You're getting this out of proportion. Readers don't even know who Ken Royce is.'

'But they *want* to, Tom. And they'll recognise his style.'

Tom replied with the absolute and immoveable authority of a prison warder. 'We don't want these personality cults. That's why we never give artists credits, and we whiten out their signatures.' He smiled to himself. 'No matter how cleverly they hide them. I always spot them and take them out.' He looked triumphantly at the two cons. 'So they can't become famous and make trouble. We've got to keep them in their place.'

'He was my hero,' said Dave.

'We have an excellent ghost artist,' said Tom. 'The readers won't notice the difference.'

'He was one of the great cartoonists of the twentieth century,' said Greg. 'He was drawing black comedy at least a decade before *Monty Python.*'

'*Monty Python?* That's for students,' Tom said with a dismissive hand wave. He looked annoyed. 'Don't care for student readers. They're pot-smoking layabouts, marching on demos and making trouble. They shouldn't be wasting their grant money on comics. *Our* money.'

Greg and Dave were unconvinced.

'Look, you two,' Tom said, jangling his keys, which sounded to Dave like a warder's keys, 'I liked Kenneth and I'm sorry to hear he's passed away. He was a good chap. Right, Ron …?'

Ron Punch had just entered. 'Right, Tom. Shame he dropped off his perch.'

Ron lit a cigarette as he recalled: 'He was a good un, all right. But he didn't know where to draw the line. He needed watching.' He looked warningly at the two cons. 'Like you two.'

Ron looked balefully at Greg in particular. He hadn't forgiven him for *Blitzkrieg!* and they'd barely spoken since that night in the Cock Tavern.

Tom had spent far longer in debate than he cared to. Normally, he avoided confrontation and conversation and preferred to laugh everything off. His office phone rang and he used the excuse to depart.

Dave recalled his happy memories of *Billy's Belly*. 'That's why Ken was so good – because he didn't self-censor. There were these huge piles of baked beans Billy had eaten that come pouring down a chute into his belly…'

Greg continued the story '… then the foreman calls the Brain department. "Anymore to come, Brains? Or is that it?" '

Dave carried on, 'Brains says Billy's eaten his fill so the foreman throws a lever for it to go into the Number Two conversion chamber. Only there's a build up of gas, and –'

'I know. I know.' Ron interrupted them. 'Billy has a massive fart that blasts all the furniture out the window. Disgusting. I was right to cancel it.'

'Okay, it's not your taste, Ron, but lots of kids found it really funny.'

'That's right,' said Greg, fuming at Ron's negativity.

'Thing is,' said Ron confidentially. 'If readers find us really funny, they'll want us to be really funny every week. Don't you see, lads?' He lowered his voice further. 'We don't want really funny, because then we might have a big success.'

'What's wrong with a big success?' snapped Greg.

Ron continued to speak quietly. 'Because then the board will want a big success *all* the time. And that's just too much work. Steady progress is what we're looking for.'

'Steady progress,' repeated Greg, rolling his eyes.

Ron saw the expression on both their faces.

'You may sneer, boys, but mediocre is best. Stories that don't demand too much of the reader. That is Tom Morecambe's vision. He is a Master of the Mediocre.'

Greg was becoming more irate, endlessly clicking his pen.

'It's why we had to calm Kenneth down,' Ron continued.

'His stories were too clever by half.'

'And clever is bad,' muttered Dave.

'Bad …' agreed Greg.

'Clever is very bad,' agreed Ron. 'Now, his final page of *Ebeneezer the Tight Geezer* was perfect. None of the indulgent stuff you 'aficionados' like. We went over it with a fucking magnifying glass. There was nothing offensive he was trying to sneak past us.'

'I'm so sorry to hear that,' said Dave glumly.

'You finally broke him,' said Greg.

All too often, Greg thought bitterly to himself, working class heroes, like Ken Royce, were eclipsed, ignored or crushed by the middle classes with their virtual monopoly on the media.

He'd first seen it in the sixties with his great hero: ex-pirate radio DJ Simon Dee. Dee would enter the TV studio for *Dee Time* to the rapturous cry of 'It's Siiiiiimon Dee'. At the outro of his show, 18 million viewers, including Greg and Bernie, watched enviously as Simon roared round one of the new multi-storey car parks at the wheel of an open E-type jag. The one-time labourer on a building site showed working class teenagers like Greg and Bernie *they* could live the dream; there was no glass ceiling.

But then Dee asked for more money and the beadle, in the form of Billy Cotton, the BBC Controller, offered him less, making him take a 20 percent pay cut as punishment. Dee ended up as a bus driver.

As Greg saw it, the glass ceiling was back in place. The lid was firmly back down on the coffin of working class dreams.

Just as the lid was firmly down on Greg's best friend Bernie's coffin. It wasn't possible to leave it open, not after Bernie's outro. Bernie, too, had leapt into an open E-type jag, only in a multi-storey car park in Ipswich. But it wasn't his E-type. Bernie, as fashionable and debonair as the cravat-wearing Simon Dee, adored fast cars; other people's fast cars. Unfamiliar with the controls, and the novelty of multi-storey car parks, he'd scraped it badly as he hurtled down it at high speed, trying to relive the iconic scenes in *Dee Time* and *Get Carter*. The damage alerted the cops. They recognised Bernie who was already 'known' to them, gave chase, and there had been that fatal crash. They *Got Bernie* all right.

Greg blocked the pain from his mind by exchanging it for equally passionate thoughts about Ken Royce. He prided himself on concealing his true feelings. It didn't suit his image. Movie stars were never angry, they were cool, they were mean, they were monosyllabic, and that's how he wanted to be. He wanted to be super-cool like Paul Newman in *Cool Hand Luke* or Clint Eastwood as The Man With No Name.

Hence his notebook, so he gave nothing away.

But he had to say something. 'Satire's not for the likes of us, guv'nor,' Greg said in his best Alf Mast voice. 'We needs to know our place. We should leave comedy to the toffs. *Carry On* films, Benny Hill and Bernard Manning are all we can understand.'

'What's wrong with Bernard Manning, son?' asked Ron. 'He's fucking funny, that bloke. When he takes the piss out of the Paddies and the Japs, me and the Major piss ourselves laughing.'

'Actually,' said Dave helpfully, 'Greg is Irish.'

'Really?' said Ron with no trace of embarrassment. 'I'd never have known.'

'How could you?' said Dave. 'I mean ...' and he snorted in derision, 'What kind of Irish name is "Greg"?'

'Lived here all my life so no accent,' explained Greg, reaching for his notebook.

'So it doesn't really count, you see, Ron ...' Dave explained. 'He's not sensitive like the real Irish. You can come out with as many Paddy jokes as you like.' He turned to Greg. 'You don't mind spud jokes, do you, Greg?'

'They do piss me off, actually, Dave,' Greg said quietly.

'But you have no right to be pissed off,' insisted Dave. 'Because you've never been to Ireland.'

'Because we can't go back. Not to the North. Not now. My dad was in the army. He'd be seen as a traitor.' Greg glowered at Dave. 'You get it ...? Okay?'

Dave shrugged, indifferent to other people's woes.

'Anyway,' said Ron, collecting his thoughts, 'I've just been to see the publisher and he wants to see you, Dave. Right now.'

'D'you know what it's about, Ron?' asked Dave apprehensively. Frank Johnson, the publisher, was a man held in fear and awe, a maverick trying to change the traditional and old-fashioned nature of juvenile publishing.

'You'd better ask him,' replied a tight-lipped Ron.

Whatever it was, Ron didn't look happy about it. Was it possible, speculated Dave, that someone had discovered what he was doing on *The Caning Commando*?

His life was already a nightmare, could things get any worse?

CHAPTER SEVENTEEN

An hour later, Dave and Greg were jauntily heading back to *The Spanker* offices, taking the steps up to the third floor two at a time, leaving the 'humour' department far, far behind.

They had been on *Laarf!* for two weeks.

Dave was humming the music of *The Great Escape* to himself. The publisher had released them. They'd been sprung. They were out of the cooler. The film theme swelled to a triumphant crescendo in his head as they proceeded along the corridor to their old office.

How his mother had predicted this was going to happen he had no idea, but they were reinstated. The boys were back in business. Steve McQueen and James Garner could not have been more buoyant than Dave and Greg at their return to the Land of the Living.

Pete Sullivan, an assistant editor on *Casino for the Man about Town* had been acting as caretaker editor of *The Spanker* while they were serving their sentence. Pete was oblivious to Dave's homicidal changes to *The Caning Commando*. He was oblivious to everything except possible sexual references in comics. Working on *Casino,* and freelancing for *Platform,* the sex magazine, he tended to see sex everywhere.

'Everything all right, Pete?' asked Dave. 'You didn't find any references to Big Ben in the issue you edited?'

'No. All clear,' smiled Pete.

'Good.' He watched as Pete collected his things. 'How's things going on *Platform*? Is your column called Raised Platform? Or Wankers Corner?'

'Spread Sheet, actually.'

'Right. You make up the readers' letters, don't you?' he asked provocatively.

'Of course. So they can have a proper punchline. That's a problem for our readers,' he mused.

'Still trying to master joined-up writing, are they?' said Dave sympathetically. 'I thought they seemed rather unlikely.'

'Not as unlikely as someone getting off on fur, Dave. Actually, it's not you sending in those letters about fur coats, is it? They're creeping us out.' And with that, he departed.

Dave turned to Greg. 'I'm just relieved we haven't been away longer. He screws everything up. *Casino* is the only publication he hasn't been able to kill. Yet.'

'That's why the *Casino* editor makes him available as a caretaker editor,' agreed Greg. 'He's desperate to get shot of him.'

'I know,' said Dave. 'His touch is like weedkiller.'

Greg thought back. 'Before he was promoted to *Casino*, he worked on comics featuring the Smurfs, Abba, Tarzan, Sherlock Holmes; and did for the lot of 'em.'

'Yes. James Bond barely escaped,' said Dave.

'I think he might have been responsible for the break-up of The Beatles,' suggested Greg.

'He is the Yoko Ono of comics,' agreed Dave.

Freed from the misery of Mirth Row, they were back talking to each other again.

Dave enjoyed his new-found freedom. There was a catch to it, though.

Their early release by the publisher was no act of clemency for Christmas: it was on condition that, alongside their regular work, they produce the scripts for a new comic, JNP 66 (Juvenile New Publication 66), in just six weeks, ready to be drawn and published in March. JNP 66 was to be modern, rough and tough, and Ron had been warned not to interfere.

The reason was that rivals Angus, Angus and Angus had just brought out modern, rough and tough *Guts*, which was selling well, and the board wanted their slice of the kids' pocket money. Faced with the alternative of losing three months of his life on *Laarf!*, Dave agreed to the extra project.

'I've got two great ideas for JNP 66 already,' said Greg.

'Yeah? Go for it, man.'

'*Car-Jacks* – about two teenagers who spend their lives stealing cars.'

'Based on you and Bernie …? Perfect.'

'And *Bent*.'

'You're finally coming out of the closet? Well, a story about a gay young man coming to terms with his sexuality would certainly fit the direction I want it to go. Mary Whitehouse would hate it, so that's good.'

'No. It's about a corrupt cop,' said Greg patiently.

'Like *The Sweeney*?'

'More G.F. Newman's Terry Sneed series: *Sir, You Bastard*. You should check them out.'

'Sorry. Can't tear myself away from *Watership Down*.'

'This time, Dave,' vowed Greg enthusiastically, 'we'll break through that glass ceiling.'

'More like break wind,' Dave replied.

But he, too, was secretly excited by the idea of a kick-ass comic for the seventies. A little later on, he intended to make a secret trip to the vaults to find a certain notorious comic strip that would be perfect for it.

Meanwhile, it was time for him to enjoy the latest episode of *The Caning Commando* due to go to press. As usual, the picture strip story was told at high speed, and began with an introductory caption:

'Because of his legendary caning skills, the War Office recruited schoolmaster Victor Grabham to be –
THE CANING COMMANDO.'

This episode was a particular favourite of Dave's.

* * *

In Victor Grabham's study in the Golden Hind Academy, the housemaster was patiently attempting to give Alf Mast an English lesson. 'Now ... what does C.O.D. stand for, Mast?'

Alf Mast considered the question long and hard, furrowing his brow in concentration. Finally, looking inspired, he had the answer. 'Cod.'

Grabham sighed. 'You really have a head like a sieve, don't you, boy?'

'What's a sieve, sir? And what's an 'ed? Is that like an 'ed of cabbage?'

'Yes, Mast. In your case, that is exactly what it is. You are more vegetable than boy. Your family album must look like a greengrocer's gutter.'

Suddenly they heard a message over the radio, a thin, nasal voice repeating: 'Longpants calling. Longpants calling.'

'It's Lord Ow! Ow!,' exclaimed the teacher. 'That's his call sign. He broadcasts radio propaganda for the Boche.'

Grabham and Mast listened to the bakelite receiver. 'I challenge the Caning Commando to a caning duel here in Berlin,' said Lord Ow! Ow!

Grabham mused on the challenge. 'It's a trap, of course, but if I turn the other cheek, it will seem like Germany are the number one thrashers. Britain has got to keep its rear end up, even if I never see Lower Belting Bottom again.'

'Who is Lord Ow! Ow!, sir?'

'Headmaster of a British public school. He was dishonourably discharged and went over to the enemy.'

'That's just like me, sir,' said Alf excitedly.

'Are you comparing yourself to the traitor Reginald Bareback-Jones?' scowled Grabham.

'I was looking at photos of bumpy men and you confiscated them, sir, in case I had a "dishonourable discharge".'

'Indeed. We don't want you having a repeat of the hot collywobbles, as your nan would say,' the Commando said meaningfully.

That night, a Lysander flew the Caning Commando and Corporal Punishment to Berlin and they sneaked inside the radio station.

'What shall I do, sir,' asked Alf, 'while you're having your duel?'

'Well, I don't expect you to disarm the enemy with your cheeky guile, Mast. But it's our duty to put this radio station out of action. Here's the instructions for a pipe bomb.'

Leaving Alf Mast in the basement, Grabham caned his way through the German soldiers waiting in ambush for him, and entered the control room.

Lord Ow! Ow! turned to confront him, an evil, menacing figure, still wearing the black gown from his teaching days.

'You know my reputation as a disciplinarian, Victor?' boasted Lord Ow! Ow!. '911,500 canings, 121,000 floggings, 136,000 tips with the ruler, 109,000 detentions, 30,200 boxes on the ear and 22,700 tasks to learn by heart.'

'That's a record of scholastic severity any teacher would envy,' admitted the Commando.

They bent their canes almost double and circled warily around each other as Bareback-Jones continued, 'My punishments have subdued even the proudest, most defiant of arses. And they will subdue yours.'

The traitor's cane looked familiar to the Commando.

'I recognise that cane, Reginald. Made by Mafeking and Jones of St James's, my own canemakers. A Windsor *Chastiser*, no less.'

'Yes,' sneered Lord Ow! Ow! 'It's the finest cane money can buy. By royal appointment. Princes' posteriors are very familiar with the *Chastiser*.'

'You traitorous swine!' snarled the Commando, outraged by this insult to the royal family and launched himself at his enemy's rear. 'An eye for an eye and a cheek for a cheek, and you will pay for your insufferable cheek, sir.'

In the deadly caning duel that followed, both men showed they were masters of their art, matching each other blow for blow, cheek for cheek.

Then Lord Ow! Ow! shook the chalk dust from his gown, temporarily blinding the Commando with the white powder, tripped him up with the crook of his *Chastiser,* and brought him to his knees.

As the Commando was bent over, blinded and helpless, Lord Ow! Ow! brought down a ferocious series of strokes on his rear end, laughing maniacally:

'I promise you endless canings as my prisoner, Victor!
Lashed for breakfast in a dungeon small,
Thrashed for dinner in the commandant's hall,
The supper time's more beating time than all!'

For a moment, it looked like it was all over. And then, to Jones's horror, the Commando got to his feet, more menacing, more deadly than ever.

'How … how is this possible?' Jones gasped.

'You forgot, Reggie,' said the Commando, a cruel smile on his lips, 'the many *beneficial* qualities of the cane, which is the reason I apply it zealously to boys.'

He advanced confidently on his foe, flexing his cane in preparation. 'A thorough thrashing stirs up the stagnating juices, dissolves the precipitating salts, purifies the coagulating humours of the body, clears the brain, purges the belly, circulates the blood and braces the nerves!'

Bareback-Jones looked alarmed.

'Which is why,' roared Grabham, 'I am now more than ready to … Carpet Bum the Hun!'

And he waded into the traitor once more. It was a most savage, superhuman caning and concluded as he broke the *Chastiser* over his knee and left Lord Ow! Ow! a broken, blubbering heap in the corner.

Meanwhile, in the basement, Alf Mast had made an improvised pipe bomb to blow up the radio station, but when the Commando came down to check his handiwork, he was disappointed to discover Alf had not followed the instructions.

'It's my fault,' he sighed. 'I forgot you were illiterate. I would give you one out of ten for effort, but you missed out vital ingredients which every schoolboy knows about when making their pipe bombs. In fact, there are no ingredients. How exactly would it explode if there's no bomb inside it?'

'Er ... don't know, sir,' said Alf looking vacant.

Grabham sighed. 'My simian young friend, I should have left you to be educated at His Majesty's Pleasure at Bircham Hall Approved School.'

Alf Mast smiled happily as he remembered: 'That's where we first met, sir. When you were visiting guest thrasher. And you took me under your wing and gave me a new start in life as your assistant Corporal Punishment.'

'With the permission of your nan who sold you for a sack of nutty slack and a new ear trumpet.'

The teacher having found the necessary explosive ingredients conveniently nearby and explained how they should be used, the bomb was primed and they were ready to leave.

'Now take your gormless stare up to the Unter Den Linden and flag down our pilot.'

'Thanks very much, sir. You're a scholar and a gentlemen, sir.'

'I am indeed, Mast. Unlike yourself: a poorly dressed but loyal chimpanzee.'

A Lysander landed along the Unter Den Linden and they climbed aboard. Moments later, as the aircraft climbed into the air, the bomb detonated and the radio station exploded so that Lord Ow! Ow! could never again make his traitorous broadcasts.

Arriving back at the Golden Hind Academy, it was time, once again, for the courageous couple to go their separate ways. 'It's your nosebag time, young Mast.'

'Ah! Me fish and chips, sir. I likes me fish and chips, sir.'

'And you deserve them, my boy. Then have matron sluice out your trough and you may retire to your tree ape nest or packing crate straw as you see fit.'

CHAPTER EIGHTEEN

Dave liked the episode because he had inserted precise details on how readers could find the ingredients and make a pipe bomb in it. His short sharp shock working on *Laarf!* had fuelled his hatred of the readers and he knew no one was taking notice of *The Spanker* anymore.

And if they did, there was the Major as fall guy. When they looked into his disreputable past and those school fees going walkabout, it would be easy to put him in the frame. He disregarded his recent encounter with the Demon Barber and was back to his old risk-taking self.

Chewing on his pipe, he recalled, from readers' letters and complaints, there had only been walking wounded thus far.

There had been that kid who tried to breathe air through the plughole and smashed his teeth. There were the two boys who tried to imitate the Caning Commando when Dave had him pushing his cane through the spokes of the Oberspankerfuhrer's motorbike. One had gone over the handlebars of his chopper bike and broken his arm. The other, holding the cane, had dislocated his thumb.

Dave had written in a scene where the Commando jumps out of a plane onto a barrage balloon. Copying him, a kid had jumped out of his bedroom window onto his space hopper, only he had missed and broken his leg. But it didn't put him off. He wrote in to say, as soon as his leg was better, he was going to jump again.

Then the Oberspankerfuhrer had forced the Commando to drink a deadly poison. Dave had Grabham saving himself thanks to inserting a balloon down his throat. It didn't work, of course, so Dave had had high hopes for that one. It never got to the poison stage, because a kid trying it out had nearly choked on a balloon and had to be rushed to hospital.

However, Dave had a good feeling about the pipe bomb. If they followed his instructions correctly, and were even a little bit smarter than Alf Mast, this could be the big one.

* * *

Now it was time for him to visit the vaults where a century of British comic art was stored. What Dave was after was on the infamous Aisle 13, a.k.a. the Black Museum of Comics: Ken Royce's legendary, banned masterpiece, *Micky's Mutants*.

In Britain, after a nuclear war, Micky is happily living in the ruins of his semi-detached house with his mutant mum, dad, brother and sister, all grotesquely but humorously mutated, but still wearing the remnants of their clothes. They jeer at Micky because he was normal and had five fingers on each hand, two eyes, and two ears.

If Dave could find it, it would be perfect for JNP 66.

Dave had had a conversation with Ron about it while he was on *Laarf!*. 'Why is it locked away on Aisle 13, Ron?'

'So people like you can't get at it.'

'What's it about?'

'If you really want to know, it's these fucking mutants who make fun of Micky 'cos he's the only one who's normal after a fucking nuclear war. Now, do you think that's funny?'

'Well, yes, I do.'

'Well, you would, wouldn't you? I don't see what's funny about mutants with three legs and one eye, who talk out their arsehole.'

'Could I see it? Purely for my personal interest?'

'No,' said Ron, regarding him suspiciously. 'That strip will never see the light of day again. It would give kids nightmares.

We'd have the *Guardian*, Mary Whitehouse, and fuck knows who else onto us. I think it's deeply offensive to take the piss out of someone with two heads and a tail.'

'But Royce is a brilliant cartoonist. He's up there with the greats: Ronald Searle, David Low, Osbert Lancaster.'

'We wouldn't put up with any of their indulgent stuff here neither,' responded a scowling Ron. 'Ronald Searle – we'd have seen him off. He'd be tunnelling his way back into that prisoner of war camp if he'd been working for us.'

Dave owed it to Ken Royce that his lost masterpiece should finally be revealed to his thousands of fans who didn't even know his name. Only hours earlier he had been saying how much he hated the readers and yet here he was, fighting for their right to laugh. The paradox was lost on him.

'You're doing a good thing,' said his mother from inside his head.

'Yeah, well don't expect me to make a habit of it,' he replied grudgingly.

But first he had to find it.

He entered the dimly lit vaults, which had a strange, eerie atmosphere like something out of *Gormenghast*. Endless aisles of classic pages of artwork, labelled and wrapped in brown paper, and famous magazines going back to World War Two, World War One, and beyond, that seemed to go on forever, were looked after by bored browncoats. This vast basement was actually much older and bigger – half an acre of arched, subterranean cellars – than Fleetpit House above it.

No one was quite sure why the former Edwardian hotel had its somewhat unfortunate name. It was claimed the site had once been a mass burial pit that massacred Romans were thrown into when Boudicca destroyed Londinium. Another theory was there had been a plague pit or a cock fighting pit on the site. Or a cesspit from which sewage poured into the underground River Fleet, now enclosed inside a giant sewer pipe, which ran the length of the vaults.

How apt, Dave had commented, that this building, built over a sewer, was now producing the worst shit in the world. As he liked to say, 'Our comics have brought shame on a plague pit.'

Approaching the entrance, Dave pretended he was looking for a harmless old page to reprint in *The Spanker*. He had forged the necessary chit. The browncoat on duty consulted a ledger. 'Aisle 9. Rack 3.' He waved Dave forward without looking up. 'Help yourself, mate. We're on our tea break.'

Dave noticed the storemen were using a beautiful, original piece of artwork, depicting a heroic British gladiator in a Roman arena, as a tea tray. 'Is that a Frank Delano original?' he asked in horror.

'Dunno,' replied the browncoat.

Dave explained to the bored storemen, 'Frank Delano was one of the finest illustrators of the 1960s. He's world famous. He's won dozens of awards.'

'That's nice for him,' said one of them, spilling tea onto it.

Close-by, another storeman was stoking the boiler. He looked across curiously at Dave, hovering by the tea drinkers, as he loaded priceless bound volumes of the history of the South African War into the furnace. They were so old, they burnt particularly well. As he ripped out the pages, depicting Britain's courageous slaughter of the Boers, his features were illuminated by the glow of the flames. He was a silver-haired, once handsome man, somewhat disfigured by an old facial injury, giving him a twisted and malevolent look.

On another aisle, a browncoat used a Stanley knife to cut some original artwork down to size, a fully-painted Crusader castle that had had appeared in *But Why?* magazine, slicing off the battlements.

The others called across to him. 'Oi! What you doing, Bill?'

'Artwork's sticking out. Got to cut it down so it fits the shelf.'

'Hurry up. Tea's getting cold.'

Dave couldn't let it go without comment. 'I suppose you have more old artwork blocking leaky drains?'

'You been spying on us?'

Shuddering, Dave headed off for Aisle 9, unaware that the browncoat stoking the boiler had left his assignment and was following him. Picking up the art from Aisle 9, Dave then sneaked across to Aisle 13.

Water, at least he hoped it was water, was slopping out of the drains. This always happened when the sewer pipe couldn't cope and the subterranean Fleet overflowed. It looked like the bottom shelves had been temporarily submerged and the artwork allowed to dry out. He prayed that wasn't the case for Ken Royce's work.

He leafed through the 'Black Museum' of forbidden comics. There were a number of *Caning Commando* banned stories that were never to be reprinted under any circumstances. The 'Relief of Mafeking' story appeared in 1963 at the height of the Profumo affair. In it, the Caning Commando visits his canemakers, Mafeking and Jones, and discovers traitorous aristocrats purchasing canes for dubious purposes, bringing his beloved profession into disrepute. Meanwhile, Alf finds a 'bumpy man' named Mandy in one of the cane-fitting rooms using a 'special reserve' cane on a member of the House of Lords.

It was embarrassing, because Mafeking and Jones actually existed and, rumour had it, the story was a little close to the truth. They supplied canes, tawses, paddles, whips, birches and other 'disciplinary devices' to teachers and security services around the world.

The Major had bought his canes from M&J when he was a housemaster, and the canemakers had no objection to him using their name. They seemed to rather enjoy the Caning Commando being their 'poster boy'. Whenever the Major mentioned Mafeking and Jones in a story, they sent him a bottle of single malt whisky.

Next to the 'Relief of Mafeking' story were the 'Belt Up Britain' posters. In 1964, in the wake of the mods and rockers riots, there were calls to bring back the birch to deal with the 'yob problem'. As the birch had only recently been banned, the publishers thought they would capitalise on the public anger. The Caning Commando fronted a poster campaign encouraging parents to discipline their children. He was depicted waving a huge belt with the captions, 'Belt Up Britain' and 'Dads Do Your Duty'.

Alongside it was the infamous 'Bumzai!' episode where the Caning Commando visits the Asian theatre of war and is awarded a 'purple arse' medal by the Americans for 'giving the Japanese a taste of their own divine wind'. It fell foul of the 1965 Race Relations Act because of the Commando's unrepeatable racist language as he battled with a cane-wielding Samurai. Clearly the Major had had a bad time as a Japanese prisoner of war.

But yes, there it was – *Micky's Mutants!* Dave tore back the corners of the wrapping paper and beheld the masterpiece as the lurking browncoat watched him from around the corner of the aisle. It was everything Dave hoped for. Micky's dad! He was in awe. And that blob with tentacles, with the skirt on: Micky's mum!

Using the reprint page of art as a cover, Dave slipped the banned pages past the other browncoats, who couldn't be bothered to sign him out or even look in his direction. They were too busy throwing darts at a priceless piece of art from *Homework* – an impressive, full colour cutaway of a Vickers Vanguard airliner.

Dave was delighted with his find. Publishing it in JNP66 would be his tribute to Ken. He might even put some words in the comic:

'In memory of Kenneth Royce, a Master of Comedy. Martyr to the "Humour" department. Sacrificed on the Altar of Shame. In the Temple of the Humourless.'

Ken would have the last *Laarf!*

Back down in the vaults, the browncoats had finished their tea break and returned to work, leaving a lone attendant on the front desk. Dave's mysterious stalker – the 'Phantom of the Fleetpit' – strode up to the desk and enquired, 'Hey, Sid, who was that git from upstairs who was looking for art?'

'They're all gits upstairs,' said Sid. 'Which git?'

'The big git who looked a bit of a shit.'

'Which shit? They all look like shits to me.'

'You know. The … fan,' The Phantom said with an air of

disgust.

Sid looked equally repelled. 'Oh, yeah. The … *fan*. I know who you mean now. Old effendi. Didn't like our choice of tea trays.'

'So who is old effendi?'

Sid consulted his ledger. 'Let's see. Dave Maudling.'

'Thought as much,' said the Phantom. 'What magazine does he work on?'

'Says here he's the editor of *The Spanker*.'

'Well, what do you know?' said the mysterious storeman. He repeated himself: 'What do you know?'

'So what *do* you know?' asked a puzzled Sid.

'I know I'm going to be paying him a visit,' said the Phantom smiling cruelly.

CHAPTER NINETEEN

Greg had been trying to get out of his relationship with Joy for several weeks. She wasn't going to show her famous dad his novel, so what was the point? He was in such a hurry to get to the top he couldn't waste any more time on her. He didn't realise she was actually a meal ticket in her own right.

Because Joy was thinking about opening a shop to sell science fiction toys, movie memorabilia and comics. There was a premises in Neal Street she had her eye on, and she'd been talking to the owner about leasing it. She even had a possible name for her shop: Time Machine. Because of her mum. Coira had auditioned for a lead role in the film, but it had gone to Yvette Mimieux. Joy always thought her mum would have been great in it.

Greg was too interested in his own future to see that Joy had one, too. However, he was sensible enough to realise his exit strategy needed careful handling. It had to be done slowly so Joy would do the dumping and he could pretend to be upset and reluctantly accept their relationship was at an end. A headbutt-free solution. But, unfortunately, she didn't seem to be taking his hints. Greg finally, reluctantly, confided in Dave about it.

'I don't see how I can end our relationship without pain, Dave.'

Dave nodded in agreement. 'Telling her is not really an option. Let's face it, Greg, you're rather attached to your lungs.'

'You don't think she'd take it well?'

Dave grinned sadistically.

'You're right,' agreed Greg. 'She'd frisbee my goolies out the window.'

'So let's get back to something more important,' said Dave. '*My* sex life. I'm getting bed sores from my lack of activity.'

This is excellent news, Dave thought. If their relationship was over anyway, he wouldn't need to show Joy the pages he photocopied from Greg's notebook after all.

Joy entered with a payment form for Greg to sign. 'The latest episode of *Feral Meryl* is out, Greg. Readers love it. It's so ... emotional.'

'Oh, yeah?' said Greg, indifferently, not even bothering to look up at her.

'See for yourself.' She opened a copy of *Shandy* under his nose so he was forced to look at the drawn version.

Greg cast a quick eye over his story and grunted, 'It's okay.'

Joy turned to Dave. 'Dave, have a read of it and you'll see what I mean.'

'Must I, Joy?' sighed Dave. 'I've really got more important things to do. Like cleaning my comb.'

'You must, Dave,' she said menacingly.

'Why?'

She leaned threateningly over him. 'You could learn from it.'

'Okay,' said Dave. 'I shall be thrilled, as always, to read it.'

He decided to skim through the episode at high speed to keep her happy.

Once again the opening caption read:

'Feral Meryl was a wild girl, brought up by wolves in the wilds of Berkshire. She was rescued by her friend Mandy who was trying to stop her being sent to a Special School.'

The gist of what he speed read was:

After recovering from being shot by the Farmer, Feral Meryl had gone to school with Mandy, who tried to pass the wolf girl off as a normal girl.

120

All was going well until she ate her maths book, bit another girl, Phoebe, in the ankle, and licked Mandy's face in class. Phoebe became even more suspicious of Meryl after she ran round the 1500-metre track at a record-breaking speed, and she alerted the Dog Catchers.

Meryl was cornered in the playground by the Catchers, who put a noose around her neck and dragged the growling, frightened girl into a van and drove away with her.

Meryl's sad face looked out the van's back window and she was pawing and howling as Mandy desperately ran after her.

Mandy lamented to herself, 'They're taking Meryl to a Special School! What will they do to her there? And … Where will it all end?'

'Yes, it's excellent,' said Dave. 'It's extremely good.'

'You read that very quickly,' said Joy suspiciously.

'I just couldn't put it down, Joy. It's a page turner.'

Joy turned her attention to Greg.

'Did you like it? Isn't it beautiful? It really made me feel for Mandy and Meryl,' said Joy expectantly. 'I was almost in tears when I looked at it.'

'Yeah? I suppose it's okay.' Greg shrugged. 'But I wrote it, Joy. So … it's not really for me to say.'

'I meant: Did you like the art?'

'Yeah, it's all right. If you like that sort of thing,' shrugged Greg coldly.

Joy tried another approach. 'You coming to the *My Gang* Christmas party then?'

'Joy, I'd love to,' sighed Greg, 'but I'm afraid I've got to get back to my novel.'

'Oh, that's a pity,' said Joy.

'Yes, isn't it? The novel you don't want your dad to read.'

'I'll come with you,' said Dave, quick as a flash.

'Sorry, Dave,' scowled Joy. 'It's Bring a Bottle, not Bring a Sherbert.'

'Would you like an edible bracelet, Joy?' Dave persisted, bringing one out from his confectionery box. 'It's got sweet lovehearts. It was given away with *Chelsea Girl*. It's really gear.'

Joy regarded it balefully. 'No, Dave. It's not really me. It's more you.'

'I thought you'd admire my thrift.'

'It's not thrifty. It's mental.'

Dave sighed. 'I take rejections from women really badly. Some of them even sent me rejection slips, you know?'

'Oh, don't look so sad, Dave. You are really sweet.' Joy looked at the pair of edible false teeth Dave was dropping into a tumbler of water. 'Like a suicidal diabetic.'

Dave opened another comic free-gift sachet. 'Joy, be honest with me. Would I ever stand a chance with you?'

He poured the brown powder inside into the glass. 'Tell it like it is. I can take it.'

'Well,' Joy replied, observing the the powder fizzing like Alka-Seltzer. 'You know ...' She watched Dave stirring it with the stick of his liquorice pipe. 'You're very ...'

Dave held the drink up. 'Toffee fizz.' He took a sip.

'You'll find the right woman,' said Joy finally. 'She's out there. You've just got to cast your net wider. You're a wonderful catch. Any other girl would be glad to have you.'

Dave looked up, a brown toffee moustache on his upper lip. 'You're not just saying that?'

'Truthfully.'

'But what about you, Joy?'

'With me, Dave, you haven't got close enough to be rejected. You're at stage one: indifference.'

And she turned on her heel and exited.

'Did you hear that, Greg?' said Dave. 'I think that was a result. She's using you to toy with me. You're going to get badly hurt.'

'If only I was,' lamented Greg. 'God. She's just not taking the hints, is she?'

'Yes, I was pleased to see you're as much of a shit as I am.'

'If only she were interested in you. It would make my life so much easier.' Greg shook his head sadly and returned to reading his magazine, *German Secret Weapons*.

'So how could I pull her?' Dave asked. But Greg wasn't listening. 'Greg? Greg? *Greg!*'

'What?'

'Sorry to drag you away from the Nuremberg Rally. *How* could I pull her?'

Greg thought about it briefly. 'Truthfully?'

'Truthfully.'

'You've no chance.'

'That's not what my mum says.'

'Your mum is dead, Dave. Her opinion doesn't count.'

'She was right about us getting our sentence on *Laarf!* cut.'

Greg put down his magazine and gave Dave his full attention. 'Even with your new look, Joy is just too tough a nut to crack. It can't be done.'

'But I need a woman in my life. Apart from my mother. Give me some advice. Throw me some crumbs from your Olympian table.'

Greg clicked his pen and looked at Dave from every angle, like a farmer evaluating a horse. 'Okay, what is it you're looking for?'

'A pulse?' Dave toyed with the sweets in his sweet box. 'A liquorice lush. A Trebor trollop. Someone to give me a walnut whip.'

Greg shook his head. 'Forget it. Double your rejections. Become bisexual.'

'Like you and your friend Bernie?'

'That is so out of order,' said Greg, his face going grey.

'Sorry, I should show more sympathy for your loss,' said Dave, thinking to himself it was five years since Bernie died. Why did he have to keep whinging on about him. It was only his best friend who died for God's sake.

Greg stared thoughtfully at Dave. 'Sympathy … yes… maybe. Maybe. Yes. That might just work.'

'What? What?' asked Dave expectantly.

Greg looked inspired. 'Sympathy shag.'

'Make Joy feel sorry for me, eh?' Dave smiled. 'Last resort of a scoundrel? I like it.'

'Yes, you see I was just admiring your insincerity over the death of my best friend.'

'I do try.'

'And you succeeded. Your phoney sympathy didn't fool me for one moment, of course, but it was still very good, Dave.'

'Thank you very much.'

'You could pull it off.'

'It will make a change to pulling myself off. Although Joy is not renowned for her compassion or pity.'

'It has been known. She's a much gentler and kinder woman than you think.'

'If you say so,' said Dave sceptically.

He leaned forward, intrigued. 'So come on. How would I reach her mythical softer side?'

CHAPTER TWENTY

The *My Gang* party had just begun when Dave joined it. It started after the dreaded browncoats had gone home. They were not cute and cuddly like the Mr Shifter chimpanzees in the PG Tips adverts. To shift a chair from one office to another was bad enough, but to pile up desks, unscrew conventional light bulbs and replace them with red ones, and precariously dangle a mirror ball from some overhead pipes was quite another. This was the exclusive responsibility of the browncoats, and the party-goers' actions could have resulted in an all-out strike.

One storeman, however, was there: the 'Phantom of the Fleetpit'. He had sensibly removed his coat so he wouldn't cause a panic. He didn't actually care what they got up to. He was only interested in Dave. So he watched him for a while as he handed over his *Black Tower* to join the *Mateus Rosé*, *Blue Nun* and other bottles assembled on a desk. Emil, the editor of *My Gang,* welcomed guests. He was standing tall in silver platforms with rainbow-coloured three-inch soles, wearing bright orange leather dungarees with a turquoise paisley shirt underneath.

'Love your orange dungarees,' said Dave insincerely, warming up for his main event with Joy.

'They're not orange, they're tangerine,' said Emil.

Dave also brought a selection of his confectionery along for the party, but none of the party-goers seemed that interested in it, apart from the sherbet. Not understanding what it was, in the semi-darkness, Emil sampled it. He tried snorting it with the straw provided, then rubbing it on his gums and told Dave it was pretty good.

Eventually the Phantom lost interest and decided to go home. There was one more thing he needed to know about Dave before he made his move.

The music started off rather badly because only the review albums none of the staff wanted were available. Rollers, Osmonds, Jackson 5 and Glitter which nobody had the remotest interest in, even though they claimed in their magazine they were crazy about these 'hunks of the month' and 'dishes of the day'.

Worse – someone had put on Judge Dread's piss-take of "Je T'Aime". In it, the Judge discovers the alluring female making advances on him is actually a 'Transmistor'. To which the latter replies, 'Oh, come on, dear! This is 1975.'

There was a chorus of 'Get that off!' from the party-goers.

Thankfully, someone had gone up to the offices of the real music magazines and helped themselves to some Bowie and Zeppelin, and the party improved to the sound of "Young Americans". But thinking about the way the staff took all the best albums home gave Dave the germ of a rather good idea for a story for JNP 66.

He moved through the throng, looking for Joy. In between sampling lasagne and nibbling pineapple on sticks, people were talking about getting away on a Laker flight to the sun for Christmas. *Y Viva España*!

Someone was describing the Sex Pistols, who were currently gigging at art colleges. He talked about John Lydon wearing an 'I hate Pink Floyd' tee-shirt and Dave tuned in to their conversation because his sister Annie hated Pink Floyd, too. He liked prog rock himself, which led to huge arguments with her.

Even so, he liked the idea of the Pistols. Their anti-establishment attitude struck a chord with him. They could also fit the story he was planning for JNP 66. It was slowly starting to take shape in his mind now.

He saw Joy, wearing a Sergeant Pepper jacket, being hit on

by Emil and realised, with a sinking heart, he stood no chance against this pinnacle of seventies fashion.

'What can I get you?' Emil asked, smiling condescendingly down at Joy. 'Babycham? Avocaat snowball?'

'Whisky,' said Joy.

'Right back.'

She rolled a joint while she was waiting and looked uncertainly around her. She didn't like teenage girls magazines very much. She described them as being for 'simps': simpering fools.

'So,' said Emil on his return, 'as I was telling you, key parties: forget them. They're just not cool anymore. The new big thing is S&M.'

'What's S&M?' asked Joy, baffled.

'Guess,' he said towering unsteadily over her.

'I don't know,' she shrugged. 'A Satanic version of M&S? Brushed nylon nighties with pentagrams on them?'

'Ha, ha. No. Some women really enjoy S&M, you know? It's the surprise, the excitement, the shock that they love.'

'The shock? It doesn't involve electricity?' she asked suspiciously.

'No, but the effect on women is electric. But it has to be a complete surprise to work. You must have no idea what is coming.'

A puzzled Joy took a drag of her spliff. 'Okay, so what *is* S&M?'

'I'll show you,' he said and gave her a resounding slap across the cheek.

She punched him back hard in the face, knocking him off his killer heels so he collapsed on the ground, blood streaming from his nose.

'Works for me,' she smiled.

She left Emil dabbing at his bloody nose with a couple of concerned partygoers gathered around him, and joined Dave. 'I'm really missing Greg,' she admitted. 'I think he's gone off me.'

'Surely not?' said Dave, looking concerned.

'I'm afraid so.'

'Well, I fail to understand his appeal to you, Joy.'

'I met him at party like this. It was the wake for *Gulp!* when it was merged into *Laarf!* He stood there silently, scowling at everyone.' She smiled as she remembered. 'He looked so cool.'

Dave tried a scowl himself.

Joy observed it. 'I said a scowl, not a stroke.'

Dave nodded and looked away, biting his lip, and shaking his head sorrowfully.

'What the fuck's the matter with you?' asked Joy.

'It was the mention of *Gulp!* being merged into *Laarf*, Joy. It brought back … memories.'

'Memories?'

'Yes. Terrible memories. It … It reminded me of when the *Fourpenny One* was merged into *The Spanker.*'

'So?' shrugged Joy unsympathetically. 'What's so special about the *Fourpenny One*?'

He slumped down onto the floor, visibly upset and Joy joined him. 'Come on. What's this all about?'

'I'm a troubled man, Joy. I need to offload something terrible that happened to me. You see, I have issues from my childhood which I've never talked to anyone about before, which I know someone as sensitive as yourself could help me with.' He looked sadly ahead of him. 'It probably explains why I'm such a failure as a man and a writer.'

Joy's eyes narrowed. 'Is this something to do with fur again?'

'Not on this occasion. It was *The Fourpenny One*. The comic every boy had to buy, or you were a pariah in the playground. But to obtain it, I had to face certain demons on a weekly basis.' He paused. 'This is actually very painful for me.'

'Go on, Dave,' said Joy, looking concerned.

And he slowly, haltingly, proceeded to relate what Mr Cooper did to him every Saturday.

How one week he saw his beloved comic attached to a bulldog clip on one of those strings of magazines high above him. He'd reached up to take it and it was just within his grasp …

Then a hook appeared and removed it.

It was held by a smiling Mr Cooper, his wife standing beside him. Dave looked desperately to Mrs Cooper for help.

'I'd like to help, Davey,' said Mrs Cooper apologetically. 'Really I would. But I don't want to walk into a door again. You'll understand when you're older.'

'Get back there,' Mr Cooper said to his wife, 'Or you'll have eyes like a panda.' She bustled into the back.

'Don't get yourself involved with women, Dave,' the newsagent advised. 'They're nothing but misery. Stick to your comics and when you're older, you can move to the spinner rack.' He nodded in the direction of the sweat mags. 'That's all you need. You don't have to backhand a magazine.'

He took *The Fourpenny One* off the bulldog clip. 'Now tell me what you want.'

Dave hesitated.

'Come on. You don't want to collect two next week.'

'Stan,' called the newsagent's wife from the back. 'Leave the boy alone.'

'It's a game we play. Right, Dave?'

'Stan!'

'I won't tell you again,' he warned her.

Mr Cooper prepared his fist. 'I'm waiting.'

'Please, sir, can I have a *Fourpenny One?*'

Once again the newsagent's fist slammed into Dave's face.

By the end of his graphic account, Dave's head was slumped forward on Joy's lap and she was stroking his head. She was truly shocked by his revelations. 'So he punched you in the face *every* week …?'

'Oh, Joy, I used to pray for a printer's strike, but it never happened.'

'It explains so much,' said Joy thoughtfully.

Dave's head nuzzled closer to her breasts.

A thought struck her. 'But couldn't you have gone to another newsagent?'

'Unfortunately,' sighed Dave, 'his brother owned the next shop.'

129

'Or complained to someone?'

'If I complained to a teacher or a policeman, they'd give me a fourpenny one for wasting their time. They'd tell my dad and he'd give me another fourpenny one for telling tales. In fact, Joy, you're the first person I've told who hasn't given me a fourpenny one.'

'No one complained?'

'Never. Particularly if the adults were in a position of authority. Mr Cooper wore a brown jacket, so he was in authority.'

'That's terrible.'

'The golden rule for kids was, you never told.'

Dave and Joy held each other even tighter, stroking each other's backs. 'Yes, Joy, happiness is a foreign country to me. I have reached the shores of Despair and settled there. I'm just six feet of emotional scar tissue.'

'Don't say that,' said Joy looking at him with such compassion. 'Don't say that.' Their lips met and they exchanged a long, slow, lingering kiss.

'Was that all right?' he asked her nervously.

'A bit liquoricey, but, aye, okay.'

Dave's hand moved round to her front and she didn't resist. 'Poor Dave. You've been through so much.'

His hand moved upwards, as they lay together on the ground, keeping up with the rest of the party-goers, who had mostly paired off by now. 'If only you'd had a father like mine to protect you. Brave, dashing, rugged.'

'Lawrence of Fitzrovia'.

'He's reported from every war zone in the world. No man can ever measure up to him. He was clubbed to a pulp by the Chicago police. Tortured by the KGB.'

'So similar to my own story, Joy. Brutality. Darkness. Privation. Physically we're very alike. Except I've got more fingernails.'

'That reminds me,' said Joy. 'Fingernail inspection. Before you go down there,' she pointed to herself. 'Which hand?'

He obediently held up his right hand.

She checked it carefully. 'Clean. No sharp edges. Carry on.'

'Where was I?' said Dave, temporarily thrown.

'You were going to tell me more, Dave. Hold nothing back. It's the only way you'll heal.'

'Yes. Neither of us should hold back, Joy ...'

Neither of them had. In fact, things were considerably advanced now.

Then Joy gently stopped his hand and whispered, 'No. Not here. Let's go back to my flat.'

'Yes, let's.' They might have gone up to his turret, but that was still his closely-guarded secret.

They sat up and exchanged another long kiss as they prepared to leave.

Joy slipped on her fur jacket, which only added to Dave's lust. This was going to be a night to remember. 'Thank you for listening, Joy.'

'You're very welcome,' she murmured.

'You're a true friend,' he said continuing to caress her.

'Mmm.'

They were glued to each other.

'You're so understanding, Joy ... Oh, by the way: you haven't got the painters in, have you?'

Joy punched him in the face. It was a fourpenny one Mr Cooper would have envied.

'Fuck off. Or I'll deep-fry your bollocks.'

Emil watched sympathetically as Dave held his nose, looking for something to staunch the blood with.

'S&M?' he asked enquiringly.

CHAPTER TWENTY-ONE

It was bitterly cold in Dave's apartment in Fleetpit House. There was hot water in the bathroom, but no radiators in any of the rooms. But he had a solution to look forward to: the Christmas present he was going to buy himself. Meanwhile, he froze.

His sympathy shag plan, as suggested by Greg, had gone wrong, but he still yearned for Joy. It didn't make sense. He had never been obsessed about a woman before. He wondered if it was because she was Scottish. He always felt drawn to Scotland and had fond memories of working for Angus, Angus and Angus in Aberdeen. The Scots seemed to understand and care about comics, whereas they were largely indifferent to them at Fleetpit.

However, his first job at Angus, Angus and Angus had been writing the horoscope for the *Aberdeen Argus*. His prediction for the week ahead for Sagittarians read: 'Bleak. Bleak. And perhaps bleaker. Looking forward to a bleak Christmas.' Not for the first time, they told him he was not taking his job seriously.

So, at age 20, he was moved to the senior citizens' magazine group, which included *Kith and Kin*, *Health and Wealth*, and *Housebound*, although the latter had closed recently, as so many readers couldn't get down to the newsagents. At least that was Dave's theory.

He had worked on *Kith and Kin* for some weeks, reading Mills and Boon-style story submissions where granny was always right and if only her granddaughter had listened to her wise advice. He would regularly fall asleep at his desk.

So he was transferred to *Widow and Wallet*, where he suggested features on 'cooking for a coronary' and 'looking for Mr Die Right.' He wrote Nurse Carter's 'Last Writes' column. He advised his readership, 'Make sure his life is insured. He could drop off at any time.' 'Buy a decent size plot before your minds have gone completely.' And, when it was cold and snowing, to invite a relative to nail up their front doors, so they couldn't go out and hurt themselves.

Sinclair Angus, the editor, explained to Dave that what he referred to as his 'Goons sense of humour' was not appropriate; the magazine gave valuable and sensible advice to widows in their time of need. Dave was trying hard to be more appropriate, but then came that regrettable business with Mrs Angus's fur coat, resulting in his instant dismissal.

But despite his differences with them, Dave had an affection for the company and all things Scottish. He felt at home in Aberdeen and missed his friends up there.

So, during the Three Day Week, two years earlier, he had tried to get his old job back. The Cold War was at its height. Everyone thought Britain was on the edge of a revolution. Rubbish was piling up and rotting in the streets. Rats were everywhere. Leicester Square was a mountain of black bin bags.

He asked to meet his old employers in their Fleet Street office. He waited in the interview room, a dim light overhead, and a single piece of coal alight in the grate. Presently, he heard the squeak of new shoes heading down a corridor. It was joined by a second pair of squeaky shoes. And then a third. Dave recognised them immediately from their squeaks as Angus Campbell, Angus Ross and Angus Murray.

The three editors entered. Angus Campbell and Angus Ross were around thirty, but looked about seventy. Angus Murray was of indeterminate age. They all wore similar tweed sports jackets, Pringle jumpers, cavalry twill trousers and squeaky, highly-polished, brown brogue shoes.

'Soooo … are you looking for a wee bit of work, laddie?' enquired Angus Murray.

'Actually, I was hoping to get my old job back, sir,' said Dave deferentially.

'Well, two years having passed; Angus, Angus and Angus are prepared to forgive and forget,' Angus Murray looked sternly at Dave. 'the matter of Mrs Angus's fur coat.' Dave hung his head in shame. 'So we will consider bringing you back into the fold.'

'Thank you, sir.'

Angus Murray looked across at the tiny piece of coal burning in the grate. 'Aye. Perhaps it is time for you to come in from the cold.'

'I should like that very much, sir,' said Dave meekly.

'But there are some matters we need to clear up.' He nodded at Angus Ross, who had brought Dave's file with him.

'First,' said Angus Ross, 'there are the Scottish jokes you've been allowing in *The Caning Commando*, about tossing cabers.'

Dave looked suitably contrite.

'And what Scotsmen wear under kilts. We have them listed in your file.'

Dave looked even more contrite.

'I would remind you,' said Angus Campbell, 'that Angus, Angus and Angus have a monopoly on jokes about the Scots. Only our Scottish jokes are funny.'

A humble Dave nodded his head in agreement.

'We don't appreciate the English mocking how *careful* we are,' said Angus Ross severely.

'I am very sorry, sir,' said Dave. 'It won't happen again, sir.'

Angus Ross made a note of this in Dave's file with the tiny stub of a pencil. It was worn down so far that he had put it into a metal extender so it could still be used. It was a device Dave remembered was commonly used at Angus, Angus and Angus.

The other two Anguses silently and respectfully watched Angus Ross do this, and Dave wondered if they had their own pencil extenders or whether they all shared this one pencil extender between them.

Angus Murray continued the interrogation. 'Now. There is the question of your private life. Have you met a lassie ...? Are you married yet, laddie?'

'I'm afraid I've yet to meet the woman of my dreams, sir, although I live in hope,' said Dave, continuing to crawl.

'You don't want to leave it too long, laddie,' warned Angus Ross. 'You could be left on the shelf.'

The Anguses all looked enquiringly at each other. 'In view of the reason you left Aberdeen, your matrimonial status, or the absence of it, is a matter of some concern,' said Angus Murray. The other two Anguses nodded their agreement. They looked meaningfully at Dave.

A subservient Dave waited respectfully for them to elaborate.

There was a long, long silence.

Finally Dave broke it. 'So have I got my old job back, sir?'

'Well, we'd have to pass this back to Old Mr Angus,' said Angus Murray. 'He still remembers what happened rather vividly, but ... nooo, laddie, you have not.'

Dave stood up and scowled at them. 'Well, you can all fuck off then.'

CHAPTER TWENTY-TWO

Dave hated Christmas. He suspected the reason was because his mother had disappeared with a lover one Christmas, and his dad fell apart. So Canon Williams came to the rescue and arranged for Dave and his sister to be looked after by an ancient Virgin Soldier: Miss Chumleigh. She did her best, and at least they were safe and fed, but she had no idea how to amuse children.

All Dave could remember was being in her living room crammed with stuffed animals and birds under glass, some in carefully recreated nature scenes. He wanted to stroke their fur and feathers to comfort them for being dead, but the elderly spinster refused to release them from their glass prisons, so all he could do was stare at dead foxes, weasels and squirrels over Christmas and Boxing Day. 'Merry Christmas, Miss Chumleigh.'

'Perhaps,' Dave said to his mum, 'if I told Joy that sob story, she might give me a second chance?'

'It *is* a bit of a tear-jerker,' agreed his mother, from the chair opposite, opening a packet of Park Drive. 'But let her calm down first.'

'So where were you that Christmas, mum?' asked Dave as she lit a cigarette.

'It's a long story,' she said hastily. 'Another time.'

'How very convenient,' he snapped.

'There isn't time, son,' she said, inhaling deeply. 'You've got to get ready to see Annie.'

Dave was visiting his sister and her family in Richmond on Christmas Eve. His mother had insisted. After all, she said, Christmases are for families. And she thought that Dave might pick up further clues as to who had murdered her. Dave doubted it. He'd tried quizzing his sister about their past before, and Annie was brilliant at stonewalling, a gift she inherited from her mother. She gave nothing away.

His sister had a successful music shop, Pie Records, in Red Lion Street, and the family lived over it. Her musical taste was very British: Rod Stewart, The Who, the Stones, The Kinks, Cream. All reminding her of her sixties youth and those incredible concerts on nearby Eel Pie Island.

She didn't approve of Dave, and thought he could be a bad influence on her three young children: Mick, Keith and Dusty.

Her husband Elliot was a mobile DJ; he was into the blues, Velvet Underground and New York Dolls, but that was rarely what audiences wanted to hear when he played at company parties, wedding receptions and bar mitzvahs.

Dave liked prog rock. Annie disliked prog rock, so Dave, with his preferences for Pink Floyd, King Crimson, Genesis and Emerson Lake and Palmer, was always arguing with her.

She especially disliked Emerson Lake and Palmer, whom she regarded as pretentious and Dave agreed. It was the reason he liked them so much, so there was really nothing to fight about, but they did anyway. As if they hadn't got enough to fight about already.

Richmond was also as far away as possible as Annie could get from Mordle Street where they had grown up, in a fading, once splendid Georgian house, just twenty minutes from King Edward VIII dock. She wanted to forget her childhood and all the bad things that had happened. And it was the norm in her parents' families to sanitise the past so that everyone who passed became a paragon of virtue. The dead had never been unfaithful; gay; alcoholic. Never had children out of wedlock or relationships with priests. Were never 'a bit odd'. Or worse.

Despite Annie being a sixties chick, she still had that ability – and need – to block the truth. Her talent ran on the female side of the family; information was withheld from the males as a matter of course. But they didn't realise that no matter how they suppressed family secrets, the shadows were still left on the wall.

The Liquorice Detective was very interested in the shadows.

So, once again, Annie was ready with her standard defensive responses to Dave's interrogation: 'Could be', 'Mum could have done that,' 'Dad might have done,' 'Yes, it's possible,' 'Wouldn't surprise me at all,' 'I wondered about that, too,' 'You might be right,' 'Oh, I wouldn't know about that,' 'Can't remember', 'It was all such a long time ago, Dave,' and 'Does it really matter now?'

And when he pressed her hard, she warned him, 'I admire people who are stoic and stop going on and on about the bloody past.'

Anything, rather than give Dave the hard information he was looking for. Annie's husband agreed. His advice had become the family motto: 'Keep it shallow'.

As they sat down to eat that evening, Elliot addressed them. 'Just to remind everyone,' he said, looking pointedly in Dave's direction, 'there's a "No talking about the past at the table" rule. We can discuss Christmas. Politics. Mrs Thatcher. Films. Football. Schools. But not the past. Let's keep it festive. Let's keep it shallow. Okay?'

Everyone nodded.

'Play nice,' Elliot smiled. Then he remembered and added hastily, 'Oh, and if we could stay off music, too.'

'What about dreams?' asked Dave. 'Is it okay to talk about our dreams?'

'Yeah, it's okay to talk about dreams, Dave,' said Elliot expansively.

'Are you sure?' said Dave. 'I mean … I don't want to break the rules.'

'Absolutely sure, Dave. Yeah. You go ahead.'

'Okay. My earliest dream,' said Dave, 'was when I was about three years old. And this dream has always stayed with me. I was in a hospital. I assume it was a hospital because it had green and white walls. Some sort of institution, anyway. Although there was no medical equipment around.'

Annie stopped drinking her soup.

'There was me, mum and you, too, Annie, and we were hurrying along this corridor. Maybe in a basement because there were lots of overhead pipes. It was hot. And mum was upset, walking very fast, pulling us along.'

Annie stared sadly down at her soup.

'Anyway, it was just a dream, smiled Dave. 'Strange dream, though. It almost felt real. But it couldn't be. Because I've never been to hospital. You were crying in my dream, Annie. I wonder why?'

Annie pushed back her soup.

'Something wrong with the soup, sis?' asked Dave innocently.

There were tears forming in the corners of Annie's eyes. Elliot put a protective arm around her and whispered, 'It's okay, Annie. It's okay.'

'So – what's the latest on Mrs Thatcher?' asked Dave breezily.

'You are such a shit, Dave,' said Annie, fighting back her tears.

'What ...? What did I say ...? It was just a dream,' protested Dave. 'And I wasn't unhappy. I thought it was a great adventure.'

'Yes, you would,' said Annie.

Annie decided she'd better tell him. She'd throw Dave this bone, so he could go off growling with it in a corner. It was Christmas after all. And there were other family secrets it could distract him from.

'All right. I suppose you'd better know,' she sighed. 'Mum had this blazing row with dad and she stormed out, taking us with her. But she had no money and nowhere to go that night, so we all went to the Langthorne.'

'Is that a hotel?' asked Dave.

'Langthorne Hospital.'

'Why would we go to a hospital?'

'Under the National Assistance Act, they put up people who had nowhere else to go.' The tears were running down Annie's face now.

'What? In a hospital?' Dave looked baffled.

'All right! It wasn't just a hospital. They'd renamed it because they didn't want to put people off.' She dried her eyes, but there were more tears coming.

'It was the West Ham Union Workhouse.'

A smile lit up Dave's face. Just as she knew it would.

'I was in the workhouse?'

'We *all* were.'

For a moment, she allowed herself some moments of sad reflection on that terrible night. 'It's awful really. People were so scared of the workhouse they had to change the name to the Langthorne. Of course,' she added hastily, 'it would have been different in the fifties.'

But Dave didn't hear that bit. 'So my earliest childhood memory is of being in the workhouse. That is great news, Annie. You've made my Christmas.'

'I knew you'd like it,' she groaned.

Dave considered the possibilities. 'Did I pick oakum, Annie? Did they stop my broth when I was bad?'

'No, Dave, although I would have, if I was the beadle.'

'Hey, how about that? The West Ham Union Workhouse, eh?' Dave turned to Elliot and the kids. 'I'm right up there with Oliver Twist.'

Only Dave would see such an event as a source of pride.

'So what was the argument about?' asked Dave, hungry for more information. 'It must have been a pretty big bust-up?'

'I have no idea,' said his sister unconvincingly.

'How long was I in the workhouse?'

'We were there for just one night. Sorry to disappoint you.'

'What happened next? Where did we go? Back home or somewhere else?'

'I don't remember.'

'Okay.' Dave could hardly say, 'Our dead mother is listening and she's just told me you're lying.'

So he let it go.

The little one had been staring intently at Dave all through dinner. Finally she spoke. 'Uncle Dave?'

'Yes, Dusty?'

'Why does everyone say you're weird?'

* * *

The next morning, the plan was for Dave to be around long enough for the kids to open their presents, thank him, and then get rid of him as soon as possible. Elliot would drive him over to Marble Arch to spend Christmas day with Joy and Greg.

Joy had forgiven Dave. He'd explained that, because it was all so new, he didn't understand the etiquette of the sexual revolution and what it was appropriate to say. Joy had relented because she needed some company – she wasn't seeing either of her parents over Christmas – and wasn't sure how things were going to go with Greg.

The kids opened Dave's badly-wrapped presents: *Caning Commando* sweet cigarettes, a crumpled *Caning Commando* mortarboard with medal and poorly manufactured *Caning Commando* toy figures. There was Victor Grabham, Alf Mast and their greatest enemy: the Oberspankerfuhrer, a.k.a. the 'Blue Man', in his underpanzer. They were still in their boxes but the cellophane was ripped and they looked like they had been played with a few times.

Then the kids saw Dave had another interesting bag alongside his overnight bag. 'Is that more presents for us, uncle?'

'No. It's my Christmas present to myself, Mick.'

'What is it? What is it? Tell us, uncle, please.'

'Okay, but I'd better check with your mum first it's okay.'

He checked. It wasn't okay. This was exactly the kind of thing Annie was concerned about and why she discouraged Dave's visits.

The kids looked anyway. 'It's a fur suit! It's a fur suit!' they cried excitedly.

Dave explained he was going to wear it when he went to Joy's.

'We want to see you wear it. We want you to put it on now.'

'Well, that's really up to your mum, Keith,' said Dave diplomatically, trying to keep the peace.

'No!' Annie snapped. 'No!'

Memories of Dave's troubled, furry childhood passing through her mind. And her fear that his strange obsession might run in the family and be handed down to her children.

'Please! Please! Please!' they chorused.

Eventually Annie gave in, even though she knew she was going to regret it, and said Dave could put the suit on when he was ready to leave.

So he did.

The kids looked at him open-mouthed as he entered the living room in his fur suit. This was not what they were expecting at all. They'd never seen *this* animal before. They were lost for words. They backed fearfully away from it.

Annie stared at him, shocked. 'Oh, fuck,' she said.

Elliot came in from the kitchen to see what all the commotion was about and the cigarette dropped out of his mouth as he, too, took in the strange creature. 'Oh, fuck,' he said.

'You have surpassed yourself this time, Dave,' said Annie as Dave, still wearing the fur suit, climbed into Elliot's camper van. She did not mean it as a compliment.

Elliot drove Dave into London. Trying not to be distracted by the weird animal sitting next to him, he talked about how, whenever he got a chance, he flew out to New York and trawled Greenwich Village looking for rare records.

He had come back with The Velvet Underground, Patti Smith and the New York Dolls. The garage band, anti-establishment music sounded really exciting to Dave and suddenly his story for JNP66 really came together. He thought it through as they drove through the empty London streets.

It would be a gang story with a similar vibe: kids fighting back against a society that offered them no future. A story of feral youth set in a near future dystopia where kids were given medication that turned them into zombies, just like they turned dad into a zombie; rock music was illegal and the cops could enter kids' houses and confiscate their outlawed vinyl.

Only saccharine muzak would be permitted. Banned albums were melted down in mobile furnaces by the black-uniformed 'Insinerators', just as Dave had seen books burnt by the sinister Firemen in the film *Fahrenheit 451*.

But a small group of teenagers would band together for musical freedom. They'd have a cool look, a bit like the gang in *Clockwork Orange* or the Sex Pistols or these American 'punks'.

They'd be called *The Damned* and they'd fight back against their oppressors.

Just as Dave felt he should have fought back against Mr Cooper.

CHAPTER TWENTY-THREE

Elliot dropped Dave off outside Joy's. Greg had told him all about her amazing flat. It was an anorak's paradise and he was looking forward to checking it out. His costume would be very appropriate, he felt, and he figured he'd make quite an entrance.

He pressed the doorbell but there was no response. So he called up at her first floor window, which was a little ajar, 'Joy! Joy! It's me. Dave.' But there was still no answer.

Then he threw pebbles at the window and waited expectantly for it to open and Joy to appear at her Juliet balcony and lower the keys down on a string as agreed.

The pebbles came from a pretty garden of winter pansies in the basket of a trade bike parked permanently outside Joy's house. It was designed to look rather cool next to the blue Georgian front door and black iron railings. Dave, however, didn't think the trade bike was cool. Despite his fur suit, he shuddered at the sight of it.

He hated trade bikes even more than he hated Christmas.

* * *

Trade bikes reminded him too much of the past. When he'd ridden one as an errand boy. After his dad could no longer afford the fees and he was forced to leave school prematurely at the tender age of fifteen. It was the only job his dad could find for him.

Dave was always on the lookout for his ex-school chums, in their posh blazers, who would take a short cut through the dock on their way to cross the river to his old school. They would spot him in the distance and wave to him. He would keep his distance, pretend he hadn't seen them, and pedal away furiously, disappearing into the grain storms swirling around the dock as the ships were loaded up from the wharf-side mills.

But even if they had seen him, they might not realise he was an errand boy, he figured, because it wasn't a real trade bike. Not like his friend Ivan's, who worked for International Stores. It didn't have a front stand or a side panel with 'M&R Pell, Seed Merchants' inscribed on it.

No, it was just a bike with a big basket on the front.

Even so, he preferred rainy days, because then he could disguise himself in his yellow rain poncho with the hood up, so they'd never see it was their old school friend.

But this was not the full extent of his humiliation. It was his job as an errand boy to hand-deliver letters and seed samples to local businesses and organisations, for which a signature was required. Mr Pell, the treasurer of the Knights of St Pancras, also had important packages that required delivery to his fellow knights, such as his brother-in-law Mr Czarnecki, the solicitor and coroner, and Canon Williams.

It was hard, constantly meeting these people from his church congregation, who smiled pityingly at the college boy whose mother had deserted her family, supposedly running off with a lover.

He liked to open packages that looked interesting, especially those marked 'Private'. He used one of the alcoves below the derelict Old Custom House as his 'office'. He would peel open the large envelopes down the side, where the glue was not so strong. Disappointingly, there were never any great revelations within. After perusing the documents, he carefully placed them back in their envelopes and resealed them, using a little amber-glue dispenser he always carried with him, that would leave no trace of his intrusion.

Reading confidential letters made him feel he had power over all these important, successful people. And he always felt that one day he might find something important in the letters, something he could use to his advantage.

* * *

Standing around by the trade bike, waiting impatiently outside Joy's house, Dave was starting to get hungry. Joy had promised him turkey with all the trimmings. It would be a big improvement on his planned Vesta curry and Angel Delight. But still not getting any response from Joy, there was nothing for it.

Hanging his overnight bag around his neck, he carefully climbed on the trade bike. A foot on the chain guard and a grab at the crumbling brickwork to pull himself up. Then balancing with one foot on the crossbar and the other in the pansies. The bike creaked, but stayed firm. He then hauled himself up to Joy's balcony.

It took some skill, but certain simian talents were expected of him as he was wearing a gorilla suit. But this was a gorilla suit with a difference. Dave had turned it inside-out, so he could have the warmth and comfort of fur next to his skin. Consequently it was its pink, polyester backing that was on display. Dave had also reversed the latex face mask, adapting it so he could eat and drink out of it.

He climbed over the balcony and stared, King Kong-like, into Joy's bedroom. She was lying asleep wearing a long silk nightdress (part of her friend Sofia's haul from Biba) that Fay Wray would have admired. There was no sign of Greg. He knocked again, but Joy was too spaced out to respond. He tried to open the window further, but it was stuck.

He knocked insistently on the glass, 'Joy! Joy! Wake up. It's me. Dave.'

Joy stirred in her slumbers, opened her eyes for a moment, and regarded the ape with alopecia staring into her bedroom. 'Of course it's you, Dave,' she said. 'Who else would it be?'

Then she turned over and went back to sleep.

'Joy! Joy! Let me in, Joy,' he demanded, knocking again on the glass. But she was gone.

He still couldn't get the window open, so he reached a paw through and grasped one of the legs of her Victorian bed and dragged it towards him to get her attention. She slowly came to her senses as her bed reached the balcony. 'Dave, will you please let me get some sleep?'

Realising he wouldn't, she got up, stumbled to the window and they opened it together. King Kong climbed in.

'Where's Greg?' he asked.

'Who cares? Fetch me a glass of water. Turn the turkey. Put the sprouts on in half an hour. Make sure you wash them first. And put little crosses in their bums. Wake me in an hour.' Then she passed out again.

Earlier, she had smoked too much Thai Stick, her special Christmas treat to herself. She had also drunk rather a lot of champagne, and had promptly had a whitey: a booze and dope-induced funny turn. With the world spinning and nausea rising, she'd retreated to bed to recover.

Dave stumbled through her darkened bedroom, barged past some huge object in the doorway, and out into the hall.

A shivering Greg was in the living room, wrapped up in his Wehrmacht leather trench coat, his gloves on and a scarf around his face. He looked alarmed and backed away as Dave entered.

'What the hell …?'

'It's me. Dave.'

'God. I might have known.'

'I kept ringing the door bell,' the ape growled. 'Why didn't you answer?'

'You can't hear it at the back. What are you doing in fancy dress?'

'Only the uninitiated call it fancy dress, Greg. It's my day suit for relaxing in.'

'You do know you've got it on inside out?'

'Of course. Sherlock Holmes liked to relax in his silk smoking jacket, I like to relax in my fur suit.'

'Well, thank God, you're here, man. You've got to help me.'

'What's wrong?'

'Everything. Joy's having a nervous breakdown.'

'Joy? Cracking up?'

'It's really bad.'

'I'm sorry to hear that. Perhaps I should leave,' said Dave, making for the front door.

'No! You've got to stay,' said Greg, grasping hold of the rubbery primate. 'And Boxing Day, too. I'm going to say I have to go home tomorrow to spend it with my mum.'

'Perhaps I should go home and spend it with my mum, too.'

'You can't. Your mum's dead.'

'What's that got to do with it?'

''Cos I need you here, Dave, so she has a shoulder to cry on. I daren't leave her on her own.'

'What about her parents?'

'Dad's in Australia with his new wife. She's going up to Glasgow for Hogmanay to see her mum. She's desperately unhappy, Dave. She's been crying and swearing. Well, mainly swearing.'

'Why? What's the matter with her?' asked Dave.

'I guess she just can't handle our relationship being over. I had no idea I meant so much to her. But I just have this effect on women, it seems.'

'You dumped her?' enquired the ape. 'That was brave of you. And rather ungallant at Christmas. Congratulations, Greg. I see you're competing with me in the Complete Shit stakes.'

'Well, no. No,' said Greg nervously, pacing about trying in vain to get warm.' I didn't actually tell her it was over.'

'You *didn't* tell her it was over?'

'No,' said Greg furtively. 'Not exactly. Well, not in so many words. But I did drop a strong hint.'

'What sort of strong hint?' the ape asked suspiciously.

Dave took off his mask and felt just how cold the air was around them.'It's bitter in here.' He looked over at the empty fireplace. 'No heating.'

'Tell me about it,' said Greg, his teeth chattering.

'Her girls don't like it, you see.' explained Dave.

Greg still hadn't answered his question.

'Well, come on, Greg! What sort of strong hint?'

Reluctantly Greg told him. 'No sex. I didn't deliver.'

Dave looked aghast. 'You do know what happened to the last person who didn't deliver?

'Yes,' said Greg wincing.

'The drug dealer who took her money but didn't come up with the goods.'

'I know. I know,' said Greg miserably. 'She got some heavy friends to dangle him over the side of King George V bridge.'

'By one leg,' added Dave.

'Normally,' grimaced Greg, 'when I stay over, we do it three times a night. So I rather suspect she knows, Dave.'

'I rather suspect she does,' agreed Dave. 'This is not good, Greg.'

'It's not good,' confirmed a desperate Greg.

'However,' pondered Dave, 'she may conclude you're queer. As I do. Joy is 'ideologically sound' so she'd never attack someone for being queer. Don't you see?'

'What?'

'It's your perfect exit strategy. Time to come out of the closet, Greg.'

Greg rolled his eyes. 'Dave, I am not gay.'

'It's the seventies, Greg. It's okay. After all, Joy has a boyish figure and short hair, which doubtless turns you on. From behind, I imagine there's not that much difference between her and Bernie. No womanly hips to put you off, right?'

Greg ignored the taunt. 'I just want to get shot of her.'

Dave thought about it and make a quick decision. 'In that case I really think I should go. I'd only be in the way. Of flying cutlery.'

He turned to depart but Greg held onto him.

'No, I want you to be in the way, Dave,' he insisted, his frosty breath visible in the air. 'In case something terrible happens.'

'To you? Or, more importantly, to me?'

'To her.' Greg lowered his voice as he fearfully explained. 'Dave, I definitely heard her say, "I'm going to slit my wrists."'

'You sure?'

'Yes.'

'That's bad. We should stay out of this, Greg. Best leave it to Cross Line, eh?'

'I rang them, but they're permanently engaged.'

'Of course. Christmas. The time for the misery of families.'

'We have to be there for her, Dave. And we have to humour her,' Greg insisted. 'Don't say anything that could push her over the edge. Okay?'

'Okay …' said Dave, taking in these strange developments.

Dave was surprised to learn Joy was in such a bad way.

She had seemed her usual self when he last saw her on the 23rd. She had just coped admirably with the perils of the Fleetpit lift, always a danger for young women and particularly at Christmas. An ornate Edwardian cage lift, it was common for predatory journalists to trap girls in it between floors.

In the sixties there had been a young, uniformed lift girl, but she had been subjected to so much sexual harassment, the company had to dismiss her and now everyone operated the lift themselves.

Joy had encountered 'Deep Throat' Barclay, art editor of *The Spanker*, who regularly rode up and down in the lift with a piece of mistletoe, asking female journalists for a Christmas kiss. Trapped inside the cage with him, they often reluctantly agreed to a quick peck, only to find his tongue halfway down their throats as his hands wandered all over them and he insisted, 'It's Christmas. It's just a bit of fun.'

When 'Deep Throat' foolishly tried this ploy on Joy, she retaliated with a headbutt and a sharp knee to the groin.

Dave witnessed the scissor gates opening and 'Deep Throat' curled up on the floor of the lift in agony, as a smiling Joy stepped over him and reassured him, 'It's Christmas. It's just a bit of fun.'

* * *

Later, Joy got up and, despite her depression, completed the Christmas repast. It lived up to Dave's expectations. He didn't let her gloomy manner put him off his food. She was wearing a Gothic Biba velvet maxi dress with balloon sleeves, which should have looked beautiful on her, but now seemed more appropriate for a funeral. She was oblivious to the cold. Dave, too, was toasty in his suit. Only Greg was suffering.

For Greg, even with his leather coat, it was colder than the Russian Front, but there was nowhere else for him to go. The Underground had shut down, so he couldn't warm himself down there. He was trapped. He was starting to feel as bleak as Joy. He had nervously brought up the subject of her lack of fire and Joy had scowled, 'You English wimp,' so he didn't dare pursue it further.

And his career was going nowhere. The writer's plans for self-advancement had worked in *Sunset Boulevard*, so why couldn't it work for him? He was ready for his casting couch. His character, *Panzerfaust*, fighting on the Russian Front, makes a pact with Satan, and sells his soul in order to succeed. Greg was fully prepared to sell his soul. Trouble was, no one was buying.

Dave wondered whether talking about the story Joy was writing for JNP66 might raise everyone's spirits. They had to do a story about a great white shark. *Jaws* was due in the cinemas tomorrow and everyone already knew it was going to be a mega hit. So Joy had asked to write her version, *White Death*, because she'd gone sea fishing with her father in Australia. She had witnessed a great white attack at Coffin Bay, so she was perfect for the job. But if they talked about Australia, the subject of her dad's new young wife was bound to come up, so maybe it was wise to leave it alone.

So Dave tried other conversational gambits. 'I was actually going to tell you about my childhood in the West Ham Union Workhouse.'

There was no response.

'Perhaps this is not the right time?'

Again, no response.

Finally Joy spoke. 'I just want to die,' said Joy, lost in her own dark, sad thoughts.

'We all get like that sometimes,' reassured Dave. 'Even me. I shall be 27 next year and they tell me that is the right time to go. I'm looking forward to my death. I shall be in good company: Janis Joplin, Jimi Hendrix, Jim Morrison, Brian Jones and ... Dave Maudling.

That didn't seem to help, so Dave tried again to make light conversation. 'You know, Joy, when you come back from Glasgow, you might want to bring back more firewood on the plane? Because firewood is actually cheaper in Scotland?'

'Aye,' agreed Joy, momentarily enthusiastic. 'Why pay exorbitant London prices, when I pick it up in Scotland for a fraction of the price?'

'And then you could have a fire, Joy.'

Later, Dave and Greg did the washing up while Joy lay on the sofa, drinking and smoking dope and staring blankly ahead of her, lost in her ever-deepening depression.

Now Dave had a chance to look around her flat, he began to see what the problem was between Joy and Greg and why their relationship had gone so badly wrong. She had every imaginable toy from *Thunderbirds*, *Joe 90*, *Doctor Who* to *Star Trek*. Many still in their boxes. The reason her bedroom was in darkness became clear now: it was so the sunlight didn't fade the packaging. The object he had barged into at the entrance to her bedroom was, in fact, Godzilla's enormous clawed foot, 'liberated' from a film set when Joy was in Japan. It was resting on a treasured square of carpet from the *USS Enterprise*.

'You've got to have a McGuffin: a shared interest,' Dave explained to Greg. 'But you were only interested in her because of her dad.'

'It's normal to network in this business.'

'But she's into toys and you're not.'

'Tell me about it. She's gone ahead and signed the lease for her Time Machine shop.'

'Whereas the only plastic you're interested in is American Express and Barclaycard.'

'I don't get it. I don't know why she wants to piss away her money on plastic retard figures,' said Greg bitterly.

'I had noticed it was like a giant plastic playpen in the bedroom.'

'It put me off.' Greg shook his head. 'I thought it was just us guys who were anoraks.'

'It's the seventies, man. Everything's changing.'

'I would have said to her it's me or Godzilla,' confided Greg, 'but I know who she'd have chosen.'

'You're being plastic-whipped, Greg. You could wake up with a *Space 1999* Eagle spaceship shoved up your arse.'

'To be honest, Dave,' and Greg lowered his voice to a whisper as he rinsed the plates, 'sex between us wasn't actually very good.'

Dave nodded sympathetically. 'She probably preferred pleasuring herself with a dalek.'

Greg paused from his washing up and stared out the window. 'I'm sure you're right. I think she even keeps condoms in their original packets.'

'Sounds like a used one would be a collector's item?' said Dave who was doing the drying.

'Oh, no. I always disposed of them,' said Greg fearfully. 'In case they ended up in her fridge.' He finished the washing up.

'You didn't want to risk the patter of tiny Gregs?'

'Definitely not.' Greg shuddered at the thought. 'Because we have nothing in common, Dave.'

'You see, Greg? You see? No McGuffin, no nothin',' said Dave as he finished, too.

They put the crockery away.

'But you, Dave, you'd be fine.' Greg looked at Dave's bizarre inside-out suit. 'Because you seem to live in a giant playpen as well.'

'Thank you, Greg. Yes. This is true. Godzilla in the bedroom is really not a problem for me,' said the man in the ape suit.

Even Dave could feel the cold now. So, as they rejoined Joy, he put his inside-out gorilla mask on again.

Joy was now sitting slumped in the wheelchair from *Whatever*

Happened to Baby Jane? It was not a good sign. Dave and Greg sat down on the sofa next to the mannequin Stella Jeanne, whom Joy had brought back from the office to deal with her skin problem. The cracking hands had forced her to dress around them, so she was holding gloves rather than wearing them. Her best friend, Stella Louise, watched from an adjoining armchair.

And then Joy hit them with the reason for her depression.

CHAPTER TWENTY-FOUR

'What's wrong with the smell of my fanny?' Joy asked, swigging another glass of wine.

'Er … nothing,' said Greg nervously. 'As far I'm aware.'

'What do you mean as far as you're aware? You should be aware,' she snapped at him. Dave spluttered inside his mask. Joy glared over at him. 'Sorry. Fur ball,' he explained. She rolled another joint and leaned drunkenly forward in her wheelchair.

'There is nothing wrong with the smell of my fanny,' she insisted.

Oh, God, thought Dave, she *is* losing it. He was terrified of mental illness after his dad. Should they call a doctor? Could they get an ambulance out on Christmas day? What was the best thing to do? Probably get her completely paralytic so she passed out. Then the ambulance men could quietly remove her without any fuss.

'Would you agree, Dave?'

'Well, I'm not familiar with it, Joy. As yet. Although I live in hope. Can I get you another drink?'

'Take it from me. I smell good.'

'I'm sure. And in my case, you may have noticed a not unpleasant whiff of Hai Karate.'

'We're not talking about body odour, we're talking about my vagina, Dave. My cunt.'

Both Dave and Greg recoiled slightly. 'Er … could we be a little more soft focus here, Joy?' asked Dave. 'I'm no longer a young man. I am in my late twenties, you know.'

'Is the whole world mad? Is that it? Am I going mad?' she asked. It certainly looked that way to Dave and Greg. 'Do I seem like a simp?' she persisted. 'That's what they want me to be. A simpering fool.' She shouted up at the ceiling. 'I will never, never, never be a simp!'

'There's really no danger of that, Joy,' reassured Dave knowingly. Greg nodded in worried agreement.

'Oh, God,' she said. 'It's a nightmare. It's a fuckin' nightmare,' and buried her head in her hands.

'It's okay, it's okay,' said the pink gorilla. 'You need to rest. Let's get back to your room.' He started to wheel the slumped figure out of the lounge, advising his friend. 'Greg, if you could just move Godzilla out of the way for me.'

'Sure, sure,' said Greg, totally out of his depth. He grasped hold of the giant reptilian foot.

'No, no!' she snapped. 'I can't rest. I can't sleep. How can I sleep? How? Tell me how? Come on! Come on!'

'Back to the dayroom,' Dave whispered to Greg, and pushed Joy back into the lounge.

'Vaginal deodorants,' she explained to them. 'Vaginal deodorants.'

'Ah,' said Dave. He was none the wiser.

'Aye,' she continued bitterly. 'Vaginal fuckin' deodorants. They have these ads for them, making lassies feel ashamed of the scent of their own bodies. And they're harmful, too. But these bastards don't care, they just want to make money. And they want me … *me!* … to be the editor of the new magazine they're appearing in.'

'Ah,' said Greg, starting to wise up. 'What magazine would that be?'

'*Everlasting Love.* Can you imagine me, boys, as editor of *Ever-fuckin'-lasting Love*?'

'Er … not really,' said Greg.

'That is a tough one,' said Dave.

'They want it to be all lovey-dovey, girly, hippy, drippy shit, to appeal to simps. So no advice to teenage girls about STDs, masturbation, oral sex, anal sex, or vibrators, but ads for vaginal deodorants are okay, oh, yes.'

'I see what you mean. Just kissing lessons. Like snogging an orange?' suggested Greg.

'You could use a few lessons yourself,' she retorted.

She hauled herself out of her wheelchair and staggered over to a cupboard and took out several cans of deodorant. 'Look. They even send free samples.'

'For you to review?' said Greg.

'Ah. Like records?' said Dave.

'For me to to try out on myself,' she growled. 'Fat chance.

'They're aimed at teenagers,' Joy read the blurb on a can with an arrow shaped end. ' "*Cupid's Arrow,* the gyno-cosmetic. Fresh strawberry flavour".' She scowled. 'Well, of course I want my vagina to smell of strawberries.' She read the accompanying blurb. ' "Your boyfriend will thank you." '

'Sounds like they're the douche bag,' said Greg, sitting down on the sofa, relieved that Joy wasn't going to kill herself after all, and determined to stay on her good side before he made his exit the next day.

Dave nodded, his liquorice pipe projecting from between his simian lips. 'We understand, Joy. We're seventies men.'

'Yes. We realise just how offensive this is to women,' said Greg.

'It's not very "ideologically sound", is it, Joy?' said the gorilla.

She read another. '*Modesty.* "Don't take risks with your natural fragrance. Be safe. Be modest. Write to Sister Brown for more information about the problems of intimate odour." Problems,' she repeated. 'Guilt-tripping bastards.'

'Just as long as it's medicated,' commented Dave.

'Personally,' said Greg, 'I love the smell of pussy.'

'Hah!' said Joy. 'You could have fooled me. I cannae remember the last time you went down on me.' Greg winced.

She read the third, pink-flowered can. '*Coquette* for vaginal etiquette'.

'Reaches the parts other deodorants can't reach?' suggested Dave.

'I tell you, boys,' said Joy prophetically, 'this is just the start, they'll be wanting us to shave our pubes next.'

'Lose the fur?' said Dave horrified. 'Surely not?'

'No. That's never going to happen,' said Greg.

'It's a turn-off,' agreed Dave. 'Particularly for someone with my preferences.'

'It's coming,' she said darkly. 'You mark my words. We're all going to end up looking like plastic dolls. Like you,' nodding at Dave's pink, hairless body.

'Meanwhile,' she continued, 'I'm working on a magazine selling this shame.' She considered bitterly. 'It should be called "*Coy, for simps*".'

'You could refuse?' suggested Greg.

'I'd have to resign and I'm not ready to. Yet. And ...' she pointed to the cupboard. 'There is worse to come.'

She went back to it and produced some photocopies of comic artwork. 'You think *The Caning Commando* is bad, Greg? Read this shit. Read it and fuckin' weep.'

Dave and Greg looked curiously through the pages. They featured *Wedding Belle*, ' "a supermarket checkout girl who dreams of finding love." ' quoted Greg.

' "She yearns to go from supermarket aisle to wedding aisle." ' added Dave.

Romantic comics were drawn by Latin artists and, consequently, they depicted British teenagers as enchanting, exotic, passionate girls with film star looks. British boys were drawn as handsome, long-haired 'dreamboat' Latin lovers.

So Belle was portrayed as an impossibly glamorous, wide-eyed, busty version of Gina Lollobrigida with 'big hair' who 'talked' with her shoulders and gesticulated with her hands.

These exotic characters were combined with the artists' rather limited visual knowledge of Britain. So Belle's working class, Cockney father was depicted as a swarthy, Chianti-quaffing Spaniard. Big Ben and other London landmarks frequently featured in the background as the only British items the artists seemed to be aware of, apart from the set of flying ducks hanging on the wall.

Fluttering her long, Latin eyelashes, Belle told the readers her story in 'true confessions' style. She wrapped the net curtains on the window around her, imagining she was a bride gliding down the aisle. But she was torn between a safe, respectable boyfriend, and a saxophone player. Which boy should she choose, she wondered, gesticulating with her hands like Sophia Loren. The saxophonist 'Hot Lips' or Steve the steady bank clerk?

The Latin-looking 'Hot Lips' had a shirt open to the navel, a medallion, and a furry chest that might have caused Dave some gender confusion. Belle watched him playing sax in a night club, with Nelson's Column impossibly visible through a window.

The heroine's father looked like Eli Wallach in *The Good, the Bad and the Ugly*. He warned her about 'Hot Lips'. 'No good can come of it, my girl. No decent boy, who can put a roof over your head, will marry you after you've been out with a saxophone player.' He looked at her clothes. 'And you've changed since you met him. You look like one of those … West End girls.'

'Oh, dad,' said Belle. 'You're just not gear.'

Later, waving her hands, Belle tearfully admitted to her father that he was right: 'I should have known one kiss would not be enough for him. He …he got fresh with me, dad. And I …I felt so cheap … But one day I'll find love and it will be … kinda like a beautiful dream.'

'Until then, keep your legs crossed,' said Eli, rolling his eyes.

A second *Wedding Belle* story was in a similar style. Now she was going out with a guy who wanted to be a writer. 'My heart turned to confetti every time I looked at him,' she told her readers. To give him his big break, she bought him his first typewriter from a mail-order catalogue and he wrote an instant bestseller.

But Belle's dad was rightly skeptical. Puffing on a dark cheroot, he observed: 'He's written one bestseller already. Flash in the pan. Can he write two? Can he fill that shelf?'

'Oh, dad, you're so ungear,' pouted Belle with a Claudia Cardinale shrug of her shoulders.

But, once again, dad turned out to be so right to warn her. Belle looked sadly out the window at London Bridge and explained. 'He's a famous writer now, leaving me to pay for his typewriter by instalments. But one day I'll find love and it will be … kinda like a beautiful dream.'

Belle never seemed to have any luck. The family moved to the seaside and she met a handsome young millionaire on his yacht when she was out swimming. A romance ensued. He was going to take her away from the fish factory where she worked, and marry her. Big Ben could be seen just beyond the factory.

A dewy-eyed Belle revealed her heart-wrenching story to the readers. 'We had a gear time together until that terrible day, a week before we were going to be married … He was racing along in his speed boat to meet me as I finished my shift at the fish factory and didn't see the rock until it was too late.'

Belle would never forget him. Dad reassured her as he reached for the Chianti. 'One day you'll find love, Belle, and it will be … kinda like a beautiful dream.'

'That is so fucking bad,' agreed Greg sympathetically.

'The readers love this kind of slush, apparently,' said Joy. 'It's *Up the Junction* or *Coronation Street* reality they hate. They prefer to escape into fantasy.'

'Same as science fiction,' said Dave. 'It's pure escapism. "Beam me up, Scottie. There's no intelligent life down here."'

'No, Dave,' said Joy coldly. 'It's not the same at all. Science fiction is the genre of speculative fiction. It is the literature of ideas.'

'I stand corrected,' said Dave hastily.

'Sometimes I despair of our readers,' said Joy.

'Yes. Always the readers,' sighed Dave.

'I don't want to be associated with something this bad,' said Joy.

'It certainly needs a little updating,' agreed Dave. 'How about: "My trousseau, my terror. I caught the bouquet … he caught something else.'

He took his mask off again, now he had warmed up.

'Definitely a wrist-slitter,' confirmed Greg.

'It feels to me like the work of the Major,' pondered Dave. 'I can detect his speech pattern.'

'The Major?' asked Joy.

'His attitude to women,' said Dave. 'It could easily inspire Germaine Greer to write a sequel to *The Female Eunuch.* Any idea who wrote it?'

'No, but he was paid in cash, apparently.'

'The Major.'

'I'm glad we've got all that sorted out, Joy,' said Greg.

'Yes. *Wedding Belle* was the gorilla in the other corner to me,' agreed Dave.

'I'm pleased in a way, though,' continued Greg. 'Because I thought you were taking, you know, us … breaking up … rather … rather badly. I was very worried about you, Joy.'

'Oh, you thought it was about us, did you?' Joy laughed a dreadful laugh. 'Dinnae flatter yourself, Greg. If we're not having sex, you're no use to me. Oh, no … you can fuck off back to Colchester on the milk train.'

Greg winced, and even Dave winced in sympathy for him.

She was cheering up now that the truth was out. 'I don't want fuckin' stupid love stories. I like science fiction. I like horror.' Her eyes narrowed. 'I particularly like violence.'

'We know, we know,' chorused Dave and Greg.

'I like chain saws. I like big guns.' Her Glasgow accent gave her words a special resonance. 'Robots having their arms and legs and heads blown off, and all the cables in their guts being ripped out.'

'Yes,' said Dave. 'That's science fiction. The genre of speculative fiction. The literature of ideas.'

'And I can't have them. Because I'm a woman.' She looked contemptuously at the Belle artwork again. 'Girls with legs bent back like Sindy dolls. No kneecaps and little pointy feet. Why don't they do some Chinese foot-binding on us, while they're at it?'

It was time for bed, but as Greg headed towards Godzilla,

she called after him. 'Wait a minute. Just where do you think you're going?

'The bedroom.'

'Come back here.'

'What's wrong?'

'You don't think you're sleeping in *my* bed tonight?'

'But there's only one other bed.'

Well, you'll just have to share it with Dave, won't you?'

'It's your chance to prove you're not bent,' smiled Dave. 'I'll report back to you in the morning, Joy.'

She supervised them as they made up the sofa bed. 'Hospital corners, Dave. What did I tell you? What did I tell you?'

'I don't know. Never do my zip up quickly? Never look a gift horse up the arse?'

'No.' She smiled a kindly teacher smile. 'Hospital corners. Now. Both of you go to the bathroom first. And dinnae flush it twice. We don't want to waste water, do we? Soap in the blue dish. Not the soap in the white dish. And not the best towels.'

Dave kept his suit on to stay warm, while Greg was freezing even with his clothes on. He thought sleep would be difficult, but then Dave regaled him with 'Amazing Facts' from *The Spanker*, introduced by Toffee Nose.

' "Toffee Nose because you don't." The Vauxhall Velux has 38,000 moving parts. And Toffee Nose, and he wishes he didn't. He's slipping out for a drink and he may be gone for some time. Did you know the Great Pyramid is made from 50 million bricks? And Toffee Nose, and has counted every one of them. Twice. Don't ask me anything that requires an intelligent answer. I was educated by Toffee Nose. It's a miracle I can put my trousers on in the morning.'

CHAPTER TWENTY-FIVE

The next day, a frozen Greg escaped to Liverpool Street, looking forward to the warmth of the train journey home to Colchester.

Dave, now in his civvies, and Joy went to see *Jaws* at the *Odeon* in Edgware Road. It had a massive curved screen, 75 feet wide and 30 feet high, and the great white shark seemed to leap out of the screen at them as Joy chain-smoked and Dave chewed nervously on his pipe. Unusually, there was no support film and every seat was taken.

The film was so exciting, Dave forgot to hit on Joy. Even though her fur was as gorgeous as she was. He snuggled up to it once or twice until she glared at him to stop. She'd taken it off, so this was understandable.

His mother had taken a back seat in his head over Christmas, ever since he had rejected her shocking new suggestion for cracking her case now that he'd drawn a blank with Annie. 'No, we're not having this conversation, mum.'

'Hear me out, Dave.'

'Sorry. I'm not listening.'

'But you want to know who the murderer is.'

'No, *you* want me to know who the murderer is.'

'Well, I'm living inside your head, so what's the difference?'

'Mum, there are some things I will never, ever do, and what you are suggesting is number one on the list.'

'But it's the best way.'

'No.'

'We'll talk about it later, dear.'

'No, mother, we will not.'

As Dave and Joy came out of the cinema, he told Joy he had a surprise for her. He was going to take her somewhere special for a meal.

'Where? Where?' asked Joy excitedly. She'd noticed he hadn't brought her a present, or even a bottle, for Christmas and this would surely make up for it.

'I want it to be a surprise,' he replied. After *Jaws*, he felt it would be the perfect end to the day and a real treat for her.

They walked part of the way to their destination on the Seven Sisters Road so Joy could smoke a spliff. She talked about her plans for *White Death*, which sounded scarier than *Jaws*. It wasn't just the opening Australian beach scenes where a bikini-clad swimmer is graphically eaten alive. Or the subsequent episode, after the fall of Saigon in April 1975, when an American gunship, fleeing Vietnam, ditches in the ocean and White Death goes into a feeding frenzy, feasting on the drowning soldiers. The follow-up episodes she described to Dave were even more nightmarish.

He definitely made the right decision choosing her shark story over Greg's, he decided. Not that he had any choice.

'Give me the job, or I'll do a dirty protest in the men's toilets,' she had warned him.

'No one would notice,' he told her.

But he admired her determination, and Greg's version was crap, anyway. His new comic was taking shape. He had really wanted call it *Street*, but he knew the board would never understand why. So he'd settled for *Aaagh!* which was now the official title of JNP66.

They continued their journey to Dave's mystery restaurant by bus. On board, Dave told her about Greg's shark story and she howled with laughter at just how bad it was. It was important, Dave decided, to make Greg look really stupid, just in case his rival changed his mind and tried to get back with Joy.

From the way she was hanging onto his arm and laughing at his jokes, he had the distinct feeling he was going to get lucky tonight.

Greg's version was called *Moby Jaw*. It featured a giant killer sperm whale that attacked and ate people.

'Did you research this story, Greg?' Dave had asked him. 'Are there, in fact, any fresh water whales that swim up the Thames to spawn? And can they crawl onto the bank of the Thames, singing their mighty songs? Like this scene where Moby Jaw attacks people in Piccadilly Circus?'

'It just crawls for short distances on its flippers,' said Greg defensively.

'Before reviving itself in a local swimming pool.'

'It's a stirring saga of the sea.'

'The river, actually. And Inspector Ahab of the Yard is determined to track him down and kill him. How difficult is it to catch a whale in the Thames? I'd have thought it was No Hiding Place.'

Joy was doubled up laughing. 'Oh, no more, Dave, please,' she giggled as the bus pulled over at their stop on the Seven Sisters Road, 'or I'll wet myself.'

'Yes!' thought Dave. 'Making Greg look a complete cock has earned me extra brownie points. I am *definitely* going to get lucky tonight.'

They walked the final short distance to the restaurant.

'So what do you think, Joy?' he smiled at her. 'Are you ready for your Christmas treat?'

'Aye, you bet,' she said happily.

And he indicated his special surprise restaurant.

'Here we are. What do you think, Joy?'

'What ... what is this place?' said Joy, looking up at the unfamiliar golden arches and instinctively backing away from it.

'It's called McDonalds. It's only the second McDonalds in Britain. There are going to be many more of them, Joy. You're looking at the future.'

Joy went white and took a step back.

Dave was concerned. Perhaps she was coming down with something? He had better get her in the warm. He helped her through the welcoming doors of the restaurant.

Inside, Dave had a quarter-pounder with cheese for 48p. He just knew Joy would appreciate his Yuletide budget choice. Although she did seem rather quiet as she ate her McMariner fish burger for 30p.

'You know what they say? "It's a difference you can taste", Joy,' he smiled.

'Aye. Aye. That is so true,' she sighed, looking miserably around her.

She seemed rather withdrawn for some reason and he wondered if her depression was returning. He sipped his coke and held it up for her inspection. 'It's the real thing,' he said conversationally.

She lit an ordinary cigarette and didn't respond, so he started to sing the famous song: how he would like to buy the world a coke. But, for some reason, this was not to her liking and she stopped him with a glare. Perhaps he was out of tune?

Then she talked about some report her father had written on Coca-Cola, Guatemala and trade unions. She was very passionate about it and got quite angry at one stage, but it sounded pretty boring to him so he didn't pay it much heed. He was too busy imagining them making love.

He wondered why the famous commercial bothered her so much. He knew she'd been at Woodstock, maybe it reminded her of it? Made her feel nostalgic? She was clearly not in the mood for 'snow-white turtle doves' just now. Maybe it brought back other negative memories of the sixties for her? Yes, that must be it.

'The peace and love thing was difficult for you, wasn't it, Joy?' he suggested gently.

'What do you mean?' she growled menacingly, her Glaswegian accent coming out.

'When you were at Woodstock? Letting the sunshine in?'

'Screw the sunshine. I was totally out of my face.'

'Yes, that's what I meant. I couldn't imagine you with flowers in your hair, dancing naked in the rain. Although I'd very much like to,' he added as an afterthought.

'You haven't got a clue, have you, Dave?'

Still in soft drink mode, he sang his reply, ' "Help me find the way." '

'Fuckin' hell,' she said.

She shook her head sorrowfully. 'You have no idea who I am.'

She started to talk about her parents. They'd met in the Bohemian world of London's Fitzrovia. Her Australian journalist father became famous for his savage attacks on the establishment: McCarthy, Malaya, Palestine. Her mother, Coira, was a beautiful and successful Scottish actress who stayed true to her working-class roots.

Joy explained that she tried to uphold the values her parents had impressed upon her. Despite their wealth, they had insisted she had an ordinary state education. Although, of course, she explained, the Scottish education system was infinitely superior to the English, anyway.

They had told her about the evils of the multinationals. 'That's why …' she looked around the burger bar and tailed off.

'Ah!' Dave suddenly realised. 'That's why you like being here! So you can be true to your working-class roots? I knew it was the right choice.' He felt very pleased with himself. 'And they taught you about value for money, too.' he added knowingly. 'As you're always saying, "Many a mickle makes a muckle." Another Coke?'

She was lost for words.

Then she tried again. She explained she had a career plan in her head. Every magazine she worked on must lead her closer to her great goal.

'And I'm going to make it entirely on my own,' she insisted proudly.

'Apart from when you got a job on *Oz*, thanks to your Dad's Australian connections?' suggested Dave.

'Apart from *Oz*,' she said hastily. 'You see, Dave, everything I write and edit has to have a purpose.'

'So what was the purpose of those dope reviews you did for *International Times?*'

'Apart from those dope reviews. I need to understand

popular culture in all its forms in order to create the future Glass business empire.'

'Ah. So working on *Everlasting Love* will be useful?'

'Apart from *Everlasting Love*. That's just shit.'

'So is most popular culture.'

'And I intend to change that.' She leaned forward purposefully, 'I have a vision, Dave. Not just one Time Machine. But a chain of Time Machines.'

'You're going to be a Time Lord?' said an awed Dave.

'And I want to be a publisher, too. I can reach the masses in a way my dad never can. That'll show him,' she smiled to herself.

'We connect with kids at the most impressionable time of their lives,' she continued. 'Look at all the stupid things they do because some idiot has put them in a comic.'

'How do you mean?' asked Dave nervously.

'Playing hide and seek in an old fridge. Putting fireworks through a letterbox. Playing on the bings. Slag heaps,' she explained for the benefit of the Englishman. 'Trying to breathe air through a plughole.'

'So irresponsible,' agreed Dave.

'We have a huge influence on them. You know what they say? "Give me a child until he is seven and I will show you the man." '

'It was true in my case,' agreed Dave. 'Although *The Spanker* readers may need longer.'

'Don't you see, Dave?' she leaned forward and whispered excitedly. 'Comics are the ultimate in subversion.'

'You … you're the enemy within?' Dave gasped.

'Yes, Dave. I am the enemy within. And I'm not talking about that episode of *Star Trek*.'

'You want to change the world? To make a difference?' These were alien concepts to Dave.

'Is that so wrong?'

'It's unheard of in comics.'

'I know. I've heard Ron on the virtues of complacency.'

'Oh, yes,' nodded Dave. 'Ron believes in stasis. Although not passionately. That would require effort.'

'There's this huge market out there waiting, and it's all mine.' She hastily corrected herself, 'Ours, for the taking.'

'I'm in awe, Joy. Speaking as a man who has always cherished failure, who knows there is no light at the end of the tunnel, who sees no future for himself, except as editor of *Budgie Mirror*, I can only admire your dream from my rungless-ladder on the wrong side of the tracks.'

Her beautiful brown eyes filled with tears. Once again she was revealing that softer, gentler side that Greg insisted she had. She leaned forward and held his hands. 'What happened to you, Dave? What did they do to you?'

'Well …' He took a deep breath.

'No. No. I know. Let's not get into all that again.' She gently removed the liquorice pipe from his mouth. 'You poor, pathetic, strange, innocent man-child.'

'You sum me up so well.'

'Come on.' She stubbed a second cigarette out on her half-eaten fish burger and got up.

'Where … where are we going?'

'Home.' She whispered in his ear, 'I am going to fuck your brains out.'

'Joy, that's …'

'No. Don't speak. You'll spoil the moment. Again. Let's go.' She turned to leave. 'Hurry. Before I change my mind.'

Dave hurried. He noted that this sympathy shag idea of Greg's really worked. He must be pathetic more often. And they should also eat at McDonalds more often.

Back at Joy's, she was unaware of the cold, as usual. She stripped off and climbed into bed. No longer wearing his gorilla suit, Dave had a sense of what Greg had been through. An icy blast whistled through the apartment and he shivered, despite himself,

'It's the open plan,' Joy explained.'I knocked down that wall with a sledgehammer.'

Dave felt it was expected of him to begin with a romantic prologue, but she quickly interrupted him, 'Dave, there's no need. Just get your kit off.'

'But …'

'This is the seventies, Dave.' She held up her hand. 'D'you see any rings? D'you see any babies? Come on. Hop in and hop on.'

He did and moments later he was embracing her. 'Oh, Joy. This feels so right. You're like exquisite white china. So delicate. So smooth, so …'

Joy frowned. 'I rejected that script of yours last week. We're going to have comic sex, are we? Rejected comic sex.'

'What was wrong with it?'

'You make me sound like a toilet.'

He tried again. 'I long for your Holy Grail, Joy …' he began passionately.

'I hope you're wearing a shield,' she replied. 'Let me see.' She looked under the covers. 'Oh. You're a hobbit.' He paused, mortified. 'That's all right. Come on. Take me, Dave. Take me now, you word beast. I want every paragraph. No editing. Punctuate me! Punctuate me!'

Then, as he eagerly responded. 'I see … bog standard …' Once again, he paused, stung by her criticism. 'No. No. Carry on,' she insisted. 'It's okay.' She looked up at the ceiling. 'If that's what you want.'

She continued to make a running commentary on his efforts, trying, at the same time, to sound seductive and encouraging.

'Have you found it yet? Dave, I'm not upside down. Not there. *There.* Where do you think you're going now? You won't get anything *there.* No. Not like that. Like *that.*'

Then, a few moments later. 'So. That's it, is it?'

Dave staggered off to the bathroom. The Christmas fare was having a lethal effect on him. His stomach was used to Vesta curries and Banquet boil-in-the bags. Not Christmas turkey and cheeseburgers.

'Hurry back,' she called after him. 'I haven't finished with you yet.'

Following a second, more successful round of love-making, Joy had a post-coital spliff and Dave chewed his pipe. He reflected that if Joy had worn her fur coat it might have been even better. But, he was still feeling pretty good about himself. He smiled across at her. 'I've been in a *ménage à trois* with you and Godzilla.'

Joy finished her spliff and turned over to sleep without replying. 'Of the two, you're easily the scariest,' he complimented her.

He mused further. 'Actually, if you include the gorilla suit, we had a fursome.'

But Joy was sound asleep.

Later, Dave slept fitfully, his digestion still not back to normal. In his dream he was inside *Billy's Belly*. There was an emergency in the processing hall. Steam was escaping from pipes and boilers. There was a distant ominous rumble. A workman warned, 'Number three sump is down.'

The Foreman checked the meters. 'It looks like the whole system is going to blow.' He tried to have an urgent conversation with the brain department, but couldn't get through. 'Brains are not responding!'

The workmen turned controls and threw a series of levers in rapid succession. 'We'll be earning overtime tonight.'

The Foreman checked the meters again. 'Methane gas escaping! Masks on, lads!' He desperately turned a wheel as they donned old-fashioned gas masks. 'Better out than in, for all our sakes.'

The rumbling increased. 'Expect the worst!' The pipes and valves began to shake violently. 'It's going to blow! Take cover!'

The masked foreman looked up horrified, 'It's a Grade 4 Krakatoa!'

There was a massive explosion as Dave's dream and reality became one.

The sound woke Joy up. It was, indeed, a Grade 4 Krakatoa. As she came to, she wrinkled her nose in disgust. That smell. It was ... *unbelievable.*

She looked up to see Dave spraying the room with her cans of *Cupid's Arrow, Modesty* and *Coquette.*

'Just dealing with my natural fragrance,' he explained.

CHAPTER TWENTY-SIX

Dave intended to celebrate New Year's Eve in The Hoop and Grapes. He had gone over there at seven o'clock, preparing for a long evening's drinking. The trouble was, his mother was endlessly playing "Death Letter Blues" by Lead Belly in his head.

By eight o'clock it was driving him crazy. He had no idea why she was playing it. It must mean something, but he didn't care. He was fed up with her trying to control his life from beyond the grave. Even though, thanks to her efforts, he had achieved the impossible and scored with Joy.

He figured it was really down to his own charm offensive on Joy, including treating her to a McDonalds, and owed little to his mother. It was his own pathetic personality that really clinched it. Albeit, just a one night stand. Joy had made that very clear. There was to be no encore, alas.

By nine o'clock, as his mother continued to play "Death Letter Blues", he finally realised why. He should go through the readers' letters. He hadn't looked at them in a long time.

The thought entered his mind: one of the readers was dead. Because of him. That must be it. That was what she was trying to tell him.

It was an exciting thought. One of his lethal suggestions in *The Caning Commando* had paid off. It was what he had always wanted and prepared for, after all. So it had finally happened.

He was finally a serial killer. He hurried back across the road to check.

As he unlocked the door to the side alley alongside Fleetpit House, he was quietly observed by the Phantom of the Fleetpit. The scarred storeman had just parked his van nearby and was taking advantage of the holiday to steal the entire bound volume collection of the *Boy's Story Paper*. He'd already had a good offer for them from an antiquarian bookshop in Charing Cross Road.

He watched as Dave climbed up up the fire escape to his apartment in the roof. He must have had duplicate keys cut. The cheeky bugger. And he was living up there in the belfry, like Quasimodo in Notre Dame cathedral. For free.

Now he could plan his next move. He rubbed the twisted side of his face. It brought back memories from long ago. It was payback time. There would be no sanctuary for this Quasimodo.

Meanwhile, Dave had taken the readers' letters from *The Spanker* office up to his eyrie and went swiftly through them, looking for any reports of the death of 'Little Johnny'. Some parent sending in a furious accusation. Some tragic tale. Some awful newspaper account of a dreadful accident.

He was all geared up to blame the death on the Major. His face would be set in stone, this time. He would give an Oscar-winning performance of shocked innocence.

Jean Maudling watched patiently as he went through the pile. She checked her lipstick in her compact mirror, pouted her lips, and made a minor adjustment. Her blonde hair shimmered in the dim light, and her face was partly in shadow, as befitted a *femme fatale*.

He was almost at the end of the letter pile. There was nothing. No death of Little Johnny. False alarm. He felt strangely relieved. That couldn't be right, he thought. Could it? What was going on?

'You didn't really want kids to die, did you, Dave?' His mother interrupted his thoughts. 'Not really?'

'What's with the Mary Poppins act? he growled. 'Of course I do.'

'Are you sure?'

'What are you? My conscience?'

'You tell me.'

He thought about it for a moment. 'No, I still want to kill them. I can't help myself. It's something I have to do.'

'Because of that bloody newsagent,' she frowned.

'D'you think it's Stockholm Syndrome?'

'I'm not sure what syndrome describes you, Dave.'

'Basil Fawlty hates his guests the way I hate my readers. Maybe it's Torquay Syndrome.'

Dave was opening his last few letters when a newspaper clipping fell out. It was from the *Belstead Herald* and the headline was: 'RHUBARB CLUB LAMENTS TRAGIC DEATH OF FATHER NORTH'.

'A group of altar boys, who called themselves the Rhubarb Club, were heartbroken by their chemistry experiment that went tragically wrong,' the article began.

Intrigued, Dave read on. The boys had been doing some work for Father North as part of their bob-a-job week, apparently, although they weren't actually real boy scouts. Their plan had been to blow up an old tree root in the grounds of the priest's cottage using a pipe bomb they had made themselves.

The boys told the reporter they were very interested in chemistry and gardening, and wanted to put their talents to good use. They had left the device in Father's car for safe-keeping while they prepared the tree.

The priest had driven off, unaware there was a bomb on board, It detonated prematurely, and he was killed outright.

The article went on to say that Father North had been very kind to the boys and had taken them on camping holidays and they often spent time at his cottage playing games. The boys deeply regretted what had happened and said they would really miss him.

It concluded with a tribute from Father North's bishop, who said he was a 'very holy, kind-hearted and humane priest, renowned for his intellect and moral rectitude and with a deep devotion to Our Lady.'

Attached to the article was a note from an anonymous *Spanker* reader written in a childish and mis-spelt scrawl.

'North only wanted to pay us a Bob a job?! With 24% inflashun? The tight barstard He sed he couldn't afford more and he was going to use younger alter boys in future. Thanks for showing us how to make a pipe bomb Caning Commando. We could never have done it without you! Rhubarb! Rhubarb! Rhubarb!'

Dave was shocked. 'Father North sounded like a good man. Why would anyone want to kill him over a dispute about gardening?'

Jean looking thoughtfully at Dave but said nothing. He passed the clipping and letter over to her.

'It certainly looks like the boys followed your instructions,' she said after studying them.

'To the letter,' agreed Dave. 'Then the priest drove off and it was "Good-night, John-Boy." '

'But if the boys had complained to an adult about him,' she mused, '*they* would have been punished, never the priest.'

'Complained about what, mum?" Dave was puzzled. 'A bob a job?'

'He got what he deserved,' she said, ignoring Dave's question. 'I don't like this new way of seeing kids as helpless victims. They're often nasty, mercenary and vengeful.'

'Like me, you mean?' grinned Dave.

'Yes. Although you were sneaky as well. Kids don't always have a moral compass. It's why they're so scary. I wonder what the bobbies made of it?'

'Tragic accident, I expect.'

'That nonsense about leaving a bomb in the car for *safekeeping*.' She laughed. 'The ones I knew would never buy that for a minute. The Soho bobbies were hard bastards.'

'Yeah?' Dave asked curiously. His mother rarely talked about her nightclub days.

'They had to be. It was wartime. All those gangs and a murderer out there in the blackout.'

'A murderer?'

'Yes. We all had to toughen up. I carried a knuckle duster when I walked home alone from the club.'

'I remember,' confirmed Dave, 'when I had a look through your chest of drawers.'

'You were very sneaky,' she grimaced. 'I bet the bobbies were keen to bring a little "physical pressure" on those boys.'

'Like when you took me to the police station and asked them to punish me when I was bad.'

'You deserved it,' said his mother unsympathetically. 'And it was normal in the fifties.'

'Locking me in a cell for the afternoon?' Dave said bitterly.

'Only for a couple of hours.'

'While you went off to do your shopping?'

'Anyway,' continued Jean, ignoring Dave's accusing eyes, 'maybe they had to accept the boys' explanation because if they investigated, they'd have turned over too many stones.'

'What are you talking about?' Dave was baffled.

'The bobbies may have known about Father North's preferences.'

'Gardening preferences, you mean? Lawns, flower beds or a vegetable plot?'

'And maybe had some secret sympathy with the clever little bastards. I guess we'll never know now.'

'I guess not,' agreed Dave. It was his first confirmed kill. He didn't feel guilty. Surprisingly, now he had a chance to think about it, the death of the priest made him feel rather good. He revealed this to his mother. 'I wonder why?'

'Because you've helped kids fight back against injustice, that's why.'

Dave eyes widened. He would never have seen himself in such a heroic role. He was flattered. 'I guess only a mother would see it that way,' he grinned.

Jean went to the turret tower window and looked out, a sad expression on her face. 'Back in Ireland,' she said, 'we were told they could never do any wrong. We thought of them like Druids, you know? They could curse you or heal you. A local priest, Father Foy, did both. We left offerings to him on his grave. Everyone believed he really could walk on water.'

'But not Father North, eh?' chuckled Dave.

They heard the distant chimes of Big Ben and a muted, rather half-hearted chorus of cheers from tourists. In the seventies, most Londoners celebrated the New Year at home. She turned and smiled at Dave. 'Happy New Year, son.'

'Happy New Year, mum.'

It was good to be celebrating New Year, just mother and son. It left him with an unfamiliar feeling of optimism for the year ahead. Growing up, his mother's bitter sister, Aunt Maeve, would join them for New Year's Eve and complain, even before it was one o'clock, 'I'm sick of this year already.' It was often said that Dave took after her.

'Now,' said his mother, purposefully, 'can we get back to who killed me? And how you're going to avenge me?'

'Avenge you? Now wait a minute, mum … I'm no hero!'

As the bells finished tolling, the Phantom of the Fleetpit loaded the last of a hundred years' worth of the *Boy's Story Paper* into his van and smiled up at the dimly-lit window at the top of Fleetpit House. 'I'll be seeing you soon, Quasi.'

PART THREE:

JANUARY TO FEBRUARY 1976

'I enjoy writing the invoice.
The invoice is the most creative part.'

CHAPTER TWENTY-SEVEN

Stoke Basing Star August 30th 2016.

MURDER IN MORDLE STREET

Police have now revealed the location of the murder house as 10 Mordle Street, where the body of Mrs Jean Maudling was recently discovered. Mrs Maudling was reported missing in 1957, aged 32. The house is just a short distance from 2, Mordle Street, where the Maudling family were living when she disappeared. Number 10 was a derelict, bombed-out house at the time, and police say anyone could have gained entry.

Police are appealing to neighbours or friends who knew the Maudling family to come forward and help them with their enquiries.

They have also released details of a knuckleduster found in Mrs Maudling's shopping basket. The weapon had blood on it and it is thought that Mrs Maudling could have used it to defend herself against the murderer before they strangled her with her fur boa. However, there is no match for the murderer's blood on the national DNA database.

In other developments, the police are considering evidence that Mrs Maudling's husband, Peter, used the house at number 10 to produce 'moonshine' alcohol, still remembered by local people, and whether this could be connected with her murder.

Peter Maudling turned the upper floor of the murder house into a lock-up containing home brewing equipment. He died there in 1970 after sampling his latest 40% bockbier that he called 'From Here to Eternity'.

Claims that he could have been responsible for his wife's death have been angrily denied by his daughter, pensioner Annie Ryan, 71. 'Mum and dad argued all the time, but he really thought the world of her. Mum had a sometimes eccentric and unconventional disposition and he was very patient with her. He would never have harmed her.'

Police have been unable to contact David Maudling, 67, Mrs Maudling's son.

CHAPTER TWENTY-EIGHT

'So you see, doctor,' said Dave, 'my hallucinations are beneficial and are having a positive effect on me. I'm more ambitious now.'

'That's good,' smiled the doctor, 'I know you suffered from low self-esteem.'

'You're right,' said Dave. 'I never wanted to be an Alpha Man or a Beta Man. I wanted to be the Omega Man.'

'You wanted to be Charlton Heston?' The doctor looked startled.

'No. But maybe one of the mutants he was up against.'

'Ah,' said the doctor.

'Plus, I'm more assertive. You remember I told you about Mr Cooper?'

'The newsagent with the great smell of brute? Yes,' sighed the doctor.

'If I came across Cooper now, I would knock hell out of him,' said Dave heroically. He stood up and paced around the room. 'I would punch that cruel bastard right in the face.' He leaned over the desk and smiled confidently at the GP. 'And it's all down to mum. I'm not afraid anymore.'

The doctor looked suspiciously at him. 'She's not telling you to harm yourself or other people, is she?'

'No, no.'

'You're quite sure?'

'No. Nothing like that.'

'Well, I suppose as long as she's not asking you to go out and kill anyone, it's all right.'

Dave thought about telling him, 'Only her murderer.' But decided against it.

Because of his father's breakdowns, he was always concerned that he, too, might crack up one day. If the men in white coats ever came for him, he needed to be ready for them, so he had researched the possible cause of his hallucinations and wanted to discuss this.

'Now I've been wondering about the liquorice, doctor.'

'As I've explained, Dave, the industrial quantities you're eating are harmful.'

'But is it possible that the hypertension caused by too much liquorice might be responsible for my hallucinations?'

'Anything is possible with you, Dave.'

'I've also read that liquorice enhances memory and can be used to help amnesia. Maybe that's why memories of my childhood are finally coming back?'

'I'm very pleased to hear it, Dave. Now … I do have other patients to see.'

A buoyant Dave left the surgery, greatly reassured by the doctor's responses.

Of course it wasn't entirely true that his mother's hallucinations were not a threat to his wellbeing. There was her latest proposition, which he was still firmly vetoing. She said it would help him find her murderer, but the Liquorice Detective didn't care. If he carried it out, and he was discovered, they would section him and throw away the key. If he was going to do anything *that* crazy, he first needed proof that she was a genuine spirit from the other side and not a Ziggy Stardust alter-ego, or a *Three Faces of Eve*-style manifestation of multiple personality disorder, or some other bizarre workings of his subconscious. So he pursued his mother's case no further, even though the Canon still seemed like the number one suspect.

And then another suspect entered his life.

He was in his attic rooms one evening in late January. He

was looking forward to watching *Make Mine Mink*, starring Terry Thomas and Hattie Jacques, about misfits who steal mink coats. It was quite chilly and he was thinking of changing into his gorilla suit to stay warm.

Then, without warning, the door suddenly opened, and the Phantom of the Fleetpit strolled in. Despite the passing of two decades and his scarred face, Dave recognised him instantly. How could he not?

It was Mr Cooper.

The ex-newsagent sat himself down in the armchair opposite. 'Hello, Dave. Thought it was time we had a little chat …'

A fearful Dave stood up and slowly backed away from his old tormentor grinning at him from across the room.

Stark terror swept over him in waves as he started silently repeating to himself, 'He chews *Sherlock's*. We choose *Sherlock's*. Everyone chooses *Sherlock's* …'

CHAPTER TWENTY-NINE

Mr Cooper smiled at Dave, who was now standing behind the sofa, keeping it between them, desperately wondering if he could make it down the steps from his turret, out into the corridor of the main attic, along to the fire escape and down into the street, before Cooper attacked him.

'Fancy us meeting again after all these years, Dave. I saw you in the vaults,' he leered. 'I liked the way you nicked that artwork from Aisle 13. You got some gumption, after all.'

Cooper didn't explain why he was no longer a newsagent and had become a storeman. That would be to treat Dave as an equal, but nothing had changed, as far as he was concerned, since 1957, when Dave would walk into his shop every Saturday for his *Fourpenny One*.

'So I'll get straight down to business, Dave ... £25.00 a week, inflation-linked, to cover your rent, otherwise I go to your boss and tell him you're living up here. And that will also cover compensation for this.' He touched his face gingerly. 'It still hurts in this weather.'

Dave looked blankly at him.

'So ... what do you know? The cow never told you, did she?' Cooper grinned.

'T-told m-me what?' Dave stuttered.

'She came into my shop that Saturday she disappeared.'

Cooper looked menacingly at his victim. 'You must have been telling tales, Dave.'

'No. No. I never told. You told me not to,' replied Dave. He nearly added 'sir' on the end.

'Yeah. 'Cos those are the rules. You never tell. Never be a grass, Dave. Never be a snitch,' said the ex-newsagent.

'I swear I wasn't,' said Dave.

'She found out somehow ... maybe the bruises on your face? Anyway, she sails in, all sassy-like, with her fur boa, done up to the nines – 'cos your mum was a looker, as you know, Dave ...' He paused. He was testing the water; waiting to see Dave's response.

Dave said nothing.

'Oh, yes. Your mum was quite a girl.' He grinned and winked knowingly.

Again, Dave said nothing, his eyes empty of comprehension, so Cooper moved on.

' "What can I get you, darling?" I asks her. 'Cos I was always very polite with customers, as you know, Dave. And she says, "I'd like a *Fourpenny One.*" "Course you can, darling," I says. "Dave not well today ...?" and I hand the comic across, all innocent like. No games with your mum. 'Cos you must never hit a lady, Dave,' said Cooper waggling a finger. 'That's against the rules. A tart, or your missus, well, that's different.

'But meantime, she's slipped some brass knuckles on her hand. She screams, "I'll give you a fourpenny one, you bastard," and next moment, she's smashed me in the gob with them!

'Well, I'm so shocked, I don't have time to give her a back-hander, as I normally would. Then she fucking hits me again. The cow. No provocation. I've done nothing, Dave.' Cooper waved his hands expansively, an injured expression on his injured face. 'Nothing. I'm innocent. Breaks me fizzog. I keel over and then she's round the counter, standing over me, stamping on me wotsits, screaming like a fucking banshee, calling me this, that and the other; not the kind of language I like to hear from a lady, Dave.'

He paused, giving gravitas to this last statement. 'Then she sails out, leaving me doubled up in agony on the floor.'

This was earth-shattering news to Dave. He had, in fact, told his mother about Cooper. She'd finally gotten it out of him, no longer convinced by his endless stories of getting into fights with other boys, walking into doors, and standing on rakes.

He had promised her he would never go into the newsagents again and, following her disappearance, he never had. He had lived a *Fourpenny One*-free childhood ever after, until he became editor of *The Spanker*, which incorporated his favourite comic.

He had no idea she had planned her revenge, using those knuckle dusters she had for her protection when she worked at The Eight Veils. Just as kids never told their parents what happened to them at school, parents never told their kids about their plans until after they were carried out. There was a mutual lack of communication. And trust.

'That was the day mum disappeared,' Dave recalled.

'Well, don't think I had anything to do with it, Dave,' said Cooper hastily. 'Oh, I would have swung for her, Dave, make no mistake, even if she was a lady, 'cos what she did was well out of order, but I was in hospital, see? So I couldn't do nothing, could I? I was laid-up. I don't know what happened to her. Poor cow. That's assuming she came to a bad end and didn't go off with a tally man. Which she could well've done, Dave. Oh, yes. I'm sorry to say this, but she liked her little bit on the side, did Jean.' He leered knowingly.

'No, no, I wasn't suggesting you were involved for one minute,' said the craven Dave. 'No, please, perish the thought.'

'It's perished,' sneered Cooper.

Dave could have said, 'Don't you talk about my mother like that, you bastard! She smashed you in the face, but you exaggerated your injuries. You fought back, killed her; dragged her body through to the back of your shop; buried it somewhere; *then* you went to hospital.'

But he didn't.

'Good,' added Cooper. ''Cos I wouldn't want there to be any misunderstandings.' He looked menacingly in Dave's direction. Twenty years on, he was still a strong, wiry figure who enjoyed violence.

But, despite himself, the hatred for his persecutor welled up in Dave's face, and Cooper saw it.

'Something you wanted to say to me, Dave ...?' He stroked the knuckles of his fist in anticipation.

Dave felt his hatred dissolve into fear, and shook his head submissively, avoiding eye contact. 'No.'

'Sure?'

'Very sure.'

'Glad we're sorted. So ... I'll be back for me wedge tomorrow night,' he grinned at the wretched figure opposite. 'Mr Quasimodo. Make sure you've got it for me.'

'I will,' confirmed Dave. 'I will.'

'You'd better. 'Cos I should hate to leave empty-handed ...' And with that, Cooper sloped off, leaving the door ajar.

Dave sat back in his chair, shaken to the core.

'It's him. It's him. It's him. *He's* the killer,' he trembled. 'It's so obvious. Oh, my God.'

He couldn't stop shaking with fear.

His mother appeared on the chair opposite. 'And you handled him so bravely,' she said sarcastically. 'Didn't you, dear?'

'No, mum,' he corrected her. 'I nearly shit myself.'

'Don't be vulgar, David,' she frowned reprovingly.

'I never knew you visited him with a knuckleduster that Saturday, mum. Why didn't you tell me?'

'Well, you might thank me for smashing his face in.'

'You attacked him, and ...and he *killed* you. Right?'

'You're the detective, dear.'

'He practically *told* me he did it.'

'Did he admit it?'

'No. But it's got to be him. It's got to be.'

'I'm pleased you're upset about what happened to me, son.'

'You bet I'm upset. He could kill me next!'

She looked up from lighting a cigarette and raised an eyebrow at his insensitivity.

Dave scowled. 'Don't look at me like that. You're all right. You're dead. And I could be if I don't pay him off.'

Dave's mind raced. 'I have to earn some extra cash somehow. But how? How?'

'It won't be easy, son. I believe Joy just turned down your latest proposal, *Penny Never Saw the Pitch?*'

'Yeah. What was wrong with a story about a blind hockey player?'

'And *Paula's Fit for the Poorhouse,*' she said, cooly blowing a smoke ring in his direction.

He irritably waved the smoke away from his face. 'Based on my life in the West Ham Union Workhouse. Another masterpiece rejected.'

She took a long drag of her cigarette. 'Then you might have to do the unspeakable and write for *Laarf!*'

Dave shuddered. 'Oh, no. No. No. I haven't sunk that low, mum.'

'Well, I'll leave you to it, son,' she said, and started to walk away.

'No! Come back. You got me into this mess: you can't leave me to sort it out. Help me. I need some support.'

She turned back towards him. '*My* mess?'

'Well, you gave birth to me. It's your job. You're my mum.'

'That's true. Unfortunately. But what can I do, son?' She leaned over and disdainfully flicked a little cigarette ash onto him. 'I'm dead.'

She disappeared into the darkness, leaving the scent of her Sirocco perfume and cigarette smoke imprinted on his mind. He was sure if anyone had entered, they would have smelt it, too, proving he was sane.

Sane or insane, he was knocked for six. Writing for *Laarf!* was the only way to get the money. Despite constantly insulting Tom Morecambe, he never seemed to take offence, simply responding with his buzz-saw laugh.

Between the time he left Angus, Angus and Angus in Aberdeen, and went to work at Fleetpit, Dave had spent a year freelancing for Tom. His stories were in high demand, possibly because there was no competition. Other *Laarf!* writers were always mysteriously ill. He learnt later that it was somehow connected with the sound of Tom's laugh. But Dave didn't have a phone, so he was protected from its lethal side-effects.

He was joined a few months later by Martin Candor, another escapee from Angus, Angus and Angus. Establishing themselves in Dave's garden shed, the two of them calculated that, in order to make any money, or indeed to eat, they would have to write a funny story for *Laarf!* every eighteen minutes.

This they endeavoured to do, using mass-production methods appropriate for a 'fun' factory. Dave discovered that if he removed a page from his manual typewriter, that he and Martin would then stop for a cigarette break, a joint break, a tea break, a coffee break, a lunch break, a cake break, a walk break, a fresh air break, a warmth break, a chat break, an argument break, a fierce argument break, a wasp-swatting break, a spider (named Fred) fly-feeding break, a game of mini-football in the shed break, a memorial service for Fred when he died from over-eating break, a game of volley ball using the washing line for a net break, anything other than the death sentence of writing for *Laarf!*

So, in order to keep the wheels of commerce turning, Dave figured there had to be a continuous roll of paper in his machine. He experimented, appropriately, with a roll of Izal germicide toilet paper. It had a suitably glazed surface but the sheets were too narrow. So he switched to wallpaper rolls instead, suitably cut down, and was soon able to churn out endless scripts for *Laarf!* without any lapse in concentration; producing sufficient stories to wallpaper an entire house.

Their circumstances were not helped by the fact that it was Aberdeen in the winter, and there was no heating or lighting in the shed. So they were muffled up against the cold. Their combined body heat in the intimate confines of the shed, together with heat and light from an old paraffin lamp, made it survivable. Dave had bought the lamp from a secondhand shop in Aberdeen, together with his wonky-legged barber's chair. The lamp was probably used by wreckers to wave ships onto the rocks and it was still lethal, pumping deadly green fumes into the shed, requiring them to take air breaks every fifteen minutes.

After a year, they'd both had enough. Despite their considerable success, they were broken by the experience; they had to get out. Martin went on to a successful writing career elsewhere, and Dave took a staff job at Fleetpit. Certainly, his experience in the shed fuelled his hatred of those mindless readers who actually believed *Laarf!* was funny, and were responsible for keeping the 'fun' factory in business.

Oh yes, Dave thought bitterly, they needed to pay for that year in the garden shed.

The prospect of returning to the dark days of writing for *Laarf!*, of eternal *Andy's Anorak*, *Billy Blower* and *Dirty Barry*, was a dismal one, but there was no alternative if he was going to save his hide.

CHAPTER THIRTY

Seeing Mr Cooper again, after all those years, Dave yearned for a drink, but the pubs were closed and he went to bed sober. But that night, he had a vivid drinking dream where he was back working for Angus, Angus and Angus in Aberdeen, and enjoying a lunch time pint in the Angus Arms.

Fortified by several pints, in full body lager-armour, he felt invincible. He was ready for anything. Even working on *Widow and Wallet*. His dad was right: the answer to life's problems was to drink your way to oblivion.

As he staggered back to work, a roadsweeper outside the Angus Arms silently observed him and made a call from a call box: 'He's just leaving now.' A mother with a pram also spotted him and hurried to a call box. She dialled a number and reported to the person at the other end: 'He has a wee bit of a stagger.'

Happily drunk and unaware he was being watched, Dave entered Bleek House, the granite-built publishing H.Q. of Angus, Angus, and Angus, opposite the old burial ground. He was fifteen minutes late and was summoned to face Mr Angus Sinclair. A tweedy character of indeterminate age, he sat grimly waiting for Dave in his funereal, Edwardian office, a bible visible on his otherwise empty desk.

'Now you should be aware we make it our business to know everything that goes on in this city,' said Mr Angus. 'So it is always better to own up and tell the truth.' He looked Dave grimly in the eye. 'Have you been drinking ...? Make a clean breast of it, Davey.'

'No, Mr Angus,' said Dave, standing before him.

Mr Angus produced a breathalyser.

'Well, now let's see if you've been an honest laddie or not, laddie.' He handed the breathalyser over for Dave to blow into. 'We'll need to take blood and urine samples as well. Although Angus the Washroom Attendant may already have them. Now ... I'll ask you one more time, Davey. Have you been drinking ...?'

Dave hesitated and Mr Angus pointed to the bible. 'We can show you Christian forgiveness if you tell us the truth, laddie.'

'Yes. I was drinking, Mr Angus,' said Dave penitently.

'You're fired. The doorman will escort you from the building.' Dave went ashen-faced. Mr Angus regarded him balefully. 'And there's no train that will take you out of this town after you've been sacked from Angus, Angus and Angus. You'll be walking back to London.'

'No. Please, sir,' Dave begged, 'please, don't sack me, Mr Angus.'

Mr Angus looked approvingly at Dave's humble grovelling. 'Good. That was just to teach you a lesson, Davey. You see, we're a family firm and we like to keep a fatherly eye on our employees and keep them on the straight and narrow.' Dave breathed a sigh of relief. 'So now ... I'd like to discuss your file with you.'

He leafed through some documents on his desk.

'Your landlady has been telling us you've been complaining about the damp and the rats in her lodging house ...?' Dave nodded in agreement. Mr Angus pursed his lips and looked severely at Dave. 'But this is a hard town, Davey. A granite town. And what did you want hot water for? Are you expecting a baby? A brisk, cold scrub-down in the yard is enough for old Mr Angus.'

'Also ...' Mr Angus checked some more reports, 'your next door neighbour tells us you had the radio on loudly *after* nine o'clock in the evening.' He paused to let the full impact of this announcement get through to Dave, then continued. 'Now, we can't order you to turn it off, but we strongly recommend you do.'

'Yes, Mr Angus. It won't happen again, sir.'

'And Angus Electrical tell us you've ordered a *colour* television, no less.' Mr Angus was clearly taken aback by this information. He checked through the various papers again. 'But there is no record of you coming into an inheritance ... your statements from the Angus Bank of Scotland do not show sufficient funds. Was it the hire purchase you were thinking of ...?' Mr Angus shot Dave a warning look. 'Because I think you're being a little over-confident of your position, Davey.'

Dave hung his head repentantly which, once again, met with his employer's approval.

'Of course, in time, we may help you purchase a nice wee granite tenement.' Mr Angus was more conciliatory now. 'But only if you play your cards right. Although,' he added hastily, 'obviously, we wouldn't approve of you really playing cards.'

Dave woke up sweating. He had been starting to have a second dream where he had blown into the breathalyser like Billy Blower, and it inflated into a balloon and he took off into the air.

His mother had been watching him. 'It was just a dream, son,' she reassured him.

'The reality up there in Aberdeen was worse, mum,' said Dave, sighing and thinking back.

He sat up in his sleeping bag. 'What's wrong with me, mum? Why am I such a coward? Why don't I stand up to them? Why didn't I stand up to Cooper?'

'That's not true. You do stand up for yourself, Dave.' She checked her make-up and hair in her mirror.

'Well, when? Tell me. I need some support, mum.'

'When what ...? Sorry, I was far away,' she said, admiring her appearance.

'When have I ever stood up for myself?'

'When Angus, Angus and Angus wouldn't give you your old job back, you told them to eff off.'

Dave shook his head. 'That doesn't count. That was a one-off.'

Jean Maudling thought again. 'When you were an errand boy, you told M&R Pell to stick their job?'

'Not really. I just posted all the letters I was meant to deliver down a drain and never went back. I couldn't face them. I never stood up to them.'

'Yes, you know, I think you're right, Dave' said his mother, thoughtfully. 'On reflection, you *are* spineless.'

'Thanks a bunch, mum,' said Dave bitterly.

But in one respect, Dave did show a certain true grit, that even John Wayne might have admired, although he had no idea where his determination came from. Because the mysterious forces that really motivated him always remained hidden in the shadows of his mind.

CHAPTER THIRTY-ONE

Ron Punch's office was an impressive Edwardian room with a fireplace, a green leather-topped desk, an antique clock, a drinks cabinet, bound volumes of past publishing successes, and photos from Ron's time in the army and the office football team he joined after the war. The walls were stained yellow from decades of heavy smoking. The curtains were drawn, so sunlight couldn't interfere while he watched the racing on TV. There was a glass top to the desk with a magnificent school shield and Latin motto engraved on it: *Deo patriae litteris*. 'For God, country and learning.'

Scattered across the ring-stained and grubby glass were racing papers, betting slips, pencil stubs, tumblers, an overloaded ashtray, a half empty bottle of Laphroaig (a Christmas gift from an art agent hustling for work), matchbooks from The Eight Veils and other clubs, and small change.

The office and its famous desk had once belonged to the editor of the legendary, but long gone, *Homework* magazine, the Reverend Julius Cambridge. The vicar had not only produced *Homework*, but established it as the template for a scholastic and sporting life, to help boys aspire to the highest positions in society. It was only sporting life where Ron and Julius had anything in common.

Julius's zeal had not stopped there; he had also set up Cross Line, offering the comfort of the Lord to troubled souls. He had set up the phone helpline from this same office and still, very occasionally, calls came through to the original number. Ron was answering one as Dave entered.

'Listen, a few beers and you'll be right as rain. Or a fucking good shag, chum. That'll sort you out.' Ron beckoned to Dave to sit down and pour himself a whisky. 'I know … I heard you, chum … you've opened the window and you're going to step onto the ledge …' Ron irritably raised his eyes and carried on giving advice. 'But if you're serious, mate, you don't fucking talk about it, you do it. You just do it. If you're going to jump, just fucking jump! Hello …? Hello …?'

Ron put the phone down and sighed. 'What is the matter with people today, Dave?'

Dave shook his head sympathetically.

'We didn't have fucking helplines and fucking counsellors in the war. You just had to fucking get on with it. It didn't do me no fucking harm.'

Ron poured himself a whisky and lit a cigarette. He had always got on much better with Dave than the traitorous Greg and the overly-ambitious Joy. Dave and he had an unspoken rapport. They had their differences it was true, but Ron was still one of Dave's role models for failure and complacency. But now his protégé seemed to be changing, and this was why he had invited Dave to his office. Dave's latest script for *Aaagh!* was lying on his desk. It was about a black footballer, a character Dave was particularly keen on.

'*Black Hammer* … You can't have a story about a black footballer, son.'

'Why not, Ron?'

'Well, you just can't.'

'Why not?

"Cos you might offend someone.'

'Who? The National Front?'

'Me. I am offended, Dave.' The war veteran waved an offended finger. 'The country's being taken over by them, Dave.' He pointed to the script. 'And this is just encouraging them to come over here.'

'You're kidding?'

'No.' Ron looked at Dave in all seriousness.

'Well, if it is, so what?' said Dave, surprisingly eager for confrontation.

Ron didn't reply. He sipped his whisky and tried another approach as he flicked through the script. 'You've got this scene here where there's all this racist chanting from the terraces at … what's his name?'

'Ernie Gambo, the Black Hammer.'

'Ernie … *Gambo*,' Ron said, rolling his eyes. 'That is just going to make trouble.'

'It happened to the black striker, Clyde Best.'

'But we can't take sides, Dave,' insisted Ron.

'Yes we can,' said Dave belligerently. 'We should. That's what *Aaagh!* is all about. It's a comic of the streets.'

Ron said nothing. He was running out of cards. His authority was already undermined and his redundancy looming. He was yesterday's man and he knew it. Frank Johnson, the publisher, had made it crystal clear he was not allowed to stop Dave's youthful path of progress, only give him the benefit of his advice.

So he tried playing the reasonable card. 'Look,' he appealed to Dave. 'I know things have got to change, son, but we need to do it *gradually*. Why not write a story about a white footballer with a young black friend who watches him from the terraces and learns from him?'

'Like the Lone Ranger and Tonto?' Dave looked incredulous.

'Now that's a winning formula,' smiled Ron.

'Or maybe *King of the Khyber*, where a native defends his beloved white master with a cricket bat?' Dave put down his whisky. It was untouched.

'Another great story,' said Ron, oblivious to Dave's sarcasm. 'It's introducing them to our traditions, our culture.'

Dave looked grimly at his one-time mentor. 'Over my dead body, Ron,' he said coldly. And he walked out.

Ron knocked back his whisky. The now powerless managing

editor couldn't believe his close ally had gone over to the other side. He sighed as he realised his time was almost up and the appalling Greg, with his camp manner and ever-changing outfits, was probably being groomed to take his place. He poured himself another whisky.

For some reason *Black Hammer* meant a lot to Dave, and he was going to make it happen, no matter what, even at the cost of his friendship with Ron. He had no idea why he felt so passionately about having a black footballer in the comic. Maybe it was connected with his parents' time in Nigeria.

He was even writing the story himself, for free, because he was only paid when he wrote for other comics. Perhaps he was just being 'ideologically sound', although that would be a first.

No, there was something else driving him to write about a black hero, something he couldn't quite get a grip on.

CHAPTER THIRTY-TWO

At the end of January, Dave put the first issue of *Aaagh!* to bed. It would be out on the streets in mid-March. Almost despite himself, he had produced the most explosive, angry, street-level comic of all time. By comparison, its rival *Guts* didn't really have any, because it was produced by Angus, Angus and Angus. But *Aaagh!* had more than enough for both of them: quantities of them were depicted in all their intestinal splendour in *Deathball,* a gladiatorial death game, inspired by the film *Rollerball* and ten pin bowling.

Then Greg revealed that, next week, he was being interviewed by the board for the job of managing editor, replacing Ron.

'Well done, Greg,' said Dave, hiding his fear and resentment that his assistant was being offered the top job.

'Thanks, Dave, but I haven't got it yet.'

'Oh, you will, mate.'

'You're right. I will,' said Greg confidently.

'And you deserve it.'

'Yes, I do, don't I?' Greg sat back in his chair, imagining the hallowed *Homework* desk was already there in front of him. 'And, when I'm in the command seat, I shall be making a few changes, I'm afraid.'

'You're afraid, or should I be?' asked Dave suspiciously.

'You should be. I'll be putting a stop to your freelancing in office hours, for a start. So I wouldn't buy any more rolls of wallpaper, if I were you.'

'But it's one of the perks of the job, Greg. And you do more freelancing in staff time than any of us.'

'Now. Yes. But on a managing editor's salary I won't need to, will I?' Greg smiled. He clicked his pen excitedly. 'I'm having lunch with the board at Rules. Isn't that fantastic? Rules! Frank Johnson told me to get a new suit specially.'

'Then it really is in the bag,' said Dave glumly.

'Looks like it,' said Greg, continuing to click. 'Although I don't actually know what's wrong with what I'm wearing right now.'

Dave saw his opportunity. 'It's maybe a little sombre, Greg. Black can be a bit depressing. Perhaps you need something more modern to make you stand out?'

'Modern?'

'If Johnson wants to get rid of Ron, you need to dress the exact opposite: young, cool – the epitome of seventies fashion.'

'Ah. Sophisticated, you mean?'

'No. Sophisticated is bad. It could make you seem old fashioned.'

'Hmm,' said Greg. 'I hadn't thought of that.'

'You've got to look hip, Greg. I could help you choose if you like?'

'I don't know, Dave. Two men shopping for a suit together. It could seem a bit ...'

'Gay?'

'Well ...'

'Come on. We're seventies men, Greg. We're both comfortable in our skins. I like fur and you like looking like Peter Wyngarde.'

Greg assumed Dave was offering his services to curry favour with his future boss. He was persuaded. Dave had then accompanied Greg to Bond Street and, every time Greg hesitated, Dave was there to reassure him.

The outfit Dave persuaded Greg to buy was a patterned, purple velvet suit with flared trousers. There was a velvet waistcoat, too, but Dave told Greg he needed to show off his Engelbert Humperdinck-style, white, Regency frilly shirt (with matching lacy cuffs) that should be worn open to the navel so the gold medallion and his hairy chest could be seen to best advantage. The silver platform shoes were the finishing touch, even if they were partly concealed by the flares.

For a moment, Greg hesitated when he saw the result in the mirror, but Dave had a final card to play. 'Bernie would have loved to have seen you in this suit. He'd have said you looked … fabulous.'

'You think so? We both bought identical blue mohair hipster suits once.'

'You see? Men do go shopping together.'

'Yes. And do you know, the seats on our trousers wore out at exactly the same time!'

'I'm sure that was pure coincidence, Greg.'

'It probably did look a little strange,' recalled Greg. 'The two of us dancing side by side with our arses hanging out.'

'You should wear this for Bernie, Greg. In his memory. He'll be right there by your side in spirit.'

'You really think so?'

'I'm sure of it. My mother is always there beside me.'

* * *

Rules is the oldest restaurant in London, specialising in serving traditional food: steak and kidney pie, beef and Yorkshire pudding, and apple crumble with custard. There was a bit of a clue there, if Greg had only taken the time to research the venue. But into the restaurant once frequented by such literary talents as H. G. Wells, John Galsworthy and Charles Dickens, had entered the face of comics for the seventies: Greg, wearing a suit Liberace would have envied.

He returned from his interview far earlier than expected, and Dave was now mining him for details, as he imagined the stunned reaction of Frank Johnson and the Fleetpit board of directors, consisting of ex-service officers, to this precursor to Austin

Powers. 'So, tell me again, Greg, what exactly did they say?'

'They didn't say much really. They were very quiet. They just kept staring at me.'

'That's a good sign, Greg. That's positive. They could see, just from your suit, you were the man for the job.'

'I hope so. You know those red plush, semi-circle seats they have in Rules?'

'I'm afraid I don't mix in your exalted circles, Greg.'

'There were three directors sitting next to me, but they all kept edging away. Colonel Horsfield was almost sitting on Granville Roberts's lap at one point.'

'That was so he could admire you better, Greg.'

'Colonel Horsfield had to leave in a hurry for some reason. He never touched his spotted dick.'

'He'd made up his mind. It's in the bag, Greg. Oh … ' Dave leaned forward to inspect Greg's chest. 'Got a little bit of steak and kidney there, mate. In your hairs. That's it.'

'Oh, no! Supposing they saw it?'

'Don't worry about it. The medallion would have distracted them.'

It was a job well done, Dave concluded. Greg had broken the rules of Rules and that was even before he opened his mouth and told them how he was going to shake-up comics. All the suits wanted was another dull suit. Dave could do dull. He figured, once the dust had settled, he would now be in line for the job and the chance to replace Ron. He would appear for his interview at Rules in a sober terylene suit straight out of 'John Collier, John Collier, the window to watch'.

Greg was lost in thought, clicking his pen, doing a post-mortem, endlessly replaying the interview in his mind, trying to see if Dave was right in his positive conclusions.

As he continued his ruminations, a sudden look of absolute fury crossed his face as he recalled the responses of the directors and what they meant. Then it quickly vanished to be replaced by a long, thoughtful stare. At Dave.

Unaware he was the subject of Greg's attention, Dave had settled back and was enjoying *The Caning Commando* in the latest issue of *The Spanker*. He had begun to read the episode, set in Hamburg, when Greg interrupted him. 'Dave, I meant to ask?'

'Sure? What?'

'That woman I saw you with the other night ... who was she?'

'What are you talking about?'

'The woman who was up there with you in your turret.' Dave was suddenly alert. He had only recently confided to Greg that he was living in the attic. Greg had become suspicious at his mysterious appearances and disappearances, so he had no choice but to confide in him and swear him to secrecy.

'I was working late, so I came up to see you. See if you fancied a pint at The Hoop and Grapes, but you looked like you were busy.' Greg looked knowingly at Dave. 'She's quite a looker, mate.' He whistled approvingly.

'Who?'

'The woman in your room. The one you were talking to.'

'What did she look like?' Dave looked suspiciously at his assistant.

Greg shrugged nonchalantly. 'Hard to say; it was dark.'

'Did she have a classic retro look?'

'Yes ... I guess that's how I'd describe her. The kind of clothes you see in old movies.'

'Which era? Thirties? Forties? Fifties?'

'No idea,' said Greg vaguely. 'I'm not a movie buff, like you. But they were definitely old.'

'How old?'

'Not sure. Let me think ...'

'About 32?'

'Yeah. Yeah. 32.' Greg clicked his pen as he pondered on the subject. 'No. Maybe a little younger. I'd have said late twenties.'

And you actually, physically saw her in the room with me? In the flesh?'

'Oh, yes. Yes. definitely,' said Greg.

Dave leaned forward and looked intently at Greg. 'This is really important to me, Greg. I've got to be certain. You definitely saw her? Sitting there? Talking to me?'

'Absolutely. There's no doubt. What's the big deal? I didn't come in, because I could see you were having a pretty intense conversation with her about something.'

'Wow,' said Dave to himself, absorbing Greg's amazing revelation. 'Wow.'

This was the breakthrough he was hoping for. Objective proof, from another witness, that his mother existed on some psychic plane and therefore his hallucinations were real. Well, stick that up your arse, psychiatrists. This changed everything. Now he would do what his mother wanted him to do.

'Maybe you could introduce me to her sometime, Dave?' enquired Greg. 'Because I have to say she looked gorgeous, mate. But, of course, if she's off limits, I understand.'

'No. I'm happy to introduce you,' smiled Dave happily. 'Why not?' Phantoms were, presumably, safe from Greg's amorous advances. And with that comfortable thought, he returned to reading *The Caning Commando*.

CHAPTER THIRTY-THREE

As always, the story began with an introductory caption:

'Because of his legendary caning skills, the War Office
recruited schoolmaster Victor Grabham to be –
THE CANING COMMANDO.'

Barnes Door, the eccentric inventor of the bouncing bum
cane and a cane that thrashed around corners, had an urgent
meeting with Victor Grabham at the Golden Hind Academy in
the village of Lower Belting Bottom. He brought grim news.

'Thrashley Park inform me they've intercepted news of
German plans to make an advanced, heavy vinegar cane
capable of striping our Russian allies with impunity. They call
it ..."The Arsenripper".'

'Those fiends!' exclaimed the Commando.

'It's vital you get hold of the plans, Grabham,' the boffin
continued. 'The Arsenripper could change the whole course of
the war.'

'You ... you don't mean ...'

'I'm afraid so, if it succeeds there'll be no stopping the
Boche. Next stop: the Atomic Bum!'

The Commando and Alf Mast were sent into Hamburg that
very night to steal the top secret plans.

'Well,' said Grabham, as he and Alf emerged from a fish and
shop in Hamburg, 'you may be as thick as a plank, but you

certainly know your way around Hamburg. You tracked down that fish and chip shop, all right.'

Alf was too busy noisily noshing to reply.

Victor Grabham looked at him disdainfully, 'Yes, we waste valuable time looking for a fish and chip shop, because otherwise you can't fight the Germans properly.' He scowled back at the shop. 'Fritz's Fishgeschäft'.

'So what happens now, sir?' asked Alf, his hunger satisfied.

'Now, lad, we find the inventor of the Arsenripper, Werner Von Vroom, who is known to frequent Hamburg's Reeperbahn, and has a preference for peroxide blondes.'

'Ah! So *that's* why I'm dressed as a blonde 'bumpy man', to lure the scientist to his doom?'

'Correct, lad. So come along. You've had your slap-up meal, now it's "slap and tickle time." We're ready to begin... "Operation Inside Top".'

'Will I do, sir? Do I look like a saucy bint, sir?'

Grabham briefly evaluated his companion for sauciness. A heavily made-up Alf was wearing a blonde wig with pigtails, a white blouse, a tight skirt, fishnet stockings and stilettos.

'Yes, straighten those seams, adjust your coconuts, and give just a hint more cleavage to entice Von Vroom.'

Corporal Punishment did as he was ordered. 'Would I entice you, sir?'

Grabham looked coldly down at him. 'No, Mast, you would not.'

'I always meant to ask, sir. Is there a Mrs Sir, sir?'

'I have no time for bumpy men, Mast,' Grabham said disdainfully. 'I am wedded to my cane.'

The Commando, vampire-like in his sinister black cloak, together with his 'female' companion, did not seem out of place as they proceeded along the Reeperbahn. Similar mortarboards and cloaks were also worn by German teachers, such as his great enemy the Oberspankerfuhrer.

They entered 'Brunhilda's Bierhaus' and ordered two steins of beer. Hardly had they sat down, when they were joined by Von Vroom. He was wearing a heavy winter coat with a fur collar and stared short-sightedly at them through thick pebble glasses. Given the unlovely appearance of Alf Mast, his short-sightedness was useful.

'Allow me to introduce myself. I am Werner Von Vroom. May I join you?'

The Commando nodded his assent and Von Vroom turned his attention to Alf. 'My, you are a foxy young tease.'

'Call me Mimi, Mr Vroom, sir. I'm a bad girl, I am. I bang like an outhouse door in an air raid. Would you care to sample my wares, sir?'

'I would indeed, Mimi. You see, we are starved of ladies here in Hamburg. They have all been sent to comfort our brave boys on the Russian Front. There is an embargo on girls working in the Reeperbahn.'

'Ooh, me nan suffers from embargo somefink fierce, Mr Vroom, sir.'

'Ach, so?'

'Indeed,' interjected the Commando. 'Your nan would appear to be mostly ailments held together by bile and vinegar.'

'Thank you very much sir. Nan always said you were a perfect gentlemens.'

'Come, strumpet,' leered Von Vroom. 'I have hired a room upstairs for just the two of us.'

'All right, big boy,' said Alf, 'show me your knockwurst and I'll show you me drawers.'

'Ha! I think not!' said Von Vroom, suddenly pulling away Mast's empty coconuts. 'You think you two fooled me even for a moment?"

'Oi!' said an indignant Alf. 'Get your sausage fingers off me thrupenny bits.'

'I knew you were the Caning Commando and Corporal Punishment the moment you entered the beer hall. I recognised you from the recruiting posters, Grabham.'

The Commando's heart sank. He had recently agreed to a poster campaign to encourage boys to join the Junior Home Guard. The posters depicted a masked Commando waving a cane with a Union Jack attached to it, exhorting kids to 'Fight the Hun for Dear Old Mum.' Somehow, Von Vroom had seen through his disguise.

Von Vroom produced secret blueprint plans from an inside pocket. 'This is what you came for, Grabham, but you shall never have them.' He flung back his coat. 'But here is the prototype I will enjoy testing on you … the Arsenripper!'

The Commando looked aghast at the awesome cane: a serrated edge ran down its entire length and there was a silver death's head on the end of its shepherd's crook.

'It is indeed an Arsenripper,' gasped Grabham. 'Not even my canemakers, Mafeking and Jones of St. James's, or the boffin Barnes Door, could devise such an ignoble rod.'

'It is years ahead of its time,' agreed Von Vroom.

'And undoubtedly against the Geneva Convention,' scowled the Commando.

Von Vroom flung Alf Mast to one side, ordering him to, 'Hande hoche, you dirty little bag.'

He then proceeded to lay into the Commando with the Arsenripper. 'When I've finished with you, Grabham, you'll be standing up from now to doomsday. I will redden your arse like the devil's cheeks.'

'Old Striper', the Commando's favourite cane, was no match for the secret weapon. The punishment Von Vroom inflicted upon him with the Arsenripper was unbearable. He cowered beneath its furious fusillade. Again and again the cane ripped down on his rear end.

Then Grabham remembered all those school-capped boys who had joined the Junior Home Guard and followed his example, marching around with their little canes, singing, 'Thrash em all, Thrash em all, the Hun, the Kraut and the Strude-all'. He owed it to them to win. It was what England expected.

His proud heart surged with patriotism. It was time, once again, to Carpet Bum the Hun. Seething with righteous rage he laid into the Nazi as Alf Mast looked on, encouraging him. 'That's it, stripe him, sir! Stripe him!'

'Take that, you Boche baboon. I'm going to bum you back to the Stone Age. It's arsekrieg for you.'

'Nicht! Nicht!'

'Yes, you're nicked all right and you're going down.'

'Donnerwetter!'

'Donnerwetter your pants, Von Vroom!'

After receiving a first rate thrashing from Old Striper, the scientist was left a blubbering, snivelling heap on the ground.

Grabham pocketed the blueprints of the Arsenripper. It had all the information the scientists needed.

But he would make it look like they departed in haste and left the prototype behind. He examined the skull-end of the secret weapon.

'He done me wrong, sir,' complained Alf Mast. 'I think I might have a Hun in the oven, like me sister, sir.'

Ignoring Alf, Grabham unscrewed the skull.

'Just as I suspected, Mast. Look… A tiny flask of schnapps. You see, it is common for teachers if they are caning a whole class, or even the entire school, to have a little snifter to keep their energy up and ensure the last pupil is given as thorough a beating as the first.'

'That's very sensible, sir.'

'Yes, isn't it? My own canemakers, Mafeking and Jones, also conceal such containers in the ends of their canes. They even make variants with a pipe or a corkscrew in the end, so we can have a break for a smoke or a glass of wine in mid-caning.'

But Grabham was going to make sure that this evil scientist could never again break the Geneva convention and he replaced the schnapps with thallium, a colourless, odourless, tasteless and lethal poison.

Back in Blighty, Grabham passed on the secret German caning plans to Barnes Door, then he and Alf returned to the Golden Hind Academy in the tranquil village of Lower Belting Bottom.

The first priority was a wash for Alf Mast. 'Get those perfumed rags off, lad, before you go blonde-happy.'

'But I'm not allowed to shower with the other boys 'cos I'm so common, sir,' protested Alf, 'and Matron complained about me being too big to have a bath in the sink anymore. Cook said the washing up was coming out filthier than it went in, sir.'

'Then it's a sluice-down in the horse-trough for you. Now be off with you, or it's a six stretch in the arse house, lad. Tell no one of our secret mission. The world must never know we are the Caning Commando and Corporal Punishment.'

CHAPTER THIRTY-FOUR

Dave chuckled over the scenes of Alf Mast in drag. The Major was a little more risqué than usual. But if anyone complained, he would remind them of Dick Emery mincing along the street as Mandy, a busty peroxide blonde, with her famous catchphrase, 'Ooh, you are awful … but I like you!'

With his knowledge of evil chemistry, Dave had added the poison details to *The Caning Commando* story and where it could be obtained. The encounter with Mr Cooper had brought out the darkness in his soul once more. But he was consoled by the knowledge that his mother was real, even if she existed on some other plane of reality. Greg seeing her proved it. His description of her was remarkably similar to the way he saw her himself.

His mother explained how it came about. 'What happened to you as a boy, Dave, opened a door in time and allowed me to come through it.'

'A psychiatrist would say it opened a door to psychosis.'

'So we must take full advantage of it,' she insisted. 'You've considered my proposal?'

'Yes, but I really think I've done enough. Look at this room,' he said. 'I've made it just the way it could have looked when you were alive.' He indicated the beige-painted apartment, full of old furniture he had discovered stuffed away in the back of one of the attic rooms. She regarded it without enthusiasm.

'You see, mum?' he said proudly. 'Not a lava lamp in sight.'

'A frumpy brown three-piece suite with antimacassars?'

'I bought the antimac-thingies for it, specially,' he interjected. 'So, if I wear brylcreem, it won't leave a grease mark.'

'And a fading floral standard lamp with tassels and a valve radio made of finest bakelite?'

'Great finds, weren't they?''

'And didn't cost you a thing,' she sneered.

'No …' said Dave uncertainly. 'I didn't want to spend any money.' He looked nervously over at her. 'Just in case you weren't real. But now I know you are.'

She pointed an admonishing finger at him. 'That's why we need this psychic merger.'

'No. No, really, I can't face it,' he protested.

'You've read Aldous Huxley?'

'Yes,' he sighed. It annoyed him that she seemed to have full access to his mind, to his memories, to his favourite songs, but he had no access to hers.

'So you know how it works.' She leaned forward purposefully. 'We have to disable the function of your brain as a reducing valve because it's restricting your conscious awareness.'

'Are you sure you're not getting me mixed up with the radio?'

She smiled a sinister smile, her lips red and lustrous, her eyes gleaming and hypnotic. 'Once your brain is disabled, *everything* will be revealed.'

'But I'll look stupid,' he protested.

'That's never stopped you before.

'More ridiculous than Alf Mast in Hamburg.'

'Just tell Greg you're taking the afternoon off,' she purred soothingly, 'come up here and try it. What have you got to lose?'

'My sanity?' he suggested fearfully. 'No, mum, I need to think about it.'

'Don't think. That's the mistake.' His mother was all-knowing; she had the confidence he lacked. He must believe in her. 'We have to bypass your brain, son. Greg confirmed I'm real. What more evidence do you need?'

Dave looked up at the shadowy *femme fatale* standing over

him, as beautiful as any of the classic movie stars in their furs and high heels.

'You're right. I'll do it,' he said with new-found determination.

In preparation for his brain bypass, Dave purchased his mother's feminine attire in a thrift shop. The shop stank of unwashed clothes the moment he walked through the door and was densely packed with old garments, piles of worn-down shoes in cardboard boxes and men's crumpled, sweat-stained jackets.

These outfits were not ephemera, but clothes meant to last a life time, and had fulfilled their purpose, right down to the very last moment before their owners died. The shop was populated by down-at-heel, little old ladies, careful mothers with children, make-do and menders, and mouth-breathers: slightly strange people who stared fixedly and perplexed at other people, with an air of mild suspicion. This was understandable when the other person was Dave.

Ignoring the mouth-breather panting close by him, Dave made his selection with a little help from his mother. Sniffing disdainfully at other options he offered her, she pointed out a classic fifties floral tea dress: square-shouldered, with little shoulder pads, a prim-buttoned collar, and flared so the wearer could dance in it. Dave held it against himself, did a twirl for her, and she approved it. He couldn't find women's shoes that would fit him, but she told him he could settle for a pair of 1950s brown, battered, lace-up shoes.

He then went on to a wig-makers in Paddington and described his requirements: a long blonde wig fashioned in a fifties style like Jean Maudling's. It was a pity the assistant couldn't see her standing next to him, but she still understood and made suitable adjustments. He tried the wig on; it was perfect. 'Is it for fancy dress?' the assistant asked.

'Oh, no. It's so I can dress up as my dead mother,' Dave replied in all seriousness. The assistant thought he was being droll, and laughed. So many people made that mistake with Dave.

His make-up, purchased from Boots The Chemist on the way home, was simple enough: red lipstick, face powder and rouge cheeks. His mother showed him how to do it. Applying mascara was beyond him, but he did have an attempt at lining his eyes with a brown eyeliner with some assistance from Jean. He had also helped himself to a pair of Joy's vintage seamed stockings from her drawer. They would only go up to his knees and he tied them with elastic to stop them falling down. That was also as far, physically, as he was prepared to go to turn into his mother. His moth-eaten fur boa provided the finishing touch.

When he was finished, standing there in his fifties-decor turret, he stared at himself in the mirror and did a double-take. He gasped that Alf Mast, dressed in drag on the Reeperbahn, looked more alluring than he did. Jean Maudling agreed, but reassured him that it really didn't matter. It was only a symbolic act. He had to believe he was her in order to have full access to her mind. He had to trust her.

He looked nervously at himself in the mirror again and the niggling doubts started to seep back in, but she was ready for them. She reminded him that, no matter what the sceptics might say, she had already transformed his life for the better. He knew she was right. So, yes, he was ready for the next great step.

She slowly walked towards him, an image of classic beauty, his dark muse, his inspiration, his mother back from the dead, and the two figures merged and became one.

And as his brain bypass kicked in, it hit him. His head spun with the power and the vision and the astonishing new reality he was seeing for the first time.

It was like being in the vaults of Fleetpit House. Suddenly, he could see endless rows of memories on countless shelves in his mind. But not in colour, in grey and white. They were coming at him faster and faster, like speeded-up film. It was hard to keep track of them. He was drowning in them, flooded by them, like the River Fleet bursting out of its sewer pipe and engulfing the basement of the publishing house. There was so much information he was now aware of, his mind couldn't cope with it all. The new mixed in with the old. The familiar with the unfamiliar. Old classics like the Queen's coronation. The Pope's coronation. Winning the Knights of Saint Pancras Christmas raffle. Nicking money out of the missions charity box. They speeded by him, along with incredible new recollections that he had once erased from his consciousness but were now recovered and startled him with their sensational and meaningful nature. They shot by so fast, but with just enough detail to recognise them; although he didn't want to pull them out of the fast-flowing memory stream yet. Later when there was more time.

The speeding torrent hurtled onwards, effortlessly tearing down the walls of repression as if they were cardboard. So many memories of his mother. Happy memories. Sad memories. Previously blocked memories. But not intimate memories. They stopped at the bedroom door. With Dave trying to enter, finding it was locked, and rattling it furiously, and Jean calling out, 'Why are you back from school?' "Cos they sent us home early. Can I come in? Mum?' 'No. I'm busy.' A man's voice, 'Tell him to go away, Jean.' 'Is that Mr Peat, mum?' 'Yes. He's helping me.' 'What are you doing with Mr Peat, mum?' 'Choir practice. Go away.'

And not just Mr Peat. There was Ernie. He loved Ernie. 'Mum. Mum.' 'Yes. What is it? Leave the door alone.' 'I saw Ernie come in. What's he doing in there?' 'Repairs.' 'Why did he come through the back door? Why didn't he come through the front door?' 'Stop asking so many questions.' 'What are you doing with Ernie, Mum?' 'I told you. Repairs. Go and watch TV.' 'But I want him to play football with me.' 'Go away.' 'Ernie will you play football with me?' Another male voice, a deep voice, 'Hey, Dave. We'll play football another time. Okay, buddie?' 'Please, Ernie?' His mother's voice. 'Don't pay any attention to him. He's got to learn he doesn't get what he wants.' 'Please, Ernie?' 'Dave, If you keep rattling that bloody door, I'm going to lock you in your room again.' 'Please, please.' 'All right that does it. You asked for this, young man.' 'Let me out. Let me out. Let me out! If you don't let me out, I'll tell dad.' 'Don't you try blackmailing me, or you'll get the hiding of your life.' Memories and feelings, too. Jealousy. Anger. Rage. 'Stop it! Stop it. All right. All right. If you promise to stop kicking your door, Ernie will play football with you tomorrow when we meet him in the park. But you mustn't tell your father. It has to be our secret. Okay?' 'Okay.' 'All right, now you be a good boy and I'll let you out shortly.'

Doors were always being locked. It was why Dave liked keys.

Yes, there was a lot to sort out.

The torrent of memories was starting to calm down now into a smooth running stream when he heard sounds of another stream from the bathroom outside, down the corridor. It was in use and his heart skipped a beat. No one had been up here in all the months he had been in residence. He listened again.

There was someone in the shower.

CHAPTER THIRTY-FIVE

Forgetting he was in female attire, he had to investigate. He descended the five steps from his eyrie to the main, warren-like attics. The corridor outside was lined with piled boxes containing failed magazines. They weren't of any archive value and therefore not stored in the vaults, but not approved for pulping either. They had simply been dumped and forgotten about. Dave slipped between them to the bathroom, *his* bathroom, unchanged since the nineteen-forties, when it was used by hotel staff who lived in the attic rooms. The door had long lost its bolt, so Dave entered.

The room was decorated with austere, now largely cracked cream tiles with black trims; its shell lights gave it a touch of Art Deco; and there was a roll-top bath with a classic Edwardian shower above it. There was a shower curtain concealing the person's identity. He stepped forward and pulled it back.

Beneath the shower's jets of steaming hot water was Joy.

She stared aghast at the Norman Bates-like figure looking at her nude body. They both screamed at the same time, in mutual shock.

Greg had told her there was a disused bathroom on the top floor of Fleetpit House that no-one used, and had plenty of hot water. Joy reminded him she had a power-shower at home, but, as Greg had pointed out to her, why spend money on hot water when it's available for free at work? She immediately saw the sense of this. So he had checked upstairs and told her the coast was clear: it was the perfect time, he said, for her to nip up and have a shower. He was very keen, insistent even, she took a shower that very afternoon.

Joy hadn't recognised "Mrs Maudling" as Dave with his wig and make-up on. He needed to keep it that way, so he turned and ran.

She had no idea who the intruder was, but she wasn't taking any chances – nor was she a victim. Wrapping a towel around herself, she sprinted out into the corridor, picking up a Stanley knife that a workman had left on top of some boxes, and pursued "Mrs Maudling". 'Come back here, you fuckin' wrong 'un!' she shouted.

Dave could see the knife-wielding Joy was in no mood for explanations: he remembered her introduction to S&M at the *My Gang* party. His only chance was to leg it further along the corridor and then down the fire escape.

She ran on after him and was gaining on him, her blood lust up. He saw he would never make the fire escape, so he dived into one of the main storage rooms instead. It was the one that had the old furniture in as well as boxes and boxes of magazines. He thought about hiding behind the boxes, but there wasn't time, so instead he ran over to a huge old oil painting propped up against a wall and crouched fearfully down behind it.

Seconds later, Joy entered, her Stanley knife at the ready. By now she knew it was a man dressed as a woman but hadn't yet made the connection that it was Dave, likely suspect that he was. All she was focussed on was that her prey was cornered and was afraid of her, so she was starting to enjoy herself. She scraped her knife along the cardboard boxes, saying, 'Come out … come out … wherever ye are …'

Dave briefly considered coming out. Joy had, after all, been surprisingly magnanimous when she found him *in furgrante* with her coat. But all his fears of being discovered, dressed as his mother, and being sectioned had built up in his mind, perhaps out of proportion, and left him in a sheer state of funk; he couldn't risk sharing his father's terrible fate. Instead, he repeated his fear mantra to himself: 'He chews *Sherlock's*. We choose *Sherlock's*. Everyone chooses *Sherlock's* …'

Still dripping wet, the woman in the towel carried on searching for her quarry, running her knife metallically along an old radiator. 'After a bit of the old in-out were ye … ye pervert?' she growled. As Dave cowered behind the massive, heavy ornate framed painting of the Battle of Agincourt that had once graced the dining room of the Fleetpit Hotel, that was the very last thing on his mind. 'I know you're in this room and I'm going to fuckin' chib ye, pal …' she warned. Joy's mother had been in some classic horror movies, sometimes on the receiving end of slashers, so she knew how these things were done.

She approached the painting: somehow she sensed her prey was behind it. Perhaps she could hear his panting breath through the battlescape. 'This will sharpen you up and make you ready for a bit of the old ultra-violence,' she snarled. It sounded much worse than Malcolm McDowell in *A Clockwork Orange*, when said in a Glaswegian accent.

Then she ripped angrily down through the oil painting. Maybe if it had been a painting of the Battle of Bannockburn, she might have shown it more respect, but she didn't care about an English battle and slashed right through it. On the other side, a petrified Dave saw the vicious blade running perilously close to his face.

He squealed in terror, instinctively pushed the massive painting forward, so it keeled over and collapsed on top of her, bringing her to the ground. Screaming, he ran from the banshee. He could hear her swearing and slashing her way out of it as he ran from the room and made a beeline for the fire escape. He ripped the firedoor open and was out onto the metal landing, breathing in the freezing February air, as he realised, to his horror, his pursuer was all too soon back on her feet and was closing in on him again. So he hared down the freezing metal steps at high speed, knowing she would be right behind him.

And she might well have done, if the weather had been more clement. But, aware she was clad in just a towel and it was February, even Joy saw she would have to reluctantly abandon the hunt. Instead, waving the Stanley knife, she stepped out onto the top of the fire escape and snarled 'Psycho!' down at him.

Entering his office floor, Dave realised it was a very long corridor to the comparative safety of his office, where he had some clothes he could change into. It would be hard to reach it without being observed, and already he could see editorial and art staff further up the corridor bustling in and out of offices. There was only thing for it: he would have to go to ground. And there was only one place to do it: the Ladies, which was just a few steps ahead of him. He slipped inside and, fortunately, there was a vacant cubicle.

With the door safely bolted, he could calm down and work out his next move. He looked around at the unfamiliar walls and was surprised to see that the graffiti was rather more verbose than in the Gents. He started to read them to unwind. 'Ladies!' one announced, 'who's your top tippy for a fuck?' A list of guys followed, added to by a number of users. The names included Greg, Emil, 'Jamie from accounts' and that 'bit of rough but tall, good looking browncoat'. Dave was mortified to see his name was not suggested.

More graffiti announced 'Emil loves Judy forever' with a love-heart. Someone had crossed this out and written, 'Emil's got a small dick.' On the opposite wall it said, 'Who's had to deal with Deep Throat Barclay?' A long list followed. Then 'I fucking hate Gilbert O'Sullivan' was inscribed with considerable vehemence nearby. Probably one of the teenage mag journalists, thought Dave, because other teen-idols were written below it with abusive comments next to them. Further graffiti requested the user to: 'Add your mark if Greg shagged you.' There were a lot of marks.

He needed to have a pee. He hadn't realised before just how loud his stream was, released from higher up, compared with the more dainty, womanly tinkle he could hear in the adjoining cubicle. To his guilty ears, he sounded like an incriminating Niagara. But, finally, everything seemed quiet outside and he figured it was safe to emerge. He could check himself in the mirror and tidy up his appearance in preparation for him to run that final gauntlet back to his office.

But to his surprise, Bridget Paris, the editor of *Pinafore*, was there. She had taken off her blouse and was washing her armpits. He saw she was wearing a surprisingly sexy, lacy black bra and had a number of unmistakeable love bites on her upper torso. This was in stark contrast to her outer sedate and tweedy image. But, even more exciting, she was endowed with a lot of underarm hair. Now she was half-naked, it came to him where he had seen her before. She was one of the stars of *Wink!*, his favourite wank magazine. And other, semi-legal classics from the world of 'mushroom publishing', so-called because they were produced in damp basements. It was her hirsute nature that had stood out to him from the other photo models.

She turned to look at the strange, blonde member of the third sex who emerged from the cubicle and he couldn't help himself. He blurted out in a falsetto voice, '*Stalag Sluts on Heat!*' The blood drained from her face and he knew he was right. 'Y-You must have me confused with someone else,' she stuttered.

'No. *White Slavers … Soho Vixens … Houkhir Hooker …*,' he continued in his pseudo-girlish tones.

She took a step back, appalled that someone knew about her closely-guarded secret past, especially as she was about to apply for a more up-market job within the Fleetpit group. She looked searchingly at "Mrs. Maudling". 'What magazine are you on …?' she asked suspiciously.

'*Mumsy*', lied Dave, still attempting a feminine voice. Then added as an afterthought, '*For Today's Young Mums.*' And shot out the door. This information about Bridget Paris could be useful, and he might be able to use to his advantage later, he figured, but right now his immediate problem was getting back to his office without discovery.

Journalists were still milling around in the corridor and there was no way they wouldn't see him for what he was, with most unfortunate consequences.

But he also saw that Vera the tea lady had left her trolley nearby, while she took some teas into an office. He'd seen countless movies where the guilty wheel hospital trolleys down corridors to escape. Why not a tea trolley?

So, head bowed, he trundled it away, and, yes, it worked; none of the staff gave him a second glance as they passed.

He sped onwards, the cups and saucers rattling, he only had to turn the corner of the corridor and he would reach *The Spanker* office – and safety.

He found himself, unaccountably, singing the TV ditty 'John Collier, John Collier, the window to watch.' He was only twenty yards from *The Spanker* when Frank Johnson's door opened and the head of juveniles put his head out and called for two teas.

For a moment, Dave hesitated and thought of making a dash for it, but then the publisher continued, 'And some digestive biscuits, please, Vera.' He was locked in conversation with a colleague within, and the tea lady's hulking and bizarre appearance had not registered with him.

Neither did Dave's falsetto, 'Coming up' as he turned the tap on the urn.

'My usual, and a strong tea for Colonel Horsfield, no sugar, Vera,' said Frank.

He returned to his conversation with the Colonel. 'Yes, ideally we should find Ron's replacement before I depart. I couldn't see him getting on with Len.'

'And I would have some sympathy with him there,' agreed the Colonel, 'but, you know, we do need Len if we are going to expand into the American market.'

'It's a pity Ron has to go,' said Johnson. 'But he's hopelessly behind the times and he will have a substantial redundancy package.

'Indeed,' said the Colonel. 'Just as long as his replacement is nothing like that Greg character.' He pursed his lips. 'That purple velvet suit. Shameful. I never tolerated artistic types in the regiment, and I won't tolerate them now.'

'Yes, on reflection, his colleague, David Maudling, would be more suited to be managing editor,' said Frank. 'Solid, conservative, reliable and not ambitious, either. He's not going to try and turn the comic world upside down.' He knew this was just what the Colonel wanted to hear.

'Now … where are those teas?' he continued. 'Ah, Vera.'

Dave had entered with two cups and biscuits on a tray. He was unaware of his appearance, not having had a chance to look in the mirror in the Ladies. Unaware that a stocking had slipped down to his ankle, one of the shoulder pads on his floral tea dress had come out, giving him a lopsided appearance, his wig was askew after his hasty descent down the fire escape, his lipstick smeared and his stubble was showing through his face powder.

Frank looked towards the tea lady, recognised Dave, and his face went white. The Colonel, however, never gave her a second glance. She was just a tea lady, after all, even if she was six foot tall.

'I like the sound of this Maudling already,' said the Colonel. 'He's the steady hand on the tiller we need. I should like to meet him as soon as possible.'

As Frank looked on in mesmerised horror, Dave brought the tray over. 'Here we are, gents,' said Dave in a piercing falsetto which alerted even the Colonel. 'I'm afraid I'm out of digestives, so I've brought you some jammy dodgers.'

The Colonel took in the grotesque, smiling cross-dresser towering over him and shuddered. 'Who … who is this?'

'This,' sighed Frank, 'is Dave Maudling.'

'Hello, Colonel,' said Dave, still in a high-pitched voice, reaching out a friendly hand towards the recoiling managing director.

CHAPTER THIRTY-SIX

There was a long moment, where the Colonel and Frank Johnson had looked towards him, waiting expectantly for his explanation. Now he was calmer, he was capable of more rational explanations and no longer feared that the men in white coats would come for him. He racked his brains for a suitable lie. The artists and writers Dave worked with were renowned for their excuses as to why they were unable to deliver their work on time. One writer said it was because rats had eaten his script, another that his leg was trapped behind a cooker for the weekend. Surely he could come up with something equally inspired?

It would have to be brilliant. Something like one of Theo Baxter's legendary excuses. Theo was another exceptional cartoonist, like Ken Royce. His excuses for late delivery were as highly rated as his artwork. There was that occasion when Theo claimed he had left his artwork behind at the Chinese laundry. It got swapped with his washing, which a bemused Ron had received instead. Meanwhile, Theo said the laundry still had his artwork and had removed 'all those dirty marks' from the pages: 'the ink was very hard to get off'. Somehow, they'd succeeded, and so the pages were whiter than white and Theo would have to start the job all over again.

That was a hard act to follow, but Dave did his best. 'It's Oxford Rag Week,' he explained.

'But, Dave,' said Frank, 'you didn't go to Oxford.'

'Oxford secondary modern.'

It was enough to get him out the door, muttering something about a long tradition of pranking with another comic, although he knew his chances of now being made managing editor were zero.

Back in his office, a leering Greg was waiting, drinking in Dave's grotesque appearance, doubling up with laughter as he clicked his pen in triumph.

'You ... you set me up, you bastard,' said Dave.

'What d'you mean?' grinned Greg.

'You made up that story that you saw my mother.'

Greg tried and failed to look serious. 'I ... I'll look more ridiculous than Alf Mast in Hamburg,' he said, quoting Dave's conversation with his mother. Then doubled up again with laughter.

'You listen at doors,' scowled Dave. 'That is contemptible.'

'Well,' shrugged Greg. 'I learnt it from the meister, didn't I?'

Joy had been the difficult one. After he had changed into masculine attire and removed his make-up, he went round to see her and explained he was the intruder on her shower and the reason he was dressed in female attire. He knew it was no good lying to her, she'd see right through him.

'Ye daft gowk,' she admonished him.'I thought this was the Fleetpit Hotel, not the Bates Motel.'

'I understand, Joy,' he said contritely.

But then he couldn't resist adding, 'Although, I have to say, it did concern me how easily you slipped into the role of the star of a slasher movie.'

'It's in the genes,' she explained. 'It goes with the accent.'

She insisted he needed professional help, and arranged a meeting with Marjorie Rayner, Britain's number one agony aunt, who wrote a regular advice column for *Mumsy for Today's Young Mums*.

Dave was fearful of her. He knew her reputation: 'Balls busted while you wait. She is the Medusa of erectile dysfunction, Joy. One look from her and I'll never get hard again.'

'Haud yer wheesht!' she ordered him, giving him a similar withering look and he knew he had to comply.

Two days later he was summoned to the office of the queen of the problem pages. Marjorie wore a pair of outsize spectacles and a very short mini-skirt. She was gaunt, late middle-aged and smoked 60 cigarettes a day. Haltingly, Dave started to tell her about his life. His obsession with fur. His lack of money. His lack of career. His lack of a woman. That was before they even got onto the subject of why he dressed up as his mother.

'Were you ever happy, Dave?' she asked him through her smoke cloud.

There was a long pause and then he replied with a more glum and deadpan expression that even Clement Freud could never hope to match. 'Not that I can recall.'

'You don't enjoy writing?'

'I enjoy writing the invoice. The invoice is the most creative part.'

'You've never liked anything you've written?'

'Well, the full stops were pretty impressive and I liked the ellipses, too.'

'Joy said you were obsessed with fur. Tell me about that.'

'It's true.'

'Go on.'

'Well, I would only date girls who had fur coats. I'd see them home, but ask them to leave their coat. I'd send it home later in a taxi.'

She interrupted him. 'Dave, will you stop looking up my clout? You won't find any fur there. Not anymore.'

'Sorry. It's just you don't have a modesty panel.'

'No. I must get onto maintenance about that. Now what about this awful newsagent?'

'I remember one Saturday, especially,' said Dave sorrowfully, 'I was walking down to Mr Cooper's and there was another boy ahead of me trying to enter his shop. He had bright purple ointment on his face; the treatment for impetigo.'

'Gentian violet,' nodded Marjorie. 'Humiliating for kids.'

'He had big bambi eyes and he was looking hopefully in

through the door at all the confectionery. Mr. Cooper ran out holding a flit gun and sprayed him with DDT, warning him: "Get back! Get back! Keep your mittens on. The shop down the road will sell you sweets."

'Then he turned to me and smiled. "You're always welcome, though, Dave. Come in. Haven't seen you for three weeks."

' "I've been off sick with mumps, sir.' I replied.

' "Well, you'll be pleased to know I've been saving your comic for you every week. You want all three, Dave? I think you do." From the back of the shop, I could hear his wife telling him: "Leave the boy alone, Stan."

'Mr Cooper called back to her: "You like being in traction, do you?"

'Then he turned to me and said, "Now, Davey, what is it you want?"

' "Please, sir … Can I have a f … f … f … f … fur … fur … fur …" '

'That's it,' said Marjorie triumphantly. 'That's it. That's the reason for your obsession with fur.'

'Fur … fur … fur … fur … fur … fur … fur … fur …' said Dave. He was like a stuck record, he couldn't stop.

'And the solution is for you to face your fear.'

'Fur-fur-fur-fur-fur-fur-fur-fur-fur-fur-fur-fur-fur,' said Dave, as he relived the memory of being given three fourpenny ones, one after the other.

'It's the only way you'll be cured of your hang-ups. Now I know it will be difficult, because you can't confront Cooper now, he's probably dead or retired, and give him the hiding he deserves. No, I don't believe in turning the other cheek, dearie. We need to fight back in this world. Never let the bastards get away with it. So you have to find a way to face your fear, because you have the strength and courage of an adult now, Dave. Do you understand?'

'Fur-fur-fur-fur-fur-fur-fur,' said Dave. He couldn't bring himself to tell her Mr Cooper was very much alive and he was paying him £28.00 every Friday.

CHAPTER THIRTY-SEVEN

The next day, back in his office, the Liquorice Detective tried to absorb what he had discovered from his psyche merger with his mother, as well as the advice Marjorie Rayner had given him. In truth, he was overwhelmed by it all. He now had all the information on his mother's past, apart from her early life, when she was a hostess in wartime London, married and went to Nigeria.

He glanced across at Greg; they were still not speaking, but he could see Greg was feeling rather good about himself, as he looked at his final episode of *Feral Meryl* in *Shandy*.

Dave could barely conceal his jealousy. How did Greg do it? Why was he so successful with Joy, who was still rejecting his offerings? It's not like they were having sex anymore. Dave desperately needed to sell her a story to pay Cooper.

'Read it and weep,' said Greg arrogantly. 'Here. See how it's done.' And passed *Shandy* across.

Reluctantly, Dave sat down to read *Feral Meryl*. There was the familiar introduction:

'Feral Meryl was a wild girl, brought up by wolves in the wilds of Berkshire. She was rescued by her friend Mandy who tried to pass her off as an ordinary schoolgirl. But she was caught by the Dog Catchers and taken to a Special School.'

The opening scene showed Feral Meryl at the Special School where a harsh, tweedy, Barbara Woodhouse-look alike teacher, Miss Thripp, was teaching her obedience. She was retraining Meryl as a seeing eye for blind people.

This included telling her to 'Sit!'

She smacked a growling Meryl on the nose when she refused, and blew up her nostrils.

Meanwhile, Mandy wanted to get into the school to rescue her friend. So she pretended to be a 'special girl' to the guards on the school gate. She messed up her hair, let her tongue hang out, stared vacantly ahead of her and talked meaningless gobbledeygook to them.

'Don't know what your special power is, love' said a guard, scowling at the drooling, gibbering schoolgirl. 'But you've definitely come to the right place.'

'Yeah,' laughed the other guard. 'Normally you special girls are trying to get out.' And they let her through the checkpoint.

Staring through a window, Mandy was horrified to see just what Miss Thripp was doing to her best friend.

Then she turned and realised two other special girls were looking strangely at her. At first, Mandy thought they were going to betray her and take her to Miss Thripp, but, instead, they introduced themselves as Jemima and Zara.

Mandy started to explain why she was here, but Jemima held up a hand. 'There's no need. I already know who you are, Mandy. You're here to save Meryl, aren't you?'

'How did you know?' gasped Mandy.

'I was sent to a Special School because I can read minds,' explained Jemima.

Mandy turned to Zara. 'Do you read minds, too, Zara?'

'No. I can bend and move metal,' added Zara, giving Mandy an example, bending a spoon, like Uri Geller.

That night, Meryl was locked in a dormitory with the other two special girls. She was having to sleep on a bed, rather than in a nest on the floor made from Mandy's old clothes. Mandy knew just how upsetting this would be to her friend.

Jemima and Zara were also being experimented on by Miss Thripp and wanted to escape. So Zara used her powers to unbolt the dormitory door. The girls then all raced down the stairs and out into the school grounds where Mandy was waiting for them.

An excited Meryl bounded into Mandy's arms. Mandy was overjoyed to be reunited with her feral friend again. The plan was now for Zara to bend back the railings around the school so they could get away.

But, as Zara went to work, Jemima suddenly warned the others that it was too late. She could sense Miss Thripp was coming. 'And she has a weapon!' she alerted them.

Zara was using her strange power to bend the railings, but it was taking so long and it was almost too much for her. The stern headmistress appeared and she did, indeed, have a gun in her hand.

'I have orders to ensure you special girls do not escape into the community. You're all far too dangerous,' she snarled.

She was about to open fire, and now it was Mandy's turn to act. She realised that Miss Thripp was going to shoot Meryl first.

'A wolf girl is the most dangerous,' Miss Thripp snapped. 'You're filthy vermin! You cannot be allowed to live.'

'I've no power left,' screamed an exhausted Zara. 'I can't redirect her bullets!'

As the teacher fired at Meryl, Mandy leapt in the way and took the bullet for her friend.

Mandy staggered back in pain, blood streaming from her arm.

'Foolish child,' scowled Miss Thripp, showing Mandy no pity. 'That's what comes of befriending wild animals.'

Next moment, Meryl leapt upon the woman, her fangs bared, ready to tear out her throat.

'No. Please, please don't hurt me,' cowered the teacher.

'No, Meryl!' cried Mandy. 'Stay! Stay! She's not worth it.'

Growling menacingly, Meryl reluctantly backed away.

Then the three special girls and Mandy ran off into the night.

Zara and Jemima said their goodbyes to Mandy and Meryl. They knew they could never go home again, the authorities would be watching. So they had decided to join a circus instead.

'And what is to become of us, Meryl?' asked Mandy. She

was using the wolf girl's old muzzle, made from satchel straps, to strap up her arm.

Meryl whimpered at the sight of her wounded friend, but had no answers for her.

'I know,' said Mandy. 'We could stay at my Aunt Violet's. She's a dog-lover and a nurse. She'll be able to deal with my wound. We'll be free there.'

But suddenly, from far away, they heard a long, strange howl.

Meryl and Mandy exchanged glances. The Berkshire wolves were calling. Meryl howled at the moon, answering their call.

She turned back to Mandy. It was clear faithful Meryl would do whatever her friend wanted her to do.

'Oh, Meryl,' said Mandy, 'if we went to Aunt Violet's, I know we'd be safe. But I'm just not being fair to you. You have to answer the call of the wild.'

Even though she knew it meant the end of their friendship, Mandy had to let Meryl go.

Meryl licked the tears off Mandy's face and the girls embraced for the last time. Her heart breaking, Mandy told her friend, 'Go on, Meryl. Go. You must be free.'

Then the wolf girl ran off back into the wild, leaving a tearful Mandy all alone.

But then Mandy looked down at Meryl's old muzzle and smiled. At least she had something to remember her by. She would never forget Meryl, her very special friend.

The End.

The story left Dave cold. He just didn't understand why girls liked it so much. But he figured this must be because there was some deficiency in his own character. A deficiency he needed to overcome if he was ever to sell a serial to Joy.

'Joy has just commissioned me to write *The Return of Feral Meryl*,' grinned Greg. 'Oh, yes, the wolf girl's coming back. It's going to be even more emotional.'

Greg was on a roll. The third story he had devised for *Aaagh!* had also worked out well. Greg's ex-army father was a barman at the officers' mess in Colchester, and he'd overheard them talking about a possible military coup and mentioned it to his son.

Theoretically, they were talking about Northern Ireland, but it was obvious, to Greg's cynical dad, at least, that the army was preparing for a military takeover in Britain. In fact, it was common talk in the media and the seats of power at the time. General Walker, recently Commander-in-Chief of Allied forces in Europe, had said openly that 'the country might choose rule by the gun in preference to anarchy'. Private armies,100,000-strong, were recruited, ready to 'restore order'. Military members of the aristocratic clubs of Mayfair were ready to seize power.

This had incensed Greg, so he had come up with a serial about Britain after a military coup. The title, supplied by Dave, was *Street*: a shotgun-carrying lorry driver who leads the British resistance against the 'traitors who stole my country'.

There were a remarkable number of British officers being blasted by the brutal Street. He wore an old flying jacket, just like the one Greg often wore.

Dave had used all his devious skills to get the story past the board, telling them that Street was the villain and, as the serial proceeded, it would be clear the military take-over was actually for the good of the country. Colonel Horsfield thought it was an excellent idea.

Pretending that he'd gotten over his latest quarrel with Greg, and to show there were no hard feelings, Dave took him over the road to The Hoop and Grapes and bought him a drink. Several drinks. He needed to get Greg drunk, so he could find out what made him tick.

Over his fifth pint, Greg started to tell all. 'Dad served his country, but we can never go back to Belfast. He doesn't deserve that, Dave. That's not right. That's not right, is it, Dave?'

'No, Greg, it's definitely not right. But why can't you go back?'

"Cos he'd be seen as a traitor. He'd be shot.'

'Shot!'

'Shot. My dad. Dear God.' Greg swayed unsteadily on his

feet and Dave helped him onto a bar stool. 'So we're stuck. Stuck in bloody Colchester.' He sighed. 'He's a servant to all those Hooray Henries he hates. He hates them, Dave.'

'Why? Why does he hate them?'

"'Cos they're useless Sandhurst gits, of course. Haven't got a clue what they're doing. And that's why …that's why … Oh, it doesn't matter.'

'What? What doesn't matter?'

'It doesn't matter. Never mind. I should be going. Got to get my train.'

'No, it *does* matter, Greg. Come on. You can tell me. Have another drink.'

Dave ordered another pint for Greg and a coke for himself. 'And that's why …' continued Greg. 'Why … I need a cigarette. You got a cigarette, Dave?'

'Only *Caning Commando* sweet cigarettes, I'm afraid.'

'That's why I had German heroes in my comic. To say *that* to them.' Greg made an angry V sign. ''Cos of what they did to my dad. 'Cos they don't care. They don't fucking care, Dave. About my dad.'

'No. They don't care,' agreed Dave.

'And that's why you'll never see any officers in my stories, Dave. 'Cos I know what they're really like. That's why *Longest Day Logan* was a sergeant,' Greg slurred proudly. 'Like my dad.'

Later, after seeing an unsteady Greg off onto the Underground, Dave considered what he had discovered about his assistant. So the answer to his writing problems was emotion and identification. *That's* what was missing from his stories. Greg was writing with so much passion because he cared about his dad.

So what about Joy's dad? He knew she was really angry with him because he was 'too busy to see his own daughter', preferring to spend time with his second wife ('that fuckin' bitch'). And, even though he was an ardent socialist, he didn't approve of Joy 'wasting her life and her education' working in comics.

That was it, realised Dave. He would write a serial about fathers who had disappointed their daughters. It would have lots of emotion and Joy would identify with it. It would be his breakthrough story. She would love it.

He had the perfect title for it already: *Pop is a Weasel.*

CHAPTER THIRTY-EIGHT

In the chemistry lab, first-year pupil Mike Davenport watched his teacher, Mr Winsley, thrashing one of his classmates with the rubber hose from a bunsen burner, and noted just how ingenious he was in his punishments. He liked to think he was equally ingenious in the way he was going to kill him.

His classmate sniffled, trying to suppress his tears after the beating.

'What's the matter with you, boy?' said Winsley unsympathetically. There was a hint of a South African accent in his voice, the teacher had spent some years in Pretoria when he was a young man. 'The kaffirs could take it. They never cried out. Maybe because,' he grinned at the two black boarders in the class, 'you've got such thick, black skins.'

For an entire term, Mike and his classmates had been subjected to Winsley's colourful cruelties. The teacher had boasted he could lift a boy off the ground by his sideburns. Mike had never seen him do it; however he had pulled Mike *down* by his sideburn, so he was almost on the ground, and then belted him across the face back up into a seated position.

Another of his favourites was to make boys clench their fist and then hit them hard with a blackboard duster. If they opened their fists, they'd get twice the punishment. But, like the Chinese burns he regularly gave boys, it hardly justified murdering him.

However, grabbing Mike by the lapels, slamming him against

a wall and then throwing him over a desk and taking a run-up to beat him to the ground with endless strokes of the slipper in front of the whole class, was rather different.

Mike was a first-year boarder at a secondary school near Reading. After the 'slippering', unrecorded in any punishment book, Mike walked out of the school grounds, went to a public phone box and phoned his army father to complain. His dad told him to wait by the phone box; he'd be right there to sort things out. Overjoyed that his dad was going to rescue him, he looked forward to seeing Winsley get what he so richly deserved. His dad was a boxer and had a temper on him. He would knock the living daylights out of the teacher.

An hour later, his father sped up in his car, jumped out and knocked hell out of his son instead. Mike had broken the golden rule still in force in the seventies: he had told. 'Don't you ever tell tales again,' he warned his sobbing son, and drove off again.

That was the final straw. Mike had read *The Spanker* since he was seven, and loved *The Caning Commando*. The institutional cruelty of the school in Lower Belting Bottom was so much like the institutional cruelty of his school. He enjoyed seeing the Germans being thrashed by Grabham, because he knew just how painful and humiliating it was. Although Mike's boarding school was no college for the elite, like the Golden Hind Academy. Rather, it was a dumping ground for kids whose parents were in the forces.

He read the episode about the Arsenripper and made a careful note of the poison the Commando used to kill Von Vroom and where to buy it. It was just what he was looking for.

Having the deadly poison ready and waiting in a phial in his satchel, his opportunity arose when Winsley carried out another of his sadistic punishments. The teacher ordered two boys, who had failed to carry out their lab experiments correctly, to drink hydrochloric acid. They knew it was heavily diluted and therefore safe, but they still couldn't face it. Winsley insisted and threatened he'd force them to drink it.

One of the boys was so scared, he burst into tears; the other tried the acid and spewed it out. The class was close to rebellion in support of their traumatised classmates, and so Winsley told them he would show them just what gutless cowards they all were by drinking it himself. While everyone was milling around, comforting Winsley's victims, no one looked in Mike's direction as he added the colourless, tasteless and odourless poison to the beaker.

Winsley began by giving the class a little lecture about how our stomachs also contain hydrochloric acid and therefore it was safe to drink in a suitably diluted form. Then, with a triumphant grin, he swigged the HCl.

He took three days to die.

CHAPTER THIRTY-NINE

With no suitable replacement, Ron had held onto his job as managing editor. But, because of Frank Johnson's backing, Dave held all the cards on *Aaagh*! and when he laid them out and Ron read them: *Panzerfaust*, *Street*, *Car-Jacks*, *White Death*, *Black Hammer*, *The Damned*, *Deathball*, and *Micky's Mutants*, he could have wept. For the end of his era, and a new world emerging, which he could never understand.

As well as editing *Aaagh!* and *The Spanker*, Dave was developing *Pop is a Weasel*, about a dad who swindles a daughter out of her inheritance, so he could pay Mr Cooper. He had to get the serial right this time. There was a further incentive: if he impressed Joy, she might let him back into her bed. He still lusted after her. She was the only woman as beautiful as his mother, and there was no competition, now Greg was out of the picture, so he might just stand a chance. Perhaps he could try for another sympathy shag? There was plenty more misery where his Mr Cooper stories came from.

Meanwhile, his mother was pressing him to investigate her murder now that their psyche merger had been successful, and demanding he look through his memory files, but, so far, he had successfully fobbed her off.

With so much pressure on him, he really needed to take time out to relax and enjoy some entertainment. Dave's idea of entertainment was rather different to other people's. He had enjoyed seeing Greg's vulnerable side when he got him drunk and was keen for more. Noting Greg was wearing his Billy Liar flying jacket and boots again, he thought he would distract himself by winding Greg up about it. He knew Greg had strong views on the ending of the film. It was about a Walter Mitty fantasist who lives in a dream world where he's a hero – a character not unlike Greg himself.

'Saw *Billy Liar* on TV the other night,' he said.

'Really?' said Greg indifferently, not even looking up.

'I have to say, I actually liked the ending.'

'What?' Greg immediately stopped work. 'How can you like the ending? It's terrible! It's awful!' he snarled.

Brilliant, thought Dave. Better than watching the movie.

'How can you like an ending where Billy turns down the chance to go off to swinging '60s London with the gorgeous Julie Christie, and instead settles for the grey, miserable streets of home?' Greg ranted. 'What is the matter with him?'

'I thought Billy was being very sensible, Greg,' said Dave mildly. 'He was putting his family first. An example to us all.'

'A no-hoper like you would think that. the message Bernie and I got, loud and clear, was know our place. Not to try. Not to reach for the stars. Even though the writer did, because the film had to be autobiographical. So why was it different for him? What was that all about, eh? *Eh?*'

'You tell me, Greg.' Dave settled back in his chair, making himself comfortable.

'Social conditioning. I'm serious. Look at the endings of most films. Just how many dreams are crushed. That's not accidental.' Greg banged furiously on the desk. 'It's bloody deliberate!' Dave loved it.

'I understand, Greg,' said Dave pretending to calm Greg down, 'but I think the ending is telling us we shouldn't take risks. *Or* we could end up being a bus driver like Simon Dee. Or worse. Working on *The Spanker.*'

'Bernie and I watched it on TV,' Greg seethed. 'We were so pissed off, we went out and stole a car to cheer ourselves up.'

'And look what happened to Bernie. You see, Greg ...?'

Dave could have been at the cinema: only the popcorn and ice-cream was missing. 'You should have concluded, as I have done, that there is no hope, there is no future for us.'

'It was my turn, so we stole my favourite car,' remembered Greg, his face clouding over again, as he thought of his dead best friend.

'And would this favourite car of yours, by any chance, have been … a Citroën Avant?' queried Dave.

Greg was taken aback. 'How … how did you know?'

'Oh. Just a wild guess really. Isn't that the same car you always see the Gestapo jumping out of in French resistance films?'

'You're right. I knew where I could find one, parked at the top of North Hill. A beauty. We couldn't get the forward gears to work, so we tried jumpstarting it in reverse. Fucked the engine, unfortunately.'

'You see?' said Dave knowingly. 'Once again, it shows how we should all stick to that straight and narrow path, Greg. I do hope your Car-Jacks are more technically proficient than you and Bernie, when they're stealing cars. We have a responsibility to our readers, you know.'

'Too damn right! I'm checking with a garage when I write it.'

'I'm relieved to hear it. And I hope your own days of joyriding are behind you?' asked Dave reprovingly.

'Not really,' grinned Greg.

'What do you mean?'

'Joy and I are back together again.' Greg revealed.

'Back … together?' Dave's face dropped.

'Oh, yeah,' said Greg, a dirty grin on his face. 'So … I'm Joyriding every night now.' And he raised his eyebrows meaningfully.

This was not how Dave had planned his little entertainment to conclude. Rather, it was the way so many movies ended, according to Greg. With dreams being crushed.

* * *

Two days later, Greg had dropped his Billy Liar look and was in Spaghetti Western mode instead. He was unshaven, no poncho, but his sheepskin vest, denim shirt and cigar stub (instead of a Sobranie) made a strong Clint Eastwood statement. For an hour or more, he switched the butt from one side of his mouth to the other as he watched Dave hard at work. Finally, Dave had to ask him.

'What is it …? What's wrong, Greg …? Did you want me to apologise to your mule?'

'I've been looking through the readers' letters,' he said, a serious expression on his face.

'Okay …'

'This one caught my eye. Here.' Greg handed it across.

Dave read it out. ' "Dear Caning Commando, Thanks for the tip-off about thallium. It worked a treat on our chemistry teacher. He deserved to die." ' Dave examined the letter closely. 'Unsigned. No name and address. Is that it?'

'That's it.'

'Well, he can't be serious?' Dave's expression gave nothing away. 'He can't really have poisoned him?'

'That's what I thought. Then I remembered a headline about 'Chemistry teacher killed by his own experiment.' So I looked it up in the news library.' Greg passed over a photostat of the news clipping. 'It was thallium poisoning.'

Dave read the article. 'Looks like you're right, Greg. Although, they seem to think Winsley got his flasks and experiments muddled up. Drank from the poison flask by mistake and it was Good Night, John-Boy.' Although Dave was triumphant inside, there was no evidence of it on his face.

'But the letter suggests it was deliberate,' said Greg, watching Dave closely. 'Because the kid hated the teacher so much.'

'Perhaps,' said Dave. 'Although it does say here the headmaster is considering a 'Geoffrey Winsley Chemistry Prize' to be awarded annually in his memory.'

'That's irrelevant.' Greg was grim-faced as he chewed on his cigar stub, more Columbo than Man With No Name now. 'It looks like this kid got the idea of poisoning his chemistry teacher from *The Caning Commando*.'

Dave sucked sharply on his liquorice pipe. 'You really think so?'

'He admits it.' Greg didn't say more, but his eyes were accusing. He stood up and started to pace the room.

'If that were true, Greg,' Dave reflected, 'then I must blame myself. I should have censored the Major.'

Greg clicked his pen. 'But was it the Major?' He stared searchingly at Dave. 'Is that really what happened, Dave?'

'What else?' Dave shrugged. 'You know what the Major is like.'

Greg leaned down over Dave's desk and looked him in the eyes. 'I thought maybe you've been doctoring the Major's stories?'

'Oh, come on, Greg.' Dave looked appalled. 'That's too weird, even for me. I'm as horrified as you are by this.'

'That's good to know,' said Greg uncertainly. 'I mean, I know how much you hate our readers and for a moment, I thought … well, never mind what I thought.'

'I do hate them, yes, but I'm not a psychopath,' said Dave reproachfully.

'Well, the Major's gone too far this time. We'll have to report this to the police.' Greg looked determined as he circled their desks. 'Whatever Winsley did to those kids, nothing justifies poisoning him.'

'I completely agree, Greg,' nodded Dave. 'On the other hand … the poor chap is dead now. And when they find the boy responsible, they will put him away for life.'

'So …?' Greg was indifferent. 'He's a psycho. Psychos need locking up.'

'You're right. But it will mean the end of *The Spanker* and *The Caning Commando*, unfortunately.' Dave shook his head sorrowfully.

'Who cares?' Greg looked at the covers of *The Spanker* pinned up on the walls. 'Good riddance to them.'

'And the end of *Aaagh!*, too.' Dave noted.

'What? Why would it mean the end of *Aaagh!*' asked Greg, suddenly concerned.

'They'll look at that, as well, just to make sure there's nothing else kids can copy.' Dave looked coldly up at Greg. 'And they'll see your *Car-Jacks*, with its presumably authentic details of how kids can steal cars.'

'Very authentic. But that's not fair.' Greg was agitated by this suggestion, endlessly clicking his pen as he circled the desks like a caged animal. 'I … I put a lot of work into that story! It means a lot to me!'

'I understand,' said Dave sympathetically. 'The secret story of you and Bernie. But it will never see the light of day now. I'll take the blame, of course. But *Aaagh!* is finished,' Dave sighed. 'I'm so sorry, man.'

Greg pondered on this for a while, rolling the cigar stub from one side of his mouth to the other again. After some deliberation, he reached a conclusion. 'On second thoughts, maybe we should let it go, Dave …? Just this once …?'

'You really think we should?' Dave looked to Greg for guidance.

'Well, we would be ruining the kid's life.'

'That's true. I'll be more careful in future. And …' Dave held up the incriminating evidence. 'I think I should rip this letter up now so the poisoning can't be traced back to us.'

'Okay,' Greg promptly agreed.

As Dave tore up the letter, they heard the rattle of Vera's approaching tea trolley.

'I'll get them,' said Dave, standing up. 'Tea or coffee, Greg? Two sugars?'

'It's okay' said Greg looking darkly at Dave. 'I think I'll get my own tea.'

CHAPTER FORTY

It was Dave's second confirmed kill. Up in his turret, Dave rubbed his hands with glee. Or rather his paws, because he had changed into his inside-out gorilla suit to keep warm. In future, he'd have to handle all the readers' letters. But Greg's suspicions weren't going to stop him. He had a taste for this now.

Dave enjoyed his sense of power. Or the demons who possessed him, who were responsible for his supernatural good luck, did. His intention had been to inflict his pain on other kids in a way he felt Cooper would have approved of, but instead, kids had turned the tables on adults.

Somehow that felt better, a more gratifying catharsis as he explained to his mother. 'I'm now, officially, a serial killer. Kids are wreaking their revenge on adults, and it's all down to me. I'm their secret leader, helping them to fight injustice.'

'And a short while ago you were trying to kill them,' said Jean sarcastically.

'It would seem the fates have something else in mind for me,' agreed Dave. He reflected on recent events. 'I suppose, in a way, this makes me a kind of super hero.'

'You …?' she scoffed.

'Super villain?'

'Villain, anyway,' she jeered.

'I've got the outfit for it.'

'A pink gorilla suit and a liquorice pipe?'

'It's different.'

'But, Dave,' said his mother, 'most heroes, or villains, change into their costumes and go into action. You change into your costume and do … nothing.'

'Because I'm more of a cerebral hero, you see, mum?' Dave explained.

'Look,' said his mother irritably, 'Can we please get back to who murdered me? There's so many files you need to look at.'

The knowledge that a chemistry teacher had met an untimely end reminded Dave of one file, in particular, that required attention. It concerned Mr Peat, his mother's lover, who some years later became his chemistry teacher.

Mr Peat was in the church choir with his mum and Mrs Czar, who played the organ. He would come round for tea when Dave came home from school. Sometimes he was already there when Dave got home, as he had discovered when his mother's bedroom door was locked.

Bill Peat had Stanley Baker cruel good looks and would smile piratically at Dave's mum as they discussed the order of service over the rock buns and Battenberg cake. His mother would stand up, smooth down her dress, and sing the Irish hymn 'Be Thou My Vision', set to the folk tune 'Slane', specially for Mr Peat.

It was so haunting and beautiful when his mother sang, thought Dave. Without the rest of the choir and the awful flat-voiced congregation and the Brueghels drowning her out.

It brought a tear to Mr Peat's eye. 'You have the voice of an angel,' he said. It was not particularly original, but he was a chemistry teacher, not an English teacher.

'Thank you, Bill,' she smiled.

'Yes, mum, you have the voice of an arch-angel,' said his rival Dave.

'Thank you, Dave,' she smiled.

The song sounded perfect to the eight-year-old, but apparently it wasn't quite right, they still needed to practise.

There was another memory of a conversation between Mr Peat and his mother. Mr Peat had called round to see Jean the week she disappeared. They argued in the kitchen, thinking he was watching TV in the front room. But Dave was listening with his ear to the kitchen door. Mr Peat told his mother, 'Jean, the good name of the Church is at stake. We must protect the Canon. This cannot get out. Be sensible, Jean.'

'No. I won't be sensible. A little boy has died. All I can think about is little Konrad. God. I need a drink!'

'They told me to warn you. You must not go to the police, Jean. Or ...'

'Or what?'

'There will be ... consequences.'

'Why should I listen to the Knights?' she retorted defiantly. 'After what they did?'

'Oh, come on, Jean. That was years ago. Let it go.'

'You were one of them. I recognised you, even with your mask and robes.'

'Of course I was there. I'm proud to be a Knight. And it was an honour for you to be chosen.'

'To be Mary Magdalene? To play the part of a prostitute?'

'She's also a saint.'

'Oh, fuck off, Bill. You were gathered around in a circle while I danced, wearing your masks and leering and pointing at me like grubby little schoolboys.'

'You can't blame us for leering. You're beautiful.'

'Maybe they should have picked someone older? Is that what you normally do, choose some broken-down tart and offer her five quid to play Mary Magdalene so you can gather round and take the piss out of her?'

'No. Our Mary Magdalene has to be beautiful,' Mr Peat insisted. 'You shouldn't joke about this, Jean. It's a serious ritual.'

'Yes. About rejecting women, Bill.'

'Not true. It was your way into the inner circle. You wanted to be one of us, Jean. You wanted to be a Virgin Soldier.'

'You may not have seen me as a whore, but the others did. The Grand Master did. He still does.'

'I thought you and the Grand Master were close?'

'He chose me because he knew I'd been a hostess at The Eight Veils.'

'I don't have all the answers, Jean. Why don't you take it up with him?'

That seemed to silence her and the conversation came to an end.

'Wow!' said Dave now looking across at his mother sitting opposite him. 'I have absolute recall of those memories. That's amazing.'

'But you can see why you blocked them,' she said.

'Sure. A private dancer doesn't fit the image of the perfect Ladybird-book mother.'

'I did try, Dave,' she winced. 'At least I didn't go out to work. I always had time for my children.'

'Except you weren't at home much either,' he looked at her accusingly. 'I was a latch-key kid, only you didn't leave the key on the latch, so I had to wait in the coal shed for you.'

She put some face powder on and checked her perfect looks and locks. 'Do you think we could get back to the Knights?'

'Them? Oh, they're just a bunch of weirdos,' he said dismissively.

'You think that's all there is to it, son?'

'Of course,' he said knowledgeably. 'They like to dress up, have some pervy ceremony, acting out their hang-ups about women, then go home to their wives and kids and lead normal "respectable" lives.'

'Really?' she said.

'Oh, yes, it would be different today,' he said. 'They could come out of the closet, go to a gay club, and sing Shirley Bassey songs.'

'Dave, they weren't gay,' she said.

'Well, why else would they dress up in weird robes?'

She looked fearfully at him. 'Power.'

Dave's flippancy left him. He looked curiously at her. 'What did you get involved in, mum?'

She didn't reply. Instead, she looked nervously away.

'Come on, mum. Give. Who is their leader? Is it the Canon? Who is the Grand Master?'

'Soon,' she said.

CHAPTER FORTY-ONE

Joy came into Dave's office to reject his latest proposal, *Pop is a Weasel*. She explained why.

'In girls' comics, Dave, you can have a cruel stepfather or a cruel uncle, but readers will never, never accept a father would betray his daughter. Fathers are good and kind, and always there for us whenever we need them.' Then her expression darkened. 'Unless they're led astray by a fuckin' bitch. Sooo … I'm sorry, but I'll pass on it.'

Dave was furious after all the effort he had put into it. He could have got through an entire roll of wallpaper in the time. 'You're not sorry, at all,' he glared.

'No. I'm not sorry, at all,' she agreed.

Then, to make matters worse, Greg entered wearing a sinister green cowl with the hood up.

'You see, Joy?' Greg said, giving her a twirl. 'I wasn't making it up. Straight out of Dungeons and Dragons.'

'Oh, yes,' said an admiring Joy. 'That is definitely a witch's cloak. You look brilliant in it, Greg. Doesn't he look brilliant, Dave?'

'Yes, he looks fucking amazing,' scowled Dave, seething from his latest rejection.

'And Mrs Thatcher really could have worn it when she lived in Colchester?' Joy asked.

'It's possible,' replied Greg. 'When she was a scientist at BX Plastics down the road in Manningtree.'

'Manningtree, eh?' said Joy. 'The home of Mathew Hopkin, Witchfinder General. Pity he missed her. Okay, let me try it on.'

Greg passed the garment across and it nearly drowned Joy.

'But the fuckin' bitch is taller than me,' said Joy. 'So it's still possible it belonged to her.'

'Which "fucking bitch" are we talking about?' asked Greg, momentarily confused. 'Oh, Mrs Thatcher? Yes.'

Greg explained to Dave. 'In the 1940s, Thatcher lived in a huge Gothic house off Lexden road that my friend's converting into a school, and he found this robe in the basement in a locked suitcase underneath a pile of coal …'

'How absolutely un-fucking interesting, Greg,' glowered Dave.

'She lived up in a turret, just like yours,' added Greg, trying to make it interesting for Dave.

'And there was this ancient book of spells in the case as well,' continued Joy. 'Written in old French, right?'

'Yes. Which my friend, annoyingly, sold to a local antiquarian book shop.'

'We lost the grimoire,' sighed Joy. 'We could have found out what kind of black magic she practises.'

Greg put the robe back on. 'But he gave me this cloak because he knows I love weird shit.' He stroked Joy's hair. 'And I know you love weird shit, too …'

'Oh, yes …' she agreed. 'And, traditionally, objects of evil are buried under coal so the demons can't escape.' She turned to Dave. 'Isn't that spooky …?'

'Actually, Joy,' said Dave, not looking up from his work. 'I don't give a shit.'

'You will when you hear about Greg's new story, Dave,' Joy said excitedly. 'It's set in the 1940s, featuring the witch headmistress, Miss Thatcher. Wearing her dark cowl, she stands in the turret of her Gothic school, calling on evil spirits to empower her, and works the orphans to death. They slave long hours, with no school milk, and any rebellion is ruthlessly punished. Tell Dave the title, Greg.'

'I'm calling it *Slaves of War Orphan School*,' said Greg.

'You like that, Dave?' grinned Joy.

Dave stopped pretending to work and looked up. 'No, Joy, I think it's sick and it's irresponsible of you to take the piss out of the leader of the opposition. It's also too scary for your readers. Meanwhile, you turn down an excellent story like *Pop is a Weasel*. I see this as clear favouritism because you're shagging Greg again.'

'Talking of shagging,' leered Greg, ignoring Dave, 'we should do it there. She lived in a creepy room with stained glass windows at the very top of the house.'

'Have sex in Thatcher's old room?' said Joy eagerly. 'Feel her darkness all around us? Now there's an idea.'

'Like *Rosemary's Baby*,' said Greg.

'Aye, okay,' she smiled. 'But you'd better take extra precautions, Greg. I dinna want a Thatcher's baby.' Dave fumed and sighed as she continued. 'And wear that robe with nothing on underneath,' she smiled. 'Naked men in robes make me feel really horny.'

'If I can interrupt your filth,' said Dave, 'speaking as a narcissist, I am only interested in other people's lives when it is to my personal advantage. This is clearly not the case here, so could you both fuck off? Go on. Fuck right off.'

'Who rattled your fuckin' chain?' asked Joy. 'You watch your mouth, you. I've made better men than you cry.' She pulled Greg away. 'Let's go to my office.'

In the Shandy office she smiled invitingly at Greg. 'I'll lock the door.'

'Maybe draw the blind as well ...' said Greg.

'Pity about Dave,' he added. 'He's really throwing his toys out of his pram.'

'Tough shit. He's not a girls comic writer. He's too heavy handed.' She pulled Greg close. 'He hasn't got your gentle touch ...'

'You mean like ... this?'

'Mmm ... Yes ... Now take your clothes off, but leave the robe on ... And tell me you are Lord of my Ring ....'

'I am Lord of your —'

'Not yet!' she interrupted. As Greg started to carry out his other instructions, he looked across at her popularity poll. 'Ah! I see my story's still in the lead.'

'Greg,' she scowled. 'Will you stop talking about fuckin' work for once? Come on! Punctuate me! Punctuate me!'

He started to caress her and she sighed appreciatively.

'So glad we're back together, Greg. And I can't wait to introduce you to my dad …'

'Yes,' said Greg lovingly. 'So you're sure he's coming to the opening of your shop …?'

CHAPTER FORTY-TWO

Mortified by his rejection, Dave gave freelancing a rest and found himself thinking about his mother's murder again. He reflected on the conversation he had heard between Mr Peat and his mother, concerning Konrad, the little boy who had died. Another memory file in his mind opened and he recalled that Konrad had been at his school. The Canon had been 'very close' to his widowed mother, Mrs Jankowski, and was often round their house. Just as he was also 'very close' to Dave's mother and was often round their house.

It looked like a promising line of enquiry and, up in his turret, Dave started to talk to his mother about it, but she told him that he must investigate the Knights of St Pancras first. She said they were central to the mystery of her murder. But, apart from being a lazy serial killer, Dave was also a lazy detective. He was no gumshoe in a grubby raincoat, asking questions door-to-door in the pouring rain. Not when he could go downstairs and check the press-cuttings library.

He found a folder on the Knights. It didn't contain many news items, just various charity events they were associated with, but there was one in-depth article from a colour supplement.

It explained they were smaller than the Knights of St Columba and the Irish Knights of St Columbanus, and very different to those organisations which had been open to public scrutiny since the sixties. The Knights of St Pancras still retained secret oaths, initiation rituals and three masonic-style degrees.

The other two orders of Catholic laymen had been inspired by the Knights of Columbus, named after the discoverer of the New World, but the Knights of St Pancras were inspired by a rather more sinister source.

'Maybe there should be a Knights of Columbo as well?' Dave suggested to his mother. 'All wearing dirty macs and smoking stogies?'

'This is serious business,' his mother snapped. 'Read!'

'But I don't have a grubby raincoat, so I don't know if I qualify.'

'You did when you were a little boy. You were always getting food down you. You were a messy little pup. I remember once …'

'All right, all right. Let's not get into that. Let me read it,' he said hastily.

St Pancras was the patron saint of children and the Knights had dedicated themselves to helping the children of the poor. The supplement had a double-page spread of them in public procession, with their top hats and canes, but, disappointingly, no photos of their apparel when they conducted their secret ceremonies. The journalist had, however, met an anonymous firsthand source, who maintained that in their closed door rituals they wore costumes modelled on penitents in Spanish Holy Week: the Nazareno robe and the conical tipped hood, the capirote.

It was straight out of the Spanish Inquisition.

There was lots more about the Knights' founder, Father Faber-Knox, but Dave couldn't be bothered to read it.

Rather, he was thinking jealously about Greg's sinister robes that turned Joy on, and how he could compete with him for her affections. The cape reminded him where he had seen even more sinister garments before, including a capirote hood.

Eleven years earlier in the apartment of radio DJ and TV star 'Fabulous' Keen.

* * *

It was while he was an errand boy for M&R Pell. Keen was a Knight of St Pancras, although Dave had never seen him at his church. Dave had to make a couple of deliveries to his penthouse in a purpose-built, nineteen-thirties block of private flats looking out over the Thames.

Fabulous, wearing a red suit with his trademark black Nehru collar, had signed for the delivery and winked at an open-mouthed, awed Dave. Awed, because Fabulous was a larger than life personality, a tireless charity worker, and one of the great DJs of the sixties. Seeing Fab's famous smile at close quarters, with his engaging manner and his cool suit, Dave could understand why he was a national treasure.

The second time he had a delivery for him, he had carefully opened the package first and examined the contents. He still recalled the title page of the document inside: 'Knights of St Pancras. Opening Ceremony. Closing Ceremony. Diagram of Lodge Room. Report of the Secretary. Order of Service.' It didn't sound very interesting to Dave, so he put it back in the envelope and sealed it. Fabulous wasn't at home, so Dave hung around for a while, waiting for the great man. Then he glanced down at the giant pot plants on either side of his front door. Sure enough, there was a spare key under one of them.

The apartment had a look somewhere between the lair of a James Bond villain, and an airport departure lounge. The dazzling white, spacious, open plan living room had stunning views looking out over the Thames. At the far end, there was a sunken 'conversation pit', carpeted in orange shag. A huge chrome ball hung menacingly, but pointlessly, above it, with far too much gravitas to be a disco ball. At the other end, near the front door, was an impossibly long white leather sofa and a futuristic TV and radiogram. Or rather, the case was futuristic, shaped like a Picasso or Henry Moore sculpture. The TV inside was still black and white.

Dave found himself drawn to the paintings on the wall. They all seemed to be paintings of Mary Magdalene. In some, she was holy and fully clothed. In others, she was still holy, but half-clothed. There were similar statues of her, as well, arranged beneath the paintings, and, on a special display unit, in pride of place, stood a truly beautiful gold bust of the saint with yellow flowing hair and a candle placed on either side of her. However, her face had been replaced with a gruesome, grey, very old human skull that looked accusingly at Dave, giving him a scare.

The fifteen-year-old continued exploring the apartment. He didn't see his intrusion as snooping: he saw it as sleuthing, although he didn't know what he was sleuthing for. At that time, he was a Detective Without a Case.

It was the bar he was especially interested in. He had never seen so many fantastic drinks, in such amazing shaped bottles. Galliano sweet herbal liqueur, in a tall yellow bottle. White Malibu rum. Blue Bols. Green Curaçao liqueur. Crème de Cassis. Naranja. Mandarine Napoleon. Grand Marnier. And more. More impressive than his dad's home brews.

He was wearing his mod fishtail parka, along with his desert boots and red socks, ready for when he was sixteen and could drive a scooter, so he decided he'd help himself to two of the bottles, and carry them in his huge side pockets. If Fabulous noticed they were missing, he'd probably think it was the cleaner. Dave figured he was so rich, and there were so many of them, he would never notice, anyway. But first he needed to sample them, to know which bottles he should help himself to.

He took a swig out of each one. That way, he would leave no signs he had been in the apartment. They all tasted brilliant. He had never mixed drinks before, and was pleasantly surprised to discover they had absolutely no effect on him, other than to make him feel happy and carefree. He wondered why adults were always warning him never to mix his drinks.

Then he checked out the bedroom. There was an impressive black leather water-bed. He'd never come across one before, so he tried it out and bounced up and down on it a few times. But the movement and the squelchy sound made him feel a bit seasick, so he quickly gave up on it. He looked around the rest of the room, but found it a little disappointing. The furniture was immaculate with expensive veneers, but it lacked personality, rather like a five star hotel room.

He opened the vast built-in wardrobe, expecting to see an array of colourful Nehru suits inside. But, as he slid back the door, he did a double-take at the terrifying object staring cruelly and menacingly out at him. An apparition of evil that seemed as if it was alive.

It was a sinister purple pointed hood, with white robes beneath. As much Klu Klux Klan as Spanish Inquisition. The baleful, black slit eyes seemed to bore into his very soul. He stared, fascinated, mesmerised, at the garment in its clear plastic, dry-cleaning bag.

Then he heard the sound of voices by the front door. He just had time to close the wardrobe door, and slip back to the lounge as he heard the key turn in the lock. He crouched down behind the long sofa as Fabulous Keen entered with a female companion.

'Now relax, Brenda,' Keen said, 'You're going to be fab. And you're going to be famous.'

Dave took a sneaky look out round the side of the sofa and saw Keen was wearing a grey suit with black leather Nehru collar and shoulder pieces. The jacket was doubled breasted and fastened off-centre. He was very Doctor No. Very scary. Dave had heard him talk on the radio about his days as a bouncer in clubs, and how he'd 'taken care of guys who were out of order'. Dave knew his presence in Keen's apartment was very out of order.

He was afraid, terrified even, and yet, at the same time, a part of him, at least, was not afraid. An ice-cold calm had overtaken him, which was surprising; not the warm fuzzy feeling that might have been expected after so much alcohol. Perhaps it was because of the mantra he was repeating: 'He chews *Sherlock's*. We choose *Sherlock's* ...' Or perhaps it was his inner demons that guided him. But, in a remote, dispassionate way, he was enjoying the drama as it unfolded, even as he wanted to shit himself.

He risked taking a peek at Keen's companion, too, before ducking back behind the sofa. Brenda was a glamorous blonde, with a plunging cleavage and big hair, about 25-years-old. Old, in Dave's eyes. Certainly her best years were behind her.

'Here,' said Fabulous. 'This will calm your nerves.' He poured her a Baileys. Dave could recommend it. It was one of the bottles he had been intending to steal. He was glad he hadn't now.

'But it's a private event, Fab,' Brenda replied. 'How will it help my career?'

'Because there will be very important people there. It's your big opportunity, Brenda. You've moved on from "Saturday Night is Crumpet Night".'

'And you want me to dance, as well?'

'Oh, yes,' Fabulous reassured her. 'We'll be standing in a circle, watching you.'

'But I get to keep my clothes on, don't I?'

'Some … It'll be just like wearing your swimsuit.'

'Oh, that's all right then.'

Dave realised that he had seen Brenda before on the telly. She was Miss London, short-listed for the Miss England competition, and Fabulous had been one of the celebrity judges.

The drinks were making him feel queasy now, so he wasn't paying full attention and he focussed, instead, on driving that sicky feeling under. When he returned to his eavesdropping and looked out at them, Keen was holding some kind of audition.

They were standing by the gold statue of Mary Magdalene with the skull. The candles were lit and Miss London was reciting from a piece of paper: 'I am the Whore and the Holy One. I am the one whom they have called Life and you have called Death.'

She paused. 'Is that all right, Fab …?'

'Oh, yes,' groaned Fab, his voice unusually dark and forbidding. 'You are Death …'

There was a long pause. 'So you really think I could make it as an actress, Fab?' Miss London finally asked nervously.

'I can get you a part in *Danger Man*, Brenda. Or, if you're a very good girl … *The Saint*.'

'*The Saint*? Oh, Fab! That would be fab!' she squealed.

'Right. My turn. Now stand behind the Magdalene as I speak the words of power, Brenda. Yes. Like that. Very good.'

Then he too recited, 'They are the ones who are called Stranglers and those who roll souls down on the dirt and those who Scourge them and those who cast into the water and those who Cast into the Fire and those who bring about the Pains and Calamities of Men.'

He was reciting with great passion and Dave was surprised to see his smile was more like a rictus grin, as he continued. 'For such as these are not from a divine soul, nor from a rational soul of man. Rather they are from the Terrible Evil.'

He placed particular emphasis on 'Terrible Evil' as he stared intently at Brenda causing her to ask, 'Fab? Are you all right, Fab?' There was no reply. Instead, he just stared at her with his strange grin.

'Why are you looking at me like that, Fab ...?' she asked nervously. 'Have I done something wrong?'

Fabulous snapped out of it. 'I'm sorry. I was far away.'

'Phew!' she said. 'You scared me there for a moment.'

He indicated the conversation pit and his smile returned to normal. 'Come on. Now you can show me what a good girl you are, Brenda.'

'All right,' she giggled. 'Could I have the gear first? It'll help me relax.'

'Sure,' Fabulous smiled. He opened his briefcase and took out a paper bag. Dave saw it was marked 'Timothy Whites the Chemists'.

But he couldn't see what kind of medicine Fab was giving Brenda, because he suddenly needed some medicine himself. He needed to be violently sick. Saliva flooded his mouth and his guts gurgled and tightened, primed to spring into action. His body was not used to being a cocktail shaker. With a supreme effort of will, he swallowed the saliva back down and inhaled steadily through his nose and exhaled through his mouth. After a few calming breaths, his stomach relaxed; appeased, for the moment.

Meanwhile, Fabulous had put on some music and he and Brenda had moved to the conversation pit and were lost from view in its depths. But, by the sound of them, they had begun having sex as the record player played Dusty Springfield's "Wishin' And Hopin'".

It was Dave's chance to get away. The auto-changer selected Cilla Black's "Anyone Who Had A Heart" as, screened by the sofa, and ignoring Brenda's cries of passion, he crawled on his hands and knees towards the front door. He figured he could reach up, turn the handle and slip out without being noticed. But, as he began to put his plan into action, he suddenly, desperately, needed to throw up. And he knew, this time, his guts couldn't wait.

But where? A nearby pot plant? But if the DJ saw the puke there would be an investigation. He would not think it was the cleaner. There would be an investigation and they might work out it was him.

Fortunately, he had the answer. He vomited into a pocket of his parka as Roy Orbison's "Oh, Pretty Woman" boomed out, drowning out the sound of his retching, and Brenda and Fab's climaxes. The package for the DJ and Dave's signature book were, fortunately, in his other pocket.

His stomach appeased, he wiped his mouth on his sleeve and carefully closed the poppers on the now full and warm pocket. He didn't want to leave a trail of vomit behind him. As he reached the end of the sofa, he checked that Fab and Brenda were still safely distracted.

Two spirals of post-coital cigarette smoke drifted up from the pit.

Yes, time to get away. He slunk out the door to the sound of "You'll Never Walk Alone". As always, his demons had been there for him. He regretted not taking those bottles; all he had to show for his visit was a pocket of sick.

He delivered the package the next day when he was sober, and obtained Keen's signature.

'What? No parka today?' said Fabulous, now resplendent in a green and silver striped Nehru suit. 'Given up being a mod, have you?'

Dave was too hungover to reply. Besides, he felt anything he said might somehow give him away. He smiled weakly.

'Sensible lad. Be a rocker. They like violence.' Keen clenched his fist and smiled cruelly. 'Violence is the best way.' He winked and closed the door.

Dave had put the spare key back under the pot plant, but not before making a copy of it, just in case it would be useful on some future occasion. After years of being locked out of houses and bedrooms in his formative years, he liked keys. It was not the only key he had made a copy of.

* * *

It was the following evening, in his office, after everyone had gone home, that Dave was able to continue his conversation with his mother. She sat opposite him, in Greg's chair. 'So you finally remembered about Fabulous Keen,' she said, and sighed. 'It was about time.'

'You knew that I knew?'

'I know everything that you know.'

'Do I know everything that you know?' he asked, intrigued.

'No. There's a lot you don't know and you're never going to know,' she replied disdainfully.

'I don't know if he still lives in the same apartment. Do you?'

'I'm sure he does,' she said. 'He's a creature of habit.'

'You knew him?'

'Well, of course I knew him,' she said disdainfully. 'We go back a long way.'

'So why didn't you tell me before?' he protested. 'Or why didn't I know?'

'Because it doesn't work like that.'

'I thought I had complete recall now?'

'You do. But we still have to sort through your memories. So I often have to wait until they're prompted by something you see or hear.'

'Consider them prompted. So what now? Is Fabulous Keen connected with your murder? He's not actually the murderer, is he?'

261

'Oh, for God's sake,' she snapped and got up and paced around the office.

'Well, my money was on the Canon, and then Mr Cooper, but I'm very open to new possible suspects. Although it can't really be Keen, of course.'

She turned and looked darkly at him. 'And why not?'

'Well, he does all that work for charity for a start. No. Fabulous is out of the question.'

Jean Maudling shook her head angrily. She looked at a drawing of the gormless Alf Mast on the wall that a reader had sent in. 'You're not much brighter than him, are you, son?'

'Come on, mum. Fab is the star of *The Keen Scene*. He won an award from Mary Whitehouse for "wholesome family entertainment". He can hardly be a murderer.'

'We all have a dark side, Dave.'

'But everyone loves him, Mum. Well … almost everyone.'

'Almost?' asked Jean as she lit a Park Drive.

Dave grinned. 'I remember an episode of *The Keen Scene* going out live. Fab turns to his audience as usual and asks them, "Who's keen?" And they all roar back "We are!". Then Fab repeats: "Who's keen?" And someone calls out, "You are, you cunt!" '

Jean wasn't amused. 'If Keen found him, he'd have broken both his legs.' She sat on the corner of his desk. 'Now. D'you think we could possibly get back to business?'

'Okay, but you do know I am not actually qualified to be a detective? I am, in fact, barely qualified to be an editor.'

'Let's try, shall we?' said his mother impatiently, 'What did you deduce from your visit to his apartment, Sherlock?'

'I'm not sure I deduced anything, mum.'

'Then let me help you,' she sighed. 'The secret ritual of Mary Magdalene …?'

'Oh, yeah, yeah, I remember.'

'They used that beauty queen the way they used me.'

'You're right. I never thought about it before.

'You didn't make that blindingly obvious connection?'

'No, wait, I did, I did. Yes, of course I did.'

262

Dave had recalled in some detail the events in Fab Keen's apartment, but the emotional significance of what he had seen and overheard had passed right over him. He was more interested in describing the colourful James Bond details of Fab's apartment, remembering all the unusual drinks on display, he could even tell his mother the names of every single bottle, his recall was that good now, and reliving how he was violently sick and made his lucky escape.

'Uh-huh,' commented Jean. She waited expectantly for some emotional feedback on his recollections. When none was forthcoming, she prompted him with another '*Uh-huh.*'

'Uh-huh,' he cheerfully replied.

There was a long pause, then Jean concluded sadly, 'It's why you're a boys comic writer, isn't it, Dave?'

'Eh?' Dave was nonplussed.

'Hardware. Uniforms. Action. Explosions. You love that sort of thing, don't you?'

'What if I do? What's wrong with that?' Dave looked defensively at her.

'It's why girls comics aren't for you, are they, son?' Dave's brow furrowed in a puzzled frown. She ruffled his hair affectionately. 'Because there's nothing there. You're just too shut down.'

'You've completely lost me, mum.'

'I know,' she sighed.

'Maybe I should start with the uniforms ...?' she said to herself. She stood up again. 'Okay, let's try that. Dave, what do those robes in Fab's wardrobe tell you?'

He looked at her blankly. 'The Inquisition?' she prompted him. 'Remember how your dad smashed the screen with a cricket bat when he saw the Inquisitor on the telly?'

'But Sir John Gielgud wasn't wearing a hood, mum,' Dave corrected her. 'However, I did like the one Fab puts on his head. It's very scary. Actually,' he mused, 'I fancy wearing something like that myself.'

Jean shook her head in disbelief as she stubbed her cigarette out in Greg's ashtray. 'Why on God's good Earth would you want to dress up like Torquemada?'

'Who's Torquemada, mum?'

'The leader of the Spanish Inquisition.'

'As in Monty Python's "No one expects …"?'

'It's no laughing matter. When you see them all assembled in their robes in a circle, it's terrifying.'

'Well, Greg looked pretty cool in his. It impressed the hell out of Joy.'

Jean lit another cigarette, and looked quizzically at him. 'D'you know, I sometimes think your stupidity – I would have said *innocence*, but you're actually rather a nasty piece of work – protects you from the horrors of the real world.'

'It's handy isn't it?' grinned Dave, selecting a liquorice pipe from his sweet box. 'I believe the technical term is arrested development.'

'You think you're Just William, or something? But it's not a boys adventure, Dave. Keen is a dangerous man. I know.' She grimaced as she recalled. 'He's done some terrible things.'

She looked up at the covers on the wall of the Caning Commando thrashing Germans and shuddered.

Dave followed her gaze. 'He likes caning people?'

'I don't want to talk about it,' she said. Her face was white as she drew heavily on her cigarette.

'Actually, you know what I'm wondering, mum?' said Dave, returning to his own train of thought.

'About Keen being their leader?' She brightened up as she circled around the desks, as agitated as Greg now. 'Because he was ultimately responsible, of course.'

'Yes, I was wondering …'

'They would have needed his approval.'

'Yes, yes,' mused Dave, chewing on his pipe. 'It should be possible.'

'Go on,' said Jean expectantly.

'I was wondering about borrowing his costume to impress Joy? Because Spanish Inquisition robes definitely trump Mrs Thatcher's cloak,' he grinned.

His mother looked aghast. 'What? No, Dave. No. That is not a good idea.'

'Why not?'

'Dave, are you serious?'

'It would take some planning, of course.'

'Planning?'

'Yes. First, I have to think up a story for Joy. And choose the right time, like when Fab's off on his travels for *It's a Fabulous World*. I can check in *The Radio Times*.'

There was real fear on his mother's face now. 'Dave – he is a hard man. You do not mess with this man. Fabulous Keen is the Grand Master.'

'I still have his key in my collection, mum. He'll never know.'

CHAPTER FORTY-THREE

Joy's launch party for Time Machine looked like being a huge success. It was her big night, especially as her dad, the legendary Lawrence of Fitzrovia, was going to be there. Dave hadn't wanted to go, but Joy said she'd kill him if he didn't attend. But he protested, 'I'm too old to be going to parties. I'm not a youngster, anymore.'

'For fuck's sake, Dave, you're twenty-six.'

'Oh, Joy, don't remind me. I'm over the hill.'

Now he was here, he definitely felt out of place. Joy was wearing a Vivienne Westwood leather outfit with fetish zips she'd bought from Sex in the King's Road. Greg, in his purple suit, was eclipsed by guys wearing ponchos, gold lurex pyjamas and tartan dungarees. Dave's plan was to compete by not competing. This was why he was wearing an old grey jumper and shapeless brown cord trousers. He certainly looked different to everyone else. Noting the bartender expertly making up cocktails (Harvey Wallbangers, Tequila Sunrises, and White Russians), he protested to Greg, 'Just what is the point of all this?'

'It's so you can pull, man.'

'But I'm self-pulling. Calling my hand 'Ursula' works for me. It's more economic. How much did your last date with Joy cost you?'

'I never count the cost, Dave.'

'Just as long as you meet her dad, eh?'

Greg, clutching a manuscript of his novel, looked worriedly around the room. 'Yeah, where the hell is he?'

'But how much is a Kleenex these days?' pursued Dave. 'It costs me less than a penny a shot and I still end up with the same smirk on my face.'

'He should be here by now,' said Greg, starting to fret.

'While you're waiting,' said Dave helpfully, 'why don't I introduce you to Barbara? I understand she's a literary agent.'

'Really? Oh, thanks, Dave,' said Greg, lighting up a Sobranie. A gold-tipped, turquoise-coloured Sobranie Cocktail, this time.

'Very queer,' said Dave, disapprovingly.

'Party time,' explained Greg.

Dave put Greg together with the agent, a glamorous woman in her late forties. A little old for Greg, Dave thought, although that wouldn't stop him. Dave knew Greg would sleep with Lawrence of Fitzrovia if it got him the gig.

The shop itself was as colourful as the partygoers. On the walls were famous clothes and props for sale. Joy clearly loved this sort of thing. The white tuxedo worn by Sean Connery in *Goldfinger*. A leather jacket from *Randall and Hopkirk (Deceased)*. A three-piece suit worn by Peter Wyngarde as Jason King. A *Thunderbirds* puppet's flight suit. Clapperboards from famous films. The genuine items of clothing were safely under glass or displayed high on the walls, but movie memorabilia replicas were also available, like sheepskin vests as worn by Clint Eastwood in the Spaghetti Westerns. Greg had been one of Joy's first customers. Joy had considered adding Greg's witch cloak, as maybe worn by Mrs Thatcher, but realised she couldn't prove it. Dave thought about his plan to borrow Fabulous Keen's outfit as the Grand Master: that would top them all.

There was a complete range of nostalgia and fantasy. *Doctor Who* Unit badges. Multicoloured *Doctor Who* production scripts Joy had filched on a visit to the BBC offices at Shepherd's Bush (the shopping trolley she brought with her should have alerted them). Daleks in every imaginable size. Japanese robots in mint condition in their original boxes: no reproduction boxes and internally-rusted robots for Joy. Mr Machine. Mr Atomic. A rare silver Robby the Robot, and the Attacking Martian robot from a scene in *The Man From Uncle*.

American comics, art and cult books of every description. Fanzines like *Just Imagine*, about movie special effects. *High Times*, *International Times*, *Mars Attacks!* cards. Everything a movie or TV buff and collector could ever want, against a backdrop of cool film music from *Get Carter*, *Bullitt*, *Easy Rider*, *The Graduate*, and, of course, the two Johns: Barry and Williams.

Joy had put in a manager and two assistants to run the shop. She needed to stay with Fleetpit until she understood the publishing business and built up her contacts. The press called her the Time Lord, although, behind her back, her staff called her the Master.

Dave sipped his Harvey Wallbanger. Joy's enterprise contrasted with Dave's sloth, and he found himself admiring, in a resentful sort of way, her energy, her zest for life, her get-up-and-go, and all these celebrities she seemed to know whom she had invited to the launch: Gerry Anderson, creator of *Thunderbirds*; Diana Dors; and Jon Pertwee, the recent Doctor Who. Diana had popped in on her Saturday night party round with her husband, Alan Lake. Joy had known her since she was a kid, growing up on the film sets, and she was like a favourite auntie to her. Dave admired the fur Diana was wearing. He had lusted after the blonde bombshell since he had seen a famous photo of her in a mink bikini, matched only by Raquel Welch in her fur bikini in *One Million Years BC*.

Looking around him at the bright, bubbling partygoers, he could see the movers and shakers of the seventies. He provided a contrast, he told himself. Watching Joy mingling with her guests, he told himself she would see through their shallow, superficial nature, and want to be with someone more solid, grounded and genuine.

He decided to enjoy himself by doing the only thing he was any good at in parties: raining on everyone's parade and sucking the light out of the room. There were plenty of opportunities. He got talking to a production design assistant, who told him he was working on an upcoming film called *Star Wars*. 'It's going to be massive. It's going to change everything,' said the assistant excitedly.

'I'm afraid I beg to differ,' interrupted Dave. 'Old battered spaceships, eh? I have to be honest, that just sounds awful. You need to understand that audiences want to escape into fantasy. Oh, no. I can't see *Star Wars* being a hit.' Watching the designer move on hastily made him feel good inside.

He then went on to praise a director for an episode of a TV series he knew he hadn't directed. Told him it was his all-time favourite episode. 'Now that episode was brilliant. Unlike the others. They were crap.'

He met a fantasy novelist whose work he was familiar with. He said how much he loved it, that it had been a massive influence on his life. He thus had the author's undivided attention who looked forward to having his ego preened. Instead, Dave proceeded to tear his latest book apart, chapter by chapter.

'So, who exactly are you?' asked the seething author, making the mistake of going on the attack.

'I work with Joy,' revealed Dave.

'She's very beautiful, isn't she?' said the writer, as they watched her laughing with Diana Dors.

'Tell me about it,' nodded Dave.

'So,' the novelist sneered, eyeing up Dave's unfashionable appearance. 'Are you one of her groupies then? One of her admirers?' He smiled knowingly at Dave. 'Do you worship her from afar …? You long for a gorgeous woman like Joy, who is just too far out of your league, but who you know, deep down, you'll never have?'

'Actually, I'm one her "screwpies",' said Dave.

'You?' said the writer in disbelief. 'You?' He took a step back. 'You've actually screwed Joy?'

'Oh, yes,' nodded Dave. The smug smile on his face told the novelist he wasn't lying.

The author stormed off, knocking over a plate of vol-au-vents.

Next, Dave persuaded a science fiction artist to talk animatedly about his work. Then, making use of his height, he deliberately looked over the artist's head, smiling and nodding at other guests.

The party was turning out to be fun. If he had anything to do with it, the room would be pitch black by the end of the evening.

There were several party girls working the room, as intent on success as Greg, looking for producers, directors or successful-somethings. He watched admiringly as one of them did her thing, Piña Colada in hand. He guessed it was Joy's friend Sofia, because she was wearing an expensive yellow and black, zebra-striped Biba trouser suit. 'You're a film accountant?' she said to her mark. 'Oh, wow! That's so exciting. So cool! You do all the balance sheets? Cool! Oh, my God! Oh, wow! That sounds so interesting. That's fantastic. That is amazing.'

She was so impressed by the excited accountant that she constantly patted him approvingly. It was only as she moved on that Dave observed she had expertly extracted a tenner from his pocket. Dave approved of that. It was good to meet someone as twisted as himself.

Then it was his turn, and Sofia checked him out, just in case he was a potential Steven Spielberg. There was no clearly identifiable dress code for directors or producers, so one could ever be sure. 'Hi,' she smiled her best party girl smile at him, leaning forward to reveal a lot of cleavage. 'I'm Sofia. What do you do?'

Keeping a hand firmly on his wallet, he responded, 'What do I do? As little as I possibly can. My name's Dave Maudling and I'm a failure.' Then looked at her glumly with a long, unforgiving, silent stare. Like Patrick McGoohan in *The Prisoner*. It was designed to make her feel very uncomfortable.

'And you're a complete cunt,' she responded with a big smile, before breezing past him to her next target.

Dave wasn't sure whether Joy had been talking about him or Sofia had made an instant assessment of his character.

An excited Greg came across to talk to Dave. 'Hey, Dave, Barbara loves the sound of my book. She's really excited by it.'

'I rather thought she might be, Greg.'

'Yeah, but what should I do?' Greg pretended there was a problem. 'She wants me to come back to her place so she can do an all-nighter on it. Then she's going to ring the publishers in the morning.'

'An all-nighter, eh? I'm so happy for you, Greg.' It was just as Dave had planned.

'I'm just concerned about Joy,' pondered Greg. 'You know? That she might not understand?'

'Course she would, Greg,' said Dave, providing absolution in advance, before Greg went off to sin.

'You think?' Greg started to click his pen.

'Definitely,' reassured Dave. 'It's business.'

'But Joy is still a woman.' Greg's pen was clicking faster now.

'You say that. But remember what the Major calls her …? A dickless bloke.'

'That's true,' pondered Greg. 'Because it could be my big break, Dave. Barbara's with one of the big agencies. She wants to sign me up.'

'Go for it, man.'

'That's good advice, Dave.' Greg smiled. 'Thanks, mate.'

Shortly afterwards, Joy came over and slumped in a chair beside Dave, drawing heavily on a joint. 'Wanker,' she sighed.

'I know,' said Dave sympathetically.

'He is such a wanker, Dave.'

'I did try to stop him, Joy, but he said he needed to see what it was like to have sex with an older woman.'

'Who are you talking about?' she looked perplexed.

'Greg. He went off with a book agent.'

'He's such a slut,' she scowled. 'But he'll be lucky.'

'I take it you mean Barbara won't be?'

Joy smiled a conspiratorial smile. 'I put bromide in his drink. Thanks for that suggestion, Dave.'

Dave grinned. 'I like to share my knowledge, Joy.'

'No, I'm talking about my dad.' She was suddenly very

sombre. 'He can't make it. He's "got to fly out to Africa". To do an interview with the leaders of the MPLA. Can you imagine? The civil war in Angola is more important than his own daughter!'

'Ridiculous,' agreed Dave.

'This is my big night,' she wailed. 'He should be here for me.'

'Doesn't he know how important this is to you?' Dave asked sympathetically.

Joy shook her head. 'He hates popular culture and despises comics.'

He tried to comfort her. 'But he must approve of your subversive agenda? Reaching kids when they're young?'

'Ha! If it was a comic coming out of Soweto, drawn in coloured chalks on walls and washed away by the winter rains, he would.'

They pulled their chairs back as more guests came in, and Joy waved a quick greeting to them.

'Does he know you're the writer of *White Death*?' Dave continued.

She looked down at the floor. 'I sent him the first script. And you know what he did?' She bit her lip. 'He sent it back, pointing out spelling mistakes and grammatical errors.'

She burst into tears. 'He blue-pencilled my love!'

Dave put a comforting arm around her. 'I am so sorry, Joy.'

She leaned into him, silently sobbing into his chest for a long time.

Thanks for being there for me, Dave,' she breathed. 'You're a good friend.'

Finally she whispered:

'Dave …'

'Yes, Joy?'

'Don't try and undo my bra strap.'

'Sorry. I was confused by all the zips.'

'They're for show. They don't go anywhere.'

'So I realise.'

'Like us, Dave.'

'But now Greg's out of the picture again,' he whispered, 'I thought you might be up for some punctuation or even … punk-tuation?'

'Ha, ha,' she laughed an awful laugh. 'Very good.'

'I am the Man with the Golden Pun.'

Then she scowled. 'No. Fat chance. You punctuated me once, Dave. That was it.'

'Oh, Joy,' he said reproachfully, 'you make me sound like a puncture repair kit.'

'You might need one: for your inflatable doll. Because it is never going to happen again.'

'I could be your rock, Joy.'

'Aye. A millstone round my neck.' And she went off to talk to Jon Pertwee.

He was making progress, he thought. And once she saw the new girls comic story he was working on, that would change everything. It was a winner. Better than *Feral Meryl* and the other stories on her popularity chart like *Hop Along Heidi*, *Nell of Doom*, and *Swimmer Slave of Mrs Tide*.

His mother was inside his head again, breaking into his thoughts, trying to direct his attention to a bookshelf. She said it was important, but getting off with Joy was more of a priority than finding his mother's murderer.

'It's in the past, Mum. You're dead. Get over it.'

'Just look at the bloody shelves,' she insisted.

'I don't see why I should.'

'Dave, is your apathy some kind of defence mechanism?' she fumed. 'Because you're scared of what you might discover?'

'Don't psychoanalyse me, mother. I've read R.D. Laing, you know.'

'So is there is a psychological reason …? Or are you just a lazy little sod?'

Dave considered the question carefully, and finally gave his opinion. 'I think I'm just a lazy little sod.'

Eventually, however, he gave in, and she directed his attention to a glossy coffee table book entitled *Blackout London*.

As the party milled around him, Dave found himself

absorbed in the book. The author described criminal life in wartime London. Juvenile delinquency was so bad that the remand homes were full, and closed their doors. Kids stole Tommy guns and held up cashiers in a series of armed raids. A teenager was convicted of fraudulently claiming National Assistance, after supposedly being bombed out of his home nineteen times.

After recent events, Dave was starting to see the criminal potential of kids. It must have been how Fagan felt, he thought, when he assembled his Artful Dodgers to do his dirty work for him.

He looked curiously at the photos. They were certainly atmospheric: smoking gave them a foggy haze, and he could almost smell the reek of tobacco in the air. But there, amongst the images, he was surprised to see a photo of Fabulous Keen in his pre-smiling days. He was looking coldly at the photographer. The caption described him as a doorman at The Eight Veils.

Even before his Nehru collar period, he looked the epitome of elegance, yet despite the hat and double-breasted suit, there was something about him that troubled Dave. Finally, he realised why. His expression reminded him of Mr Cooper.

There was another photo of worse-for-wear revellers at The Eight Veils: a drunk aristocrat, a gangster, British and American officers and two glamorous beauties.

With a startled thrill, Dave realised one of them was his mother. The caption described her with her maiden name: Jean Ryan, a nightclub singer. Dave stared at the grainy black and white photo, studying the young woman who was to become his mother. She was looking straight into the lens, unlike her companions, who were caught mid-pose, smoking; laughing; drinking. Not Jean. One slender, penciled eyebrow was arched sardonically, and a small, secret smile played on her lips. For all her youth, Dave could see she exuded … what was it? Confidence …? Yes … but it was more than that. It was power.

The other glamour girl was Jenny Clarkson, described as an exotic dancer and singer, Jean's best friend.

The text explained that this was the last photo taken of Jenny before she was murdered by a Soho serial killer, the Blackout Strangler, who was never caught.

Dave read the accompanying chapter for more details. Between 1942 and 1945, four women, two of them possible sex workers, had been killed by the Strangler. The murder weapons were an electrical flex, silk stockings, copper wire and, in Jenny's case, her own scarf.

CHAPTER FORTY-FOUR

Mr Cooper was putting the squeeze on Dave. But he just couldn't face writing for *Laarf!* anymore, even though the alternative was starvation. He was already living on his sweet box and instant meals, whose cardboard packaging had more nutrients. Perhaps he'd do what hungry kids did in the past: look at vast, delicious repasts in comics, and imagine he was eating them. It was the origins of the famous 'big feed' final picture in comics. In the depression of the 1930s, comic publishers had discovered that starving kids loved looking at pictures of slap-up feeds. They could, at least, dream of filling their bellies. Fleetpit and Angus, Angus and Angus had been happy to help them, as long as they had the price of a comic.

Dave dug out some Angus, Angus and Angus comics and decided to try it. He would treat himself to a feast for the eyes. He began with a vast, gravy-dripping, steaming deer pie, with antlers sticking out of the crust, as favoured by Knuckles Duster. He followed it with Wee Cheeky's favourite food: a mountain of delicious bangers and mash. Then he joined Scratch and Sniff for some huge, mouth-watering bowls of jelly and custard and endless plates of cream cakes. And finished off his imaginary repast with a six-foot-high ice-cream cornet, as supplied by Cap Puccino, the crazy Italian.

He stared and stared until he couldn't stare anymore. He discovered his eyes were definitely bigger than his stomach.

'D'you know? It seems to work,' he told his mother. 'I actually feel full-up.'

'Perhaps you should try the same thing with families?' she suggested.

'How do you mean?'

'Well, to make up for all the traumas, the cruelty, and losses in your childhood,' she explained. 'Why not look at some pictures of happy families to make you feel better?'

'You mean look at pictures of a perfect Ladybird-book mother, a sober father and a big sister who didn't ignore me, to feed my voracious, desperate need for a happy family?'

'Yes. That's the idea.'

'I'd just want to throw darts at them,' said Dave.

* * *

Dave, Joy and Greg gathered after work in The Hoop and Grapes to talk about future plans for *Aaagh!*, three weeks before its launch on Saturday March 13th. It was also the launch date of *Everlasting Love*, although no one talked about it, in case Joy cracked up again. Greg and Joy were excited, but Dave was uncomfortable with the thought of success.

Greg and Joy were also fired up because they had been to see the Sex Pistols at the Marquee the week before; the support band for Eddie and Hot Rods. Dave had declined to join them because he said he was too old to be going to gigs anymore. But they saw *Aaagh!* as being a punk comic: another sign the old order was about to be swept away.

Dave noted Greg's new punk look: his hair messed up, a jacket with lots of zips and a T-shirt featuring two cowboys with their penises hanging out.

'So you've climbed on the latest bandwagon, Greg,' he scowled. 'You don't think you're just a little old to be a punk ...?'

'You're never too old, Dave,' interjected Joy. 'Even you could wear a T-shirt with 'I hate Pink Floyd' scrawled on it.'

Dave watched Greg light a Sobranie Cocktail. 'Pink cigarettes. Definitely queer.'

'I like to stand out from the crowd,' shrugged Greg.

'Punks smoke roll-ups,' Dave said reprovingly.

'I have no brand-loyalty,' smiled Greg.

'I know. You have *no* loyalty.' Dave switched his attack. 'So what happened to your big literary breakthrough?'

'What do you mean?'

'Joy's launch party. Barbara, the hotshot agent who was going to read your novel?'

'Ah. Yes.' Greg avoided looking at them. 'We didn't really ... It didn't quite ... You know ...' He grasped hold of his pen for reassurance.

'You're clicking your pen, Greg,' observed Dave. 'Do I detect signs of agitation? Did something, perhaps, go amiss with your all-nighter?'

'Well ... for some reason ...'

'Was it ... *hard*?' asked Joy innocently.

'I was ...tired,' said Greg defensively, not quite sure where this was going and wondering how Joy could possibly have known about his erectile dysfunction. Assuming that was what she was getting at.

'You didn't ... connect?' suggested Joy.

'You drooped a bit?' suggested Dave.

'Come on, Greg,' said Joy, 'Out with it.'

'No, no,' said Dave hastily. 'I don't want to see his sex pistol.'

'We need to know, Greg,' insisted Joy.

'Yes,' agreed Dave. 'Did you or did you not punk-tuate Barbara?'

'Unfortunately,' said Greg, avoiding the question and possibly dangerous fallout from Joy, 'Barbara said I wasn't famous, so the agency couldn't take me on.'

'Well, if you can't break through the glass ceiling, at least you can spit at it now,' Dave reassured him. He leered at Greg's T-shirt. 'By the way. Is that meant to be you and Bernie? I know you were a couple of cowboys.'

'What did I tell you?' said a grinning Joy to Greg. 'It annoys him, so you got it right.'

'Yes!' laughed Greg, punching the air.

Joy smiled at Dave, '*You* really should buy more clothes.'

'Oh, I can't afford it, Joy.'

'What do you spend your money on?'

Dave shrugged nervously. Cooper had increased the rent to £30.00 a week in line with inflation. He didn't want his shame shared with Joy and Greg.

'No. Don't tell me,' said Joy, putting a hand up. 'I know it will be something weird.'

'Anyway,' said Dave, 'I'm hoping what I'm wearing will see me out.'

Dave was preoccupied trying to switch off Bob Marley's "Get up, Stand up", which had been endlessly playing in his head ever since they entered the pub. He knew his mother was responsible, but had no idea why she chose this track.

'How was the TV ad?' asked Greg.

'I regret to say it was very good,' admitted Dave, always more comfortable with failure.

He had just seen the commercial for *Aaagh!* at the advertising agency offices. 'Geiger counters at max! We're radioactive!' the advert proudly declared to a generation of kids living in the shadow of the bomb. 'Great free gift with Issue One: The Super Nuker. The Red Terror from the skies.'

It showed exciting flash images of *Panzerfaust*, *White Death*, *Black Hammer*, *The Damned* and *Deathball*, all to cries of 'Aaagh!', and ended with the Super Nuker hurtling towards the viewer.

'Yes,' said Dave. 'There are 250,000 Super Nukers waiting for take-off at a warehouse near Dartford, more than the combined airforces of the Warsaw Pact.'

'They had to do something with them after the plan to give them away with *The Spanker* was cancelled,' said Greg.

'Yes, I'm afraid it looks like *The Spanker* is not long for this world,' said Dave grimly.

'Mary Whitehouse will hate *Aaagh!*,' said Greg gleefully. 'She lives in Colchester and was sitting opposite me on the train scowling at my T-shirt.'

'I can't imagine why,' laughed Joy.

'So I wrote in some extra blood and gore in a script; had

Street blasting old Etonian traitors, as I muttered, "This one's for you, Mary." '

'I'm looking forward to the episode where Street breaks into Buckingham Palace,' said Joy.

'The "We've come for you, Queenie!" scene,' grinned Greg.

'After I'd seen the ad,' Dave continued, 'I asked if I could see it in black and white.'

'Course,' said Joy.

'You know what the Suit said to me?' Dave imitated the Suit's snooty accent. ' "The majority of homes in Britain now have colour televisions." '

'What did you say?' asked Joy.

' "Good point. Who gives a fuck about poor people with black and white tellies." '

'You see,' said Joy,. 'You're a punk, Dave. You just don't realise it.'

'Oh, no, Joy,' said Dave shuddering at Greg and his new image. 'I despise exhibitionism.'

'Look at the way you're proud to have been in the workhouse,' she insisted.

'And not just any workhouse, Joy,' Dave said. 'The West Ham Union Workhouse.'

* * *

And then Mr Cooper came over with an attractive, brassy woman, her arm in a sling. Dave was startled to see him. Firstly, because The Hoop and Grapes was the journalists' pub and the browncoats' pub was up the road. Secondly, because he was drunk, doubtless on Dave's money.

'How are you, Quasi …? Aren't you going to introduce me then …?' slurred Mr Cooper.

The Liquorice Detective shook his head. Too afraid even to speak to the monster who was still ruining his life.

'All right. I'll introduce meself. Stan Cooper. I work over in the Fleetpit vaults. But me and Dave go back a long way.'

'You're not Cooper the newsagent?' asked Joy.

'That's right. Dave's talked about me, has he?'

'Oh, aye,' said Joy grimly.

'We had a laugh in those days, didn't we, Dave?' Cooper indicated his partner's sling. 'Slipped on the ice. Bandy old cow, aren't yer? Very accident prone.' His partner looked down miserably at the floor. 'Cheer up,' said Cooper. 'Still got the other arm. Still push a hoover.'

'What happened to your wife?' asked Joy. She was looking for a cue to nut him.

Greg shifted uneasily from one foot to the other. He might look like a punk now, but he didn't like to be seen drinking with a browncoat. It was one thing for him to talk about the injustice of what happened to Simon Dee, while Billy Cotton's super-yacht was moored in Poole harbour, but it was quite another for him to mix with the lower orders himself.

'Oh, she disappeared one day, you know?' replied Cooper. 'Never even took her handbag. Steaming cup of tea on the table and no dinner in the oven. Cheeky mare. Like the *Marie Celeste* in my kitchen. The police were baffled. I often think of her when I'm out on the allotment. Probably ran off with a darkie.'

He winked knowingly at Dave. 'They often do, you know? How's the fur coat, by the way?'

Cooper must have listened to the gossip, thought Dave. 'I can see where you're coming from,' Cooper said. 'Fur coats don't answer back. I wish I'd thought of that meself. You're a smart little bleeder, aren't you?' He was talking to Dave as if he was eight years old, which is how old he felt.

Cooper turned his attention to Joy. 'You all right, doll? He doesn't give you too many backhanders?'

Cooper grinned at Dave. 'Looking at your one, I should sleep with your wallet under the pillow if I was you. I used to.'

He looked back at Joy. 'No offence, darlin'. But you birds are all the same.'

'What about your shop?' she enquired coldly, closing in on him.

'I'm out of the newsagent business now, love. Pakis took it

over. I had a bit of bother with the police. I probably shouldn't talk about it. Anyway, we used to have a laugh every Saturday, didn't we, Dave?'

'N-n-no,' stuttered Dave.

'Come on. No harm was done.'

'I … I …' Dave managed to force out the truth. 'I … hated you!'

'Now that's no way to talk, son,' warned Cooper, clenching his knuckles, reminding Dave he had the power. 'Come on,' he said. 'Let's do it again. Just for old time's sake.' He turned to Joy, Greg and his companion. 'Watch, everyone. This'll have you in stitches. It did him.' He turned back to Dave. 'Now … what was it you used to like, Dave?'

Greg was about to catch his train, but this looked too good to miss. Dave was about to be seriously humiliated, and he lingered expectantly.

'Come on,' said Cooper, stroking his clenched knuckles in preparation. 'What was your favourite comic?'

'A Fourpenny One,' snarled Dave, smashing his fist into Cooper's face as "Get up, Stand up" exploded inside his head.

It was a punch Carstairs the Fag-Master, would have admired. It was Dave's Popeye moment, but liquorice wasn't his spinach. Rather, it was his mother who had awoken the man inside the boy.

'You'll pay for that,' said Cooper, blinking away the shock, and wiping the blood from his split lip. His age hadn't limited his appetite for violence.

Dave grabbed him by the lapels. 'Yeah? Yeah? *Yeah* …? Come on then, you bastard. *Come on!*' He slammed the storeman back against the wall, towering over him. 'Let's be having you!'

For the first time, Dave knew what he was capable of, and Cooper knew it, too. His face went ashen. 'It's all right. It's all right. Calm down, Dave. Calm down, mate. Easy, big fellow. Easy.'

'And that's the last money you're getting out of me,' growled Dave. 'If you tell *anyone* about me living over the road, I will have you. I mean it. Do you understand?'

'Yeah. Yeah. Sure, Dave. Message understood. Your secret's safe with me, mate.'

'Because I will kill you,' warned Dave. 'Understand?' Cooper was too terrified to speak. Dave banged the ex-newsagent's head back against a wall. 'I said … *do you understand?*'

'W-won't breathe a word, mate.'

'It will be your last breath if you do.'

'We …we were just having a laugh, that's all,' said a craven Cooper to Joy and Greg as he staggered towards the door with his companion.

Dave pursued him and hissed viciously in his ear. 'Yeah, and I reckon you killed my mother.' He stabbed his finger into the storeman's chest. 'Your card is marked, pal.'

A terrified Cooper didn't answer; instead, he just slunk away into the night.

Dave turned back into the pub.

'Respect,' said Joy admiringly.

She reminded Dave so much of his mother, and he suddenly realised that must be why he was attracted to her. Both were beautiful; not interested in him; and violent.

'Yeah … respect,' said Greg, grudgingly, hiding his surprise, disappointment and jealousy.

"Get up, Stand up" was playing louder than ever inside Dave's head.

Cooper was now higher on the list of suspects, with his near-admission he had done away with his wife, whom Dave had always liked. So it could be the ex-newsagent, along with the Canon, with other possibilities being the Knights of St Pancras, their Grand Master, the Blackout Strangler – whoever he was – or even his long-suffering father. Any one of them could be his mother's murderer.

'I think this calls for a choky sherbet to celebrate,' said Dave. He produced one from his pocket, sucking up the white powder through the liquorice straw.

'You're not still on the sherbet, Dave?' said a concerned Joy. 'It's really bad for you.'

'Almost at the bottom of the sweet box,' he confided. 'Just

one last hairy gobstopper to go.' And then collapsed into a coughing fit as the sherbet did its work. Washing it down with a pint of bitter, he was soon his usual self again.

'That's a pity,' leered Greg. 'I was looking forward to carrying out the Heimlich manoeuvre on you ... giving you some abdominal thrusts ...' He grabbed Dave from behind and lewdly demonstrated what he had in mind.

'Get off me, you bummer,' said Dave, shoving Greg back.

'What's the problem?' said Greg.

'The Heimlich manouevre,' said Dave primly. 'Sounds German, so I'd have to refuse it. I'm a post-war baby-boomer, you see?'

'Even if meant The End?' asked Greg.

'What would your last words be, Dave?' enquired Joy.

'Fourpenny One,' said Dave triumphantly.

CHAPTER FORTY-FIVE

There was much for Dave to reflect upon after his victory over Mr Cooper. In the shadowy pub, through the tobacco smoke, he had seen his mother watching, beautiful as always, in a 1940s suit with a fur stole. But the expression on her face was not that of an admiring mother who had seen her cowardly son finally turn into a knight errant and defeat the Dark Lord.

Rather, for a moment, the mask of her beauty dropped and he saw a vampire, a princess of the undead, a *femme fatale*, a dame from the pages of a pulp fiction novel laughing wantonly as Cooper slunk away. Whether or not Cooper had carried out his homicidal intentions on his mother, there was no doubt of her homicidal intentions towards him. That much was clear from the surge of violence within Dave when he punched the ex-newsagent. That same surge of violence he had felt when the priest had confronted him in the church, and he had torn the chalice from him and drank the blood of Christ.

He was still pondering on her true nature when, the next day, he and Ron were summoned to meet the new publisher who had just been appointed to head the juvenile and teenage publications group. 'Who is it, Ron? Do you know?'

'His name's Len Lang, Dave. American. He was a publisher for an American magazine company.' Ron noticed Dave's bandaged hand. 'Sprained it? Gave yourself one too many off the wrist?'

'Something like that, Ron. What's this Len doing here?'

'The board headhunted him. They want to break into the American market and he's got the know-how. Had a big success with *Heroines* in the States.'

'Oh, I know. Bit like *Cosmopolitan.*'

They entered the publisher's office where the browncoats were putting framed magazine covers on the wall, in preparation for Len to move in.

The magazine was entitled *Tampon*, with a top line above the logo. 'It's that time of the month' said one. 'Your favorite periodical' said a second, and 'Your monthly treat' proclaimed a third. Dave noticed one issue came with a 'Free map of where to find your G-spot.'

The covers all featured the same tall, statuesque, blonde model. In one, she was skiing, in another about to go deep sea-diving, in a third, at the controls of a light aircraft. They were all eye-catching, although Dave's eye was actually caught by a magnificent fur coat hanging next to them.

Ron was mystified. 'Have we opened up a branch of Boots? Or am I in the women's bogs? I'd hate to be pissing up the wrong wall.'

Embarrassed, he looked away, as a woman entered. She was in her mid-thirties, very tall, statuesque, blonde and power-dressed. Dave recognised her as the model for *Tampon.*

Ron didn't. 'I'm Ron Punch and this is Dave Maudling. We're here to meet the new publisher. Put the kettle on, would you, darling? I could murder a cuppa.'

'I am the new publisher,' she smiled, towering over the little cockney and stretching out a hand. 'Leni Lang.'

'But … you're a woman,' gasped Ron.

'Observant,' said Leni.

'You sound … German,' he gasped again.

'Ja. But I left Munich when I was a teenager.' She saw Ron looking open-mouthed at the framed covers of *Tampon*, finally realising Leni was the model. She explained. 'It's my joke, Ron. I like to see people's reactions. I like to shock.'

'I get it,' grinned Dave, shaking her hand, as Ron clearly

wasn't going to. 'I like to wind people up myself.'

'So relax, Ron. It's not real,' smiled Leni mischievously.

'Thank Christ,' said a relieved Ron. '*Tampon* ...! For a moment, I thought the world was going mad.'

'Actually, it *is* real, Ron,' laughed Leni. Ron looked furious.

'Ha, ha, ha!' she waggled a finger in his shocked, angry face. 'Caught you, didn't I?'

'Prove it,' he glowered.

'Okay.' She pointed at the pilot cover with 'Free map of where to find your G-spot', took out a chart from a filing cabinet, and spread it across her desk. 'This is a gynaecological map, presented free with issue one of *Tampon*.' Ron and Dave looked mystified at it.

'It was easier to find my way up Sword Beach,' said Ron.

'It's how you can pleasure your wife,' smiled Leni.

Ron looked outraged. 'My wife? She's the mother of my children.'

He still hadn't shaken her hand, so Dave felt an explanation was called for. 'He's a D-Day veteran. He needs time to adjust.'

'Ah.' She smiled. 'Normandy. Yes. My daddy also. He was on the Atlantic Wall. Perhaps you met?'

'If we had, you wouldn't be here,' scowled Ron.

'Oh, no, I was born in 1943,' Leni replied cheerfully.

Dave had to get Ron out of there before he reopened hostilities. He pulled him away. 'Needs his pills,' explained Dave. 'Suffers from blackouts.'

'Blackouts?' asked a puzzled Leni.

'You know: blackouts, like when London was bombed,' growled Ron.

'London was bombed ...? Now Leni was mystified. 'Who by?'

'Your fucking lot,' snarled Ron.

'Really ...?' She was genuinely surprised.

'You're taking the piss out of me again?' scowled Ron.

'No,' she said, looking shocked. 'I really did not know London was bombed in the war.' She put her hands to her mouth. 'Oh, that is so awful.'

Then she saw Ron's fuming face. 'But you are angry with

me,' she smiled. 'That is good, Ron. It is very good. Because it's your chance to heal. We must lighten your frequency.' She produced a bundle of dried herbs and set them alight. 'Come, let me smudge you. I can release the negative energy from your chakras.'

'Leave my fucking chakras alone,' said Ron, backing away as the giantess advanced on him with the smouldering herbs.

'Later,' said Dave to Leni, escorting Ron out the door. 'Love the fur, by the way,' he added, as he looked longingly back at it.

'It died of natural causes,' Leni explained.

'Heart attack farm in Siberia …? Oh, good,' said Dave.

Ron and Dave retreated to the Gents. Standing in the Edwardian urinals they commiserated with each other.

Ron, a calming cigarette in his mouth, explained his view on women. 'They wear mini-skirts. They make the tea. They don't talk about jam rags. And now this. I'll be fucking ironing next. If you see me with a fucking vacuum cleaner, Dave, put a fucking bullet through me head. I stormed Sword Beach for this? I'd rather have stayed on the fucking landing craft. The Germans won, didn't they? When did that happen?'

'And she wore a trouser suit,' Dave added. 'And you can't send her home.'

'I'd like to. Back to fucking Germany,' agreed Ron.

To Ron's horror, Leni put her head around the door of the Gents. 'Hello …? Am I interrupting anything?' Receiving only a stunned silence, she entered. 'I like to be where the decision-making is happening.'

'What is she doing coming in here?' asked an outraged Ron.

'Germans, Ron.' Dave explained. 'They don't have our hang-ups about bodily functions.'

'Well, they fucking should have,' said Ron.

Leni stood in the empty urinal that separated Ron and Dave, happily chatting to both of them. 'I need my finger on the pulse. There is much to discuss. Firstly, I require an end to smoking in comics.'

The cigarette dropped out of Ron's mouth with unfortunate consequences. He yelped in pain.

'Then this violence towards Germans must be toned down,' as Ron looked murderously at her. 'The war has been over a long time.'

'You'll be pleased to know we have a German hero … Panzerfaust,' said Dave, keen to suck up to his new boss.

'Fucking collaborator,' Ron snarled at Dave.

'Very good,' noted Leni. 'Now, I have been reading *The Caning Commando* and I found it both stupid and offensive.'

'We do our best,' said Dave, going over to the wash basins.

'This character, Corporal Punishment, who refers to women as "Bumpy Men"? Has he never seen women's breasts before?'

'We lead very sheltered lives in Britain, Leni,' Dave explained. 'I'm a little confused by the statues in the park, myself.'

'I require changes to *The Spanker*,' she said imperiously as they washed their hands. 'Big changes.'

Ron couldn't take anymore. He stormed out as Greg entered and took in the modern day Brunhilda. Dave sighed. This was all he needed.

'Tell me who this lovely lady is, Dave?' said Greg, his eyes glued to hers.

'No, I don't think I will, Greg,' said Dave coldly.

Greg opened a packet of Virginia Slims.

'Women's cigarettes …?' scowled Dave. The final, damning evidence that Greg was queer.

'My purse pack,' Greg explained to Dave, knowing it would infuriate him.

'I am Leni Lang. I'm your new publisher,' smiled Leni.

'Our new publisher, eh? I'm Greg.' They shook hands, and he only slowly let go of her hand as he looked appreciatively at her. 'Where are you from …?'

'California,' she replied.

He looked deep into her eyes as he replied in smooth and honeyed tones. 'You've come a long way, baby, to get where you've got to today …'

'Ja, originally I am from Munich.'

'Of course,' said Greg, drawing on a Virginia Slim. 'Leni. Like Leni Riefenstahl? *Triumph Of The Will*.'

'I'm afraid I don't know it,' she said.

'Really …? It's a pre-war film. I've seen it … ah … a couple of times.'

'Our history teacher taught us very little about the war.'

'That is so interesting,' said Greg predictably.

'Ja. He said it was much better to forget everything that had happened in our past. Not to think about it anymore. We had to start again and build a new Germany.'

'Sensible advice,' said Greg. 'Although unusual for a history teacher.'

'Then, unfortunately, his wartime past caught up with him, and they took him away.'

'You know, Leni, I'm fascinated by your culture …' Greg purred.

'Oh, Jesus,' said Dave.

EPILOGUE

Detective Inspector 'Fiddy' Ferguson finished his Sidney Sheldon novel and leaned back in his deckchair with a satisfied smile. It had been a real page-turner, and he hadn't been able to put it down since they'd arrived at Sol Tower Hotel, near Estepona in Spain. Now he was looking forward to picking up James Clavell's *Shōgun* the next time he went shopping.

He liked the hotel: it reminded him of the tower blocks on his old manor. For the same reason, he liked the beach chalets nearby, used by the Spanish army as holiday homes: they reminded him of Butlin's chalets. While they were staying at Sol Tower, he and the wife were looking around for a villa to buy. He felt really at home on the Costa del Sol. There were so many retired villains and retired cops like himself there. He had never really wanted to retire, but had been persuaded by his superiors. Especially when they pointed out the alternative.

He was tall and silver-haired with piercing, Husky-like, pale-blue eyes that had scared the bejesus out of more than one villain. There was just a hint of heavy drinking in the burst blood vessels in his cheeks. He was quite anonymous in the multi-national, Costa del Golf community. It was only when he got onto the subject of Enoch Powell and told his favourite racist joke that anyone realised he was, of course, British.

He watched his seven-year-old grandson, Tim, the apple of his eye, running around on the stony beach in front of him. The boy was wearing a teacher's mortarboard and was wrapped in a black cloak. He had insisted on bringing this outfit on holiday with him. It was some comic book character he was crazy about. Now he was lost in make-believe, waving a stick and yelling something Ferguson couldn't quite make out.

He fell asleep in the warm winter sun. In his dream, he was back in the Flying Squad, once again drinking with Dennis Waterman and John Thaw. To prepare them for their starring roles in the TV series *The Sweeney*, the actors had spent many happy hours drinking with the lads on the squad. The detectives were huge fans of the series and, after watching the show, they'd all go into work the next morning whistling the famous theme tune.

Ferguson was suddenly awoken by cries of pain and saw, to his dismay, that Tim was caning a sunbathing holidaymaker on his bottom, and snarling at him. He could make out his battle-cry this time: it was 'It's time to Carpet Bum the Hun!'

Fiddy quickly intervened, restrained Tim, and apologised to the tourist, who turned out to be Norwegian. That was how the problem had arisen. Tim had heard the Norwegian talking to his wife and believed he was German and therefore a legitimate target of someone called the Caning Commando. It was all rather embarrassing, but the Norwegians were very good about it and said 'boys will be boys'.

But it set Ferguson wondering just who was this Caning Commando his grandson admired so much? Later, in the hotel, Tim proudly produced the latest issues of the *The Spanker*, and the policeman decided to take them back to his room and have a read of them. He had nothing else to read, now he'd finished *The Other Side of Midnight*.

He found *The Caning Commando* stories amusing enough in a *Carry On*-film sort of way. But then the story of Lord Ow! Ow! caught his eye. In particular, the way the Caning Commando described to his half-wit companion, Alf Mast, how to prepare and detonate a pipe bomb. It was completely authentic, and showed the readers, in precise detail, just how they could construct such a bomb themselves.

He looked at the stories more closely now, and then he came across the Commando's battle with Von Vroom, the inventor of the Arsenripper. He saw, once again, there was detailed information on how kids could obtain and prepare a tasteless and odourless poison.

He recalled there had been a story in the newspapers about a chemistry teacher drinking that very same poison by mistake. Yes, it would have been shortly after the comic appeared. Coincidence ...? Or maybe not ...?

He stared thoughtfully out the window for a long while, looking at the crashing winter waves hurling themselves at the beach.

His family were keen for him to join them down in the bar and normally he would have done so. He liked to extol the virtues of Enoch Powell with other expats and talk about just why the old country was going to the dogs. But he needed some time to himself to work out what was really going on in *The Caning Commando*. Just who was including these lethal ideas in a kids' comic, and why? The writer? The editor? Old instincts and old habits were kicking in. He couldn't help himself. He had to figure out what was going on.

Finally, he joined the dots.

Then he made a phone call to Britain, to one of his old colleagues on the squad. As he waited to be put through, he whistled a certain theme tune.

APPENDIX

From: AngusAngus&Angus@Angus.com
To: Pat Mills; Kevin O'Neill
Date: 20 September 2016 13:30:15 GMT+01:00
Subject: Read Em and Weep

Dear Mr. Mills and Mr. O'Neill,

Thank you for sending us an advance copy of *Read Em And Weep 1: Serial Killer*, which you asked us to review. I am sorry to say it was not to our liking. Or anyone's, frankly. What were you thinking of? You describe it as 'humour', but I found it deeply offensive. Are you well?

At the centre of your story is David Maudling, whom you allege is a serial killer; a notion that you seem to think is funny. You suggest that his homicidal tendencies and strange obsession with fur is due to a childhood trauma involving comics and his mother. For shame!

You also refer – with some glee – to the brief period of time when Maudling was employed by us as a sub-editor, before moving to London to work for Fleetpit Publications, with which your account is primarily concerned. Our records show he was summarily dismissed in 1971 for gross misconduct. And what could be more gross than the incident you describe, with such unpleasant relish, involving Maudling and Mrs Angus's fur coat?

I turn now to the comics Maudling was responsible for, commencing with *The Spanker*. As a former serviceman, I took particular exception to the comic-strip character you enthuse about, known as *The Caning Commando*, a teacher who canes his way through Nazi hordes to Berlin and proclaims, "I see Germany as one big a*** that needs a colossal thrashing." I found his obsession with caning Germans unwholesome and suggestive of what I believe is referred to as 'The English Disease'.

The series denigrates Her Majesty's Forces to the point of libel. May I tell you, sirs, my father gave up a leg for his country? His good leg. Mr. Gordon Angus's father gave up an arm. And Mr. Brian Angus Sr, an eye. Between us, we lost an entire Angus in the field. Many Anguses gave up their limbs in the service of their country, and they are spinning as we speak.

Furthermore, in the girls' comic, *Shandy*, there was *Feral Meryl*, the story of a Wild Girl brought up by the Wolves of Berkshire. You clearly have very sick minds to think a young lassie choke-chained like a rabid dog by her best friend is a cause for amusement.

As if this were not enough, you say you intend to relate, over four books, the story of British comics, through Maudling's involvement. Commencing in 1975 with *Blitzkrieg!*, the abortive and unpatriotic war comic featuring German heroes, then the notorious *Aaagh!*, followed by the truly warped *Space Warp* and, finally, the unwholesome *Raven*, a girls horror comic.

I believe you both to be a menace to society and certainly a menace to publishing and I give *Read Em And Weep 1: Serial Killer* one star, the lowest possible rating it can be awarded, and that is one star too many.

Yours sincerely,

Sinclair Angus
Maj. (Ret.)

General Manager
ANGUS, ANGUS & ANGUS & Co. Ltd
Bleek House, Caber Passage, Aberdeen, Scotland

COMING SOON!

Read Em and Weep Book Two:

GOODNIGHT, JOHN-BOY

• Dave, the Liquorice Detective, investigates Fabulous Keen, the Grand Master, and draws closer to discovering his mother's murderer.

• Detective Inspector Ferguson investigates Dave.

• More kids avenge themselves on adults and it's Goodnight, John-Boy!

• Dave is summoned to canemakers Mafeking and Jones: with painful results.

• Can The Caning Commando thwart the Oberspankerfuhrer's sinister plan to capture and thrash Winston Churchill?

• The genesis of *Space Warp*, the legendary science fiction comic.

• An enemy from Greg's murky past finally catches up with him.

• Joy's empire-building brings her a bitter rival.

• Feral Meryl returns, but Mandy has found a new, special friend. Where will it all end?

For the latest updates on *Goodnight, John-Boy,* check out www.millsverse.com!

DID YOU LIKE THIS BOOK?
WE NEED YOU …

Without reviews, indie books like this one are almost impossible to market.

Leaving a review will only take a minute: it doesn't have to be long or involved, just a sentence or two that tells people what you liked about the book, to help other readers know why they might like it, too, and to help us write more of what you love.

The truth is, VERY few readers leave reviews. Please help us by being the exception. If you bought *Serial Killer* online, you can leave a review at the retail site. Or you could leave a review at Goodreads, or on a blog, or even just tell your friends about us!

Thank you in advance!
Pat and Kevin

BIOGRAPHIES

PAT MILLS, famed as 'the Godfather of British comics', started his freelance career writing stories for *The Spanker*, *Everlasting Love*, *Shandy* and *Laarf!*. He went on to create *2000AD*, featuring *Judge Dredd*, and wrote many of its key stories such as *Judge Dredd*, *Slaine* and *Nemesis the Warlock*.

Subsequently, he co-created the anti-superhero character *Marshal Law*, with Kevin O'Neill, for Marvel Comics, and wrote the satirical French bestselling series *Requiem Vampire Knight* with art by Olivier Ledroit, now published by Editions Glenat.

His acclaimed anti-war series *Charley's War*, with artist Joe Colquhoun, has been the subject of major exhibitions in French war museums. He was made an honorary professor by Liverpool University for his contribution to popular culture. His series *Accident Man*, co-created with Tony Skinner, is currently being made into a film starring Scott Adkins (Lucian in Marvel's *Doctor Strange*).

KEVIN O'NEILL began his career in British comics aged sixteen as an office boy and art assistant at Fleetpit Publications making art corrections and colour separations on *The Caning Commando* in *The Spanker*, and *Feral Meryl* in *Shandy*. After a brief spell on *Laarf!*, he left Fleetpit and became art editor of *2000AD*, creating with Pat: *Ro-Busters*, *ABC Warriors* and *Nemesis the Warlock*. Subsequently, they produced the superhero hunter

Marshal Law for Marvel comics, described as 'the freshest re-examination of superhero mythology since *Watchmen* and *The Dark Knight Returns*.' It is now a New York Times bestseller, reissued by D.C. Comics.

In 1999, O'Neill, with writer Alan Moore, began the popular *League of Extraordinary Gentlemen*. He is currently working with Alan on *Cinema Purgatorio* from Avatar Press, before embarking on the final *League of Extraordinary Gentlemen* volume.

O'Neill is also the author of *Published and Damned!*, a Fleetpit history (pulped due to legal concerns), and *Ron Punch: A Boot in the Privates – A Biography* (a work in progress).